NOAH THE WITCH
BOOK I

Noah the Witch
Book I

SENOVIO C SPARROW

Senovio C Sparrow

Front Cover Design by Aaron Herrera

Library of Congress Control
Number: 2020918874

ISBN: 978-1-7352959-3-0

First Printing, 2020

For my amazing husband and our two
beautiful and brilliant daughters.

Contents

Prologue

It is a recurring dream. Although my eyes remain shut, I know there are people surrounding me, but I do not feel fear. In its place, is an insurmountable pain and heaviness in my chest, it desperately bargains for some change in reality, but the past cannot be undone.

We began rocking, their movements are gentle, I do not hear a single harsh step against the ground, and I think for a moment we may be floating. The people begin chanting incomprehensible words. At first quietly, but their voices grow louder and turn into an enormous siren.

Their chants quicken and the wind changes direction. A sure sign of a storm brewing. I am swaying in resistance to the push and pull of the swift breeze.

The air begins twisting and pulling at me with sturdy hands, its touch has the consistency of water.

I have had this dream hundreds of times before, but for the first time, I am able to open my eyes.

I see myself hovering above the floor, my arms and legs lay limp beside me, and there is a slight rise and fall of my chest providing the only evidence I am still alive.

There are three people, shrouded in black, with their hands raised to the sky and myself in the center.

What I thought was wind that cocooned my body was something else entirely, some sort of translucent force or energy, only made visible by the distortion of space that seemed to exist within it.

At the call of the three strangers the energy begins circling at random, invading more of the area around us. It sizzles with genuine menace, until it blurs the vision of the entire clearing including some shack of a house in the back.

The chanting stops and the house begins to slowly deteriorate until it is near collapsing upon itself, then gives one final shudder before exploding into a million pieces.

My eyes open in a flash. It is three in the morning. I try to hold onto the nightmare, but it floats away like dreams do, leaving behind only the heaviness in my heart.

Chapter One

To replay a home's story, mark a double lined circle sigil, light three candles, and cast the incantation thrice fold. Beware ghosts.
Trae daisana Martafiks

The night of February second, just before midnight, a random firefighter found me in downtown Seattle, Washington. On an unseasonably warm and rainless night, the firefighter had stepped out for a walk when he saw the abandoned antique stroller outside the station's front door with a baby tucked away inside. They say that following day the cold and rain returned with freezing winds from the Pacific Ocean that brought a deluge upon the seaport city.

There was no note or evidence to give an indication of family members or some origin of my birth. I had nothing, not even a name. They had to create a birth certificate to document the start of my life. The original form identifies me as, Newborn Boy February Second. A child seemingly born of my own accord in the rainy city.

Bright side, at least I wasn't left in a dumpster. The firefighter notified the Department of Family Services, who sent a random caseworker to monitor my care. Joan Masterson, my first turn of fates, an East Coast girl who was only in Seattle to complete her Law degree at her beloved alma mater, The University of Washington. Never one to stay idle, she also worked part-time for the Department.

Her husband made a name for himself in the stock market, she would say, "Thank god for that man's income, Lord knows there ain't no money in saving the world." She intended to return to their home in Massachusetts after graduation that spring.

She brought me to a hospital, where the doctors estimated I was one to ten days old. That would make me 13 years and 46 weeks, as of today, then again, who knows? I could already be 14, but I'll go with it.

She visited me every day during my time at the NICU, while the medical staff completed their observations. Later in life, she would tell me how I must have had a guardian angel, "Thank goodness they found you the night they did, because the very next day it poured so hard I thought the world was going to float away." That is why she named me Noah.

My last name was a result of her fondness for Ellis Island. Joan's husband had invited her to tour the place for their first date. Smart call on his part, she had always loved Ellis Island and would often refer to the symbolism behind the Statue of Liberty, with her torch held up high inviting the unwanted and rejected for a chance at a better life. She said it reminded her of love and hope.

Joan was a Christian woman, church every Sunday without exception kind of Christian, singing gospels loudly and proudly as if no one and everyone was watching. She didn't take the bible literally or push any kind of agenda on others. She was just genuinely good. If needed, I know she would have adopted me, but anyone that knows anything about the foster care system, knows that babies do not stay foster kids for long. According to Joan, a sweet single woman named Nancy Amiri adopted me almost immediately.

Unfortunately, life with Nancy did not work out. She died shortly after I was twenty months old. Cancer, not her fault and I truly believe not mine either. I sometimes wonder if maybe that is when I learned to push people away. Or maybe because of her, I ended up not an entirely terrible person. I am still not sure which.

After Nancy, there was a period when many families applied to be placed with me, back when I was at the appealing age range of "six and younger".

None of these families would maintain my placement. Usually after an onslaught of certain peculiar events, the prospective parents would begin to describe me as "strange" or expressed concern for my mental health. Little things really, all the cabinet doors found opened, chairs stacked up on top of each other, constant lightning in a single spot. Inevitably, they would voluntarily disrupt the adoption process. I have the paperwork to prove it. Each time I would return to the residential center and the cycle would continue.

As Joan would put it, "It didn't help that you go off spouting out stories about car accidents that would happen the next day or reveal some affair one or the other was having."

She said it was my childhood curiosity. "Noah baby, you are so smart and figured things out quickly. Maybe you did have Angels speaking to you through God, but people can't handle the truth and prefer to leave some things unsaid."

One foster family went so far as to petition the courts for my adoption, but before finalizing, they began reporting serious concerns about my tantrums. They said that during my outbursts the walls would shake and the windows cracked. Believing I was cursed, they even requested approval from the State to perform an exorcism on me, but the Department said no. After their house burned down and a tornado demolished their entire town, all except the willow tree I stood under during the disaster, they rescinded their adoption request. Still though, it is somewhat sweet they were at least willing to try.

Most of the information I have about my childhood was from Joan, who secured a position as my legal representative known as a Guardian Ad-Litem. Even after she moved back to Massachusetts, she would always return to Washington when a placement fell apart. With Joan, no matter how blaring the evidence was, I could never do wrong by her, "Oh my god, I cannot believe that woman, blaming this innocent baby for her food being rotten. Buy food that's not expired, bitch."

She always thought it was happenstance, or God, or me adjusting to the place.

"Like they didn't know what they were getting into. Who signs up for a child only to give them up, the hell is wrong with people?"

And so it went, families would get scared and shut me out. I can only recall a few fleeting things, like trying to help or just wanting to learn more about a family, but what I remember the most was a feeling of no control. It felt like there was an ocean living inside me, with tumultuous waves ready to crash against the world or me. I was powerless against it. Maybe circuit wiring did explode because I was refused extra snacks, but even if it did, I was just a child.

At some point, I learned how to shut my mouth and block out these things that lived in my mind, but by then it was too late. I had turned seven years old. Fewer and fewer families were willing to consider me for my age, let alone the concerns regarding my psychological state. Not many families are looking for grown children that may potentially grow to be delinquent teenagers and possibly even more degenerative adults. I became quiet and introverted. At one point I was evaluated for Autism, they deferred to the all-inclusive diagnosis of Attention Deficit Disorder.

Joan could have adopted me and would condemn herself later in life for not doing so, "That would have been the Christian thing to do, Noah, and I failed you."

In the end, I do not think it was because I wasn't important enough to her. Joan had so much hope in humanity; she honestly believed I would be fine. If she had only known what would become of me, I know she would have tried harder, gone further, hell she would have kept me.

I would still receive the occasional interest despite my age, pale skin and sickly-looking appearance. Who wants an unhealthy kid? Joan would tell me at each referral, "It's the eyes Noah, they fell in love with those beautiful blues."

The one thing everyone noticed about me were my eyes, they said it looked like I had stars in them. I hated them, or at least the attention forced on me because of them, but there was something different about their color. I once saw a picture of deep space, some sort of cosmic sky, and it reminded me of them.

My eyes may have brought families in but something about my way sent them out. I think it was deliberate, my attempt at saving myself from continued disappointment and rejection. At that point, I thought I couldn't care less, but that was until a lady named Anne volunteered to foster me.

I lived with her and two other foster kids, Sam and Nina. They were biological siblings.

Anne drank so much that it never phased her when one of my unusual events occurred. She just kind of laid there. Her drinking would not have been much of a problem, but Anne brought along the most sinister of evils.

She was once a semi-functional adult, employed at a local discount store and married to a nice man who happened to be the manager. By her own fault in character and inability to remain monogamous, he divorced her. He left town with a younger woman, a nurse with a pretty face. After that, Anne was really no good to anyone or herself. In one last act of utter negligence, she chose to remarry a monster of a man.

Charles Daley moved into the deteriorating home that Anne inherited from her deceased parents. The house at the end of Grayson Road, isolated in a shrubbery of decaying woods.

Shortly after their marriage, Anne added a cocktail of painkillers to her daily regimen. For two years, she would intoxicate herself to the point of unconsciousness half the time and was at the bar for the rest.

It would take two years for the State to find out what Charles Daley was doing to us. Two whole years in that hell hole, before Nina would make the outcry. Too late for her and her brother, but not too late for me.

God or whoever, rest their souls.

A caseworker said he died shortly after the removal. May he burn in hell and hopefully something worse.

After that, Joan, along with her husband Kevin, would save me. Them and their sweet biological son, he was only a couple of years older than I was. The nicest family I had ever met. I didn't think I deserved it to be honest, not after everything.

Chapter Two

A simple fire and flood prevention charm:
Place one portrait, family or self, in the exact spot where the light of the sunrise first touches inside the home.
Then bury three stones found over three days where the last light of the sunset leaves.
For both rituals, speak the incantation four times for equity:
Ommm, Freya, Ommm, Gaia, Ommm, Aradia

The authorities removed me from Anne's home, she was charged and convicted for severe negligence of a minor and will spend the remaining years of her life in prison. Joan could not easily secure approval for my placement with her but worked furiously, traveling back and forth from her home in Massachusetts to attend the legal proceedings in Washington while I remained at the Children's Shelter. The Department of Family Services finally authorized my placement with Joan and her family a month later.

At ten years old, supposedly, I came to live with her family in Westchester, Massachusetts. Escorted by one of the trillion case managers in my life, I stepped onto the porch of their craftsman home. In my left hand, I held a trash bag lightly filled with the few possessions I owned, while my right arm hugged a cardboard box with holes punched at the top. It contained a black cat that found me the day I arrived at the shelter and refused to leave my side. I named him Morgan.

I can clearly remember knocking at their door, greeted swiftly by Joan along with her husband, Kevin Masterson, and their son Jake. On his right side was a Great Dane, Rocky, their family pet.

Morgan was not a fan.

"Hi Mr. and Mrs. Masterson, thank you for inviting me to your home," I said as they embraced me into their arms and family.

Joan said her biggest regret was not taking me in on that fateful day she was assigned to me. She cried into my shoulder and I remember desperately trying to reassure her, with all my ten-year-old might that it really was okay.

Life was good with Joan and her family. They treated me like their own, with love. Rocky, who seemed to simultaneously adore and fear Morgan, respected his personal space and stayed perfectly still whenever Morgan was near.

Years had gone by, and there had not been a single strange occurrence since I came to live with the Mastersons. It was like it all went away the day he died, taking away most of my memories, which were now fuzzy at best. A gift, I think, saving me from the past.

Like Joan, a part of me wanted to believe all the peculiar experiences of my life were merely by chance. Freak events, coincidentally occurring during my presence. A belief I held onto, especially these days with the Mastersons. We live in an ordinary town with ordinary people. I have a semi-ordinary life that would be plain if not for being a foster kid. I don't need to be normal, I have good people taking care of me, and very soon I will no longer be a foster kid. The Mastersons are nearly complete with the litigation for my adoption. After that, they will be my family, permanently.

So naturally, it came as a surprise when I was reminded of how profoundly different I am. A few months ago, my foster family and I were leaving the home to run various errands. Jake was upset about some team losing some game or another and was yelling. I don't know why, but it terrified me.

He was about to walk outside, but his frustrated rants became louder. Jake, as gentle as he was, became ominous with his towering height. My breath was trapped in my throat, but I forced the air out and the front door suddenly closes on Jake's face and refuses to budge, leaving him stuck inside the home.

Mr. Masterson pulled at the door for nearly an hour, "Jake, what did you do?"

Jake says, "I didn't do anything. It just closed, I think it was a ghost."

Mr. Masterson sighs heavily, "Don't be ridiculous, did you break the door?"

"No, I promise."

Eventually Jake just had to go out through the garage. I apologized profusely to the Mastersons out of habit, unnecessarily so, they merely laughed about it and made jokes at Jake's expense, his challenges with a door would go down in history.

He took it in stride and paid Mr. Masterson back in return with sarcastic remarks regarding his father's own ineptitude. After all, Mr. Masterson took two hours to open the door himself.

The strangest part was I could feel the door the entire time. Somewhere inside me felt tied to it and that would be the beginning of the end.

Things like that continued to happen, mostly in minor and insignificant ways. Doors shutting and closing, a pencil rolling toward me, or the TV turning on. There were other things as well, experiences not so easily dismissed.

I was having Visions of unfamiliar far-away places. They seemed harmless at first, not so different from daydreaming.

Unfortunately, these Visions seemed to be increasing in frequency and duration. Teachers would call on me multiple times in class before finally reaching my consciousness and pulling me out of the images. Joan received multiple reports concerned over my inability to concentrate. She laughed at the notion, "Tell them to talk to me when you don't get straight A's."

Worse were the unfamiliar thoughts that would intrude on my own, like the lucid plans of our neighbor, Joe. He would tell his wife he was playing basketball with his buddy Mike, when really he and Mike were having an affair. They would rent a room at a sleazy motel in the next town over every Tuesday at 7pm, "guys' night out". Nothing against being gay, I'm gay, but that's just wrong. Get a divorce Joe.

It was all a bit concerning. As far as I could guess, I was one of those Abnormal kids, the humans with extra gifts. Some Abnormals could float or even walk through walls. There were not loads of Abnormals, but there were a few in town. I figured my gifts consisted of moving things with my mind and being a bit psychic.

The scary part was that these things were difficult to control. These abilities seem to operate on my emotions. It was like that feeling of the ocean again, the more intense I felt about something the more powerful the waves would become. The worst was when the tide changed direction, a sure sign of a hurricane, and all I can do is witness the event. It is not just fear or anger that can trigger a reaction, even my good moods can cause a disaster.

About two months ago I nearly destroyed the Mastersons' home. My foster parents held a party to celebrate me winning first place in a Tri-District writing competition. I still had trouble getting used to being treated that way, being celebrated just for winning something, let alone having a party just for me.

It felt incredibly awkward having all this attention and happiness around me. The sporadic times I lived at the Children's Shelter, caseworkers would host monthly birthday parties, a way to celebrate all the kids at once, but never just for one. It doesn't help having to deal with the Mastersons' friends and family. People get this annoying, pitiful face with tearful eyes and upside-down smiles once they find out about the whole "abandoned foster child" stuff.

They act as if I have some terminal illness, not aided by the fact that I am smaller than most boys my age. They think I am malnourished and maybe I was once, but not anymore. I feel like telling them to stop feeling sorry for me, that I am fine so they can get over it and go away. I don't, that's the foster in me, a constant reminder to behave.

You wouldn't know I was bothered by much. Holding up a false half-smile, expressing gratitude appropriately, reading the scene; also the foster in me.

They sang, "For he's a jolly good fellow" and I felt intensely unsettled, and a little dumb to be honest, but then I saw Joan. She was there singing along and had been doing her absolute best to make sure everyone was enjoying themselves and, in that moment, I knew she was doing it all for me.

Mr. Masterson gave me a high five and I awkwardly returned it. We both smiled and laughed at my poor attempt to return the gesture.

It was strange for me, having a celebration like that, what was even stranger was the feeling inside me. Despite the sense of being pitied by the Mastersons' friends and family, I felt happy.

I knew what it was like to be happy but not like this, I thought maybe it was love. Thank god everything else happened when the party was over.

Joan and Mr. Masterson were on their weekly date night, Jake was with friends, and I had the house to myself. There wasn't anything special or particularly scary, just a usual Saturday night, except I was in an unusually good mood and that was apparently enough.

I was cleaning up the house, a gift to the Mastersons, and I had my favorite station playing on their stereo system. As I washed the dishes, I turned up the volume and swayed to the music. I swept and mopped excitedly and started dancing as I cleaned different sections of the floor.

At the peak of the upbeat song, with a short head start, I ran and slid on the wet floors and spun at the end as if I was ice-skating. I catch my balance and return to the chore. It was the first time I felt this degree of being content. There was no monster waiting for me behind the next corner, or impending doom scheduled for tomorrow afternoon.

I felt safe. Consumed by a sense of comfort, I had not noticed how the room pulsated. Not until I saw the movement from the corner of my eye. Quickly turning around, there it was, the Mastersons' large five-piece sofa set in the family room was floating in the air as if they were balloons held down only by the limits of the ceiling.

As for the rest of the house, I am not sure how to describe it, but it was as if the room held a heartbeat. The air was vibrating and it rippled back and forth against the walls. One by one, more pieces of furniture and objects floated up to the ceiling. What is this? What have I done?

An hour later, with the Mastersons interior property still floating all over the house. I was on the verge of a full-blown panic attack.

I could only assume my excitement was the cause of this phenomenon, because the objects descended the minute my good mood turned anxious. Like a mad man, I ran from room to room trying to prevent precious heirlooms dropping from the air. Thankfully, the objects floated downwards in slow gradual deflation.

It seems my gift was disproportionate in its impact, as some objects remained weightless longer than other items. Altogether, it took two hours for everything to return to the ground, leaving me to scramble as I return the various objects to their respective homes. The headlights of Mr. Mastersons' car shined brightly through the living room windows just as I finish resetting the couches.

After that day something changed in me, I became eager to test these abilities and wanted to know exactly what I could do. I began practicing them at every possible opportunity. If I have these gifts, I might as well use them.

At first it worked infrequently, and was usually dodgy at best when it did. I couldn't repeat the feat of floating furniture the night of my celebratory party, but I managed to do some lower scale, still neat, things like float a centimeter above the ground. So tiny, I wasn't sure I did anything at all. Gradually I noticed small improvements, a bit more strength and precision, and centimeters became inches for exactly two seconds.

One day, from the roof of the Mastersons' home, I stepped off to try my new trick only to fall straight down. I narrowly avoided a broken skull, my face hovered inches, literally inches above the ground. I think my nerves got the best of me, but instinct is automatic.

It continued like that, eventually I was able to levitate a ball and even have it bounce for Morgan. I restricted any practice of hovering my own body to the safety of my room, and could now impressively last a whole 15 seconds.

Even the psychic stuff received time and attention, ever respectful of the privacy of others, I learned how to shut out the unfamiliar thoughts from people near me, and my Visions were no longer like daydreaming. They were clearer and increasingly elaborate and I was even gaining more of a handle on steering the Vision, like lucid dreams. Except unlike dreaming, I was able to recall what I saw and could retain some awareness of myself. Although they remained relatively random, I was at least able to return to the present moment, like when Mrs. Niesche called on me for my turn in reading.

The Visions were always of specific events. Things in the future like Jake fumbling the ball during a game, only for it to come true the following day. Sometimes they were of things happening at that very moment, like Seeing exactly where Morgan was hiding in my mind's eye. Most recently, I had a Vision of the neighbors fighting violently inside their home. I called the police, and an hour later from my upstairs window, watched the police arrest the man and haul him away. The best part though was no more unplanned bizarre events. At least until that fateful day at the park.

It was one month before my birthday. One month before this chasm would form in my world, figuratively and literally breaking the ground beneath me. One more tribulation that I would have no choice but to carry by the compulsory forces of life. I guess some people's lot in life is to struggle. These are the cards I have been dealt, cards of hardship. All I can do is play my hand.

It was a clear, bright, ordinary morning. A strange thing given my life would be irrevocably shattered in a glorious catastrophe, and all before my morning cereal.

Jake and I were at the neighborhood park. We had taken Rocky out for a walk, who had a habit of running into people for his version of a hug. It was cold. The unyielding winter still held tightly onto the earth. Jake, who always carried a football around, wanted to play catch.

"Alright buddy, let's do this," Jake said.

Unsure of how to act around Jake, I awkwardly tried to play along. I shouldn't feel uncomfortable around him, like his parents, Jake was kind to me and treated me like family. The way he genuinely smiled and laughed helps me relax and try to enjoy the moment, no matter how inept I felt. We were having fun. I was having fun. Even if it was technically at my expense, as I uselessly tried to retrieve the ball in mid-air and clumsily threw it back.

Jake was laughing but it did not make me feel self-conscious, there were no cruel bones in that boy's body. Besides, it was not a secret that I had athletic deficits.

"Okay, one more time. You gotta go long," he says.

"What does that mean, like run back?"

"Yup, that's what they mean by, go long," he says chuckling to himself.

"Okay," I ran back feeling only slightly like an idiot. I tried to "go long" secretly desperate to convince him I could play well and be a good brother, like I was auditioning.

That's when it happened. Rocky, that sweet giant of a dog saw Jake throw the ball and I am sure in his dog-mind thought Jake was throwing it to him. He came running in the direction of me and jumped up in that lumbering loving beast kind of way, but he was so big, and in my fear, all I saw were his large wide jaws and danger.

I felt the same feelings that twist at my stomach and make me think of Charles Daley, and then nothing else.

There it was, my ocean inside me, it was too late the wind had changed directions, a hurricane.

"Stop," my voice sounded strangled somewhere between screams and cries. I pressed my hands forward, preparing for the impact that would not come. Rocky went flying into the street. I hear Jake's own cry, and then the sound of screeching tires and metal crashing, with a final squeal from a dying dog. Then more yelling; a woman rushes out of her car, not bothering to close the door. Rocky is lying still on the street.

I felt like the world just might end right then and there. My breath, my damn breath catching like it does, stuck inside me. I wish, harder than I ever wished for anything before, to wake up from this nightmare.

"Please, don't be real. Please, don't be real," I say to myself compulsively. This can't be true; he can't be dead. Rocky was like another child to my foster parents; I can't do this to them. I beg and plead with some higher power to change reality, and then in one quick flash there is nothing but bright white light and the sound of destruction.

The ground shakes and literally cracks beneath my shoes, and I know it is because of me. I try to stop myself, but fail miserably. I cannot fight the waves.

The crack in the ground spreads past the playground and into the street, making its way toward Rocky until finally meeting his limp body. I felt him the moment it touched him, it was as if I was holding him in my arms, and saw red, dark red. I wished and prayed harder. A bright light seemed to shine in some distant place. A place that existed in Rocky, me, and the Earth itself. I clawed at the bright light as if it could change this day and my mistake. I felt Rocky's limp body one last time and the bright white light changed into red sizzling, blinding light and burned out suddenly in one final burst.

Boom.

I was dizzy and with heavy eyelids, I dropped to the ground. The last thing I saw was the thin crack in the earth resealing itself, the wound healed, and then nothing.

The next day I found myself in a hospital room, Joan sat beside me. She was reading but looked up when I stirred and seemed strangely small. She wore an expression I didn't quite understand, something sad. Underneath her eyes, were deep dark crevices etched into her normally smooth brown skin.

"Hey honey," she says with a kind smile.

I attempted to speak but struggled against the deep scratching in my throat. Preemptively, she gave me water. It feels better within seconds. I clear my throat, "What happened? Why am I here?"

Her eyes began to swell up with tears and it seemed they would overflow into streams, but Joan recomposes herself in an instant, dabbing her eyes and inhaling deeply, as if those tears were never there.

"There was an accident, with Rocky and you." She stumbled on her words and I struggled to make sense of her.

She pauses and her face is empty, but her eyes dart back and forth, searching for the right words to say.

"You were scared," she says decidedly, but her absent smile makes me think she is also talking to herself.

"You killed Rocky," then a deafening pause for the briefest of moments, "It was an accident. You didn't know what you were doing."

There is a feeling that accompanies terrible news, the two go hand in hand, one inviting the other. I have that feeling now. It lives inside the pit of my stomach; it twists and tears me into pieces, dragging me into some void where there is no return. It is a sign of the world ending, but the instinct to survive is powerful, and I attempt to deny reality.

"No, I didn't, that's not true," but as the realization and the flood of memories return, the ineffable truth comes to life.

I shudder and that feeling comes in full reckoning, pulling apart every seam in my body. I hear myself wailing and clutching at my stomach, my attempt to put the pieces back together.

"No, god no," I cry.

Joan, in all her utter kindness, rushes over and wraps her arms around me, rocking me back and forth. She is a good woman, but I wouldn't blame her for no longer wanting me. I don't want me.

Then she says, "He's alive honey." She remains quiet for an unusually long time, "You saved him."

Her words confuse me and seems oppositional with all that happened. She should be angry, not sweet and gentle.

"The Doctor explained to us what happened. Did you know you were a Witch?"

I laughed at the absurdness and irrelevance of the question.

"What," I say quietly.

"A Witch, did you know you were one of them," she waits for me to answer before speaking further, "We didn't know you were one and we didn't think you knew either, not that it matters. We still love you. I just wasn't sure."

"What are you saying," slowly coming out of the thick clouds I seemed to be in, "What are you asking me? No, I'm not a Witch."

I would think being a Witch is the kind of thing a person would know.

"Noah, you used magik."

"I thought I was one of those kids, the Abnormals," I confess to her.

She looks at me with those kind eyes, "Abnormals can't do what you did babe." She explains that Abnormal humans generally only have one mild or moderate ability. Not like Witches, whose powers far surpassed that of even the most talented Abnormal.

I remembered a time when I was eight years old, when I was with Anne. She was visiting her friend who lived in a nearby trailer park. Her friend never wanted kids inside her home so we stayed outside while they drank the day away.

A young Witch lived nearby. She could not have been any older than thirteen. One day, the cops came and there were ambulances. The rumor was she had killed someone. As the police dragged her away, the trailers started catching fire and the metal roofs twisted from the sheer heat of her power, apparently not something typical of an Abnormal.

When an Abnormal was identified, it was a visit to the hospital, and they were set up with some tutoring on how to control their gift. They did not get escorted away, never to be seen or heard from again.

"That's why her daddy had to save her," said Anne, with her yellow teeth and sunken face. I always wondered if her family even bothered to bury her.

Witches were rare. I am sure there weren't any in Westchester, but I knew there were Witches elsewhere. Other than the girl at the trailer park the only other Witch I knew was Charlotte Tucker, the star of The Real Life beWitched, a reality show about some famous Witch that was beautiful and rich. The show was more drama than magik, apparently most Witches usually keep their powers secret.

I would have thought I'd be excited about being a Witch. Like any other kid, I had fantasized about having magikal powers, and Witches were amazing, but they were also scary. I remembered the history lessons on the Witch trials that were common at one point. Even though Witches had magik, they were not all-powerful and could not overcome entire mobs. Over time, Witches became a resource to seek for opportunity and are now thought of as allies. However, in classic American hypocrisy, they are still seen as a threat and even kindergarteners are taught to avoid them.

It is times like these I wished I knew my biological family. Maybe they would know if I had some distant relative who was also a Witch, like a great grandmother on my father's side.

"I don't have magik, believe me. If I did, I would have used it a long time ago."

She laughed. It was a beautiful sound.

"Many Witches don't have or aren't able to use their powers until they're a little older, like you."

"You said I saved Rocky. What happened exactly, and is he alright?"

"Yes he's fine. Noah, you were scared. You somehow pushed him into the street." I wince and she quickly adds, "By accident, with magik I guess, and then you brought him back to life," she says incredulously.

I began to piece the memory together. Rocky was running toward me, or at me. I closed my eyes and the physical memories return making my body flinch automatically, preparing itself for the imaginary impact. I recall seeing Rocky's limp body on the ground, the crack in the earth, and the dark red light.

I felt him, I felt Rocky. I knew it right away. It was like admitting some undeniable truth, it was his blood, I felt his blood, churning it and ultimately changing it. Was I holding onto his life?

The loud boom I heard was not the earth breaking. It was the sound of his heart beating once more. I had brought him back to life.

How is that possible?

The monitors began beeping, reacting to the rising panic within my body, and activating an alarm. A rush of nurses charge into the room. One injects something in the IV sack connected to the vein in my arm, and I begin to feel sleepy all over again. The new round of sedatives take their effect, spiriting me away.

My mind turned to Morgan, my handsome boy, and I thought for a moment that I saw him purring in the distance. A moment's reprieve, in his kitty-way, I think he tells me to shut my eyes. This was too much for one day.

Chapter Three

Ribbon Binding Charm
Maintains close physical proximity, especially helpful for keeping young children near in crowded areas.
Caution: Length of ribbon is literal for the charm.
Example: 10 inches of ribbon equates to a maximum distance of 10 inches between the person or object.

My fainting episode resulted in the hospitalization and, subsequently, unwanted attention. Apparently, it would have been better if the Mastersons kept me at home. My first lesson as a Witch was that any attention was bad attention.

It is a federal, F-E-D-E-R-A-L, law that the Council of Witches be alerted when a Witch youth has something called a Manifestation. It is when young Witch children reach the age of maturity and receive their magikal abilities, kind of like puberty.

The steel-eyed doctor didn't bat an eye to Joan's protests, "It's policy, ma'am."

"Well, what are they going to do," remarks a flustered Joan.

"His kind will come for the boy and take him to their compound."

A compound, what the hell is that, it sounds like a concentration camp. It sounded like I was in trouble, and then a much worse thought came to mind. What if something happened to the Mastersons for having me in their home? Not just with the Witch Council, but also the local authorities, they couldn't possibly blame them for me being a Witch. I prayed they did not suffer any consequence on my account, and as I prayed, I wondered if that counted as a spell. Do Witches have to think about that sort of thing, do I? It was an uncomfortable thing to admit.

The physician finished his explanation of the policy, "Witch youths with no immediate Kin or Witch relatives go directly to the Witch-people."

Basically, these Witches can sweep in and abduct foster kids and we become their property and registered citizens of their nation. It felt like someone was holding my heart.

After twenty-four hours of post-sedation monitoring, we were finally able to return home, well past any respectable dinner time. The entire time it felt as if the hospital staff were antsy to discharge me. Not one nurse looked me in the eye as they rushed through the final vitals, not even bothering to double check, let alone triple check their numbers. It made me wonder why the hell they didn't kick me out earlier, instead of waiting until the end of the damn day.

At least the Mastersons were home, the obligation to stay with me was no longer necessary. It had now been two days since the hospital discharge.

The whole debacle seemed unreal, like I was living someone else's life. The Mastersons pulled me from school, which was also not the best idea in terms of maintaining secrecy, gossip flew fast in Westchester, but that was the least of my worries.

For those brief days, I convinced myself it was all a bad dream. The phone rang earlier that day; its chimes broke my temporary delusion. As the hospital physician promised, a representative from the Witch Council contacted us that morning. And per the snobby sounding woman that Joan placed on speakerphone, we were made aware of what lay ahead of me as an alleged Witch.

"Thc Council was alerted to Noah's Manifestation at the time of the incident, his level of power set a reaction that traveled quite a distance," she sounded impressed. "The Council would have investigated the incident regardless of being notified. A group of chosen assessors will arrive in three days' time by the setting sun. We will screen and verify his Witch status. Should he be of our kind, we will take him to our realm."

Joan asked about the "compound", and the woman laughed condescendingly, "Mortals are quite limited in their knowledge about our facilities and ways."

I wondered why the event with Rocky was considered a Manifestation and why the other times I used these powers were not. It seemed I "Manifested" some time ago, but I guess those acts of magik went under the radar.

Joan tried to argue, demanding information on the location, but the woman who said things like "the setting sun" refused to answer. Joan persisted, and demanded to know the woman's name. "Abigail Tetson, ma'am, and again, the location of our realm is of no concern to those of non-Witch lineage. As I said, when we arrive we will test the boy. Should Noah be verified as a Witch, we will initiate and assume our nation's rightful custody of him. He will attend our Academy for his magikal training and that is all that I choose to say on the matter," cutting Joan off with the click of a button, leaving the endless dial-tone behind.

They would force me to attend their Witch school.

Joan has not stopped crying, and is currently out cold thanks to her forgotten painkillers. The medicine was prescribed during her recovery from a recent hysterectomy, but she never used them, a strong woman that one.

Mr. Masterson hasn't said a word, neither has Jake and with Joan asleep, nobody is talking. I feel like I am going to explode.

In all honesty, their reactions surprised me. I guess they had grown close to me and maybe even loved me, it did feel like what a home ought to feel like.

Night arrived graciously, ending this day from hell. I lie in my bed that will soon no longer be mine, uncertain about everything. I've often wondered why all the bad things that have happened to me, had to happen. I once blamed the world, then some higher power, but in the past few days I've come to the idea that it must be my penance for some crime in a past life or something heinous I will do in the future. Somehow, it makes it easier to feel like I deserved it.

Slowly and then all at once, I break entirely. Treacherous tears make their escape, falling freely as I crawl into a ball, desperate to keep the parts of me together. I don't remember falling asleep but when I opened my eyes, the room was still dark and I was on the floor. A hint of effervescent blue slowly lines the top of my window. I get up, and halfway to the bed, all the realizations of the day's events buried by my half-stupor, come rushing to the surface and it feels like death.

A soft rap at the door, "Can I come in?" Mr. Masterson takes a seat beside me, "Are you okay? Dumb question. Sorry."

My dreams and fears must have spoken for me while I slept.

I can smell the lingering alcohol on his breath, and I think of Charles Daley. The thought is like a fire, burning the oxygen in the room. I struggle to breathe, but remind myself he is a good man, and exhale. I can tell by the deep streaks of red webs in the white of his eyes that he is not only scared for me, but hurting too.

"I thought maybe we could stop this, I thought we could fight it. Noah, I am so sorry, I don't think we can."

And just like that, this great man, who I have always thought was doing such a kindness by taking me in based on his wife's wishes, breaks down in front of me. As he crumbles at his genuine defeat and extraordinary grief, I realize this man truly does love me like a son and that it was not just Joan who wanted to save me. So I broke down along with him, it is my grief too.

"It's going to be okay, I'll be okay," I lie and I do not know where those words came from, but it seemed right to say.

As promised, on the setting sun of the following third day, there is a knock on the door. Joan and I were drinking tea while Mr. Masterson obligatorily opened the door, incidentally inviting my captors inside.

A rather tall man with a large belly and broad smile, dressed to the nines, is the first to enter. Doctor Vance Huebner, "Doc, if you please?"

He winked at me when he introduced himself, I could have thrown my tea on him, but his gesture was more than a means of reassurance. The tea began to swirl in upon itself, twisting, and transforming into the shape of a castle, a ballerina, a dragon, and finally a Witch on a broom.

Two others joined him, a middle-aged woman and a man who looked to be in his 20s. Both wore placid faces, indifferent to anyone else but the good Doctor. The man barely said a word, but the woman was a real treat.

The Doctor had a boom for a laugh, and talked with his hands. He explains his role and reviews his magikal and non-magikal accomplishments, an attempt to convince us of his altruistic nature and competence in effectively helping others. However, he did not seem arrogant, something about his enthusiasm and theatrics made his self-praise reassuring. He tries to introduce the others, but the woman interrupts him before he can speak further, leaving the Doctor unable to sing their praises.

"Abigail Tetson and my apprentice, Pedro Flores." The younger man nods in agreement.

Dr. Huebner chats with the Mastersons as if they were old friends. Worst of all, he seemed to genuinely get along with them. Even Rocky became fast friends with the Doctor, which was more than I could say for the dog and me. Our own relationship seemed strained, based on his indistinct growls toward me that started the day after I killed him. I would think the damn dog would be grateful, after all, I did resurrect him.

Just then, Morgan sleeks in, all black and attitude. Jumping onto the kitchen table, hissing at Rocky, who yielded with sad whimpers and backed away, hopeful Morgan would not get feisty and scratch his eyes, again.

Doc perked up, "A Faemalyr! Well there you have it, no test is needed. Noah is clearly a Witch."

On the defense, Joan rises and challenges the Doctor, but Kevin beats her to it. "What the hell? That is a bogus test, how does that prove anything, lots of kids have cats?"

And the Doc explained he could "sense", an albeit mild, connection between Morgan and I, which allows him to screen me as a Witch.

Joan spouts out, "Bullshit!" The two no longer seemed like old pals, "How the hell does that prove anything?"

The Doc sighs and then does something that surprises everybody, "I know this is a difficult time, and I truly am sorry. I wish I could tell you that you could keep your son, but you can't, he is one of us. What I can tell you is you do not have to lose him, entirely."

Even though I was miserable, I found myself kind of liking this man, a bit.

Ms. Tetson interrupts the Doctor before he can further explain, "Excuse me, Doctor Huebner, their concerns are legitimate. Despite his Aura, our regulations require official testing, we have to produce evidence that supports his Witch lineage through trial and examination."

Although my Manifestation, the figurative bat signal, reached the Witch Council, it was still insufficient for their protocol. Whatever tests they were going to give me were required by policy, not necessity.

Dr. Huebner concedes, "Very well, I was hoping to avoid putting the boy through it."

Joan and Kevin frantically look at each other then at the Doctor, but before he can open his mouth.

Ms. Tetson says, "There are three tests required to verify his Witch status. Biologically, Witches are different from Mortals, as evidenced by our abilities and extended life, therefore the first exam is a magikal version of genetic testing."

"What are the side effects? Has this been FDA approved," Joan challenges.

The Doctor answers, "There is no way for your scientific tests to evaluate the serum we are giving him; however, there are some side effects, a chemical reaction."

"You'll need a blood sample and we'll have to go to a lab," Kevin says but Ms. Tetson interjects the conversation to avoid being silenced again, "The insolence, you know nothing of our methods, so please refrain from any further interruptions."

The vein in Kevin's forehead is suddenly distinct and I swear I can see it pulsate.

Pedro pulls out a vial filled with a brilliant, glowing gold liquid. I worry it might be poison and should fear it, except I don't, and cannot understand why. Everything in me wants to run away, but I do not, instead I just stand there patiently waiting for the drink.

Joan, Kevin, and Jake all squander about, but their voices seemed distant. Ms. Tetson says something, and everyone becomes silent. I don't know where they went, because all I can see is the curious light in the vial in front of me. Everything else seems dark.

The apprentice, Pedro, asks the Mastersons if they would like to experience the test to verify its non-lethality, explaining to them that if they are not of Witch-kind they will experience nothing.

Joan volunteers, despite the resistance from Kevin and Jake, "I am doing this."

Pedro grabs his bag, walks Joan to the side of me, and fusses about for a few minutes. Even though he took the vial with him, I am still left in somewhat of a daze and do not even think to turn around.

Joan sharply gasps, and I thought maybe that she might be a Witch too. I optimistically hoped she could qualify as my Witch relative, but the thought is fleeting. Ms. Tetson gives no facial indication, but her petulant sigh indicates that Joan is obviously not of Witch lineage. Joan returns from the corner, tucking at the crease of her elbow, her face filled with dread, "If he is a Witch, what will it do to him?"

"It will make him feel pain," the Doctor says, with an edge in his tone. "It's a savage tool. I wish it were different."

I hear them, I see them, but the man has put the vial back on the table in front of me, and it's so curious looking. I feel miles away, some shuffling about happens around me as the Mastersons argue and before I know it, the other man grabs my arm.

I will not be drinking the bright gold potion. Instead, they will inject it into my veins. My panic rises gradually, but it wakes me from the trance. Tired of needles and terrified of these Witches, I start to flail. Ms. Tetson grabs me with nonsensical strength and her apprentice tears away at the plastic of the new syringe and fills it with the vial's remaining contents.

In a flash, he plunges the needle into my vein and I go numb.

It flows into my body, warm and heavy, I feel like I am floating in empty space for one second.

The reason Dr. Huebner was hoping to avoid this test arrives immediately after, the darkness dissipates into nothing, replaced with white-hot fire.

I burn. I am on fire and I am screaming, begging, pleading for mercy, but I continue to be burned alive.

"Trial by Fire," with obvious shame on his face. "To a Mortal, this would be the equivalent of fluids being supplied through an I.V., but to a Witch, is a toxin, non-lethal in this quantity. It reacts at the cellular level of his Witch genotype that separates us from Mortals. It is designed to mimic the Witch Trials of Salem."

I beg for death and after five eternal minutes, the burning begins to recede, finally ending ten minutes later.

"Time for the second test," says Ms. Tetson with a sickly-sweet tone.

I tried to refuse, but the golden neuro-poison isn't just to make a Witch suffer, but also to encourage obedience. I find myself succumbing to its persuasion. If I don't, the burning comes back, compelling me into submission.

The second test is a demonstration of an innate skill. Every Witch has at least one. I choose to use my ability to move things with my mind. I take advantage of my anger; it fuels my power and sends Abigail flying toward the wall.

Mid-air, she flicks her hand and stops herself abruptly, completely still in an upside-down position, but effortlessly floats back upright, then descends to her original location.

I stare at her, refusing to break eye contact, she remains unfazed, "Time for the third test."

The last test is a simple spell, one used to illuminate the dark. It requires crushing a few herbs, one stone, some words, and poof I have a magikal flashlight.

I am almost proud when the spell works, it is after all my first. The pride quickly recedes having remembered what completing the spell means. I have to remind myself that my fate was inescapable. They already knew I was a Witch. I was never getting out of this, and my hate floods back into me, especially for her. The destructive feeling has a vague familiarity.

We were sitting at the dining room table, as Dr. Huebner and Ms. Tetson reviewed the details of their next course of action.

I try to plead with them, "I'm not even a good Witch, why would the Council want me anyway? Yeah, maybe I had a breakdown and a magikal outburst as a result, but that was it, I can't control it. Even if I wanted too, I couldn't make it happen again. Look at me now, I'm mad and still, nothing."

Dr. Huebner insists, "Because all young Witches start off as low level, with time and training, your powers will grow. You will become stronger, but without training you will become a threat to yourself, your family, and the Witch nation. Ultimately, this is for the best."

Abigail, with her permanent resting bitch face chimes in, "The order between our kind and humankind is a delicate balance. The survival of Witch-kind depends on the careful nurturing of our young. The Mortals, in their infinite insecurities, are constantly searching for a threat to justify their fears, and a single uncontrolled Witch provides them all the evidence needed to threaten that balance."

She pauses to look directly into my eyes, "This is bigger than you, Mr. Ellis. You are a Witch, more specifically, you are now our Witch."

My skin crawls. I belong to no one.

"I don't have any money," I argue with the Doctor. "I can't afford to go anyway," to which he scoffs and waves at the air, swatting away my statement like a bothersome bee. The younger Witch, Pedro, explains, "Every Witch is fully funded by the Council. Even Non-Legacies, excuse me, I mean Recessive Witches such as yourself."

He clarifies that Recessive Witches are born without any known Witch ancestry, and the same is true for Non-Legacies, but the term is used to differentiate Witches without biological or legal guardians with the authority to interfere with the Council's orders.

Regardless, all Witch children must go to school, even "Legacies," Witches with an identified magikal bloodline. However, Non-Legacies become Wards of the Witch nation.

As far as funding goes, Pedro explains that no Witch or Mortal parent was expected to pay for their children's magikal training. This was done in an attempt to reduce contact with Mortals. I wondered how many Witches existed and how this Witch nation was able to afford this entirely free education.

"Witch children have no business in the Mortal world the moment they Manifest," Ms. Tetson says without invitation.

In any case, Non-Legacies are assigned Guardian Crowns, like a legal guardian. Doctor Huebner elected himself to the role, and he referred to me as his "Crown Ward", Witch language for foster kids, which coincidentally is the same title used in Ontario.

Oh, foster care, will I ever escape you?

He said being a Crown Ward was an "absurd, inconceivable, deplorable and futile attempt to put restrictions on a Witch, but policy, unfortunately, must be followed."

Ms. Tetson, loving to hear herself speak, adds, "Time has run away from us, no more discussion. Pack your bags, we leave first thing in the morning."

Joan began to cry while Kevin started to argue. Jake and I were silent as he hugged my shoulder. I remained still, frozen.

I see Kevin. He reminds me of the kind of man who you would see host a children's television program. High energy and a seemingly endless supply of smiles, he was just that, full of genuine kindness. It breaks my heart to see him breakdown, and I begin to cry as well. It still surprises me to see him care as much as he does.

The Doctor, responding to our distress, is the reason we are given a rare extension, two days to prepare for departure. If it were not for the circumstances, I think I might have liked Dr. Huebner. He seemed kooky, that's the best word I can think to describe him. A man that danced to the beat of his own drum, all height and belly, full of mania, like he gave a damn about life.

The rest of the visit is hazy, information exchange overload. I barely remember walking to my room, let alone falling asleep. Like the night before, I wake up in the middle of the night and open my eyes to darkness. Except tonight I woke up with a crisp awareness that I was not having a nightmare but living in one, there was no relief, not even in dreams. I was going to the school they called St. Philomena Academy, a school for Witchcraft, whether I liked it or not.

Another goodbye to another place, but this time was worse, quite possibly the worst. This time I was leaving my home.

Joan and I went shopping that morning. She started acting erratically and had stayed up all night engaging in full online shopping binges with 24-hour delivery services. A slew of packages began arriving at the front door. We had spent the better part of the morning zip lining through local stores for clothing, luggage, and other objects of comfort.

We returned home to organize and pack the supplies she purchased for me. We were packing my ninth piece of luggage with books filled with various literary content, many of them were her personal favorites. She had written several notes to me, life lessons she called them. It was as if she was trying to fill my tank with as much of her wisdom and love in the briefest amount of time.

She started talking to me about boys, which she never does. It wasn't a secret that I was gay but discussing it outright, with anyone really, made me incredibly uncomfortable. Under normal circumstances I would have refused out of embarrassment but, with my upcoming removal on the horizon, there was no time for shame or hesitation. I did not know when or if I would ever see her again.

She warns me of the danger of boys.

"Some boys won't like you, love, and that's okay. Baby, the real problem is when they do. Knowing which boy is the right one, now that is a challenge. Be careful with your heart, don't trust easily, but trust all the same. If a boy shows you who they are, good or bad, believe them."

"Why are you telling me this?" I ask.

"Cause you're leaving me, I won't get to see you off on your first date, or hear about your first love, or console your first heartbreak. And here's a secret, you will fall in love, and will be disappointed, hopefully only once. You are so beautiful Noah Ellis and I don't mean beautiful because I-love-you kind of beautiful, but God spent some time on you dear. I even think he put a little heaven in those big blues of yours, and believe me there will be many boys telling you all sorts of sweet things to have some of that beauty, just to own it, they won't care so much about you as a person. So, find the boy that will fall in love with the most beautiful thing about you, it isn't your eyes, or your pretty smile, it's you and this," as she points to my heart.

I promised to follow her advice and she hugged me tightly. Not wanting to worry her, I fought back my tears while her own fall freely.

Dr. Huebner arrives later that evening to inform us of some unexpected news. Turns out the Doctor was a good man after all. Not only did he modify my departure but, in an unprecedented move, also modified the law.

By some miracle, the Doctor was able to secure authorization from the Council to approve the Mastersons partial custody over me. Close to midnight, the Doctor and the Mastersons signed paperwork on the arrangement.

Before all this, the Mastersons had prior legal guardianship over me but could not finalize adoption due to various legal complications. Joan had been working out the details for the past two years. She was close to securing authorizations for them to move forward prior to the whole Witch fiasco.

Apparently, the Witch Council has special mechanisms for beelining bureaucratic red tape and state-to-state clauses for custody rights that had kept the Mastersons from adopting me earlier. They would maintain significant rights, like the right for me to stay with them during breaks, the right to be kept informed of how I was doing, as well as the right to consent for education or medical services I received. As promised, Dr. Huebner would be my Guardian Crown, and he assured the Mastersons that he would enforce these custody rights on behalf of them, and me. He promised to do so for the remaining years of my training.

I finish packing the night before I am to leave. I have more stuff than I have ever had before, suitcases filled with clothes and other electronic toys. Kevin even purchased a new smartphone for me. The Mastersons promised to maintain services despite Dr. Huebner explaining to them, "There is no service in the city of Tarias," the realm of Witches, "But not to worry, there are other ways of communication." Kevin persisted, "We are keeping the phone." Joan followed with, "For when he visits during breaks."

That night, for the first time since this all started, I fell asleep without tears in my eyes.

At dawn, Dr. Huebner, Pedro, and a young Witch that I have not met arrive in a small sedan. They must have used magik to pack my entire luggage into that small trunk; it should have taken up the entire space of the car.

Joan hugs me on my right and Kevin on my left. Jake cries non-stop but joins for a group hug. Morgan meows loudly, confined to his kennel; he hated that. Then Rocky whines at him in sympathy. Kevin places his hand on my shoulder, "You take care of yourself now."

All I can do is smile. I gather all my strength and try my absolute best to be brave for them, so they may send me off with a little less worry. I pack it all up, my fears and devastation at the loss of life that could have been mine. I pray it will be enough.

I step into the car and say goodbye to them from the window. As these strangers drive me away from my family, I cannot help but feel a little less secure that I will see them again. Once out of eye-view, I allow my tears to rain down.

Chapter Four

Walk-Easy
Walk Thy Path for 30 days and 30 nights
Channel solar and lunar forces.
Refer to the following texts for further details: Mastering Fate, Space, and Time through Temporal and Translocative Magik.

The Doctor offered to chaperone my trip to the Academy. It seemed strange this group of Witches chose to drive a generic car from an ordinary and mundane company, and it left me with paranoia over their intentions. However, I found it relieving when he forced me to sit in the back, uncertain of the Mortal safety protocols for children, "Better safe than sorry." Despite his prominence, he seemed to always manage to remain polite and generally pleasant.

Pedro sat in front while the Doctor drove, at least for all intents and purposes, not once have I seen him actually touch the steering wheel and I was certain he was paying no mind to the pedals. He used some sort of sophisticated spell to operate the vehicle independent of him, which granted him the time to engage in many conversations. I was quickly learning that talking was the Doctor's most-favored pastime. It appeared he could go on non-stop, all the knowledge of the world seemed to be at the tip of his tongue, and I wondered how much he knew.

The younger woman I did not recognize was actually the Doc's assistant. Her name was Darcy Hutchins. She sat with me in the back and looked to be in her mid-20s. She was blonde, small-framed, and her face held no smile.

I thought it would be more fantastic going to a magikal school, flying on brooms instead of driving in a sedan on a regular road trip.

I uselessly try to rest my eyes to disappear and pretend none of this was happening, but fail miserably. I was too wound-up in anticipation and worry over what was in store for me in the city of Witches called Tarias.

Once more, I try to reason with them over my abduction. The Doctor insisted it was an "opportunity." I repetitively debate moot points. "Why does the Council want me? Why do I have to go, I barely did any magik? The whole Rocky thing was a fluke."

I was talking louder than I expected, almost near shouting. Darcy told me to calm myself but the Doctor just smiled sympathetically. He must have known my desperation, I breathe in and out to settle myself.

The Doctor patiently reminds me, "Regardless, you are of Witch-kind. Please be mindful all young Witches require education to manage their abilities. Believe me Mr. Ellis your powers will grow. This is beyond your juvenile tantrum. One day you will become stronger and you will contribute, as is your birthright and duty."

"I don't want it, I don't want any of this," I want to scream and curse, but out of respect, or fear, I contain myself.

He adds, "Hopefully this will appeal to some sensibility. Without proper tutelage, you will become a threat to your loved ones. Mr. Ellis you are still a child, and whether you like it or not, you are also a Witch. You are gifted with skills you cannot yet conceive and with power comes responsibility. A child's actions are the obligation of its caregiver. In your case, it is mine as your Guardian Crown and the Council's. It is our duty to manage your training and development until you come of age to take that responsibility for yourself. Lest we forget, you have been provided the most fortunate chance to maintain your Mortal ties, who also are held accountable for you. Do you want to hurt your family?"

"Of course not," I interrupt him. Was he threatening me? I know they signed paperwork, but I still have difficulty believing that a piece of paper could truly bind us. Who knows what would lie ahead of me in this new world? What promises would be kept, and which would be broken?

He pauses to allow me to speak further but I say nothing, and he goes on, "You need training, without it, you will hurt them. Not on purpose, but the dog incident would only be the beginning. You do not belong to us, but you need to be with us. We have the capacity and competency to give you the tools you need to master yourself and prevent repeats of the past unfortunate events from occurring."

It was only one incident, why did he say events?

"Fine," I said.

"Now, time is running out, no more discussion," the Doc says, "Pip-Pip," his way of encouraging haste, "we must journey on," as he pulls into a familiar parking lot.

There is a state park near my house, well, old house, it is only 10 miles past town. I had noticed we seemed to be using routes closer to town instead of the highway. I chose not to say anything, naively hoping they would realize their mistake and return me home. He parks the car and steps out of the vehicle along with the others. Perplexed by the whole scenario, but I follow suit without thinking.

I opened the door and, although it is made of lightweight aluminum, it feels oddly heavy. I must be depressed because every move requires effort and concentration, my fear of what was to become of me clearly taking affect over my body. It was a familiar sensation, change and hardship were not new to me. There was always a bit of apprehension and uncertainty when I was moving from home to home in the foster system, but this was different. At least back then, I generally knew what lay ahead of me.

We stand on the pavement of the parking lot; I ask the Doctor why we stopped at the state park.

"We must go on foot. It is too far east to go by sea and you are far too inexperienced to use a broom. That would be an absolute safety violation and I will not allow it," as he waves toward the direction of a nearby nature trail, leaving me with more questions than answers. He suddenly turns back toward the car. It has been fully unloaded by Pedro and Darcy.

Dr. Huebner extends his arms, palms facing the sky, and raises his hands vertically. The suitcases follow his instructions and levitate up into the air, rising above us. My mouth hangs open as my nine large suitcases follow us onto the trail as if they are on an invisible conveyor belt.

There is a historic cemetery in the park, back from the days of battles on these lands. I see Georgia, a large stone statue of an angel holding two small children. I have always thought it was one of the most beautiful things in the world. The Doctor places his hand on the angel, expressing his similar revere, "The magnificence of all things."

As we walk out of the cemetery, we come across a man jogging. He gawks at us and the expression on his face is in-between shock and excitement. Surely surprised at the sight of the outlandishly black and flowing clothes of the three Witches. Then again, he was perhaps more preoccupied with the flying luggage set at our backs.

Pedro twirls his hand like he was changing a light bulb and the jogger has this shift in his face, from surprise to confusion.

He searches his body as if he has forgotten his keys but then looks around his perimeter and it is plain to see on his face. He is lost.

"What did you do to him," I demand to know.

"A simple memory spell, he will only forget the past two minutes," Pedro says in response. A revelation grows in his eyes as he spots a landmark and remembers the way, jetting forward in full stride. Pedro whispers a few words that sound similar to Latin and a breeze disturbs the loose leafs on the ground as he speaks. We continue our walk and others pass us by, but they pay us no mind, as if we were never there.

So there I am, walking toward some unknown world, altogether different from how I arrived at the Mastersons. This time I held Morgan in a trendy cloth kennel that Kevin purchased for me. He meows softly from inside his temporary home.

Darcy and Pedro are a slight bit ahead of me, talking to the Doctor of science, math, and magik, using words that held no meaning to me.

The sun shines brightly above. It must be close to midmorning and I recognized the direction we were currently taking, the path leads to a more heavily wooded area that quickly clears out, cut down for a parking lot near the main road. That is where we should be, but instead we were back at the beginning, at the entrance of the old cemetery. We approached Georgia once more, as Dr. Huebner places his hand on her for a second time. I thought I might be going crazy and was feeling more certain of it with each passing minute.

"Doctor Huebner, we are going in circles," I finally say.

"Are we now?" the Doctor replies, and then urges me on, "Thrice is the price, a lesson you will learn well as you flutter off to soar the skies my young Witch."

We continue the path and come across Georgia yet again. Once more, he rests his palm on her, and we continue our cyclical trip through the park for the third time, but when we return, Georgia is no longer there. In her place is a stone entryway encircled within the ground with steps leading to the depths of the Earth itself.

"This way Mr. Ellis," says Doc.

My eyes must have shown my combined fear and intrigue. "There are many secrets to this world Mr. Ellis and I would very much like for you to know them all, if it is quite alright," asked the Doctor. He held his hand out toward mine through the stone hole, helping me take my first step below.

Sconce torches illuminate the narrow tunnel and our path ahead. We walk further downward, the floor becomes level, leading us right and then left. Until finally the steps return, and we ascend toward a small circle doorway where the sunlight shined through, revealing the outside world.

Pedro said we were in the Canadian Rockies. It seems impossible, yet there they were, mountains that were more like stone giants. The cold was unlike any I have felt before. It seeps into my bones and makes it difficult to breathe. Dr. Huebner gently touches a large boulder just like Georgia.

Using strange words, Darcy cast a spell, and the cold no longer bit at my skin. The feeling of death, gone in an instant. Instead, a comfortable warmth surrounds us and melts the snow only to instantaneously re-freeze as we walk away.

We circled the path three times, returning to the spot where the boulder once was, replaced by the entrance for the stairs hidden in the ground. These lead us to the Redwood forest of California. Dr. Huebner touches one of those giants, the one we would pass by again, soon enough.

It was dusk as we walked deeper into the woods. I had always wanted to visit the Redwoods, although under different circumstances, the shadows of these tremendous trees cloak the forest floor in darkness, a task made easy with nighttime quickly approaching.

I let Morgan out so he could stretch his legs. He had mostly slept since we started this journey; Morgan would not stray far from me. A moment later he returned to the pretty cloth kennel for what I guessed would be continued sleep. Even he knew this was not our destination, and I unequivocally ached to be back home.

We continued making our way through the forest while Dr. Huebner reviewed Witch history with me, explaining how Witches have been researched and written upon for eons, citing Hecate, a favored Witch deity, and her followers.

He differentiates non-magikal witches from the Witch-species, explaining that Mortal witches practice their abilities but at a significantly lower level of power. As it turns out, every human is capable of magik and he described it as, "Just enough energy to push at chance and probability, a mild influence on the odds or course of fate."

He goes on to explain the evolution of Witches, "Our ancestors far surpassed that rudimentary sorcery, transforming themselves in the process into what we are today, glorious practitioners of Witchcraft. No longer Mortal, but still unlike other supernatural forces that exist, we became the bridge between these worlds. However, we are also unlike the other supernatural forces that exist in this world."

"How so," I ask, unable to resist my curiosity.

"For one, our magik is different. We have our own natural abilities, but we have the capability of accessing and utilizing other forces and do occasionally tap into them for our own devices. We have learned from our supernatural brethren, and as a result, our Craft has been responsible for the evolution of other species like the Pegasus, and birth entities that are not found in any common mythical lore."

"Wait, Witches created those? Pegasus, the horses with wings?"

"Yes, that is correct Noah," Dr. Huebner responds.

"That's a bit like playing god, don't you think," I ask, not sure if I am probing too far.

Dr. Huebner laughs loudly at my rhetorical question. "No, not at all. It is no different than Mortal scientists researching cures or cross-breeding their non-magikal Faemalyrs."

"You mean pets," as I smile at the idea of Rocky being a Faemalyr.

"Yes, fur babies or what have you," chuckling to himself as he goes on, "Now it is true our ways are not always agreeable to other supernatural beings for various reasons, often because our methods are more complex. Quite frankly our ways can sometimes be inefficient and, at times, redundant, at least by the standards of other supernatural beings. With that said, in many ways Witchcraft can reach far beyond the imagination and limits of these beings. That is the purpose of us utilizing these forces. We learn from one another and in doing so we can advance to limitless horizons."

Limitless seemed wrong to me. Everything should have limits.

Tired and frustrated my filter began deteriorating. I started asking all the questions that had been building in my head without hesitation. "What about fairies and mermaids and dragons?"

Confused, the Doctor asks, "Yes, what about them?"

"Are they real, is it all real?"

"I do not know about *all* the legends but yes, it is true there exist such beings. The Faelin are what you would call a fairy and technically the Myre-people would qualify as the fabled mermaid, although they are significantly dissimilar from the mermaids described in popular culture. They exist along with a myriad of other various supernatural beings."

"Where are they? Why is it I have never seen one?"

"Most choose to remain hidden from Mortals and some exist outside of our reality, while others find clever ways of bridging their world to ours, like petulant poltergeists. On occasion, Mortals do see some of these beings, but the few that choose to share their experience are often discredited and find themselves labeled as either bizarre or insane."

He continues laughing to himself, surely lost in some memory, "The Faelin are exceptionally skilled at crossing realms, notorious for their natural power of crossing great distances in seconds."

"Are they friendly? Will I meet any," I try to ask nonchalantly, attempting to mask my fascination.

"Remember, these beings are not the same as the ones commonly described in children's stories. Their shapes and sizes all vary tremendously, whether they be creatures of the sea, giants, or fiery salamanders with all their secrets."

Trying my very best to hide my disbelief I ask, "Do they tap into Witchcraft, I guess," unsure of what I was asking.

"Yes, in some ways. They utilize our advancements, accept our offerings, and in repayment lend us their own power resources. We operate on an economy of magik. As they say, there is no free lunch and everything has a cost. The life force of a supernatural being mixed into the body of a Mortal is said to be one of the four origins of the Witch. It is not such a surprise that Witches talented in Weather Magik would share a kinship to beings such as the Faelin, what with their natural gift of aerokinesis. Through this connection, both parties receive benefits, the supernatural force now connected to the ultimate manifestation of magik, the physical world. While we Witches gain a connection closer to the source of magik, known as the metaphysical world."

"What does that even mean," utterly dumbfounded by what the Doctor is trying to teach me.

He chuckles at himself, "I do apologize Noah Ellis. I've gone ahead of myself; magikal theory is something you will understand in time."

Reluctant to end the lesson, I try to clarify what the doctor tried to explain to me, "You said a supernatural mixed their life force with a human. A Mortal, I guess, and that created a Witch. What did you call it? One of the four origins, what does that mean?"

He is clearly excited I was showing interest in the Witch world, "Ah yes, I have already mentioned the first origin, the binding of life forces between a Mortal and supernatural entity, known as the Blessed Origin. The second is known as the Devout origin, it is the practice of developing magikal ability through perseverance, a Mortal who has pushed their limitations to the advanced level of Witchcraft. The third origin is that of heredity, any Witch born from magikal lineage, known as the Legacy origin. The final origin is the most mysterious, a Witch born with magik, but with no known Witch ancestry. This is the Recessive Origin, occasionally referred to as the Non-Legacy Witch as we previously discussed. Some theorized they are the accumulation of Mortals developing their lower level magik throughout the generations, eventually creating a Witch. Others believe that at one point, a Witch's magikal gene may have become dormant or 'recessive' in their descendants and reactivated in a later generation. Although, it is still unknown."

I remember Pedro's earlier reference to the term, but he first called me a Non-Legacy as if I was last to cross some finish line. The whole thing was a reminder of my inadequacy. A bitter taste grows in my mouth along with the sickening feeling of being inferior, an old friend. My face must have given me away, because he then said, "You my dear, could not have the power you wield without being chosen, in some way or another. It could have been your biological parents, a distant relative in your ancestral line or something else entirely, but I would guess your origin has a unique and beautiful tapestry beyond any Witch of your class."

I can't help but wonder if my biological parents were Witches too, and if I am so great, why didn't they want me? I guess I will never know.

We continue walking, but I now remain silent, processing all that I have been told. I allow myself to be lost in thoughts.

Doctor Huebner calls for my attention, "Noah."

I realize that I have unintentionally, but perhaps subconsciously, wandered off.

"Are you alright," Dr. Huebner says, tethering me to the present moment instead of my mind. The majestic forest loses its beauty due to the harsh reality of my life. I suppose Dr. Huebner might be nervous of me running off, but where would I go? I wouldn't even know how to make my way out of these woods, and I would never jeopardize the Mastersons well-being. As Abigail Tetson had previously informed me, "The consequences of not obeying Witch laws were severe."

Time had gotten away from me during my ruminations. The forest had grown completely dark but Pedro manifests several orbs of light to illuminate our perimeter.

Darcy speaks up, "Mr. Ellis, we must walk on, we are nearly there."

"Yes, sorry, I was distracted," it was the first time the young Witch spoke to me with kindness, truly acknowledging my presence. There is something comforting about the way she looks at me, it was in her eyes, pity. As a foster kid, pity is something I am intimately familiar with, and normally I would be annoyed, but today, with her, I don't know. It was nice.

I appreciated that at least one of these wicked Witches recognized that this wasn't a dream come true. It was not some fantasy played out in which I was to be rescued and taken away. I was already living a dream come true.

No, that was too sad. None of that.

Back to this walk, we must have been walking for hours now, "How much longer?"

Doctor Huebner repeats himself, "Mr. Ellis, thrice is the price, do the math my young Witch." Great, a riddle.

And thrice more we walked, the third loop, arriving where the landmark tree ought to be, but now instead is the stone hole in the ground once more to which we all step down, following the stairway path below.

Thrice is the price, this would be our third time using these stairs, our third time descending into the ground. How many more repeats of this game would there be?

The stairs started shifting in a way they had not done so before, no longer turning right or left. Instead, they started spiraling higher and higher toward something dark and bright blue, opening into a world of stars.

"Thrice is the price, three times three, nine trips all together. We're here, aren't we Doctor," I state more than ask.

"Powerful, beautiful, now add brilliant to the mix! You shall be a force to be reckoned with Mr. Ellis."

We climbed the ascending staircase toward the large opening, held outside it was the constellations of Aquarius, the Water-Bearer. We approached the opening, and I loudly gasped at the sight of it. Tarias, the city of Witches was beyond my imagination.

Chapter Five

Map spells for the frequent traveler:
Pour sand or dirt of the land on a flat surface.
Repeat 13 times: Abraxi Artemis Atlas

In the far Eastern corner near the state line of Colorado, tucked away in the rolling mountains of the Rockies, is a hidden formation that no human or hovering satellite has ever seen, Mt. Tarias. Rising in stages from the valley up the slope, into the high cliffs, and all the way to the Peak is the city of Tarias, home of the Witches.

We stood inside the cave's hole, staring out at the wonder of it. A semi-transparent force barricades the cave opening. We cannot pass and suddenly I would like to pass, I want to see Tarias.

"You must say the magik words Noah," The tower of a man lowers himself to my ear and whispers the word for me to cast.

"Tah-Ree-Yah-Sss"

Tarias

Nothing happens.

"Thrice is the price young one," Doc reinforces.

"Right," I say it two more times and the invisible force shatters into sparkling bits of ethereal glass, flowing out and up into the night sky. Amazing.

Dr. Huebner touches my shoulder softly, "Come Mr. Ellis, lots more to see and the hour grows late." We walked out of the hole in the ground, the cave releasing us to the glittering sky. The path leads us into a stone courtyard of similar design to the mouth of the cave, with symbols carved into the rock that glow unnaturally against the bright Moon that hangs low in the vast sky.

And there it is, the most spectacular sight I have ever seen.

"The city of Tarias," Doctor Huebner explains, "The land of the Witches. Specifically, the Witches of the Americas; well to be politically correct, the Witch Union of North and Central Earth, meaning Canada, the U.S., a portion of Mexico, and a few segments of Europe. W-U-N-C-E, or more commonly referred to as ONCE."

"It is beautiful."

"I'm glad you like it Mr. Ellis," Pedro catches me by surprise, I didn't realize I was thinking out loud. "It is not all a loss, life here can be grand."

"This way my young Crown Ward," says Doctor Huebner, as he leads me toward the entrance of Tarias. We walk the ascending trail up the cliff, heading toward the capital city of the Witch Union.

The bright skies of the oversized moon reveal the glowing windows of the houses and buildings sprinkled throughout this wonder. It is vastly different from the compound that the staff physician initially described when he reviewed his report over my Witch status.

After all, I had never been a Witch before, so I had no idea what to expect.

We meet a Coachman, a Witch who transports other citizens of Tarias around the mountain with the use of a buggy, a sort of flying taxi-service. Although that meant little to me, as I was entirely preoccupied with his magikal horse-like creature.

"It is not a Pegasus," Darcy explains, as if I thought this creature was anything like a horse with wings.

Although its body type was similar to a horse, it had the agile nature of a feline, bending and stretching effortlessly and gracefully. On its back were six, rather aggressive looking, wings. Its feathers could oscillate from loose and soft to pointed and sharp, like blades.

Dr. Huebner states, "It is called a Corrorabador, a creature not found in Mortal lore."

The Corrorabador was gentle, curious, and focused on retrieving a snack from the Coachman, sniffing about a large cloth bag attached to the buggy. Regretfully, the man allowed me to feed the Corrorabador.

"His name is Tiny, why don't you give him a snack. He will love you for life, I reckon," said the Coachman.

A Corrorabador's diet included large rodents and small animals. Tiny carefully licks the dead ferret out of my hands and into his mouth. I tried not to gag.

We hopped aboard the buggy, and per my request, the Coachman kindly undid the leather rooftop so I could better see the city. The interior is lit by a glow that emanated from the very table, seats, and structure itself.

Once we were sitting comfortably in the plush interior of the buggy, Tiny took flight with ease carrying us along by only a few straps that attached to the saddle-like vest wrapped around his body. Dr. Huebner voluntarily provides his services as an impromptu tour guide. He says, "The Coachman's own magik levitates the buggy itself. The Corrorabador aids only in steering the vehicle."

My stomach rolls upon itself as we lift off. It was like the drop off of a roller coaster and it was unforgettable. We soar over Tarias along with other peculiar objects traveling in the night sky.

The isolated city was enormous. It started at the low ridge of Mt. Tarias, making its way up to her peak. The sun rises over the city and it sets over a large lake on her far western corner. Small rivers and forests snake throughout the buildings, which are built atop uneven grounds.

It reminded me of treehouses, a thing that combined invention and nature perfectly. Tarias was the same with its earthen passages, like Roman tunnels connecting buildings and sections of the community. There were roads and random plateaus that served as natural courtyards. The buildings were a hodgepodge collection of various architectural designs.

During the flight, one large stone structure flies past us at a higher elevation, traveling unaided through air in a perfect line. It was like the frame of a house during construction but shaped in the form of a simple geometric cube, its edges and floor were made of a material that reminded me of the pyramids.

A group of people stood inside and I wondered why they did not fear tripping through the wide openings. Maybe there was an invisible barrier containing its passengers, like the entrance to Tarias. I noticed several more identical structures carrying large groups of people or supplies through the night sky, each seemed to have specific routes like ski lifts. They traveled to and from various towers similar to lighthouses that were scattered on the mountain. It appeared they were the more frequently used means of transportation.

I then turned and saw two women flying on brooms further below us. Outrageous, there were real Witches on brooms. “That’s a thing? I thought you were joking earlier. Witches actually fly with brooms?” I asked in disbelief. It was unreal, but I guess my belief system on what is or is not possible will require some recalibration.

“Oh yes, sometimes,” Doc replied as I see other Witches flying but not riding anything at all, traveling in the same lower sections of the sky. It appeared that certain elevations were reserved for different modes of flight, as our current elevation was exclusively used for other flying buggies.

"It depends, some Witches like to enchant carpets or cars to carry more items at once. Difficult process enchanting, using that type of magik. However, we Witches of ONCE are making rapid progress streamlining methods to manufacture these magikal objects."

Supply meeting demand, even Witches rely on a balanced economy.

The Doctor discharged Darcy and Pedro for the day and we land near a cluster of large buildings that appear to be apartments.

"We're almost there Noah, our next stop will be your new home," says Dr. Huebner, as he directs the Coachman, "To St. Philomena Academy, Manor of Delphi please."

Darcy and Pedro wave goodbye as we lift off once more. I think I was in shock, overwhelmed by it all, not to mention the relief I felt that the modern city of Tarias was nothing like the medieval destitution I had envisioned. I thought about the Mastersons, and felt shame for feeling relief at all.

It carries us further up the mountain, the area is far more deserted than the lower sections of the formation. We rise higher and higher and, for a moment, I think that we may fly over the mountain's peak. However, my worries were needless. Up ahead is a looming building that reminds me of an extravagant doll house.

"This is to be your new home during your time at St. Philomena Academy," says Dr. Huebner as we fly closer toward the structure.

It looked like a house straight out of the 1920s, but renovated for modern use while maintaining its decadence for nostalgia. The Victorian home was built in a form that looked like the letter L, but in reverse. More castle than house, it was five-stories by my count at least and towered over the land.

Several turrets hang from various levels of the structure, and the largest one surpasses the height of the entirety of the home. It has a parapet placed at the very top, the twinkling lights inside it shine bright in the dark night sky.

Most of its size is allocated to its eastern body and, per the Doctor, is reserved for the majority of student housing, with a few of the facilities designated for staff and faculty.

Apparently, large houses often have names for different areas inside for points of reference when navigating the structure. The living quarters were named Madison Hall.

The Coachman begins to land for the final time, at least for me. There is a slight bit of turbulence due to the wintery high-speed winds at this elevation, but the Coachman waves his hand and it dissipates quickly, allowing us to land with ease. Dr. Huebner stands and exits the buggy, signaling me to follow suit. The Coachman offers his assistance and I accept his hand as I step down, more for manners than need.

My horde of flying suitcases rapidly approached the buggy, they must have been behind us the entire flight, which would have been fascinating if not for the cold.

One of the last places anyone wants to be in the dead of winter is near the peak of a mountain, which I am informed is nearly 2,000 feet taller than Mt. Elbert, the supposedly highest summit of the Rocky Mountains in North America. This would be true if not for the magikally hidden mountain of Tarias.

This must be the birthplace of winter, a vortex of angry winds cost me the sensation of all ten fingers. I was not sure I still had them and was semi-convinced the same of my face. I brushed off my wet tears in their valiant attempt to shield my eyes from the sharp air.

Dr. Huebner leads the way towards the home. He opens the door and, to my immediate relief, the warmth of an oversized fire set in the entryway wraps me in a blanket of heat, leaving a fading memory of the winter hell behind me.

We enter a room that appears to be the home's foyer, inside were several scattered large crimson sofas and dark brown coffee tables. A lean boy reads a floating book near the adjacent wall, the pages gently turn on their own as he sips tea.

"Mr. Haimus," said the Doctor, and the boy jumped up almost immediately and rushed toward us. The Doctor turns to me, "Urgent business my dear," then introduces me to the young man, "Noah, this is your House Lead, Leroy Haimus." The Doctor provides his instructions, "Mr. Haimus, please take care of Mr. Noah Ellis. Do be sure to provide a thorough tour as this is his first night with us," Dr. Huebner pauses to check in on me, placing his hand on my shoulder, "You'll be fine Mr. Ellis, you are in good hands." Dr. Huebner walks out the door, returning to the buggy. Tiny's wings stir the winter air, steering the buggy up and away, disappearing into the night sky.

The extravagance of the home was endless. Long draped curtains, winding staircases with sharp turns, and sudden exits and entries leading to endless hallways. It reminded me of an article I read on the Winchester Mystery House, the allegedly haunted mansion.

William Winchester, a man who secured his wealth through the sale of firearms, widowed Sarah Winchester. After his death, Sarah Winchester funded nearly perpetual construction to her home for the span of her life. The project consisted of several additions and renovations, each project lacked rhyme or reason. The result was a nonsensical layout of the residence, hallways and staircases that lead nowhere. Many claimed she built the home to provide residence for the ghosts of the victims of her late husband's rifle company.

Leroy rambled on, taking his assignment as student tour guide very seriously, and provided a bonus lesson in Witch history.

"Mt. Tarias was discovered and used by our ancestors many centuries ago and was originally designed to be a haven for Witches to practice in peace and without disturbance or fear of persecution. The city of Tarias, the one we know today, was established in 1508, founded by a group of Witches who arrived well before the British colonists, eager to claim ownership of uncharted territory. Due to its difficult terrain, it remained untouched by the natives at the time. As the years went on, buildings were erected of various and evolving shapes and sizes, which you may have noticed upon your arrival. Their designs vary from gothic, colonnade, to French chic styles. True time capsules, reflections of the evolving nature of fads and various trends throughout the past few centuries. Some deteriorated buildings were replaced to meet more modern needs, but most were simply repaired and enhanced. They all have history and stories to tell."

"Doesn't seem very safe, building a city on the cliffside of a mountain," I say.

"Correct, our ancestors protected Tarias by their own enchantments from troublesome occurrences like landslides, avalanches, and the ever-shifting topography of the mountains. In addition, those enchantments created magikal barriers that separated our kind from intrusive Mortals who sought our magik for their personal gain, or simply desired our destruction. This created ideal circumstances for our great Witch nation's development. Tarias, and other Witch cities like it, became avenues for Witch-kind to work and contribute to the magikal community. It became a place where we could connect and socialize with one another. As we grew in strength and presence, so too did our influence. The need for focus on sanctuary lessened, affording our race the opportunity to create ground-breaking advancements in Witchcraft."

I interrupt him, trying to find some useful information like directions to my first-class tomorrow morning, "What is the school like?"

"St. Philomena Academy," he offers, but to my disappointment, responds with more useless historical facts, "Incidentally, as I was saying, Tarias was no longer exclusively a haven and became a bustling community. Witches from the globe over could practice and develop their Craft. Witch-kind experienced a rapid development in magikal ability. As our numbers grew, and further advancements in magik were made, our ancestors were forced to address the most critical need for any nation, the need for education. A need most conveniently met through the protection of Tarias. Pioneers in the Witch community successfully changed policies to mandate the development and execution of formalized training, thus the creation of St. Philomena Academy, founded in 1633. Prominent Witches came from distant lands to lead the way in the future of magikal practice through their research and education of young Witches, specifically of Witch children; after all children are our future." He laughs at his joke and I try not to roll my eyes, and he goes on without reprieve.

He shared other various facts as he walked me to my room, but at least showed me where the kitchen and other critical areas of the house were located. "I think you'll like Spirit Manor."

The wooden floors creaked beneath my shoes as we walked, "Spirit Manor?"

"Sorry, that's just a nickname. Every place is named here, the correct name is Manor of Delphi. Emma Tetrazzi, the Witch who founded the house, named it after one of our Coven's most prominent sisters, the Great Oracle Delphi."

"Coven?"

"Yes, the Coven Divina Diademate, St. Philomena's student body is divided into several Covens. Most of them are based on your innate abilities." He either saw my confusion or realized the obvious, that I knew nothing about being a Witch.

"Some Witches have innate skills toward certain power or magik types. Seers, the more clairvoyantly inclined, are placed here. That is why you are here Noah, this is your Coven."

"Wait, so everyone here can read minds," panic rose within me, clouding the memory of my own visions and ability to hear thoughts. They would all know everything about me, I couldn't do this. Dread rose from my belly, constricting my airflow like a python and it felt as if the room was spinning.

Either anticipating my fears, or reading my mind, Leroy eases my anxiety, "Generally speaking yes, but I wouldn't worry about another Seer reading your mind, there are charms to maintain boundaries. Secondly, we Seers operate on the unspoken rule to keep our minds to ourselves. Lastly, even for the few that aren't so ethical, I don't know anyone here that could get inside your head."

"What do you mean?"

"Oh, well maybe you haven't accessed your full abilities, but Seers have a glow that only other Seers can perceive, and I guess you can't see yours yet, but you're glowing brighter than anyone else here, dude."

I hated being called dude, but it gave me some relief. I allowed myself to believe that I would be safe. What else could I do?

Leroy talked quickly and I asked only a few questions that he responded with, what is in my opinion, an excessive amount of information required for a home tour. I tried my best to keep up, but I was tired and hungry. Not just physically exhausted, but also heavy from all the change and loss.

He seemed to notice this and kindly opted to speed up the tour. He promised to make-up the time the following day at the Academy.

"It's tough when it's new, but it wasn't that way for me. Both my parents are Witches, so I always knew I would come here, or the Colleges of Avalon. I have a friend who goes there, she doesn't have any Witch relatives in her family either, and it came as a complete surprise when she Manifested. It wasn't easy for her, but it got better with time. I hope it gets better for you too."

We climbed up a set of stairs only to return to the same hallway on the opposite side, Winchester house; then continued to ascend the next flight, but somehow arrived at the tall tower on the other end of the home.

Leroy leads me to the fourth floor, at the farthest end of the jagged west wing, and we finally reach our destination. I opened the door to what would be my room during my time here at Philomena. For what seemed like the hundredth time today, I was once more in awe.

"Looks like you won't be at Madison Hall, you get the best view in the house."

"Thanks."

My room was directly under a pitched roof and had the semblance of a fully finished attic, more loft than storage space. It was located at the top of the home's tallest turret and topped with a cone-shaped roof, ironically called a Witch's cap. The high slanted ceilings merged into the walls, but do not diminish the room's size.

"Laundry goes here", he points to a basket nestled in a large cabinet in a nearby corner. I let Morgan out of the kennel and set up his litterbox underneath an end table near the door. Leroy exits shortly after, wishing me goodnight, and I extend him the same courtesy. He seemed to genuinely want to help. Morgan explores as I take further stock of my surroundings.

The room curved in the circular shape of the tower itself. There are large high arched windows, with a living mural that surrounds the window frames and stretches from floor to ceiling. The paint magikally reflects the winter snow falling on the ground and the flowing branches of the leafless trees just outside my window and above it was a miniature version of the glowing moon. Tall curtains were wrapped elegantly to the side, revealing the city below. Leroy was right, this had to be the best view in the house, a town made of stars.

I change into my night clothes and drink some water out of a pitcher set aside for me on a coffee table near the bookshelves. Each already filled with books, oak perforates my sense of scent.

I place my cup back down, too tired to eat the meal underneath the silver tabletop, but I am reminded to serve Morgan water along with his dinner. The hardwood floors creak slightly at my every move, despite the oversized white shag rug that lay underneath. I even have living room furniture in the form of two large armchairs that I assume are for guests.

Across from the furniture is a gigantic bed. A king, I guess, although it was bigger than any bed I've ever seen. It was beautiful, if a bed can be beautiful, covered in sky blue linens and many, many, exceptionally soft looking pillows. An iron frame, plain, and yet there was an intensity about it, like the person who created it suffered on each lattice, ensuring its perfection.

Morgan stretches himself on the mattress; great minds think alike. This couldn't all be for me. It was over the top.

I finally fall into bed, exhausted, yet despite my fatigue still have difficulty falling asleep, as I replay the last 15 hours of my life in my head. Where had I been 15 hours ago? The Mastersons, yes, I was with them exactly 15 hours ago. I bite my lip so I don't cry.

I hear the soft crack of fire burning at the inner portion of the room's wall that I had no recollection of igniting. The day had been too long. Sleep offered me time and rest, time I needed to organize the pieces of my life, time to accept the dreadful truth of the loss of one life in exchange for this foreign one. A strange life that I could not help but be terrified over, despite its mysticism.

My thoughts, like a train, continue in rebellion of my desire for them to stop. They do so for minutes, hours, I am not sure. At some point, I am pulled into the gentle embrace of white sheets and pillows filled with soft cool air. The warm cloud of fluff I laid upon absorbed me, pulling me in like quicksand. Graciously, I was suffocated by sleep's embrace, gifted a quiet temporary death, peace. The type of sleep that came with the kindest act of all, an absence of dreams.

Chapter Six

Skyclad: Ritual Nudity
Enhances most attraction and desire spells, but be warned, exposing the body increases the risk of accidental self-enchantment.

The small antique clock rings sharply with an odd off-white glow that shines brightly, revealing the outline of the bed I lay in. Deep in sleep, it screams for me to wake up and I sprawl in and out of consciousness.

Closer to awakening, I try to pay it little mind, but the alarm has no sympathy and brings me forth from the safety of slumber.

I slowly opened my eyes and began to recognize my unfamiliar surroundings, starting with the absurd softness and equally ridiculous oversized bed.

There are strange and complex feelings when you wake up in a strange place, especially one that you would rather not be.

First, there is panic and then derealization, the feeling of disbelief, followed by denial, a futile refusal to succumb to reality. And as realization sinks into consciousness, then comes a nauseating awkward sensation from the displacement and rejection accosted to me seemingly by the place itself.

It feels as if the walls and floors and even the slumbering inhabitants of the home scream for my intrusion and collude for my immediate eviction.

I tried to turn on my phone the Mastersons gave me, but as Dr. Huebner promised, there was no signal to be found.

I hear two quick startling knocks. "Good morning," I hear a chipper woman say from behind the closed door, "May I come in?" Tentatively, I say yes. Miss Penelope, the House Master, who seemed to have an unpleasant tendency to sing while she spoke, a personal pet peeve of mine that made my blood boil.

How can people be so goddamn cheerful? "Rise and shine," chiming the last bit.

"And how are you today, Mr. Ellis?"

"Fine. I'm fine."

Propping myself up, I took note of the clothes Miss Penelope had draped over her forearm, and the slight downturn her smile carried, "The rest of the students have left for Morning Meditation. I suspect you may have to be there as well," chuckling awkwardly, with a look of tension around her eyes. "I am sure Madam Reyna will...understand."

She began busying herself in what I assume is my closet, walking in and out of a door tucked away toward the inner part of the room, opposite the bay windows. She begins hanging up foreign sets of clothes, confirming my closet theory, and laying various options before me.

"What's that?"

"Why, you're uniforms dear. Dr. Huebner ordered them, along with your school supplies. I'll set them beside your desk."

"Where's the bathroom?" I asked while eyeing the small mountain of things magikally floating into large piles across from me.

"Well right here love," pointing to a door to the right of the entryway. "I have my own bathroom," I ask.

"Of course, every student at the Manor of Delphi must have their privacy to set about honing their precious skills."

"Oh, thank you." I ask her to let me put the things away, feeling guilty for making this woman do work that I could easily do myself. She questioned my decision, apprehensively looking back at the room, her face filled with concern.

Finally, after several attempts of reassuring Miss Penelope that I could in fact use a hangar, she begrudgingly left me to my own devices. Standing there, in an empty room, with a bizarre sense of appreciation that I had yet to feel since this Witch business started.

I felt spoiled by all the luxury. I had my own room at the Mastersons, but this was like a small apartment. Even the bathroom was more spa than restroom. I have lived in houses not nearly as nice as this bathroom.

It had a separate shower and an oversized, stand-alone, claw foot bathtub placed in the center of the room. I had never seen anything like it, let alone the fact that it appeared to lack any type of plumbing connection.

There was even furniture. What bathroom has furniture? There were chairs placed at the wall with side tables and lamps at each corner. A floating sink attached to the wall, and on the right was a floor to ceiling mirror.

I began to put my clothes away and enter the impossibly large walk-in closet, and I realize that, given the house's structure, it really was impossible for this amount of space to be available. I walk outside several times to verify, but based on the location of the door, the room should be taking up space in the hallway but instead there is only emptiness. My closet is easily the size of my room and is fully stocked with various items.

Uniforms, many uniforms, black and grey sweaters, trousers, blazers, and sweater vests. With the exception of the white oxford shirts and deep purple ties, Witches apparently do like black, some gray, but mostly black.

At the very back of the closet was a rack covered with silver pins. Each held a purple diamond in the similar shape of the North Star only with several more lines, more cosmic-like than the geometric symbol.

Having clothes was nice, but I brought my own. The Mastersons had always treated me very well.

Once I put the clothes away, I look toward a food tray left by Ms. Penelope. There was an assortment of breads laid out, at least three juices, and a ceramic teapot that remained warm despite the mountain's stagnantly cold air.

My stomach growled at me with a ferocity I did not recognize. How long has it been since the last time I ate?

I made a mental note to be nicer to Miss Penelope going forward. I pour the juice and stuff one pastry into my mouth, grab two more, and then start rummaging through the various items Dr. Huebner ordered for me. That was nice of him, I made another mental note to say thank you.

No joke, there was an actual cauldron. How much of Witch life was true and what, if anything, was myth?

Beside the cauldron was a large cedar chest and inside it were vials and glass containers that held liquids, stones, and dried up plants that I assume are herbs.

There were also other items including a serious looking knife set, with one ordained blade set aside in its own box; I suspect it was not for cutting.

I looked over the pile of books. A note was placed on top of the stack; it was a list of my courses.

Divination:

- Divinacion, Ilisos, y Conexion
- Understanding Sight: A key to the past, present, and future

Spell Theory:
- The Fundamental Science of Basic Spellwork
- Witchcraft: A foundation
Transference:
- Levitation: Skills
- Transference: Controlling the world around you for the novice Witch
Abjuration:
- Barriers and Banishing: A Beginner's Guide
- Curses, Hexes, and other dark spells
Elemental:
- The Cardinal Powers: For the Non-Innate Witch
- Healing and Restorative Magik Meets Eastern and Western Medicine
Evocation:
- The Encyclopedia of Evocation
- Summoning Spells: A guide for the practical Witch
- Working with Daemons, Faelin, and the Other Worlds
Conjuration:
- Charms and Enchantments (Books I, II, & III)
- Sympathetic magik and Voodoo too
Alchemy:
- Herbalism: The power of plants
- Potions: Student Witch Edition
Versation:
- Transformations and Mutations
- Physicalize: Shape-Shifting and Enhancements
Astronomy and Celestial Magik:
- Temporal Magik and Translocation
- Cosmic Magik: Master Your Fate and other Events

I perused the pages of the spell theory textbook. It was written in various languages, some I recognized, like Latin and Spanish, and some with languages and symbols foreign to me.

Surprisingly, I found familiar algebra algorithms and based on my brief scan of the book the equations were used in calculating the effectiveness of herbs using lunar cycles. It seemed the stage of the moon affected the magikal level of plants. I was blown away, was all this real?

My door bursts open just then, and in comes Dr. Huebner, rushing in obvious panic.

"Oh, thank heavens Noah, I was worried sick. You are late for Morning Meditation, where have you been? I thought you may have been abducted or worse, deserted us. Spirit forbid!"

It is my first day at the Academy and I am in hell. It was some nonsense about a ridiculously early class called Morning Meditation. I had quickly gathered the items for each class into my bookbag, trying my best to be prepared for the troupe of courses lined up for the day.

The thing about bouncing from home to home like a piece of luggage is that you get real good at figuring things out rather quickly. Not that I was happy about it, but I know how to go through the motions, that was survival.

I take one last look in the mirror. There, staring back at me is a blue-eyed skinny boy with pitch-black hair. I chose to wear a grey sweater, white button up shirt with a gray tie, and black fitted trousers. Unfortunately, I have to wear these ridiculous pointed black boots. All I was missing was the black pointy hat to complete the ensemble. Regardless, the boy in my reflection does not feel like me.

I give Morgan a kiss on the top of his head, scratching gently the back of his ears as he purrs, and rush out, losing my way as I try to recall the setup of the strange house. Eventually I make my way through its maze of hallways and nonsensical staircases, finally walking out the back-porch door that reveals the trail that ascends and weaves into a thick micro-forest.

At its end, is a plateau used for the morning class. There are large stones that serve as makeshift seats and tables and, in meditative style, a woman sits cross-legged at the center. She is floating. She is beautiful, a bit too thin, but her long-hair and deep copper skin detract from her frailty. She reminds me of peace that is until she opens her eyes.

Her melodic voice is low, and her words illogical, initially I thought she might be high, “The sun knows no watchtower for it is its own keeper, and yet a stupid boy can’t arrive on time.” I do not think she is high anymore. Her voice now crisp and short in her instructions and it appears she has a physical deficit, an inability to smile.

They call her Madam Reyna.

I walk toward one of the open spots, but she demands for me to stand still, “New boy, smiling as if you just didn’t miss half of class, tardiness is utterly and entirely unacceptable.” Unsure of how to respond, I look up and then away, “Boy!” Her raised eyebrows lift so high that I think they may actually lift her face clear off her head, “You don’t deserve to be in this class, or have me as an instructor. Do you know who I am?”

“Yes Madam,” and for the life of me, I cannot remember the woman’s name. “Um, yes Madam.”

“Reyna, R-E-Y-N-A, insolent child,” pausing for effect, “Come here, little Witch.” She points toward the floor by her side, as if I was a dog.

“Now!” I shakily walk toward her, “Yes, Madam Reyna,” I say correctly.

“Do you think you are special? You cannot even be bothered to arrive on time. You should arrive 30 minutes prior filled with enthusiasm for the opportunity to train in the gift of Sight. The degree of insult made by you arriving late is a personal assault against all Witches. Your irreverence toward the gift insults your peers along with all the other rudimentary young Witches who lack our abilities. You are not special, just ungrateful. I suggest you learn quickly to get over yourself.”

What. The. Actual. Hell.

"Where is your pin?" she barks.

"My what?"

"You're pin!"

She points to the nearest student's vest, the silver pin with the diamond star, I guess it's part of the outfit.

"I forgot," and stared at my feet, "I am very sorry."

She looks like she wants to kill me, literally. She says one last thing to me behind gritted teeth, "Sit down and pray."

I sit in silence and pretend to pray, sometimes actually praying, at least for it to be over.

Now intensely missing the Mastersons, even the dog, and I decide to use this opportunity to try to have a Vision of them, but it goes nowhere. After five minutes, she finally rings a silver bell that sounds like an acapella choir more than a chiming instrument.

Once released, with not actually understanding the point of Morning Meditation, Leroy offers to continue his second portion of the tour of St. Philomena. I was grateful for his help; at least I had some directions to my classes and could try to avoid getting lost on my first day. Hopefully, I could prevent future repeat incidents of tardiness like with Madam Reyna.

St. Philomena Academy was a conglomerate of several campuses and residences all located toward Mt. Tarias' Peak, fittingly titled, Cat's Peak, which remained snow-capped all season long. I walked into the homeroom for Abjuration, a class focused on things like curses and hexes.

I felt their eyes on me the moment I walked into the room. I was used to people staring. Usually they would comment on my eyes and occasionally other students would make fun of me for being skinny. Either way, it always made me feel uncomfortable, being noticed in school is the worst thing when you are a foster kid, and all your secrets become increasingly difficult to hide.

The thing that bothered me the most was the fact that all these kids were Witches, yet even they stared. What does that say about me?

"I love your eyes," said a girl named Tiffany. "Are they real or just a glamour?"

"Real," I say a little too quickly.

"Yeah, right?" she scoffs and looks away.

Not off to a great start in the friend's department, someone thinks I am a liar now.

To top it off, the class is a bit of a disappointment. I was hoping that at least the magik bit of this gig would compensate for the disaster. The classes apparently incorporate traditional school studies. In my next class, the Alchemy professor explains that along with the mystical side of magik, "Potions, like any magik, involve a combination of Witchcraft and Science. Alchemy requires the use of chemistry, biology, arithmetic, literature, and other general studies."

We were reviewing formulas for assessing the biological chemistry of Betel nut. Naturally, my mind starts to wander, and I start thinking about all the reasons to feel sorry for myself, my very best gift.

"Mr. Ellis, Mr. Ellis, are you with us?"

The sound of the teacher calling my name comes in slowly, softly jarring me from my train of thought, until I finally realize he is talking to me.

"Yes, sorry," I say shyly and apologetically. I hate that about me.

The class giggles. It seems like a roar of laughter filled with ridicule, more sinister than giggles.

"Ah, so pleased you could join us," more giggles.

"Yes sir, Mr. Whinn, I mean, yes sir"

"It's Instructor Williams," like it matters.

I smile politely, but I am angry now, so I stare directly into his eyes and with a severe tone, "Yes, Instructor Williams." He shifts, and I am not sure what to make of that. Finally, he looks away, the class stops giggling, and then returns to his lecture.

This sucks.

He drones on for the remaining portion of class and I remind myself to pull it together and deal with it, like I have done many times before. Okay, I force my brain to think positive. After all, there are some redeeming qualities.

One, I am a Witch, that is kind of cool. Two, I have an awesome setup, and it's not like I am not being taken care of. Three, I have only been to a couple of classes, there was the potential of making some friends here. Hopefully, things will get better. My next class, Astronomy, was a bit more interesting. The professor magikally created miniature stars that glowed throughout the room.

Before I know it, the morning ends, announcing noon and lunch. Leroy does not meet me after class. He had a special assignment to cover for Madam Reyna. Apparently, she can be nice, if she likes you. I am sure he has his own friends. Even so, I doubt we would get along even though he was good-natured.

Food was served in a pantheon that the other Witch children called the Pillar. Leroy previously provided me directions to the building. It was surrounded by what I thought were Greek statues of gods and goddesses.

Closer inspection reveals names of famous Witches that contributed to the Witch Nation. One stood out, a fountain with a sculpture of a woman with her hand held to the sky. The inscription identifies her as Hai-Ti Wussein, High Crown – 1204. The statue is unique because a small living tornado forms from her stone palm and rises into dark miniature clouds above her, pouring rain heavily into the fountain below.

I make my way inside the Pillar where laid an assortment of generic to gourmet cuisine, buffet style. There was food that I did not recognize. I ended up choosing something called a quiche. I was all about it, egg, cheese, and bacon. It was like eating a piece of heaven.

Four, the food here is phenomenal, adding it to my stop-feeling-sorry-for-yourself list.

There is a common square where both the students and staff eat. It opens to the courtyard. Despite the cold, it is a pretty day, clear skies and a bright sun. There is a lingering sensation in the air, like the temperature was being raised a degree or two, a sign of a seasonal change. I wondered if the rolling mountains would carry multicolored flowers to welcome spring.

I was putting my things together when I saw him. Everything blurs around me, everything except for him. The most beautiful boy in the world.

He stands still, seemingly to allow me to admire him. Although we seem to be about the same age, he stands much taller than I do. His smile leans to the side revealing a perfectly aligned bright grin with a crease in his cheek, dimples, forever marking him in his perfection. His dark shaggy hair made it seem as if he just rolled out of bed, but it was still a handsome mess shooting out in various directions. He could not have been more accidentally gorgeous even if he wanted too.

It was then I realized he was not moving, in fact, no one was, time seemed to have stopped. All the other Witch students stood like statues, eyes unblinking. The water from the fountain is suspended in mid-air, as if frozen like the sculpture of Hai-Tai Wussein. A soccer ball, tossed between two students, sits perfectly still in the air. Has time stopped?

I exhale, not realizing I was holding my breath. As if in response, time starts up once more. The other students resume their actions, engaging in their private conversations or making their way to their afternoon classes. The water from the fountain splashes into its pool. The two boys resume their game with the ball. It happened so quickly; I wasn't sure it happened at all.

It was something that would have understandably concerned me under different circumstances, but for some reason does not, as my attention is wholly focused on him.

He is walking toward the Pillar with the steady confidence of an athlete, laughing with a group of friends that seemed to belong in a photo shoot, and he would be the star. They follow his lead and I, unable to help myself, continue to stare. I uselessly try to stop myself from looking.

That is until we make eye contact and he stares back. He is now fully aware of my shameless gawking. I quickly gather my things and speed out of the courtyard, not sure where I was going, but certain it was anywhere but here.

Luckily, I ran into Leroy, he guides me to my next class and unintentionally offers me an immediate exit strategy. Thank you to whatever higher power for him. Peppy as ever, he walks and talks as he leads me into a large building, "How's it going, exciting stuff, right?"

"Yup, thanks again for helping me learn the lay of the land," I say mostly to distract myself. I kept replaying the eye contact event in my head, embarrassed for how enamored I was with the beautiful boy.

Leroy informs me that my next class, Spell Theory, has been temporarily relocated. The normal classroom was under construction. Apparently, serious damages occurred the day before. He explains that a spell, that involved some temperamental magik, had gone terribly wrong, but assures me the repairs should be complete by the end of the week.

We walk through endless hallways until we are at the back of the building. A large door sits between two windows. The door should exit to the outside. He opens it for me, revealing a large hall.

I double-check the windows to be sure.

Outside, directly where the door should be, is a small garden and empty space.

Leroy laughs at my befuddlement over the magikal doorway, "This is the East Aceaclytes Labrynthe, East Lab for short, it has a small library supply, but it is one of the four exterior sections of St. Philomena's official library, known as the Castle. We call it the Castle because, well, it looks like a castle."

I laugh slightly, "Not the most creative nickname, I'll give you that," he said in response.

The East Lab is about the size of a soccer field with several bookshelves and tables. If this is what Leroy classifies as small, I cannot begin to imagine what the actual library looks like.

Leroy explains the East Lab is an extension of the Castle, connected by a magikal tunnel, exactly like the tunnels I traveled through during my journey to Tarias.

"There are four Labs exactly, each are placed in different locations throughout St. Philomena, with individual functions. The East Lab is reserved for Preparatory students, think of it as a study hall."

"Preparatory," I ask.

"Oh, I am so sorry Noah. I forget about you being a Non-Legacy."

And he looks truly sad over his statement. Interested in what he had to say, I reassure him it is fine and ask him to go on.

"Yes, Preparatory meaning the equivalent of the Mortal's education received prior to, what's the word?"

"College," I offer.

"That's the one, we are considered Preparatory students until we reach our Ascension, the Witch version of a High School graduation. Although by the time you finish your training, you will have an education more like that of the Mortal's version of college. Once complete, you can then choose to pursue higher education, known as your Dedication, although I wouldn't worry much about those things, you have plenty of time. You can take as long as you like in the Preparatory stage of your training."

I wasn't worried because I didn't care, but I was confused, "How long will it take to complete my training?"

"That varies from Witch to Witch. I extended my own training by a few years, making this my twentieth year here."

"Twenty years! It's going to take me twenty years?"

"No, it could be as little as seven, but it's not uncommon for it to be extended up to twenty-five years. It is a matter of specialization. For Witches, it's not quite as big of a deal to be a bit older in your Witch education as it is in the human world. Since we live longer, age is less important."

"That's right, Dr. Huebner had said that, but I was tranced out when they performed the Witch gene test. I completely forgot about it; how long do we live," I ask with big eyes and an open mouth that I remind myself to close.

"Yes, sorry, I still can't believe that I keep forgetting what it's like to be a Non-Legacy Witch. It must be a lot for you, but yes, Witches live far longer than humans. I guess that is why they seem so removed from us. Our life span can vary of course, just like the Mortals, but typically we live around five or six centuries. The oldest Witch on record is said to have lived a little over eight centuries."

Suddenly the sound of bells chime throughout the halls, and an object taking the form of a large orb of light streams by, making its way through the hallways and reaching every corner of the school announcing that lunch has ended, and another period awaits.

The orb is accompanied by the sound of thunder. Still standing outside the magikal door, I look out through the window and see from the distance purple lightning. It comes from somewhere closer to the Pillar but seems to come from the ground itself. The magik orb flies by again for the second time, then a third, and not once more.

Leroy leaves me here with my head swimming with thoughts. I want to ask a thousand more questions. So many questions, that I do not know where to start.

Chapter Seven

Scanning Whole Texts
Levitate quartz crystal, centering on the Third Eye, while placing palms over the book. Recite the incantation:
Dexia Pa Tearanog
Caution: May cause nosebleeds

The days fly by and it is now the start of my third week at the academy. I was overwhelmed and missed the Mastersons terribly. My saving grace were the letters between the Mastersons and I, all thanks to Dr. Huebner. Unfortunately, the mail delivery system outside of Tarias was sporadic in its efficiency. The sun shined a little brighter for me the days I received their letters, and my heart broke a little on the days I did not.

I tried my best to move forward, but the work was impossible to manage and for the life of me, I could not seem to adjust to the harsh schedule. My classes varied by week.

Week A: Abjuration, Transference, Alchemy,

Elemental, and Spell Theory.

Week B: Divination, Versation, Evocation,

Astronomy, and Conjuration.

Each class hosted some portion of generic study that was not intrinsically magikal, but were also atypical of human studies like Witch history, dead languagcs, and practical matters related to being a Witch.

Each morning I was forced to wake up before dawn for Meditation. I had no idea the time of dawn changes every day, but certainly do now. Every student in Spirit Manor was required to attend the session to hone in our Seer gifts, even though we were all assigned a standard Divination course as a part of our core requirements.

Every day I wake up with enough time to prepare for the day and arrive 15 minutes early to Morning Meditation and the ever-changing time of dawn. Morning Meds, as I like to call it, seems like an utter waste of time. I mostly just sit there and contemplate on my misery.

This morning, after Meds, a cute housemate with bushy brown hair named Earl Miller says, “Hey, new guy,” and then proceeds to offer me a leather manual with the same cosmic star that was embedded on our Coven pins. He said in his heavy Brooklyn accent, “It’s a manual, man. Should help you with the meditations and psychic stuff.”

It would have been sweet, except he went on to say, “It's obvious you don’t know what you’re doing, thought I’d help you out. It’s annoying to see you struggle to be honest,” and walked away. Thanks a lot, Earl. Who names their child Earl anyway? Frodo-looking jerk, obviously we will not be friends. It is a shame Earl was such a dick, since I continue to struggle in the friends-department. I haven’t even made close friends with any of the Seers in the house. To be fair, there are only a handful of us, and the few I have gotten to know are in higher levels, the equivalent of upperclassmen, allowing for few interactions.

Thankfully, I got my first social break in my Spell Theory class. The Professor assigned new seating arrangements. A pretty, fair-skinned girl with blonde hair and green eyes sits opposite me at our conjoined desk.

"Hi, my name's Maria, how's it going?" She smiles pleasantly and talks with ease.

"Hello, I'm Noah," I smile weakly.

"I thought so! I didn't recognize you before and at this place people know everyone," rolling her eyes and sighing loudly at the thought.

"But it's okay, most people here are pretty nice. It was kind of rough for me when I first got here. I didn't want to leave home, but it got better. This is my second year here, a year and a few months to be exact, but whatever I just love learning about magik."

"Yeah, to be honest, I am kind of worried. I haven't really learned anything yet or seen people do much since I arrived. What's the point of a magik school if you aren't learning magik?"

"Exactly! I am always asking for the teachers to focus on more practical-training stuff, but they just lecture, like I might as well be at my old school, Eleanor High."

We both laugh slightly at the irony, which surprises me since I haven't been in a laughing mood for some time now. Maria's relaxed and authentic nature encourages me to do the same. I felt increasingly comfortable as our conversation continued.

"There is actual magik practiced here, we will be doing some today, after our exhilarating lecture," rolling her eyes just then, making no attempt to hide her irritation, "We go into technical and practice some real spells," she said excitedly.

Professor Abraney taught Spell Theory. Although informative, his method of teaching is basically a non-interrupted lecture reviewing every detail of a magik theory, section by section. Like a construction project, he starts from the foundation, until reaching the rooftop. Most found it difficult to remain engaged; especially when he would try to explain a theory that had the equivalent complexity of the architecture of an enormous high-rise tower.

Maria says he is dry, but I find everything he says fascinating and take down every word, a task made easy with one of the supplies provided by Dr. Huebner; a magikal pen that finishes sentences as I write. It works based on my intention and subject of focus. The ink spreads across the page, catching up to the Professor, who can talk faster than I would normally be able to write.

"Central to all magik are the elements of control and connection. You can think of connection as receptive, accepting of something. Similar to physical perception such as vision or touch. Our senses are meant to receive information, connecting us to the outside world. Control is active and influential, our ability to walk or magikally move objects, all forms of control. Take for example Transference, the study and practice of moving and manipulating physical matter, also known as telekinesis. All magik requires a Witch to make a connection with that which they wish to manipulate. Most Witches train using vision as their method of connection. Through physical vision, we can extend our magik to the selected object, establishing our control. Developing psychic abilities enhances our magikal potential to connect beyond our physical proximity, to remote distances."

He continues on, "Telepathy, for instance, is a standard skill for any Seer. Most Witches that develop their psychic abilities are using physical perception such as vision or hearing to connect to another's thoughts at the neurological level. Rather than call them telepaths, a more accurate term for these Witches is nearby-paths."

He laughs at his own joke, but the class remains silent. He clears his throat, "Seers can connect through the physical realm and the metaphysical realm, also known as the Spirit world."

A student raises her hand up. "Professor Abraney, what is the difference between a Seer and a Witch with psychic abilities?"

"A Seer can connect through the metaphysical realm innately whereas a non-Seer Witch must train to master those skills."

"Is it possible a Witch can be born with the innate skill of connecting to the metaphysical realm?"

"Why yes, that would make that Witch a Seer, now would it not?" The class chuckles at the Professor's unintentional jab, as he pauses to drink water. I myself couldn't help but laugh, although I do not consider myself much of a psychic these days, I seemed to be suffering some sort of mental block.

Professor Abraney then provides his instructions for the remaining portion of class, "Please pull the supplies from underneath your desk, instructions on page 354-355, a subchapter in the Elemental Section of the book. You will need to complete your work outside. Please submit your spellwork in two hours and then you will be dismissed for the day."

I opened my book.

Witchcraft: A foundation

Beginner's Fire Magik: Candle Flame
Supplies: Single white candle, Garret stone dust
Instructions: Draw the pentagram sigil, representative of
the Elements. Place the candle in the center
and recite the incantation with poses.
Incantation: Ignitia
Poses: Using your non-primary hand, circle the candle
while speaking the incantation.
Repeat until candle flame is ignited.

Maria and I walk together. She was in this class last year and is extending the course, what would be considered a repeat in the Mortal world. In the Witch world, this was a common event. Now that I think about it, I have seen her in a few of my other classes as well.

"I mean, don't get me wrong, I am very powerful," she said aggressively. For a moment I thought she was mad at me, and that I may be losing a friend before I had one. "Sorry, I am just a little sour having to repeat this class. Technically, I am not repeating the course, it's an extension." I realize she is talking more to herself than me.

"I don't have a lot of control over my magik even though my mom's a Witch. My dad's not, he bailed on her when he found out about her powers. I guess that makes me a little less-Legacy," she says bitterly.

"Anyway, I didn't grow up in places like Tarias. My brother and I lived in a small town in Texas. My mom didn't really like to talk about magik, so this is all kind of new for me. I still feel like an outcast, but I am going to figure it out, for my little brother and me. He's already showing signs of magik and I'm sure he'll be Manifesting soon."

We sit down and start setting up for the spell. "Anyway, what about you? Are your parents Witches?" She tilts her head slightly, the question fresh off her lips. The worst question to ask a foster kid is about their family. Even these Witches, who people fear are monsters, still have a family to call their own.

"I grew up mostly in foster care. I never met my biological parents."

Subtle signs of understanding grow on her face, simultaneously wrecking my world of pretend. I had thought that maybe, here, in the land of the bizarre, I could be normal. She looked like she wanted to gag over her own words, as if she spoke some poison. "I am so sorry, I don't know what to say," she says, desperate for redemption. "It's fine, really," eager to offer it, hopeful we could still be friends, "Besides, technically, I'm not a foster kid anymore."

I inhale sharply at the sound of my own words. I am not a foster kid anymore. Up until then, I suppose I had not fully realized it. The Council had partial custody of me, but more importantly, so did the Mastersons.

"That's the first time I said that out loud," I explain to Maria my backstory, fighting back tears all the while. Surprised, I trusted Maria, a person I'd just met that day.

Comforted by my emotional, yet non-defensive response to her initial question, she tells me more of her own experiences here at Tarias. She explains the subtle differences between her and the other Witches, the ones raised in the Witch world. "The most important thing to all Witches is power and money."

"Guess Witches and Mortals have more in common than I thought."

She laughs then and it sounds like a bell.

"It's a big deal to be born from a powerful Witch family. They have all the status and wealth. My family doesn't have much in the way of money, but I have the power."

I laugh, here I am just trying to survive, meanwhile people like Maria are trying to rule the world.

She asked me to make a pact with her. "Let's promise to become the most powerful Witches of all time."

"Deal," and we shook on it.

It is time to attempt the spell and Maria goes first. Witchcraft was difficult to control, as I found out moments later when I completely bombed the spell. Professor Abraney had to cast a spell on mine to avoid further fire damage. At least Maria's fared just fine, her spell went off perfectly.

What is wrong with me? Suddenly I found myself hoping I could keep the promise I made with Maria. Once the danger of my explosive spell had been extinguished, Maria and I said goodbye.

I make my way to Bexar and Gruene Hall. Since I was behind on all things Witch, along with my normal schedule, I had two additional weekly supplementary courses, held every Tuesday and Thursday evening. No rest for the wicked. Fortunately, Dr. Huebner taught these courses, making the experience tolerable.

Dr. Huebner would wait at the door and, apart from the Mastersons, he was so far the only person who routinely checked up on me. Even though I made friends with Maria, I still felt incredibly alone.

As far as I knew, I was the only Witch in Philomena from the Recessive origin; a Witch without a known magikal bloodline. Not to mention, I was also a Crown Ward of the Council, a Non-Legacy. It felt like I had a spotlight on me. Look at this weird kid without Witch parents or even a family.

All the other students were Legacies.

There were some Crown Wards here at Philomena. Dr. Huebner tried to get me to join their support group. It is true, they may have come from the foster system, but they were not like me. They at least had some information on their magikal lineage, a way to verify their Legacy.

Maybe, there are other Witches who had no bloodline to account for their powers. In theory, they could develop their magik in secrecy while living in the Mortal world. After all, even a Recessive Witch with adopted or biological parents were required to complete magikal training. In any case, I would not blame them for wanting to keep hidden, being a Witch had exceptional repercussions.

Dr. Huebner was assisting me with my Astronomy homework that focused on Celestial magik. Specifically, he was helping with language translations. All spells and incantations can and are created from a litany of varied backgrounds. Whether it was a dead language or modern English, it all worked, if you got the logistics right.

I was exhausted from the day but thankfully, the session finally ends, and as I exited the building, I saw Leroy taking notes by the door. He saw me too, and preemptively opened his mouth, ready to talk.

"Hi! I stayed late to work on the Divination project for Madam Reyna. It has to do with analyzing the stars, really exciting work." Drooling with enthusiasm, he then asks, "Headed back to the manor?"

Obviously. "Yup."

"I can walk you back," he offers.

"Sounds good."

I feign interest as he begins to describe, with excruciating detail, the origins of his own life. I continue to nod politely.

I think it was his attempt to reconcile his assumptions of my knowledge regarding Witch-life, a product of my "Non-Legacy" background.

"I'll try to be better at explaining things for you Noah, I promise".

I thought Leroy might be a little neurotic, excessively "Type A".

We returned to the Manor. It had been a long day and my regard for social graces were wearing thin, but I decided to help Leroy out. He was after all sincerely trying to help.

"It's okay. I think you're doing great. Honestly, you've really made this easier for me."

Here is your A plus, Leroy, I think to myself.

"Ready for dinner?"

"I am so tired," I proclaim while grabbing a sandwich and pouring a healthy serving of milk, "so I think I am going to eat upstairs and head off to bed," and that put an end to it.

Leroy was nice but was less of a friend and more of a teacher. I was grateful that I made friends with Maria. I didn't think I could be happy about returning to my room, no matter how luxurious the space was, but at least it was mine and I found myself feeling a bit relieved. My old room at the Mastersons may not have been as nice, but it gave me the same kind of relief, the thought leaves me longing to hear their voices, and I scold myself for thinking such a thing.

I wasn't being dishonest to Leroy. I ate my dinner alone and went to bed shortly after, grateful for the quiet. I needed to spend a little time with my thoughts and a few obstinate tears.

Chapter Eight

Love spells distort the mind and senses, creating false attachments. They do not create love, a common misconception.

He stares at me from the hall. The light of the fall moon casting his face in shadow. He moves, every step, bringing him closer. It cannot be.

I hear a noise, it grows louder and louder, my alarm perhaps, graciously disturbing my sleep, rescuing me from bad dreams. Until I realize it is not the blaring of my alarm making the noise but me screaming, waking myself up.

"Noah."

I wake up in a flash, sitting straight up, my breath fast and body flinching, half-asleep and shocked by the sight of an unfamiliar person at my bedside. Ms. Penelope stands beside me and cautiously touches my shoulder, her face riddled with concern. "Everything is alright love; you were having a nightmare. I will fix you some of my special tea tonight to get rid of those nasty buggers."

Still in disbelief that I was not dreaming, my body remains rigid with fear. I compose myself, forcefully slowing my breath and, consequently, my pulse.

"Dr. Huebner has arranged a surprise for you, an accommodation, and it is ready to be installed."

I am still unable to speak, still breathing.

"A special way to communicate with your family, dearie."

"What, really, how?" My mood rapidly changed.

"Yes, love. It's all right here, come and see."

My heart lifts to the moon! "When can I talk to them?"

"Well now, I suppose, love," as she waves toward the ancient, rather large rotary telephone plugged into nothing. The contraption hops like a kangaroo onto the nightstand.

There were telephones in the common areas of every Coven's residences. They were set up like phone booths, with sliding doors for privacy. Although they were limited and could only make calls to other residents of Tarias or Witch families with magikal access.

"I didn't have a chance to install it last night. Your family has been calling non-stop. I apologize Noah, I did not want to wake you. Since the nightmare did it for me, I figured why not now," she says brightly.

I want to tell her she should have woken me up, but I bite my tongue. After all, it was five in the morning.

She hovers her hand above the telephone, rapidly whispering words that I cannot discern, as they live somewhere under her breath. There is a brief pause, followed by a brilliant multicolor tapestry of bright lights. They shine from mini bulbs scattered on the device. The various golden symbols molded on the machine begin to glow in the same measure. The Mastersons had apparently received their own identical telephone the night prior.

"Go on love, give them a ring. Oh, and happy birthday Noah! Tonight, I am going to make you a special cake."

Tears welled up inside me when I heard Joan's voice.

Ms. Penelope interrupts the conversation, "Noah, would you and your family like to try the special feature?"

Annoyed, but unable to help myself, "What special feature?"

She takes the receiver from my hand and instructs Joan to, "Place the phone in front of the nearest and largest mirror in your home, love." Ms. Penelope picks up my own telephone and walks into the bathroom, motioning me to follow. She places it in front of the floor-to-ceiling mirror and the phone glows purple, while the mirror ripples like water and the Mastersons look at an image of me from Joan's large cheval mirror. While I stare back at them, in love with the vision of my family, I cannot help but cry more than I think I have ever cried in my life.

The sight of their beautiful faces, that I feared I would never see again, is almost too much to look at. Joan said her own tears were from pure joy, "I am so grateful to hear your voice and see those beautiful blues again!" Jake said he was happy and thankful that I was okay, that they had been worrying and praying for me every night.

Kevin said, "We miss you buddy." Joan snaps at him in a very Joan-like fashion, "Kevin, of course we miss him, don't make him feel bad. Oh my god Noah I can't with this man." Kevin laughs as Joan goes on to ask a million questions. She barely gave Kevin or Jake time to get a word in edgewise. I cried and laughed. This was the happiest I have been since arriving at Tarias.

They were sending me gifts for my birthday, along with more care packages that usually arrived with their letters. "Dr. Huebner was able to arrange the delivery. That man has stayed true to his word and kept his promise. Thank God for him," cried Joan.

More tears came then, not because I cared about what they were sending me, but because they thought about me. I still mattered to them. It was nearly impossible to say goodbye and only after a promise to speak again soon did we end the call. My heart was filled with happiness and I think it may have even fixed some of the cracks that lived within me.

Even Morgan was excited, purring violently as he bumped his head against the mirror's surface and the ancient telephone. I am grateful for it too, handsome boy.

Despite the nightmare, I felt refreshed, and stretched. After all, it was just a nightmare.

Oddly, I find myself looking forward to the day, that's a first for me here at Philomena. I rushed to wash up and after a bit of grooming, I am satisfied with the finished product.

On my way out to Meds, I found a small package laid out for me. It was wrapped in a pretty metallic paper that felt oddly fragile. This was not the first gift I received from a stranger. I was receiving packages from a few, random, families all welcoming me to the Witch world.

Robes, brooms, jewels, and even a knife. Doctor Huebner asked me to wait for him to open any gifts and to place all the items in a special safe that sat in a back corner of my closet. He told me it was a precaution against curses. He still had not given me an explanation as to why someone would want to curse me, but I am sure he would, and I made a mental note to ask him once more.

I place the box inside the magikal safe as the Doc instructed, but not before reading the card.

To: Noah Ellis. From: The O'Faolains.

I was in Versation, a class focused on transformation, and I am partnered with another student, a boy named Luke Stein. We were supposed to be reading the chapter titled,

> Initiation of the Mechanism of Transformation for Shifts in Color.

Instead, Luke asked, “Did anyone ever tell you how beautiful you are?”

In my hometown, I was openly gay but I didn't talk about it, and no one asked. Here, at Philomena, it was the same, but for entirely different reasons. Needlessly, I came out to Leroy and some other Seers during dinner one evening.

Leroy informed me that Witches do not distinguish sexual orientation the way Mortals do, "We view our relationships more fluidly, but that's not to say every Witch is bisexual. Many Witches have their preferences, but the idea is that sexuality isn't some concrete thing on which to base any moral or ethical judgment." He theorized this was the result of our extended life. I guess the longer life made people more open-minded to novelty and the unknown.

Luke was the obvious kind of handsome, an All-American blonde athlete, and he just blurted out this random and ridiculous comment to me.

It was extremely strange. I wasn't used to guys saying that kind of thing to each other, let alone to me. I feel terrible admitting this, but I was embarrassed. Even though I knew it was not, it felt like a man liking another man was some terrible crime, and I was uncertain of his authenticity. He could just be tricking me in some devious attempt to humiliate me. How could anyone like me?

"I hope that's cool," Luke says to me, reminding me that I have yet to respond to his statement.

"No, it's fine, sorry. It's just that no one has ever said something like that to me," apologizing automatically, a habit of mine.

"Impossible! Man, you have the prettiest eyes I have ever seen, and the sweetest smile," he says in a whisper, "even though you don't seem to smile all that often." He looked away then, a bit embarrassed himself, I think. It is a nice change of pace, not being the only nervous one.

And then I say the strangest thing, "Sorry, I guess I should smile more often," then nervously giggle, but it comes out sounding more like a cough than laughter.

Immediately I want to kick myself. Firstly, admittedly, it was probably true that I was generally the Eeyore type and could stand to be more positive, but even then, I didn't have to say sorry for it. Primarily, though, I was shamelessly flirting with him and now feel like an idiot because I don't know the first thing about flirting.

"It's cool. So, after this, you want to maybe hang out? We can skip class and go to the Bridge?" He was referring to the skybridge that ran across a steep gorge and valley that held the great Lake Osage. It connected Mt. Tarias and her lower hills on her northwestern mountain face. The stone bridge offers easy passage to the other side, accessing the shore of Lake Osage, at least for those traveling on foot.

"I can't, I have individual sessions with Dr. Huebner, booster sessions." I am glad I didn't say sorry for having plans. At least I held onto a little self-respect.

"Oh, well maybe this weekend," he asks.

"Yeah, maybe," I notice his unique pin attached to his coat, the one that identifies his Coven. It appears to be made from gold, and in the center of the small pin is a carved-out design of a tree. I attempt small talk, "What Coven does that pin represent?"

"The Coven of the Pentacle, we all have some form of innate Elemental magik."

"What kind of Element magik do you have?"

"All of them," he says proudly, then nervously adds, "I still have a lot to learn though," for what I assume is to avoid appearing obnoxious.

"That's really neat, a lot better than being psychic," and we smile at each other but are interrupted by Professor Periniea, he prompts us to return our attention to the assignment.

With my head down, I begin reading the chapter. I want to say yes to Luke, but in my experience being alone with another male inevitably ended up in something inappropriate happening. I wanted things to be different here.

Wow, how sick am I? Who said that is what he wanted?

My morning classes come to an end and I make my way to the Pillar. I wrap myself tighter in the standard mid-length black coat. It is still cold out, at least by my standards. Underneath, I wear grey slacks, black tie and sweater, and the same pointy black Witch dress shoes. Most importantly, I wore my pin that held a cosmic star on the front pocket of my sweater. A matching symbol is embroidered onto my coat to distinguish me from other Covens.

I bundled myself in extra layers including scarves and a pair of gloves, and I am the only Witch to do so. I never was one for the cold and tended to avoid it under all possible circumstances. However, the weather was changing, and becoming increasingly tolerable. After all, I wasn't even wearing my parka. Warmer days would soon arrive along with a promise of romance.

An energy seemed to pour out of the bright clear skies above, electrifying the student body. Activating some internal magnetism, people seemed to gravitate closer to one another, in search for adventure.

Meanwhile, I am alone, typical. I hate this mood I get into, isolating myself, and then complaining about it.

Thankfully, I find Maria, my one and only friend. She's great, when she is free. She has a boyfriend, Todd Ointeros, who she is currently spending time with, at least until she sees me. She waves her hand up with all five fingers spread out; reassuring me she will be over in five minutes. She returns her attention to the handsome boy staring intensely at her, then consoling him briefly before giving him a hug and then walks away. She does not look back, not even for an instant.

At that moment, I think that Maria may just be the most fabulous girl in the world, and I am full of gratitude for her.

"He's cute," I say.

"He's alright, a little needy." We talk a bit about school but mostly we spend our lunchtime complaining about Todd. Well, she mostly complains, while I listen, I have absolutely no experience in the way of relationships. Even so, I do not think their relationship is long for this world.

I knew the class bell was coming soon so I packed up my lunch in preparation. I hate the sound of thunder.

In anticipation of the bell, Maria and I stand up to leave for class. It is then that I feel it, like there are eyes on me. Sure enough, people are staring at me. Confession time: I had this secret, and probably irrational, fear that these Witches might sacrifice me to some horned god. I try not to let paranoia get the best of me. A task made easy when I heard him call my name, the actual reason people were staring.

"Hello, Noah."

The most beautiful boy in the world is standing in front of me, smiling politely.

"My name is David O'Faolain," he says with a Scottish accent and I fall apart, stunned by the fact that even his voice was handsome. Silence.

I despise my social anxiety. Catching it, I apologize too quickly, rush a "hello" back, and laugh uncomfortably. "Small school, I guess," I say awkwardly. He looks perplexed.

"Because you knew my name," I try to clarify, uselessly attempting to sound casual. "It's a little unnerving," invariably making the situation worse, wishing I could stop myself from speaking at all.

But the handsome boy only laughs, "There are not a whole lot of Non-Legacy Witches, and not many that are Crowns."

I cringe at him knowing so much about me. How does he know about my Non-Legacy Status? I hope that is all he knows, some secrets I get to keep, and what was up with that odd reference to Crowns, was he referring to me being a Crown Ward?

"No worries, ummm," he grabs at his hair, as if thinking, and then asks, "Did you get our gift? Sorry, I know it's a dumb tradition, sending gifts to you like that, but my family really wanted you to know they were thinking of you. It should've arrived today."

At first I said nothing, until I remembered the gift and the card from the O'Faolains that sat with the other gifts in the safe.

It was from him or his family, a rather sweet albeit still slightly creepy gesture.

Maria chimes in, "What gifts," distracting me from my vision of the beautiful boy with brown eyes.

"Gifts for his Manifestation. It's tradition for members of Coven Ius Divinum to send a gift to Crowns when they come of age."

"Like a bar mitzvah," asks Maria.

He chuckles and his smile breaks my heart.

"Sorta, anyway, have you got it, Noah?"

"No, I mean yes, I have, and I am sorry I haven't opened it. Dr. Huebner wants me to wait for security or something."

"Oh, you're alright, nothing wrong with being careful." His friends call him over. "Right, I best get going. It was nice talking to you, Noah. Have a nice day. See you later, Maria."

He turns his attention back to his group of friends who are playing a magikal version of hacky sack, levitating the pouch a mile high into the sky at each kick. They all wear the same silver pin with one golden and one diamond Phoenix circling one another, just like Maria's. I wonder how well they know each other.

The sound of his voice lingers in my mind. Maria speaks first, alerting me to my silence, "That was nice of him. I'm sorry

I didn't get you anything, I had no idea about that tradition for Crowns. I promise to make it up to you."

"No, please don't, I don't need anything." A question brews and a moment later boils over, "What did he mean by that, the tradition and Crown stuff," not so discreetly, adding, "Who was he, again?"

"Oh, that's David O'Faolain, the most gifted Witch in all of Philomena. It's kind of annoying since he hardly ever trains, I kind of hate him." We both laugh at her peevishness. Her tenacity and deep desire to surpass the Witches of Tarias can make her rather competitive.

Collecting ourselves, she sighs as if she has lost a race, "He's nice enough though, I guess."

"What did he mean earlier, when he called me a, what did he call it," pausing to remember, "A Crown, what was he talking about?" I am nervous now and dare not ask any more.

"The Witches of your Coven, Divina Diademate, are known as Crowns," Maria says, as if that explains it, but the class bell rings interrupting our conversation.

Purple lightning erupts out of the stone hands of the Fountain of Hai-Tai Wussein. The sound of thunder surges across the grounds. The magikal orb whizzes by, the volume of sound rising as it approaches. It gradually fades as it travels to the various buildings of Philomena, reaching every corner of the Academy, exactly three times.

The lightning is only used to mark the end of lunch. I half believe it is to ensure that no student considers skipping afternoon courses. Its thunderous boom reminds Philomena students of the significance of punctuality.

As we walk toward our classes, we run into another first for me in the magik world. An actual flying fairy, no that is not right, a Faelin, mentally correcting myself. Only it is more bird than anything I imagined, covered in feathers with large yellow owl-like eyes. It had a miniature version of a human body with intricate antlers atop its head.

It flew up to me and stared directly into my eyes. The way its wings moved reminded me of a hummingbird; although it was much larger than any hummingbird I have ever seen and was at least the size of a basketball. The Faelin, now remarkably close to my face, starts speaking a language unknown to me. Its words sounded extra-terrestrial, and then I wondered if it was an alien. I started to question all that I thought and understood about the world.

What else existed in this magikal world? What other differences existed from Mortal myths and supernatural facts or was the lore an entire contradiction of magikal reality? Such was the case of the aggressive Faelin that did not look like Tinker Bell or any other fairy found in storybooks.

The Faelin's voice now raises in volume. I was fascinated and deeply uncomfortable, afraid it would try to claw my face with its sharp talons that served as appendages. I try to create space between us, a futile attempt to mind my bubble. Faelin or not, it needed to learn some manners.

Meanwhile, Maria is having the time of her life, laughing at my expense and discomfort with the Faelin's proximity.

Maria chants a few words, and then a quiver rippled in and out of me. She must have cast some sort of translator spell because suddenly the Faelin's gibberish transforms into coherent statements. It still sounded the same, only it now made sense to me. Impressive, I would have to ask her when she learned to do that, and how to do it myself.

The Faelin introduces herself. Her name is Aeduou and, in a nutshell, she wanted my lunch, a brie and turkey sandwich. She was trying to bargain with me for some sort of exchange but I just gave her the sandwich. She refused at first, but then resolved to settle the debt sometime in the future. She would repay in the form of a favor. Apparently, she was exceptionally reliable at speedy deliveries.

Once her promise was made, Aeduou did something in-between a curtsy and a bow, and quickly flew away. She carries her sandwich effortlessly and, in a wisp, turns into air and vanishes.

I arrive late to Divination and, as a result, have lost my preferred backrow seat. Worst of all, Divination is taught by Madam Reyna.

"Mr. Ellis, hurry up, take a seat immediately!"

"May I sit here," I ask an unusually tall girl with short red hair. On her pinafore sits a silver pin with a golden Phoenix and diamond one in the center.

She stands, "Yes, my Crown," nodding to the desk, motioning for me to sit. She wears this look of anticipation, and I felt as if I was missing something. After a painstakingly long three seconds, I mumble out a "Thank you." She whispers to me the correct protocol, "You say 'Thank you, my Lord'."

A little too late. Madam Reyna shouts at me. "Mr. Ellis, mind your manners."

"Thank you, my Lord."

Madam Reyna scolds me, "A Crowned one does not look at his feet Mr. Ellis, never look away. How incompetent are you? Do it again," I look right at the girl and repeat myself, wary of Madam Reyna's rage, "Thank you, my Lord."

I just stood there, not knowing what I should do next. Madam Reyna audibly sighs from the front, "A Crowned one does not initiate, but always leads."

I remain quiet, confounded by what this crazy woman was going on about. More exasperated sighs, "You sit down first, by the Spirits. Don't be rude and make her wait and further delay class with your incompetence."

All the students' eyes are on me, causing my anxiety to blur my vision. I quickly take my seat, trying to ignore their stares.

They are obviously perplexed by my reaction to an apparently routine conversation between this girl and myself.

"Hey, you okay," she asks, her voice soft. Her name is Amelia Sycamore.

"Yeah, I am fine, nice to meet you. I'm Noah. Sorry, Noah Ellis." I pause, uncertain of what to say, "Why did we have to do that?"

"Oh, that's because of Madam Reyna," as Amelia rolls her eyes, "I don't know why she's like that. She forces us to practice this stuff, she's even worse when the Esbat rolls around."

I nod and pretend to know what she is talking about, returning my eyes to the crystal ball in front of me.

An hour later, the flying bell rings and I see the orb zoom by and away out the window for the final time today. Outside I meet Maria and we walk back together to our respective houses for Ending Circle, the Witch version of a house meeting that was mostly to serve dinner.

I tell Maria about the Crown and Lord incident. She says most classes do not follow that formal etiquette, "Madam Reyna is such a bitch, probably has some tarot card stuck in her ass."

With my tongue-in-cheek, Maria explains, "Your Coven has the rarest of all Witches. You all are said to be descendants of the source of magik, or the Spirit. It has something to do with you all having divine access. I know, so weird."

She pauses to adequately roll her eyes, and adds, "The name, Divina Diademate, basically translates to Divine Crown, but only the members of my Coven refer to you all as Crowns."

"That's ridiculous, why? Also, why am I supposed to call you all Lords?"

She explains, "My Coven, Ius Divinum, translates to 'divine right', like the explanation used to justify ancient monarchies, hence the whole 'Lords' nomenclature. We are said to be chosen by you to be the Hand of the Spirit."

Reading the confusion on my face, Maria explains, "Our Covens in the Witch nation are considered elite, think ivy-league. Your Coven is known for rarity, and mine for talent; only the most powerful Preparatory Witches are admitted into the Coven Ius Divinum."

She elaborates, "The idea is that we are the most powerful Witches because we were chosen by the Divine, the members of your Coven. You 'Crowned' us, making us Lords, and we are supposed to honor all of you."

"That makes no sense," genuinely baffled by the lack of logic.

"Oh, it gets worse. Even creepier, our Covens are supposedly betrothed to one another, like we are married or something. I know, so dumb."

"What?" I cannot help but laugh at the absurdity of it.

"Right, but that's Witch life."

We mock the irrational tradition until we reach the end of our walk. As we were about to go our separate ways, I remember another question, "What's an Esbat?"

"The one tonight?"

"I guess."

She explains, "It's this lunar cycle ceremony thing, but like also a monthly school assembly."

"Do I have to go?"

"Everyone has to go," frowning, "Especially us."

"Me and you?"

"No, our Covens. We have to do our part. Speaking of, I have to run home and get ready, and so do you."

"What do you mean, 'our part'?" but she was already jogging away. I assume she is running late. "Sorry, your House Lead will explain it to you. See you tonight," she shouts as she waves goodbye. She hurried to her own residence, which was located on the eastern end of Mt. Tarias' summit, opposite

Spirit Manor. I wondered what it looked like, her home, where she and David lived.

Chapter Nine

Luminaries: Cosmic light bodies to include the Sun, Moon and stars. All excellent power sources for Evocation and Conjuration, especially during strenuous spellwork.

"Noah," Leroy says, standing in front of me. I don't remember him walking into my room, regardless, he came in without knocking.

"Please, get ready, we leave in twenty," he says anxiously.

"Leroy, I'm exhausted. I was wondering if I could skip this one?" Truthfully, I was tired but the unappealing idea that me and the rest of my Coven play some role in the production of tonight's ceremony only worsens the issue.

"No one skips the Esbat Noah, it's required, the rules." Unable to argue, "Okay, I'll be there in five."

"Don't forget to wear the uniform zipped up in the suit cover," he then disappears, literally. It was a psychic visual of him known as an Altar. He did it without permission, the act felt invasive like magik voyeurism.

My frustrations are all but forgotten the moment I opened the bag that contained the uniform. It was a full-on Witch's outfit. Included with a decorated hat that looked like a crossbreeding between an Easter Sunday headpiece and the stereotypical cone-shaped Witch's Cap. It was mortifying.

Maria called me from her residence's communal telephone. She wanted to be sure that I had all the information I needed for tonight.

She elaborates on her explanation of the Esbat, "They say it's meant to be a joining of minds and time to reflect with other Witches on spellwork, for each other's magikal development."

"Why do I have to be there? Or, I guess, why do we have to be there? Why is that so important?"

"I don't think it is important, just pomp and circumstance more than anything, if you ask me," she says in a half-sigh. She continues, "Here at Philomena, it's tradition for our Covens to attend any formal event where there is ceremonial magik, like during the Esbat. Think of it as a fancy tea party, because like most traditions, it's all for show. We are technically part of the party, the opening act and the ending scene." I can hear the annoyance in her voice, "That's the crappy thing about being us, our freedom is kinda limited. Just sit where they want you to sit."

After a few minutes of her venting she says, "I know it's embarrassing, but they don't play around when it comes to these kinds of things. You have to grin and bear it, and besides, I'll be there, we can try to make the most of it."

We promise to, at least, attempt to have fun and then say goodbye. I placed the receiver back on the antique phone's hook, pausing to admire the contraption. Deciding to take a little more time to appreciate the golden gears that coordinated phone calls, but really I was just stalling, a hopeless endeavor to delay the night. Leroy's voice echoes throughout the Manor, "LAST CALL."

With that, I place the pointy embroidered hat on my messy hair and walk to meet the other Seers downstairs. Together, we make our way into the dark night.

The Moon is high in the sky as we walk toward the Bridge. We carry lanterns with small candles held inside. It lights the path ahead, illuminating an unnaturally broad circumference, far beyond the scope one would expect from a standard candle.

We wore large hooded capes, bonded at the neck by the pin of our Coven. Each of us wear various elaborate versions of the traditional black pointed hat. Every single one held a unique design. My own was decorated with silver symbols representing the full lunar cycle, speckled with diamond dust that was meant to look like stars.

Oddly, I could not help but have a small sense of reverence toward the experience. In the dark night, with only our lights revealing the world around us. Yes, I was still embarrassed, but there seemed to be some grand sense to the event.

We arrive at the Bridge and walk across the crystal lake beneath. The light of the lanterns creates the effect of a small sun approaching the destination, leaving the darkness behind. We walked past the wooded clearing and entered the Palladium; a mammoth sized stone amphitheater located on the carved-out ridge on Tarias' northwestern edge. It was built in the shape of a crescent moon with natural stone rows serving as both stairs and seats and cascaded vertically against the cliff.

The Moon stares at us now, bombarding us in its spotlight. It seemed to brighten as we approached. Did magik do that, did we? The sight of the young Witches casting their spell immediately answered my question. Leroy had explained earlier our role in this ceremony. We were to arrive at the call of the members of Coven Ius Divinum, something known as the Drawing of the Moon.

The Lords of the Divinum stand together in the center of the Palladium. They are on a small pavilion on the ground floor and they are singing. Their voices are in unison, a perfect blend of various pitched sopranos and tenors. The song was melodic and hypnotizing. I am pulled by it, by him. I swear I can discern David's voice out of the choir.

Lost in my wayward thoughts, Kady, a housemate, places her hand on my shoulder, calling my attention to the task. She prompts me to follow her lead and we make our way toward a round stone table that is wider than my bedroom and nearly as tall as I am.

The other Seers each take their turn setting their lantern on the edge of the table, encircling it with light, and I follow suit. As I approach my designated spot, an indentation suddenly appears in the stone for my lantern to rest, a superfluous coaster, at least in my opinion. The song ends and our lantern's light transforms into bright, magikal orbs. The orbs leave their home and scatter into the surrounding area, unveiling light to aid the procession of tonight's festivities. It was as if our arrival provided some protection and blessing from the darkness.

We stand still, as the student body and faculty take their seats. The Witches of the Coven Ius Divinum remain standing. There is an electric buzz in the air, and I am convinced this is a result of the ceremony.

I follow the other Seers toward a set of chairs placed a short distance from the table. They are set up at the front and center of the stage, forcing us to face the audience. I silently scream as each Seer takes their seat. We were going to sit there while the entire student body of St. Philomena watches us. This had to be some form of hazing.

Maria waves at me, and then so does David, and I just want to crawl into my oversized Witch hat and die. I try my best to remain calm, hoping that my face is not turning several shades of red. Distracting myself, I stare out at the audience, focusing on nothing in particular.

I turn my attention to the colors in the crowd and the colors of the other Coven's pins. Seas of multiple and separate colors reveal obvious factions. I didn't know if this was because of some Witch protocol-thing or the typical high school clique phenomena.

I knew the pins were representative of the Coven's craft, which can sometimes be related to power type, level, and other factors, but I thought that served as a function, not a separation. Like with Seers, it was useful to place us together, as we could prevent unauthorized mind-readings.

I did not see her walk toward the table and onto the higher podium. She was serving as the Interim Dean, while the Acting Dean was on sabbatical researching Transdimensional magik in Argentina.

Voysieur Eternealisum

She speaks, her voice amplified by the spell, resonating so as to be heard throughout the entire auditorium. The familiarity of that stern voice was unmistakable, Abigail Tetson. My eyes narrow in absolute loathing at the sound of it.

She provides a general update on quarterly obligations, even more evidence this was more of an assembly than a gathering of magikal prowess. I was beginning to allow myself to believe there would not be a sacrifice. Yet, that did nothing to reduce my animosity toward that vile woman.

Abigail ends her announcements with a spell.

Ugusta Impuies

"Now what," I ask Kady.

"Cakes and Ale," she says. As if on cue, floating plates manifest throughout the Palladium. They are filled with various hors d 'oeuvres and accompanied by flying flutes of champagne providing food and drink to every Witch in the outdoor auditorium.

She laughs, "Now, we eat, drink, and be merry."

Leroy rushes over to me, mid-chew of some puff pastry. He instructs me to, "Mingle." He reminds me, "When you see a Witch from Ius Divinum, the ones with the pins that have a gold Phoenix, you do know what a Phoenix is, the bird made of fire?"

Annoyed, I respond, "Yes, I know about the Phoenix." "Right, the pins with the gold Phoenix and," I interrupt him, "And a diamond Phoenix."

He does not look convinced; Leroy is quickly becoming more hindrance than aid.

"Okay. Anyway, if one of them approaches you or bumps into you, or you bump into them, you call them Lords and they call you Crown. They address you first, that's their job. Then you end the greeting and try to do it quickly to avoid making it awkward. Oh, and they can't sit down until you are seated."

My scowl must have given me away. "Look, I know it's stupid, I get it, but it's a big rule with the Chair of our House." Good old Madame Reyna, "So just go through the motions, and we won't have hell to pay for it."

"Okay, I can follow the rules, trust me," I reassure him.

"I won't fail you, or us," I correct myself, "One question, why does it have to be this way, this formal?"

Leroy explains the Esbat is old ceremonial magik, the power was found in the ritual. He reiterates what Maria said earlier today, with the Seers representing the source of magik and Maria's Coven representing the action of the spell. Unfortunately, all that talk about ritual has me re-thinking my fear of being sacrificed.

I attempt to mingle but end up walking aimlessly through the crowds. Eventually, I run into Maria, but she is preoccupied with her boyfriend, Todd. From the look of it, things do not appear to be going well as she is waving her hands in the air and talking loudly. She sees me, but not wanting to interrupt what appears to be a very serious conversation between the two, I politely raise my hand up to let her know I would see her later.

I do not really feel like talking to anyone from my own house. Maybe it was our thing to not like each other. No one was overtly rude, but we were not all that friendly with each other, either. I file that away for me to think about later.

Ironically, I end up making small talk with a few Lords, engaging in the further social dividing that had concerned me earlier. Perhaps there is some truth in this supposed union between my Coven and theirs. The wind shifts and I turn to my right and find David O'Faolain walking toward me. Lean and broad, in his tailored suit with a bright smile. His dark eyes now peer down directly into my own, while his black hair remains messy and perfectly dashing.

"Hello," he says to the crowd. To my embarrassment, he puts his head down, bowing slightly toward me.

"And hello...to you, my Crown," the other Witches in the group buckle under the apparent obligation of his act.

"Damnit David, seriously," says one boy. The group is forced to follow the protocol. They bow their heads in solidarity. I hear David laughing, and under his breath he tells the boy, "rules are rules, mate," grinning all the while.

"To the knee, in honor of the Divine," says Dr. Huebner, his voice booms from a magikal intercom.

Every Witch including Dr. Huebner and Abigail bow. Only fellow Seers, Madam Reyna, and I remain standing. I hear David laughing loudly and I get the feeling Dr. Huebner took David's practical joke to another level. The sound of David O'Faolain's laugh is a glorious thing.

Every Witch stands back on their feet, including David, and with his beautiful accent, his voice soft and low, "And how are you, Noah?"

Lost in the moment, I somehow do not care about the humiliation of having all these people forced into that act of obeisance. He is stunning. He literally stuns me and I seemed incapable of coherent thoughts. He stares at me blankly, waiting for me to answer.

I manage to rush out a few words, "Okay, I am okay, you?"

"Just fine, Noah, thank you for asking. My family wishes you a very happy birthday," and hands me a small blue box, "For you, a small token from my family."

"Oh, that's right. I had forgotten about it."

"You forgot it was your birthday," he asked incredulously.

Pausing, "Yeah, I guess I did."

We sort of just stare at each other, until I realize he is still holding the box in his hand. "Anyway, I couldn't, you have already sent me something."

"Please, it would break me mum's heart if I had, excuse me, if we had to return it."

He speaks sheepishly, which seems uncharacteristic of him. Then again, I barely knew him, so who am I to say? With incredible apprehension, I agree, "Thank you, you all really didn't have too. Please tell your family I said thank you."

"No worries, Noah, glad to do it."

As I start to unwrap the ribbon, he softly clasps my hands, and whispers in my ear, "Not here, it's part of the rules. Maybe at home?" He winks at me and I wonder how I am still standing.

He turns to the rest of the group, "So, my fellow Lords, having fun?"

They change topics, starting a new conversation. A silver flask is tossed between the group, which I refuse. I have learned to never take a strange drink this late at night.

An hour later, Maria joins in, just as the Dean closes the ritual with a toast and a spell.

Luna Nexxus Nyx

We repeat the Dean's words and cast the quiet spell that ignites the sky into a deep bright purple, a token meant to honor the Moon.

"It's time to head back," says Leroy. "Crowns first, then the general student body, and Lords and faculty last."

We began our walk back to the Manor, I spy Maria as we leave, and she is talking to Todd. My guess is she is trying to comfort him. He looks like he is close to tears. Right before we enter the shroud of woods, I turn back and meet David's eyes. He smiles broadly at me, waving goodbye, and takes the slightest bow. I turn around and walk with the rest of my group. It takes me nearly a minute to realize I am holding my breath.

I opened his gift once I was back in the safety of my room. It was a silver charm in the form of a cat, just like Morgan. The Mastersons had gifted me a locket attached to a necklace, and inside was a picture of us. I link the charm to the pretty chain and wear it to bed.

My birthday had been extraordinary. I could now talk with the Mastersons, compliments of Dr. Huebner staying true to his word. For the first time since I arrived here, I was starting to feel a bit of hope. Maybe things would be okay here.

I lay down peacefully for the first time in what felt like a long while, yet I could not find sleep. My head was swimming with thoughts of David. Unable to help myself, I imagined him coming to my window in the middle of the night and scolded myself for my shameful adoration of the boy I barely knew.

Chapter Ten

Protection charms require Divination for foresight, Temporal magik for influencing future chance events, a Celestial invocation for a power source, and Transference for manipulating the physical environment should barriers be incorporated into the charm.

We were in Transference, the class focused on telekinetic magik. It was held in an expansive gymnasium filled with various contraptions that served as an obstacle course. The class was padded from the floors, walls, and ceiling; a necessary precaution for training this type of active magik.

I stood inside a transparent room-sized cube. It was enchanted to mimic any type of weather. Sir Yung, the Transference Professor, prompts the mechanism to create rain.

My eyes were fixed on the drain, where the water pooled. I paid special attention to the water pooling at the center, reassuring myself that I would not drown inside this entrapment. I was supposed to produce a magikal barrier.

It did not have to be visible to the naked eye, just secure enough to prevent water flowing, like an umbrella.

There are hosts of issues that can interfere with magik, including simple limitations in skills or power. Even psychological interference or stress can disrupt a Witch's magik. Spells compensate for these barriers and help create the effect, if done correctly.

Dr. Abraney, the Professor who taught spell theory, says any magik can become innate and readily available without the need for spellwork, what is known as wordless spells. However, he also says no Witch can have innate gifts in every magikal ability, so at some point every Witch requires the aid of rituals and incantations.

Even the Witches with an innate talent still have practical limitations such as time constraints, stress, or plain old forgetfulness. Witches often purchase magikal objects, choosing to skip the whole enchantment fuss entirely.

Charms and enchantments are simply spells to give objects or areas a specific power and are often used for convenience. Mops and brooms that are bewitched to clean the floors at sunrise or dishes that self-wash once dirtied are real timesavers. Efficient Witches often use brooms to travel rather than using their own power to fly unaided, like choosing to drive rather than walk.

The problem was that literally nothing about Witchcraft was simple. Spells required considering things like physics, astronomy, even posture, and of course a sound mind. All these factors can influence the effectiveness of a spell.

Sir Yung prompts me to take my turn at the spell. My skills are not innate and require lots of magikal convenience.

> Six candles set in an Aquarian star pattern.
> Purified rock salt to define the line.

It was a simple spell. In fact, the candles and sigil were really like training wheels. Ideally, I should be able to conjure the barrier with only a few words.

Secundum signum corporis obiectu

"Visualize, Mr. Ellis!"

I was the only one in the room unable to produce even a modest effect. Thelma Chase, who was forever daydreaming, produced something that at least acted along the lines of an old tattered roof, preventing most of the water from coming through.

As I stood there, repeating the words, I felt a pull at my fingertips, like a magnet to some metal within the salt that formed the symbol on the floor. I was supposed to pull the energy, like a rubber band. Once it was at its most taught, then release, the energy should have bounced back and formed an invisible barrier around me. Yet it was only a mild sensation, it felt like I was trying to help a sack of potatoes stand upright.

The water, with just the slightest delay, falls steadily through the "umbrella", like the way water drains from a sink, and leaves me looking like a wet dog. Anyway, without a functioning barrier, I might as well feel nothing, and maybe it was nothing.

I arrived at Spirit Manor for Closing Circle. Tonight was a booster session with Dr. Huebner, so after dinner, I changed into jeans and a tee shirt that is one size too large. On my way out, I see a notification on the magik message board. Every residence at St. Philomena has one placed in their main common room, independently writing and rewriting messages as needed, and notifying the school of general announcements.

Evaluations
(Gymnasium B)
February 11th at 12PM
Preparatory Students:
Chris Laurel
Ridge F. Taygue
Elliana Ridge
Maria E. Pedraza
Katherine Zilberman

The names were erased, replaced with the second set of names, and continued to change until completing the entire list, there must have been 50 students selected. The message repeats itself and will probably do so until morning. None of the names were mine, thankfully.

I recognized Maria and David on the list immediately. Also on the list was my housemate, Katherine Zilberman, who goes by Kady and is in the common room with me at the time. She is reviewing her own hard copy of the message. I asked Kady about the notice.

"Just the invitation for the Evaluations," she answers nonchalantly.

"What are those?"

"No one's told you about them?"

Duh, Kady. "No, not yet."

"Wow, okay well, they're like a magik IQ test, a good rating could change everything for a Witch. This is my second one. It's kind of a big deal." She goes on to explain that they are held quarterly for volunteers and required at least annually.

She allows me to read over her notice as it has additional information such as the skills to be tested, skills that I did not have. Reading the worry on my face, she adds, "You'll do fine when it's time for yours. It's just to get an idea of where you are with your magik, and it probably will not be until the fall for you. Most students are trying to earn privileges, like private bedrooms. It's not a big deal for us because we already get our own, but most other Covens require students to share a room. More importantly is qualifying for certain opportunities. Personally, I am hoping to get an internship with the Royal Healers."

Worried over the likely scenario of failing these exams, I immediately think of the Mastersons, what would happen to them? I wanted to ask Maria more about them, but I was afraid of bothering her too much, or making her worry over the exams. Besides, she was spending her extra time with her new boyfriend, Nathan Uman.

The Doctor and I were supposed to train on my Seer abilities, but I thought I would take the opportunity to ask him more about the Evaluations.

To my disappointment I arrived at an empty room. I take a seat and decide to wait. It was not uncommon for the Doctor to run late. He had a corner office with floor to ceiling windows, grand bookcases filled to the brim, magikal objects of some fashion in every corner, and several elaborate portraits hung on the remaining wall space. His office extended into the floor level above, creating an upper story loft just above the hallway on this floor.

Dr. Huebner shouts out from the hallway, "On my way, Mr. Ellis, grabbing some tea and biscuits, care for some?"

"Yes, please," responding as loudly as I could without sounding rude.

After I take my first sip, I ask about the Evaluations. He had sat on many review boards, so he was well-versed in the requirements. He immediately, and rather eagerly, provided a detailed overview. "It is a comprehensive assessment that tests for the Three C's in a Witch: Capability, Capacity, and Competency. The Evaluations are meant to assess a Witch's talents per stage of development, identify current and potential innate skills, and determine rarity, range, level, and expertise."

Mine would likely be scheduled in the coming fall, confirming Kady's estimate. In any case, Dr. Huebner volunteers himself to provide tutoring sessions to prepare me for the Evaluations.

"Albeit, this is rather early and a bit preemptive, Mr. Ellis."

"Doctor Huebner, if I were to fail, would I be expelled from the Academy?" He tries to reassure me, "It is positively unlikely you would do poorly!"

"I know you think that, but what if I do?" The volume of my voice is much louder than I expected, but I do not pause, "If I do fail, would something happen to the Mastersons? I couldn't live with myself if they were hurt because of me." Damn these tears and their infernal treachery.

Doctor Huebner seems wistful just then. His voice softens, "No Mr. Ellis, nothing will happen to them in that unlikely scenario," he says without theatrics.

"Okay, good...thank you."

He further reassures me in a stone and sober voice that there wasn't much need for worry. As it turns out, the more critical Evaluations were performed closer to a Witch's Ascension. As the prior assessments were generally testing for core skills as the more advanced abilities are rarely developed for younger Witches.

"Although there are some Witches that begin their studies at a much earlier age, not to worry, a late start is a start all the same."

I know Dr. Huebner would never intentionally try to hurt me but that whole "late start" comment stung a bit, like something was wrong with me because I was not up to pace. It made me second guess, not just the exam, but me.

"Dr. Huebner, one of my housemates told me that doing well on the exam may grant certain privileges, could you tell me more about that?"

"Well, doing well on the exam can pave the way for your position in the Witch nation, such as the Royal Guard or the Coventry of the High Crown, which is especially significant for you and the other young Witches of your Coven."

"What is a High Crown?"

"Ah, yes, the High Crown is a symbolic monarchy, a nod to tradition, like the royal line of the United Kingdom. Although the High Crown does serve a role in coordinating internationally between our sister and brother nations, including the Witches of the Eastern Lands that include most of Asia and Japan, or the European Unionized Witch Government, not including the United Kingdom, Scotland, or Ireland, which are territories of ONCE. Some Witch Nations have their own High Crown Representative. Such is the case for the Egyptian Council's Descendants of the Pharaoh and Africa's long line of Rain Queens. Others, like the Australian Council, choose not to participate as they have dissolved most of their governing powers, save for their required annual extended holiday."

Unable to help himself, he adds, "They say it is to pay respect for the Order of Magik, but just between us, I think they just want a reason to vacation. An absolute atrocity if you ask me!"

I laugh slightly then, "So like royalty, but symbolic. Why have it at all?"

"Well that comes from tradition. The High Crown is said to rule all Witches. Legend has it, in times of peril, either from internal strife or external threats, supernatural or Mortal, the High Crown rises to restore order and peace. Historically, there have only been a handful of identified, potentially legitimate, High Crowns. The last testimony of a High Crown was in the early centuries of the second millennium, a talented weather Witch who is said to have used her powers to open the gateways for what the world would know as the Renaissance. If the few corroborated stories are accurate in their descriptions of her feats of power, well you might find me a believer."

"But Doctor Huebner, what does that have to do with my Coven?"

"Well, with no true Chosen One, the High Crown has been divided into Nine Seats. The policy of the modern High Crown is to elect members in every generation, these new chosen ones represent the order. The connection between your Coven and the High Crown is that thc Witchcs of Divina Diademate are frequently elected as members, securing a Crowned Seat of the Nine or even the Crowned Chair itself, the highest-ranking member. The Seats are elected through several assessments to include Evaluations, which are used to screen extraordinary abilities beyond the average of our kind. However, one tradition remains from the legendary High Crown; the Vilix Despirir."

Dr. Huebner further explains, "The Vilix Despirir is considered pure awareness, the ability to connect to ultimate reality also known as the Sight. It is incredibly rare, in fact, not one of the current Nine possesses the gift, but each member is required to possess a component of the Vilix Despirir, one of its children."

He must have sensed my confusion.

"Essentially, all psychic gifts are children of the Vilix. Take for example these three, mind-reading, visions of the future, and communication with the dead. All require some form of extrasensory awareness but are contained by limit of vision. Those gifts are pointed in different directions, vantage points, if you will. The Vilix is all the vantage points, beyond what is above, below, within, without, and everywhere else." Pausing to ensure I was following, he continued, "The Coven Divina Diademate, with its strict admission requirement of innate psychic ability, is a convenient supply source for the High Crown."

"That makes us sound like cattle," I say candidly.

He chuckles, but I was not saying it to be funny. "It is an honor to be at the High Crown, you would be very blessed to be selected, even as a general member," Doc adds.

This was all interesting, but I failed to see how it had anything to do with me. My main objective is to complete the exam with a shred of dignity. Powerful and talented Witches make the team, not Witches like me, whose spells either do not work or cause an explosion.

"Speaking of psychic gifts, it is about that time that we resume our focus on your own abilities, is it not, Mr. Ellis," says Dr. Huebner.

With that, we spend our remaining portion of the session practicing some of my Seer gifts. I manage to sense the people around us, feeling their movements, their change in directions, and even the subtle movements in their body, from agitated, to fatigue, to indifference, and excitement.

One Witch is cleaning an office on the floor below. She uses her magikal gifts, sending rags and chemicals flying about while she listens to Spanish rock. It was as if I was wearing the young woman's earpiece. I can still remember the melody, but not the words; I was always terrible at remembering lyrics.

We wrap up our session, "Have a good night Dr. Huebner," as he waves from his office, while on the phone with some congressional representative. I make my way to Spirit Manor, an end to a very long day.

Chapter Eleven

Judgment Call
Supplies: Silver traditional scale
Instructions: Place at your center and cast
Incantation: Ammut Ahemai Ma'at
Legend: Right for Innocent and Left for Guilty

I am bleeding. I cannot stop it. The bad man is here, and my screams wake me from the nightmare. I sit up in a gasp. My mind is no longer on red alert, no longer shutting everything down but the priorities, I realize my bad dreams have returned with a fury. It is a sure sign of me adjusting to this place.

It was Saturday and despite it being four in the morning, and the weekend, I decided I would work on my studies. It was better than worrying about bad dreams.

I was reviewing the different types of magik and their respective foundations. Interestingly, teleportation or Translocation is often accomplished through powerful cosmic magik, a type of magik that harnesses the might of the Celestial giants, from stars to planets.

There are plenty of Translocation devices in the Witch world, like the Walk-Easy that Dr. Huebner used to transport me from Westchester to Tarias. There were other similar contraptions, all requiring extraordinary power to charm. It worked by creating a vortex of sorts. The spellwork sometimes required years to complete.

One chapter covered a type of Witchcraft that dealt with emotions, called Empathic magik. What surprised me was how much our thinking, Mortal or Witch, was purely emotional. The energy of it all. I found a spell that addressed deficits in emotional depth and moral reasoning.

> Sondropsis - a perspective spell that creates a realization of the complexity of other people's lives.

Maria's phone call interrupts me before I have a chance to read the rest. She needlessly begs me to go to the market with her, located within the city of Tarias.

"Absolutely," I say excitedly! She meets me at the Manor, and we hike down the paved descension of stairs, "It's not so bad going down. It's a monster going back up, but we'll take a buggy for that."

"Are you nervous about the Evaluations," I ask. It was scheduled for her that following day.

"Hell no," sighing to herself, "A little," she admits.

Surprised, I say "But all your spells seemed to be going off without a hitch." It was true, Maria had advanced in a noticeably short amount of time. Once she put her mind to something, she was a force to be reckoned with.

"Thanks, it's just my first one you know?"

"Yeah, I guess even if I was really talented, having someone critique me is still nerve-wrecking."

"That's exactly what it is. I get it, they are there to figure out what strengths and weaknesses we have, but it's still degrading. I am not here to dance in front of you." She adds, "But, also, I'm a ballerina, so I will, but only if they absolutely love me for it."

We laugh together.

We stopped at a small candy shop and reveled in the opportunity to control our diet for once, a job ordinarily left to the whim of our House Masters.

Good as the food was at the Manor, thanks to the ever-attentive Ms. Penelope, there is something to be said about eating the food you choose. She would never serve these kinds of sweets at the Manor.

We laughed and jumped up and down. Excited over generic candies and enchanted soda, called *pop*. It caused the briefest moments of weightlessness at every sip, allowing us to jump, in a figurative pop, higher than we typically could using our own strength.

We decide to go to the Port.

Importing products to Tarias was a complicated process. Most things were locally sourced until freight day. We waited by the harbor to see it. Visibility is low as a result of a dense mist that looms about. This mist is dissimilar in movement to a normal, generally well-behaved, one found in the Mortal world. I think this magikal mist is a bit cantankerous. Gradually, its image slowly forms as it floats closer, until the colossal freight ship comes into full view, all noise and steel. Finally, it arrives onto the harbor of Lake Osage, which is interesting since Tarias is landlocked. I wonder what secrets lie behind that cloudy veil.

Workers began levitating large crates filled with goods, delivery orders, and everything else under the sun. We wait for them to unload the daily mail as we stand in line at the Post. It is Tarias' central location for mail delivery and Maria was expecting something from her mother. Unexpectedly, I also had a care package delivered from the Mastersons. It was filled with gifts and treats for Morgan and I. Normally Dr. Huebner had these packages delivered directly to me, it made me happy to receive it firsthand.

On our way out of the harbor, I overheard one of the Witch-sailors discuss the difficulty the crew experienced on the voyage. It was something about battling a dimensional Daemon. The Witch talked of the Daemonic threat as if it were a roach problem. Could it be true, what the sailor said about battling dimensional Daemons, that it was some annoying but easy task? Or, was that some false bravado speaking?

"Are there actual monsters," I asked Doctor Huebner later that week. He modified my schedule to rotate our sessions from evening to early morning.

"By what definition do you use for monsters?"

"I don't know." Geez, what kind of circular logic? "I mean, bad, like things that are evil," duh.

"Ah, in that case, in terms of good and evil, no and yes. Anyone can be a monster, Witches or Mortals. I think you might be referring to the more animalistic of the supernatural world. Such as the beast-like dragons, not to be confused with the highly intelligent Draegons, whose cognitive skills far surpass any Witch I know, including my own. Perhaps you mean the degenerate Vampyres and Wyrewolves, who have been made primal by the infectious curse placed upon them. It is all quite unfortunate. The answer is yes; but that does not make them monsters, at least in the way most think. They are more like animals, operating out of instinct more than conscious decision. There are Witches and Mortals that deserve the description of evil, but both are deviant in their forbidden actions and are stains on society."

"What about Aengels and Daemons," I ask.

"There are Aengelic and Daemonic forces, only differentiated by their capacity to either nurture or destroy, but both forces are necessary. And as you will find out, young Witch, all forces have their time and place." My curiosity overwhelmed my confusion and my questions rambled out without conscious thought, "Where are they? What do they look like?"

"They live in the various Realms with all sorts of beings. These forces vary in both form and powers. Now, with that said, I do believe it is time for class."

He left me with more questions and truly little answered. We say goodbye and I leave for Divination.

The class was held in the Observatory, an immense atrium, on the top floor of the Shrine, a building held more for spiritual practices of magik. A large portion of the space was dedicated for studies on healing. In fact, the Shrine included St. Philomena's hospital, known as the Infirmary.

The building is nearly half a mile in length and is divided into three buildings that are connected through skybridges. The center has a dome-like design and on the right and left side of the dome are the remaining structures. The buildings curve into crescents, altogether they form the shape of a triple moon. The architectural design reminded me of photos I had seen of London's clock tower, Big Ben. The Shrine hugs Tarias' western corner, sharing the mountain's face with Spirit Manor, which is seated at a much higher elevation near Cat's Peak. Creeks flow through the building past the well-maintained courtyards with mature trees and into Lake Osage and onto the Colorado River. The drainage network was so sophisticated that it had to have been engineered by magik so as not to disturb the natural course of the weather and rivers that pour inland. The charms of Tarias were designed to work with nature, not against it.

I meet Maria at the door. Divination is one of the courses she had to extend, which she says, "Is bullshit." Apparently, Maria has significant limitations in Sight and psychic spellwork. She had recently transferred to have the same class schedule as mine. I am exhausted after another restless night. For once, I am grateful to have Divination. The best part about class is when Madam Reyna routinely enters her psychic-drugged state, allowing for, easily, a 30 minutes power nap.

We walk in and, fortunately, Madam Reyna is in one of her zonked out states. Unfortunately, David O'Faolain is there along with all his disabling charm. He stands tall, smiling from ear to ear when he sees us, and waves.

He is wearing a black sweater and a grey tie, and dress shoes that are, suspiciously, far less pointy than mine, which makes me want to investigate the matter with Dr. Huebner. Still, though, his presence unravels me. It is incredible how just being near him can both distract and ground me. Why was he in this class? I thought he was a grade above me.

David walks up to us and I feel my heart quicken. I could barely function when he was near me. I remind myself to breathe in and out.

He and Maria do most of the talking, discussing a new house rule regarding evenings out and the use of flight. Gradually, I entered the conversation. I find out David is the same age as me but only for a few more months, his birthday is in May. I already know Maria is 14 and her birthday is in October.

David says, "You just turned 14, isn't that right Noah? Your birthday was only a couple of weeks ago. I suppose I got the timing right. So, you like it, my gift? Err, my family's gift, I mean," half-smiling, now looking at his feet.

"I loved it," I say too quickly! I realize my locket was loose against my shirt with the cat charm attached closely to it. I hoped the shades of red I was turning were at least a little less bright than blood.

"Yeah, I really appreciate it." Why can I not shut my mouth to save my soul? I at least manage to say thank you, "It was a really good birthday."

"I'm glad to hear it, Noah," he says with the softest smile I have ever seen, and my heart wants to break at the sight of it. I refocus, trying to recuperate from the effect he has on me.

Mirrors and a clear glass pane for a ceiling that reveals the sky surround the Observatory. The room is made bright with natural sunlight.

Dark plush couches are scattered throughout the room. There is an earthy aroma in the air, and I am more convinced Madam Reyna is actually high. She has yet to acknowledge a single student in the room.

David looks toward us and then at Madam Reyna. He nods toward her, a subtle question over her bizarre behavior. Maria scoffs, "This bitch is crazy."

I laugh a little too loudly.

Returning to herself, Madam Reyna screams, "Noah Ellis!" I guess no breaks will be given to me today, she is going to kill me.

"Come here now!" She points toward the front of class, motioning for me to stand there. I obey, lest I suffer another verbal attack. "I'll deal with you later." As she turns her attention to David, her tone suddenly softens.

She introduces him to the class, "Mr. O'Faolain has demonstrated exceptional spellwork in Divination during his most recent Evaluation. I have asked him to offer special mentoring as an assignment for his advanced course. He will be offering individual training for Witches without innate Divination skills." She then announces to the class, "Today we will be practicing defensive and offensive use of Divination. Each one of you will partner up."

She turns and looks directly at me. "Let us start with Noah Ellis, who is apparently a psychic protege." I feel as if I am swimming in a passively violent sea. "Since you can laugh and play games during my class, I am left to assume you know all there is to know about psychic awareness. Please share with us your incredible skills, oh gifted one." She commands me to call a basic psychic connection.

Breathe Noah, breathe, I silently remind myself.

Divination requires a meditative practice; skills I am forced to strengthen every morning before dawn. Who knew Meds would give me the advantage? I contact the present moment and raise a spiritual consciousness. We, the students of Spirit Manor, are trained in Receptive Modus Operandi. It is a step-by-step psychic manual; the one Earl Levi gave me several weeks ago. Granted, he only did it to help himself, but I find myself suddenly grateful for bushy-haired Earl.

It is sort of like following a yoga sequence, only in your mind. The first steps are used to access the Sight. The next are to connect to the reciprocal system of balanced energies. The tasks open the doorway to my natural gift. Although it is an entirely metaphysical activity, there is a physical sense to it. Visions and sensations for Seers often surpass the vividness of the physical senses.

All at once I feel it. The air around me shifts. From multiple angles, I can See the surrounding students and myself from a broad point of view. I had some successes in the past with my Sight, but this was a clear image beyond any other Vision so far. I hear Madam Reyna tell a student to initiate a psychic attack against me. The young Witch, a non-Seer, named Yeurie, approaches.

Through my Vision, I can See Yeurie's energy winding within and around her. It is sloppy, more like Transference magik. There are only hints of Divination magik required for the act. I felt bad for her, it seemed unfair for Madam Reyna to have Yeurie challenge a Seer. It was like expecting a one year old to have table manners. She chants a spell to address the deficit in her abilities.

Madam Reyna prompts me to counter her spell. The way she pitted us against each other, it made me mad. No, it enraged me. She wanted to see how powerful we were, how much of a resource we could be, to use us. She wanted someone to psychically attack my mind, or the reverse, to see who would win. She did not care about us. We were like dogs-in-training to her. I could feel the coldness on my face, evidence of the rage-driven tear trail.

Everything started feeling off. It felt like I was falling. My Vision changed, the colors grew dull and the psychic sound of the room seemed very far away.

Only Yeurie's image remained undisturbed, and then I realized it, she was attacking me, pushing me into the astral void. Her eyes had fittingly grown black, a result of the poor execution of her spell.

I felt more out of body. Desperate to refocus my Vision I attempt to latch onto random energy trails, anything that would lead me back to the room, to my body. My Vision shifts from darkness to various angles of the room, then to images of strange houses, followed by someone's messy room that seemed oddly familiar. Other images persisted, friendly faces that I do not know, and some other things, secrets, that I will be bound to keep.

Words and sounds bled into a tangled mess. And then, nothing, black or the absence of light, the Betwixt. I read about it in the Receptive Modus Operandi, and although I have not been here before, I now know it is true; I was in psychic hell. I thought I heard a man's voice that sounds disturbingly familiar, or did I actually hear it? Terror takes over me.

NO!

I can sense my physical body, my breathing has become rapid and my heart is racing. I See her, somewhere far away from this lost place, Yeurie. She continues to chant her spell, trying to ensure my suppression, and I feel red-hot light. You don't get to hurt me!

I hold her in my mind's eye. Her power is like thin gray smoke, sloppy, so many ways inside, what a weak thing. I grabbed her from the darkness and dragged her inside. White-hot light flashes and I am transported.

I See an Asian woman looking down on me. She carries love on her face as she lifts me up and I am filled with joy. It shifts again, I am eating ice cream and surrounded by friends, laughing. It shifts once more, now I am holding an invitation to St. Philomena Academy, an Asian couple jump with excitement, and I feel the same exhilaration.

I was inside Yeurie's mind, in her memories, seeing them from her point of view. I mentally step back, and it is like I tripped and fell back into the Observatory, still out of my body, existing in the space between Yeurie and my physical self. I am holding her mind along with her heart. I understand now, it was like learning to navigate my way in a new city, suddenly aware of how the streets connect. It all became clear and I knew my way.

I feel them, the others. The images and sensations of their complex lives and experiences, all within my reach. It was as if they were toys. Their lives and minds were like building blocks that I could move around if I wished. What else could I do, where else could I go? Worst of all was the sick pleasure I experienced when I played with them, these things. I wanted to keep playing with my toys.

I pushed my way into their hearts and, graciously, I felt something again that ached in my chest. It was guilt trying to restrain me. Something else persisted, something beyond my control. A desire to stop this feeling, a desperate act of avoidance. Something about all this felt vaguely familiar, like déjà vu.

Suddenly, Madam Reyna forces my psychic evacuation from their inner thoughts, returning me back to the room. I remain out of my body, but I am still holding the other students in my mind. She seemed to be on fire. Her magik was raging despite the absence of color. It was visible in my Sight, a transparent force disturbing the air around her, like giant vapors escaping from an exposed gasoline tank. It had the slightest tint that was more felt than seen; it was anger.

She was going to attack me. Initially, I am scared, but then I felt my own power and it was nothing like vapors. Instinctively and without conscious decision, my magik shielded both my body and psychic presence in a dark black blue, the color of the deep sea, where the light barely touches. It creates a dome over my physical body and coats the entire room in a pulsating glow where my mind exists in time and space. Her energy tried to snake into the dome, coiling itself on my power, attempting to find a vulnerable opening, but there was none to be found.

She takes a breath, seeming both surprised and annoyed. "Stop it this instant Noah Ellis!" She tries once more to stop me. She casts a spell that seems to target my psychic presence.

The dome transforms into billowing smoke and flame, pulsating crimson red and black. It strikes Madam Reyna, poisoning her. I felt her thoughts as my magik consumes her like fire. It was like I was becoming her, it felt foreign and wrong. I tried to stop myself. I tried to return to my body, but it was too late; I was beyond myself.

I do not know if I was in shock or rage, maybe both. I felt numb and unreal.

Deep within, I knew I had to stop. Once more I attempt to return to my body, but my internal struggle seems to complicate all my senses. The other students' streams of consciousness became loud and erratic. All the stories confused me, intensifying my aggravation. Within my mind I scream for them to be quiet. Instantly, the noise shuts off, leaving only silence behind.

What seems like a very long time goes by before I realize that I am no longer in the room. It's all blank and I feel far away. At first it was difficult to recall what had happened, but gradually, the pieces came together. I remember the challenge, the one between myself and the other student, Yeurie. I was supposed to stop her. Where was she? Where was Madam Reyna? I do not feel them anymore. I don't feel anything. Then I hear her psychic yell from the distance. I know right away she is in the Betwixt. Yet, even in psychic form, she still manages to scream through gritted teeth.

Noah.

Ellis.

Sit.

Back.

Down.

Chapter Twelve

Possession: Exceptionally challenging magik, for in one psyche, whether they be Witch or Mortal, exists an entire universe.

It was like she crashed into me. All at once I was back in my body, hands and knees on the ground, panting, sweat dripping from the bridge of my nose.

It was a room of about 20 or so plus Madam Reyna. I looked around, they were all just standing there, unblinking like statues. It was all just so implausible. I blink my eyes slowly to provide some sort of reassurance that this is happening.

The people around me are motionless, only time continues to move forward. I see their bodies continue to take shallow breaths. What did I do?

Amelia, the Witch who helped me with the Crown and Lord fiasco, is leaning back as if she were about to run away, yet she remains perfectly still. She has her hands up defending her face from something. I realize she is defending herself from me.

From behind me, I hear him, "What the hell?"

I jumped at the sudden noise. I turned around to the source, David, the perfect boy.

"I'm sorry, I'm so sorry," I say pathetically.

I didn't know what to do. "I'm sorry," I say in panicked repetition. My racing thoughts were scattered and left me unable to think.

"It's okay, it's going to be okay." Something in his voice, I am not sure why, but for whatever reason, I believed him. I started to think again, realizing I was still on the floor. My face felt flush, and I realize I am crying.

The beautiful boy kneels down in front of me, his pretty brown eyes staring directly into mine. I control my breathing to build a temporary dam against my stubborn tears.

From my right, another scared voice speaks. "Oh my god," says Maria, no longer frozen.

Gasping for air, holding on to the desk to stay steady, "What was that? I was lost, I was lost in this," as she breathed heavily "darkness. Complete darkness."

"I'm so sorry," and start crying all over again, filled with shame and anger.

David softly takes a hold of my shoulders, "It's okay, it's over now. It'll be alright." Why was he being so nice to me, was he that good?

My head began to clear, as if sobering up from a drug induced trance.

"What did I do?"

I hear the crisp, distinct voice, "It's called a domination."

"A what?"

"A psychic domination, do you not read your textbooks?"

Madam Reyna, no longer frozen, speaks in clear agitation.

From the hallway I hear them coming. The footsteps, running, growing louder as they approached the classroom. Now acutely aware of myself, I stand back up.

The Dean, Abigail Tetson, rushed inside the room. The sound of her heels echoed intimidatingly in the large area.

A man and a woman that I did not recognize accompanied her, and immediately began studying the room. The Dean looked at me, I could not discern if she was mad, but another string of desperate and tearful apologies pours out of me anyway.

"That's enough," she said abruptly.

"What did you do?" She sounded more intrigued than furious. I went over what I could recall. I stopped talking when I remembered how much I enjoyed using that kind of power. I thought to tell them, but at that exact moment, I looked up and saw David looking back at me. He wore the world's most gentle smile and I cannot bring myself to disclose anything further. Instead, I start stumbling over my words and eventually change the subject. I try to excuse this avoidance, reasoning that I was only trying to protect myself.

She then asked, "Have you ever done anything like this before?"

I looked away at Madam Reyna and the other two Witches, avoiding the Dean's question. Their hands hover over my classmates' statuesque bodies. They are Reading them to determine the best strategy for addressing the affliction.

When the male Witch says, "A full domination, Ms. Tetson." I thought about how awful that sounded, domination. Finally, I answer the Dean's question, "No, nothing like this." I am not sure why, but it felt as if I was lying.

Dean Tetson looks back at me and then to Maria and David who are standing next to me, "Can either of you tell me what happened?"

They nod their heads. "I didn't get affected," said David.

"I did. I was in a black room, or world, I'm not sure where I was, exactly," adds Maria.

Madam Reyna and the other Witches walk toward them, hands outstretched. The man attempts to speak but Madam Reyna silences him, flashing a sympathetic grin for his attempt to explain anything about the psychic world, "You were in the Betwixt, a realm absent of sense or conscious thought," she says as she completes her scan. "What," I say, with pressured breath, sounding more noise than language. "How are the others going to get out, what did I do, what's wrong with me?" I felt an old, but familiar sensation, a combination of nausea and disdain. My fingers tense, my nails ready to sink into my own skin to punish the bad.

"Enough," Madam Reyna says roughly. "You need to be stronger and pull yourself together."

I don't know why but I obey and steady myself. They shift the topic to David as the other Witch places her hands inches away from his chest.

"He hasn't. Noah's magik touched him. Strange, his energy shifted from the coercive nature of the psychic attack to the natural passivity of Divination."

Dean Tetson asks us to step out of the classroom while Madam Reyna and the older Seer Witches work on the remaining students.

Several hours later, we continue to wait in the large central lobby of St. Philomena's primary campus, appropriately titled the Pyramid. Despite its polygon structure, the outer surfaces of the building maintain a relatively triangular geometric form, and ultimately converge to a primary peak at the top. Its floor levels are clearly distinguished and remind me of building blocks placed on top of one another. They grow smaller and smaller as they reach toward the sky.

David and Maria remain with me and we have spoken very little. David tries to make conversation, but I don't think even he really wants to talk, or at least doesn't know what to say.

"Jesus, it's okay," Maria says randomly, directly facing me. Her green eyes flash, their color and intensity reminds me of power and grace.

"You didn't do it on purpose. Madam Reyna is right about one thing, it's time to get over it," smiling at me. I smile back. One treacherous tear fell, but this time, only one.

"Yeah, mate, this kind of thing happens, and honestly Noah, it is right spectacular what you were able to do. You must be very powerful."

"Students," Dean Tetson interrupts, "Come with me."

We entered her office a few minutes later. If you can call it an office, the space took nearly the entire floor. Several divided areas serve as meeting rooms, available at the Dean's whim. A young Witch, the Dean's secretary, with an agreeable nature greeted us at our arrival and offered us Nulang tea. It contained several magikal sedative properties, nothing in small quantities that would incapacitate a Witch, but enough to ease the nerves. Naturally, we all graciously accepted.

Abigail Tetson explains what she thinks happened. She says that my powers are rapidly developing and something about passing an internal barrier, and how it's very common in young Witches.

As it turns out, Madam Reyna was the one that stopped me or "woke me up". She broke out of my psychic hold and cast a spell from the Betwixt that blessedly reached me in the physical world.

It made sense.

Although her awakening was delayed compared to Maria, at least she was no longer frozen, unlike the remaining students in class.

"The students are all being cleared at the Infirmary and will be headed to their residences within the next half hour."

"What," I gasp and say in a rush, "Is everyone okay?"

"Yes Noah, every Witch has been returned to their normal state," she said matter-of-factly.

I miss a few things after that, still stuck on the fact that they are all going to be okay. A huge weight lifts off me and I say a silent prayer of gratitude for the miracle.

Maria asks, "What about us, how did I get out when the rest stayed or were dominated? And why didn't it affect David?"

"One thing at a time. We don't really know why you two had different effects. It may have been that Mr. Ellis experienced a depletion of power. Madam Reyna theorizes that there may be a psychic rapport or a personality congruence between each of you and Noah. Potentially, his psychic impression, for whatever reason, did not view you two as a threat. The shutdown of his underlying psychic defenses would explain why the both of you had little to no impact."

Maria is quick on the draw and is about to ask a deluge of questions, but the Dean is faster, silencing Maria, "But with that said, you two are now free to go."

Madam Reyna walks in just then, they both give me lingering glances as Dean Tetson escorts them out.

"Mr. Ellis," says Madam Reyna.

"I am so sorry Professor; I don't know what happened."

"I do. You attacked me, and you synchronized almost everyone in the room's life force and then, apart from Ms. Pedraza and Mr. O'Faolain, entirely dominated those energies, unhinging their minds. Mr. Ellis, that type of Witchcraft would be difficult to manifest for even the more advanced Witch. However, as a Seer, you must learn to master these gifts. It is my recommendation you receive training from a student with expertise in Transference, and with advanced training in Sight related skills and spellwork."

She clicks her heels and turns to walk away, but looks back and adds, "You impressed me today, Mr. Ellis. I can't wait to see what you have in store for us."

My mouth was wide open. Impressed? I felt like the scum of the earth and she's impressed. I really am in the Witch world.

Dean Tetson smiles at me slightly and informs me that I am to require temporary bindings during specific classroom training exercises until I gain management over my abilities.

"You will receive further instructions on your tutorship and class modifications at your next meeting with Dr. Huebner. You are free to go now."

I paused, unsure of what to do, despite the clear instructions.

"Go Mr. Ellis, now."

Chapter Thirteen

Wyrd magik: Witchcraft exclusively focused on influencing probability. In popular Witch culture, this type of magik is also known as tempting fate.

"Is there something wrong with me," I ask Dr. Huebner. Per Dean Tetson's instruction, we were reviewing the accommodations I would receive for my magikal education. My remorse and insecurity restrained me from viewing these accommodations optimistically. Instead, it was only confirmation of the ineffable truth that has lived with me since I can remember. Yes, there is something wrong with me.

"No, of course not. Mr. Ellis, you have extraordinary potential. Unfortunately, you are delayed in mastering your skills and as a Witch, that is a dangerous combination. However, with frequent and intensive training, that delay can be easily remedied."

I remain silent, refusing to believe any words out of the Doctor's mouth. He goes on to compare me to someone with a high IQ who does not know how to read, adding, "But with a bit of intervention, that person can flourish."

I think the doctor just said I had special needs, or at least that I was disadvantaged compared to the other students. At least he didn't call me a sociopath; that would be infinitely worse.

I felt slightly insulted but I shake it off, partially because I do not have a say in the matter, but primarily because Joan would be furious at the idea of me thinking negatively of disabilities or of needing help. So, I refuse to think of it that way.

The Doctor must have seen the discomfort written on my face, "You cannot help where you've come from, that is beyond even the most powerful magik, but you can do something with what's right in front of you Noah Ellis, with or without magik." It was his way of telling me to move on. "Okay, sounds like a plan."

My accommodations consisted of increased one-on-one sessions with Dr. Huebner, magikal binds during psychic spellwork, and tutoring with a qualified peer, a tutor.

My tutor would train me in learning the nuances of connection and control. These concepts are best compared to acceptance and change. The idea is to acknowledge the issue in order to work toward the goal. In magik, it is connecting to your personal power and forces beyond you and then using that power to create change. The truth was I needed help with both. Right then and there, I decided to start "Project New-Me".

"Thank you, Dr. Huebner. I'll do whatever it takes to get better," accepting the help. Our meeting ends along with the morning. I say goodbye and make my way to class, ready to address my "deficiencies".

Maria saves me a seat in Alchemy, easily my most difficult class. It requires a broad understanding of multiple sciences, including biochemistry, certainly more knowledge than I cared to possess.

Maria and I stuck together. She switched classes to attend as many with me as possible. Who knew I would get so lucky to have a best friend like her? Although this was probably not the best idea for Alchemy. Neither of us were exactly leading the class in scientific expertise or even basic math. I think I might be holding her back, but I dare not say it aloud and risk losing the only friend I had, even if it was just for one class.

We were working on Euros Atifea, a love potion, and were completely floundering the experiment. The floral scent of the concoction was starting to smell more like bleach and was turning into a thick brown matter that did not remind me of love.

We weren't helping ourselves by having side conversations when we were supposed to be weighing ingredients and calculating boiling times. Maria was explaining my tutor selection process. It turns out it is a tradition for our Covens to help each other out whenever there is a time of need, something about our "companionship". I ask to confirm, "So, the tutor will be from your Coven?"

"Yup, our House Lead held a full meeting with the rest of the Lords. Even our Chair attended." Her eyes widen to emphasize her point. I nod my head enthusiastically and rather awkwardly. I assumed it was a big deal for the Chair to be present. Witch policy and procedure was still foreign to me.

"Tom, our House Lead, tells us there is a new Crown at Spirit Manor, AKA you. By the way, he also described you as 'sickly powerful'," winking at me just then, like I just won an award, "And that you needed help to control your powers. That's when the Doc asked for volunteers to serve as your tutor."

"Wait, Doc as in Doctor Huebner?"

Maria responds nonchalantly, "Yeah, Dr. Huebner, our Chair. Anyway, he is the one who..."

Interrupting her, "Wait a minute, Dr. Huebner is your Chair?" She sighs, slightly annoyed with my repetitive question. "Yes Noah. The one and the same, he's like my Coven's greatest alum."

Based on Maria's casual response I assume it should have been obvious, after all, he was well-respected and obviously superior in terms of magikal talent, a key requirement for her Coven.

"Anyway, Dr. Huebner tells us the volunteers have to qualify, so someone that is equally powerful as you and has some psychic skills, which ruled me out." Maria rolls her eyes and I think they might fall out. "I still volunteered, I told them that you were my friend, and there was no one better for the job."

"What did they say?"

"No."

We burst into laughter.

"Believe me, Noah, I tried. I argued every damn reason I could think of, but the Doc refused, with my 'limited psychic prowess'," she said mimicking the Doc's tendency for histrionics, and continued, "Apparently I don't have any significant psychic skills and that, in his words, 'simply and regretfully are of no use to you!' I'm like ugh, thanks, could've stopped at prowess."

We laughed so hard we had tears in our eyes. "Oh my god, who knew Doc was such an ass," I proclaim.

"I know, right?"

We laughed some more. It was then that I realized that I loved Maria like I have never loved a friend, although if I am honest, I have never really had friends before. Guess my luck is changing after all.

"Thanks Maria, that means a lot to me. I mean, at least you tried."

"Of course, but either way there weren't many Lords that qualified. The Doc listed those who did, which was Ian Gutierrez, who is just the worst, David O'Faolain, Amelia..."

"Amelia, how is she?" I was still feeling terribly guilty over the whole domination incident.

"She's fine, Noah. Everyone else but you are over it," rolling her eyes once more and making no attempt to hide her irritation. "Anyway, that's when David casually volunteered, which is totally unlike him. It was weird that he was even there. He doesn't even bother to attend Closing Circle. We all laughed. It's like get real, it's David O'Faolain, but Madam Reyna agreed that David would be a suitable tutor because of his high scores in Divination on the recent Evaluation."

"So he is going to be my tutor?"

"Yeah, looks like," Maria confirms. David O'Faolain is going to be my tutor; this wasn't sounding so bad after all.

"I am supposed to meet him today. I didn't know who it would be, only that we were meeting at the official library. It's called the Castle, right Maria?"

"Yeah, you're right, that's what everyone calls the library. Well he better be there, if not let me know," she says, her tone flat and serious.

"You don't think he'll show up?"

"I don't know, I think so, if he remembers. The thing is everyone in my Coven are, how to say it, assholes." We both grinned at each other. "They're not mean, just entitled, at least a little bit. The whole Lords thing gets in people's heads, and David is like Witch royalty. He's normally 'volun-told' to do things, him volunteering on his own is just bizarre. Not to worry, me being the wonderful friend I am handled the situation."

Smiling at her, "What did you do?"

She flips her golden hair back, "Your main girl is always looking out for you. I told David, and everyone else there, that I thought he was lazy and wouldn't help you."

"You didn't," I say in half-gasp.

"I sure did, David just laughed. He claimed his reason for helping was because he is getting bored these days. He also said something about how his parents want him to be more involved in some extracurricular activity and this mentorship can get them off his back."

"Sounds promising," I say flatly.

Maria smiles excitedly, I am glad she does not notice my disappointment. She reassures me that I do not need to worry. "The Doc reamed into him and told him that he needed to take the assignment seriously. He even threatened to notify his parents if he failed to maintain his duties to you, who by the way are also alumni of Ius Divinum. Honestly, I think that got to him."

My heart sinks. It was just a task for David, "Awesome." I felt silly for being so excited. Even though he technically volunteered, in a way, he was still being "volun-told".

Looking at me sympathetically, Maria intervened, "Don't get me wrong, he is easily the most talented Witch at Philomena. I think that's what makes him lazy. Everything is just handed to him."

"Oh great, just what I need, some extra-entitled guy who doesn't know the first thing about struggling."

Maria wears a concerned expression on her face and tries to comfort me. "He is sort of a prodigy. I think it makes me a little jealous, well I know it does. To be fair, David is a nice guy, spoiled, but never mean, and pretty much gets along with everybody. I am sure he will help you," and without smiling, "Or else." She made me promise to keep her updated on David's attendance before we walk away to our separate classes.

Several hours later, after the school day ends, I arrive at the East Lab located within Bexar and Gruene Hall to meet David, assuming he shows up. I enter the underground tunnel that serves as a magikal bridge and is nearly a mile in length, connecting one of four sections of St. Philomena to the Castle.

The low ceilings and dull fluorescent bulbs provide poor lighting. It would have been less terrifying if it were not just me walking down this long empty hallway. My footsteps echoed loudly against the bare walls. I could not see the exit of the seemingly endless tunnel. Fear clutches at my legs, urging me to turn back, but I force myself to step forward through the stone mile.

Thankfully, I was too tired to panic, too many hours of reviewing Alchemy, Astronomy, and Spell Theory. Memorizing everything from star plots to mineral and elemental charts, all in preparation for Test Week, had taken its toll on me.

My mind felt like mush, and my body was heavy as I dragged it along to complete the last task of the day. My stomach ached from hunger.

I devour the sandwich Miss Penelope stored in my bookbag earlier this morning for just this occasion. I think there may have been magik in that sandwich. Although small, it hit the spot but did little to decrease the drowsiness that dulled my senses.

I kept reminding myself, it was just one more thing to be done. I repeated this like a mantra, attempting to buy into it as if the message could magikally transform into reality.

The light from the opening came into view as I walked the gradual curve of the tunnel, revealing the exit, along with him. He stood there, in all his glory, in a red pullover and khaki shorts.

His neck was craned, and his hands were deep inside his pockets. He was shuffling about and there was something about his face, as if he were upset. We make eye contact and in an instant that look he wore fades away. His frown transforms into a slight but glistening grin. I smile back at him, at ease to see him relieved. That grin grows large and wide and suddenly I wasn't worried about the day ending.

I walk up to him and he says, "Hi Noah, guess I am to be your tutor. I suppose that class debacle got you in a bit of a spot."

"Yeah, I guess so," I try my best to compose myself, being this close to him affected me, but being this close and alone with him, was like an overdose. With an honest sentiment I added, "I do need the help. I don't want to do something like that again," a moment of awkward silence follows, until the claws of lingering winter scratched at my skin in its attempt to fight away spring. I am in my school uniform, and although I am wearing my heavy winter-coat, the cold still manages to infiltrate its way inside.

David, in all his beauty, stands there in shorts in defiance of the cold air. Even though his legs were muscular, he had to be just as uncomfortable.

"It's pretty chilly out here, aren't you cold," I ask out of concern.

"It's a little cold," he says as he digs his hands further into his pockets, conserving warmth. I couldn't help but laugh. He looked miserable, cute, but miserable. It was precious and hilarious at the same time.

"Why are you in shorts?"

"I'm alright, just fine," and was literally puffing out his chest in playful bravado.

"Do you want to go back to your house to change?"

He refused, claiming that he was warming up as he moved about. I, however, was not doing as well. I hated the cold, it felt like death. My teeth, in loud chatter, were fist-fighting one another.

Even then, I did not want to go back. I wanted to stay out here, with him, even if it meant freezing in the process. Being here with David, I don't know how to describe it, but it felt like something was changing into something good. It's hard to explain and I am not even sure I understand it.

David, having observed my body trembling, asks, "How are you holding up, mate?"

I nod attempting to display a brave face, "fine," but concede just as quickly. "Not really, I'm freezing, but its fine, I'll be fine."

"Not to worry, I can fix that, if you let me?"

The combination of tenor in his voice and Scottish accent derails my thinking. My face must have carried a question mark, to which he responded, “Magik, we can use it for the cold, if you like?”

“Oh, really? If it’s not too much trouble, go for it, please?” Up until now, I had not found much use for magik, mostly because I had not been looking. I was so busy trying to learn it that I really had not thought of a reason to use it.

Nevertheless, there he went, muttering a few pretty words under his breath and rubbing his hands together. I could see the steam gradually growing, first in wisps, and then in contrails twisting around us.

“May I,” he asks as he opens his hands towards my own. I place mine in his palms, which are far larger than my own. He holds them tightly and all at once, I feel the warmth of his magik. It regulates the temperature around us. I could still feel the winter air but, dulled by his spell, it had lost all its bite.

The touch of his skin was tender with a slight roughness to him. If his hands could tell a story, I am sure they would talk of his love for adventure.

“You need something of mine to keep the spell connected to you. I cannot hold the spell without a charm. Well, that’s a lie. I can, but it’ll hurt you, so let me give you this,” he takes off his watch and wraps it around my wrist. It’s too big for me. Still, he fastens it as best as possible and mumbled a few more magikal words. It tightens slightly, fitting perfectly now.

I wore his heavy watch, that I think is made of gold, while I stood there watching his extraordinary skill, and suddenly felt small and inadequate. Even then, there was something about David’s way, his easy-going and confident nature that reassures me that everything would be alright. In full sincerity, I express my gratitude for the warmth.

“No problem at all, honestly. Would you like to sit down,” he says in response.

"Absolutely," the word comes out impulsively and I want to kick myself for being so eager. David and I take a seat at a lonely table in an area near the entrance of the massive and gothic Castle. I comment on its imposing beauty, "It's incredible."

"Sure is, it was built in the 1800s, in honor of one of the founders of Tarias. They say it was built to honor her Parisian heritage."

The building was grand and intricately designed. The architecture is a stark contrast from the skyscrapers of the modern world, a glorious nod to the past.

I return my attention to David, an easy enough undertaking. "So, what should I expect or what should we be doing," I ask him, unsure of what would be the next step for our time together.

"I guess since Doc thinks you need some help in Transference, we should focus on that. Honestly, I think the whole thing is a little ridiculous, I am sure you'll be fine, but I am glad to help, regardless." I look away from him as he adds, "Since most of my specialties are in Transference and I have some Divination skills, powers more similar to your own, that makes us a perfect fit."

The comment makes me blush. "What skills in Divination do you have, if you don't mind me asking?" I ask mostly to change the subject.

"Telepathy, mostly, although more on the mind control side of that type of magik. I do use actual telepathy instead of how most other Witches practice mind-control." David was explaining the difference between true telepaths, Seer or not. Genuine telepathy involved connecting to the physical, and metaphysical level as well, only then could one See the essence of a living entity. "It feels a bit like skipping ahead, if you don't have both," he concludes.

Mind control requires a minimal amount of telepathy and is considered a rudimentary Divination skill. Still it is impressive that David possesses actual telepathic ability, an uncommonly developed gift in Non-Seer Witches.

"The whole thing is pure quality. Personally, I can only last a few minutes in the experience. I don't know how you Seers do it." David is referring to a Seer's natural resilience to the overwhelming and sometimes harsh experience of reality through psychic senses.

He smiles and looks straight at me, his brown eyes distract me as he adds, "I can also do a bit of retrocognition, you know looking-into-the-past, that's probably the most Seer-like ability I have, although it is a bit limited. I have to touch something to see it. Not to mention, that the few times I have connected to the past, I've done no good at navigating the thing. I could not go where I wanted to go. Still, it is one of my favorite skills. The past, and everything connected to it, really is a beautiful thing."

"What do you mean?"

"The beauty in its chaos, I guess. Do you not think so," he asks.

"Maybe, I think I have been more focused on getting used to being here, at Philomena. Not to mention that my last major psychic experience resulted in me over-turning the psyche of the majority of my classmates, which still makes me feel like the worst person in the world. So, I haven't had much reason to appreciate the experience."

We pause for a moment in awkward silence.

"Sorry, not exactly like the pretty picture you painted of the past connecting to the present," I say honestly.

"Geez, you really do hold onto things, don't you," he laughs, at what I don't really know, but I cannot help myself and share in his smiles.

After that, we plan my magikal training on how to best assist me in developing my skills. David asks me several questions during the process. He finally asked the question, the one that I am always trying to avoid.

"Do you know anything about your biological parents?"

He quickly looks down and exhales. He must have realized he crossed an invisible line and stepped onto a landmine, one that is ready to explode within me. Although it should not surprise me that he knows this much about me. I am after all a Non-Legacy Witch, but the fact that people could know this much about my life, without me saying a word, felt invasive.

He looks directly at me, "Forgive me, I am sorry. I just thought I'd ask."

His question is actually a benign thing, at least in terms of planning my magikal training. It can be helpful to know mundane genetic predispositions; like vulnerabilities to certain medical conditions, or even personality traits; these factors can often influence certain magikal strengths and weaknesses.

The thing is, I learned early on in school that it was easier to not be the foster kid. People treated you differently once they knew. Students either looked at me with pity or ignored me altogether. It was as if being unwanted was a contagious thing.

As I look at David who is looking to the ground like a puppy that got into the trash can, pathetic and endearing all at the same time, I cannot help but answer.

"I don't know anything about them. I was in foster care since I was a baby. Nobody knows who my biological parents are," I paused, not sure what to say next but not wanting to stay quiet. "They abandoned me. I have thought about looking for them with my Sight. Which, if I am being honest, I am not sure I could even if I tried. The thing is, I'm not so sure I want to, why look for someone that didn't want me to begin with?"

I felt a sharp sting prickle my eye and quickly looked away to recompose myself. If David had any inclination of my emotional reaction, he showed no indication. I remind myself that I am not a foster kid anymore.

"Their loss," David was looking right at me, "Fuck 'em." His words were sure and certain, and his face held no smile.

"Fuck 'em," I parrot, laughing slightly.

We talked further into the night, and to my surprise, I shared more with him. I told him about the Mastersons, how wonderful they are, and that I am now technically adopted. I tell him the story of how I found out I was a Witch, including the events that led to my enrollment at St. Philomena. I even share some childhood stories about some of the homes I lived in, giving some half-truths occasionally. I told him I did not remember much about the last home, the one prior to the Mastersons. I felt bad lying to David, but there are some wounds best left unshared.

We ended the night having agreed to a general training plan to address my magikal deficits. We would focus on Transference. David wanted to spend time specifically on Transvection, which was the equivalent of levitation and personal flight, an advanced skill in this type of magik.

We said goodbye awkwardly, and he headed off to his Coven's house. He offered his watch to keep me warm until I returned to the Manor. I wanted to stay there with him, at least a little bit longer, but instead I accepted the watch for the night and promised to return it to him the following day.

Later that evening, I am on the phone with Joan. I explained the whole debacle resulting in my need for tutoring. Predictably, Joan chastised me for being resistant to receiving help, "Noah Ellis, don't you dare think so much of yourself that you can do all of this alone. It just isn't true, everyone needs help; none of us are our own islands. You tell every single person that has offered their assistance how much you appreciate them first thing tomorrow morning. This world gets built on us helping each other, not us turning away from each other."

After a well explained scolding from Joan we say goodnight but only after we say, "I love you," along with Kevin and Jake. After a long day, I was not in the mood to talk much more, but just as I was falling asleep, the rotary phone clicked its odd version of ringing. I drag myself out of bed to answer.

"Noah," Maria shouts before I can say hello. I mumble out a "Yes?"

Maria starts a ten-minute, uninterrupted rant about an extra coursework Madam Reyna assigned to her, "I just hate that bitch."

She is talking rather loudly and it makes me wonder if she thinks she is talking to Madam Reyna instead of me.

She tells me how Madam Reyna came back with her usual derogatory and dismal evaluations of Maria's skill. Apparently, the oh-so-pleasant Divination teacher has doubled Maria's assignments to address her "shortcomings". Maria fought her tooth and nail, not letting Reyna off the hook for a second, and cleared her throat to re-enact the event, "I raised my hand up for an entire minute, I even called out her name multiple times, but she completely ignored me. So, I stood up and started yelling at her. I told her I didn't deserve to be punished for not having the skills of a Seer. I did all the work needed for the spell and it's not my fault if I couldn't perform the magik."

"What did she say?"

"She said I missed the primary focus, whatever the hell that means. Honestly, I think it's just because I am not one of her precious Seers. That doesn't mean I should fail."

It is true, Madam Reyna is known for favoring Seers, except me. She considers the Sight superior to all magik, a sentiment she reminds me of at least once each class period. Even then, Madam Reyna wasn't one for giving special treatment to anyone, Seer or not, and if anything she was harder on us.

Maria continues, "Reyna said I had six weeks to redo the spell, along with completing the extra assignments, I even have to start going to something called Morning Meditation."

"Oh! You're going to be in Morning Meds with me," I ask a little too excitedly judging from the layer of bitterness in Maria's flat response, "Yes. Even if I get to hang out with you Noah, it's still not fair what she is doing."

Fifteen minutes into her rant, Maria started swearing in Spanish, "Por favor, pinche pendeja."

Despite the problems I've had with Madam Reyna, I wasn't that upset with her. She was a bitch, but she never seemed unfair, she was a bitch to everyone. The rest of the Seers just learned to toe the line with her. Yeah, she gave me hell for being tardy, but she did the same to every other Witch that arrived late. Nevertheless, Maria is my best friend, technically my only friend. On that note, I decided to hate the professor too.

In solidarity, I harshly comment on Madam Reyna, joining in on her war against the Instructor. "You know her purple 'dresses' that she claims are for comfort during meditation," I ask?

"Yeah."

"I am sure that hag is just too lazy to change in the morning, she probably just rolls out of bed in her nightgown and calls it a freaking day."

"Exactly! It's probably because she's a whore. I am sure she spends all night at a bar and sleeps with whatever trash she can find and barely manages to make it to class."

I had a hard time understanding how her alleged sex life had anything to do with her ability to teach. The two seemed separate, but I do not want to cause a rift between Maria and I, and it's not like I am Madam Reyna's biggest fan. Moreover, Maria was only saying this out of anger. It wasn't really how she felt.

I am reminded of David and his own immediate response regarding my absentee biological parents, "Fuck her."

"Yeah, fuck her," Maria said emphatically.

Maria goes silent for a moment before adding one last retort, "Dumb whore," this time more calmly, her rant at an end. Maria surprises me with a complete change in topic, "How was tutoring?"

"Oh, uhm good, I guess. David was nice. He helped me understand magik a little bit more."

She breathed out, sounding relieved.

"Good, that's really good to hear. I was so worried that he wouldn't treat you right. I was ready to kick his ass."

I laugh and she joins in, after that our conversation swiftly comes to an end. We swear our allegiance against Madam Reyna and say goodnight. It made me suspicious that her intentions for calling tonight had nothing to do with Madam Reyna and were rather just an excuse to check up on me.

She was worried about me. And that damn thought must have aligned itself with my subordinate tears, giving them enough boost to spring for freedom despite my lack of agreement.

I hold on to the watch David let me borrow for the evening and the locket given to me by the Mastersons, with the pretty charm also from David O'Faolain. I held onto his warmth as I cried myself to sleep and, for the life of me, I do not understand why.

Chapter Fourteen

Elixir of Rejuvenation
Incantation: Doa Nay Fae Rai Omm Tut
At sunrise, perform the Seven Poses within a circle of thirteen gold candles while chanting.
Repeat as needed. Each day practiced will progressively restore youth.

The course portion of my day was over and I was now finding my way in the mysteries of magik. Dr. Huebner, who had a habit of modifying our sessions scheduled time on a whim, now prefers my booster sessions to be completed directly after my last class. He was illuminating his theories on interdimensional sorcery and the principles of the multiverse. I might have been bored, or at least his ideas would have gone way over my head, if not for his presentation.

Dr. Huebner demonstrated the concepts through illusions, in this case a magikal projection of the solar system. Cosmic giants presented themselves in front of me as if I were in a 3-D movie. Only his images had a soft tangibility, making the experience even more realistic.

He waves his hand and a miniature cluster of stars appears. He identifies the plane of twinkling lights as our universe, scaled down of course. He waves his other hand and several more clusters appear as our Universe settles between others like itself.

Dr. Huebner explains, “The universes can be thought of as variant dimensions, some are relatively similar to our own with only the slightest of differences, and others are antithetical in every dynamic.”

I do not know what was more entrancing, the illusions or the sheer impossibility of these theories. The clock tower chimed once, reminding me of the time. I was late, Dr. Huebner and I say goodbye and I quickly rush out of his office.

David was waiting.

We met at the exit of the underground tunnel. He was eyeing his watch with an odd and intense perplexity. It looked as if he had serious concerns over its reliability. I call out to him immediately, and without regret, begin to apologize profusely for running late. He grins and reassures me, “You’re alright, just glad you made it.”

I am exhausted from the day and my fatigue must have shown.

“Forgive me for saying, but you look like you’ve been through hell, Noah Ellis.” He grins as he says it and his smile was infectious. I laughed despite myself, “Sorry, you’re still bonnie, I just want to make sure you are alright. Are you alright?”

“I’m fine, I promise,” and I am not lying, spending time with David gave me a second wind and I no longer felt tired.

“What does bonnie mean?”

I swear I see his cheeks turn slightly pink, “Oh, that.” He briefly pauses, but then offers the explanation, “Bonnie is a Scottish word, slang honestly, for pretty.”

“Oh,” my words fail me for a moment, “thanks,” I say with a smile as my own cheeks return the favor. That was the first time I had seen David O’Faolain behave awkwardly.

He asked to take a slight detour from our usual training spot. He wanted to show me something special. We climbed a trail that led us toward a specialized class he was enrolled in, it was held semi-outdoors. It surprises me to find Maria there, she happened to be a student in the same cohort.

She stands with a small group of faces vaguely familiar to me. Most of them wore the same gold and diamond Phoenix pins as David and Maria.

They were standing on the cliff's edge. It faces a gigantic structure built of both rock and stone. There are trees and vegetation growing from various cracks within its form, reminding me of a treehouse. Centuries ago, this building served as the formal town hall for the citizens of Tarias. It is now partially deteriorated, a result of diminished magik originally cast to sustain the structure.

It had a semi-intact exterior staircase that wrapped around its frame. Its towering height and various openings made it the ideal location for training on Transvection magik. It was affectionately called, the Birdcage.

Witches in the flying class used the drop off to enter its hollow walls and would take flight from the various locations and heights scattered around the stone treehouse. The Birdcage functioned as a magikal hangar. Only the students with advanced training in Transference met the prerequisite to enter the raised structure.

Brooms were only used once a Witch mastered the skill unaided, as in broomless flight. Sensible, if a Witch falls from a broom they could at least save themselves by propelling their own flight until able to return safely to the surface.

I stared down at the ground below as David stands beside me. He estimates the drop to be about 8,000 feet and predicts a fall would result in certain death, but denies the likelihood of the scenario of that happening to me on all accounts.

"Might be a bit terrifying, Noah. But not to worry, I won't let you fall."

"Thanks" I say, changing the subject, trying to hide the rush of emotions coloring my face. "Why is Transvection its own class? I thought every Witch learns how to fly, like a driver's ed course?"

He chuckles softly at the question, "Most do, but they receive their training in the standard Transference class and it's not quite the same," he says with a quizzical look on his face. I am sure he is uncertain of the purpose of my question.

"Then what's the difference?"

He pauses to think, "I suppose it's a bit of a specialty."

"How so," I ask.

"Well, Transvection is a specialization of Transference, and in all honesty moving objects with magik requires fairly standard spellwork, there really isn't a whole lot of forethought needed to push your standard household items around. Hell, the same could be done with your arms and legs. You'd get the same result." We laugh at his small joke.

He goes on, "But levitations and other more advanced techniques are right more complex, making something float or fly requires dealing with powerful elements like gravity and other forces. Most just learn basic levitations, enough to be able survive falling off a broom or something."

"Uh-huh," I say, still somewhat confused.

A flash of brilliance shines in his eyes and smile, "Think of this like football," he says excitedly, "The Mortal kind."

"Like the NFL?"

He laughs and smiles my favorite smile. I keep my face straight to hide the effect he has on me. "No sorry, real football, what Americans call soccer?"

"Oh, right," like that cleared things up.

"Anyone can run or kick a ball and train all day long, but if someone wants to play football, err 'soccer', you have to do more than just those things. You gotta combine it all, and something else, something special." He struggles to find the words to explain himself, "Like football, you have to move but you also have to think and work with your mates in order to play the game."

Surprisingly, I think I get what David meant by something special. In order to be good at soccer, I mean football, you must learn to work with it and not against it, "Like a team."

"Exactly, and just like there are different types of magik there are also all sorts of sports people can learn to play."

"Thank you, Coach O'Faolain, for the information session," Maria says as she lands next to us, rolling her eyes, overhearing his sports analogy. She reviewed the "correct principles" of Transvection, but mostly confused me. I pretend to understand so she would not go on and further argue with David, who was far more interested in the doing rather than explaining.

"Alright, come off it Maria, Noah's got to be able to complete a full lift if he is going to be able to start classes next month."

"Next month, are you seriously expecting him to be able to do that, there's no way, he's still not able to..."

She stops herself from speaking any further. She did not have to finish her sentence. I still had difficulty doing the most basic magikal skills. She and I both knew that, but David refused to believe this and would not accept it.

"Nonsense, he's got this, you'll see," David chimes in, assuredly.

He said it smiling, half-laughing, but there was a ferocity in his tone and something about it made me believe him. David did not doubt himself or me. His presence and opposite attitude had a way of affecting my own perspective and it made me think twice. Maybe I could do this, one day.

David stays with me as the others begin their training. I watch in awe as I see Maria and her friends lift off in dives and leaps, floating gracefully into the top floor of thc Birdcagc. Moments later they would rapidly ascend into the high skies, either on brooms or unaided.

Maria said she liked brooms, that they made her feel nostalgic. It was glorious. I think even more significant was the look of exhilaration they held on their faces, the sheer joy of flight. I wish I knew what that was like.

David tells me it will be me up there soon enough, "Speaking of which, best we get to it, aye," reminding me of today's lesson. We continue my training back at the Castle. David covers a quick lesson on magik theory, "If you are to learn to control your powers you need a basic understanding of spellwork. It's science. That's all there is to it," he says casually, oversimplifying it. Maybe it was easy for him, but it was not for me.

"You'll figure out the logistics part, just do your homework, it'll all make sense."

For the first time I was annoyed with David O'Faolain.

He was way too nonchalant. I had a hard time using magik at the basic level. Either nothing would happen or some extreme event would occur as the result of my spell. There was no middle with me. Such as the case of my explosive fire spell and, more recently, the domination. I don't trust myself anymore. "In that case, can you help me with something? In Conjuration class, I was supposed to create some kind of magikal camera."

I handed him my book already folded to the section on the spell I needed to recreate. We review the instructions as I unpack the supplies, including a small cauldron out of my enchanted bookbag.

Use ashes of incinerated birch bark to draw the
Transcendent Sigil with a double lined circle.
Summon the Daemonic spirit of Erishal.

"Daemons David, like the devil!"

He laughs so hard just then.

“It’s not really like that, just a name for something destructive. Authors of spells come up with all sorts of random crap when they whip something up. It’s their call, just a label.”

He provides me an example of Agatha Belalz, the inventor of an unrelated but infinitely more popular cloaking spell that achieved nearly 100% invisibility. She refers to the destructive energy required for the magik as the Daemon *Rikhards.* A jab to her then deceased, and notoriously unfaithful, ex-husband Richard.

Omni Pertart Ruki Nah
Until the Sigil begins to glow.

To my chagrin, it does indeed glow. “Oh, I misread the instructions. I thought I was supposed to do two circles side by side.”

“Honest mistake, Noah. I can see how you thought that.” Although David smiles politely, I have the feeling he is struggling to conceive how I misread the directions.

Mix the following herbs inside a standard cast-iron
cauldron: African lillius petus, amphetamiy, belladonna.
Pour dragonbee honey on the herb mix and place the tip
of a white candle inside the cauldron.
Tip: Length of candle determines duration of spell
Repeat the following incantation thrice:
Achi Nay Soot Swen
Etch Nay Bay
Nemi Ershi

“Oh, pour while you chant,” I say to my sincere surprise.

David's eyes open wide with incredulousness, but he remains silent.

"Okay, so I have a hard time doing two things at once David," which is followed by laughter.

Concoction will burst into flames.
Caution, extremely hot.

I had to back away.

Drop the jar of bloodstones.

"Oh, I thought just dropping the berries would be good enough," further laughing as I toss the jar into the cauldron.

It shatters and the substance inside begins to swirl, glowing a fluorescent dark blue. Gradually, the liquid takes an orb-like form and hovers above the magikal pot until it is at eye-level. There, before my very eyes, was this little ball, balancing in the air, seemingly alive with its twinkling lights.

Direct with candle.
Spell is wick remaining.

"Meaning until the wick burns out," says David.

"You know, I kind of figured that one out," which has him engage in an onslaught of chuckling.

And there it went, like a hovering mechanical camera. The ball of light traveled through the forest of Tarias. The images seen through the orb were reflected in the clouds of smoke that continued to be produced by the small cauldron. We saw visions of animals and the other fantastic things that lived in the forest of Tarias.

The spell took a lot of work, but all that work pays off in the end. Under the right conditions, with all the pieces in their place, timing, and ingredients, the magik within the spell will flow naturally.

The spell cannot help itself. It is like setting up Christmas lights, you buy them, you get your ladder, you staple them into the roofline and presto-chango, an ordinary house transforms into a dream.

"Once you master this spell you won't need to fuss about with the instructions and ingredients."

That turned my attention, "Master a spell?"

"Why do Americans do that, ask a question with a statement? That drives me crazy."

"Sorry," I say with my eyes to the ground, not knowing where else to look. Was I annoying him? I continued to find places to stare, worried that I would further irritate him.

"You don't need to apologize. I meant nothing by it, promise. That kind of silly little stuff bothers me, but I'm not bothered by you, Noah."

He stares at me with this pleading and nervous look, and with a very unlike David laugh adds, "Oh, come on now, stop looking like that, like a lost puppy. You gotta believe me."

How was he calling me the lost puppy? "Yeah of course, sorry, I apologize a lot, it's a bad habit. Oh, I just did it again, just now. I'm working on it," I say hurriedly, "Anyway, do you have any other pet peeves?"

He smiles from his eyes, "No, not really. I have a couple, like chewing loudly, why do people do that, not chew properly? Drives me crazy." He silences himself for just a moment, "You don't chew loudly though, Noah, just so you know."

"Have you seen me eat?"

"No, I don't think so, but I can tell," now turning bright red.

I smile, "Well I don't think I do, and I hope I don't, for your sake." Beaming at him, "With that said, let me try to accommodate your sensitivities by asking my question correctly. What do you mean by mastering the spell?"

He reminds me that for various reasons, Witches are not always capable of using certain magiks, especially the complicated ones.

David teaches me that mastering a spell is another term for "wordless spells", a process in which the function and specific type of magik within a spell becomes innate to a Witch. The herbs, stones, and language used in spells are just conduits for the user to channel the magik needed to achieve the desired result.

It is overwhelming, there are so many spells that I need to study. "Am I expected to master them all," I ask him with a small sound of terror in my voice.

"Not at all, you don't have to master a single spell if you don't want to; you just have to learn certain basic spells. Besides, no one can master all magik. That'd make a Witch a true Jack of all trades and there's too much out there."

I guess he sees the nerves still frazzled over my face because he adds, "Noah, all this stuff is meant to give you a basic understanding of magik. Like how to start from scratch when you need too, let's say one day you need to conjure some rain and you, my wee psychic, have zero natural talent for Elemental magik."

"Thanks," I say flatly.

Grinning, "You know what I mean."

I smile, "Truth hurts." We laugh together.

"With all this training, you'll be able to whip up a spell using all the right supplemental ingredients for that type of magik." Unable to help himself, he continues his speech. "It's like learning how to read and write, love. Once you have that, you don't have to worry about the rest."

I lost track of the conversation when he called me "love", too busy trying to hide my excitement and actively pretending not to notice him saying the word is hard work for a teenager, Witch or not.

Shortly after we say goodnight and I return to the Manor. I lay in bed replaying our conversation, trying not to dwell on the "love" comment. I think of how our talk made me feel less stressed and surprisingly hopeful.

Yes, it was hard for me here at Philomena, but maybe it wasn't as hard as I made it seem. Maybe I could do all this magik stuff after all, maybe?

Chapter Fifteen

To Reveal a Secret
Prerequisite: Mastery of a standard wind spell.
Whisper to the Ayre while holding an object belonging to the person whom you seek the truth.
Send crushed autumn leaves soaring into the conjured wind.
Repeat seven times: Nichnven Vevaes Miestra Iaoapen
In your native tongue, ask for what you fear to know.

He lays on top of me. I try to scream but he has his hand over my mouth, blocking my breath. I cannot get him off and I think he might kill me this time. I wake up in a full sweat. Just a dream. I refuse to call it a nightmare, unwilling to give my fears the satisfaction of acknowledgment.

Although it was midnight, I decided to get up and prepare for the day, checking under my bed only once, just to be sure. Morgan runs underneath to the opposite end, jumping back onto the mattress, reassuring me of the absence of monsters.

I found myself at the main concourse of Bexar and Gruene Hall, inside there is a large portrait at the center of the two famous male Witches, for which the building owed its namesake. They had fallen in love with Celestial magik and each other. The building held a planetarium that was said to have access to the powers of the cosmos.

It remained open to accommodate the needs of the students but was relatively empty after classes were dismissed and instructors returned to their homes. There were many floor levels and I had made a habit of walking these halls when I couldn't sleep. Tonight I decided to practice a spell David and I had been training on.

I made my way to the East Lab's study hall and unloaded my bookbag when I arrived. A spellbook, several quartz stones, and dove feathers. If I was going to be up all night, I was at least going to get something out of it.

Nearly an hour later, with the help of an exceptionally large cup of coffee, I effectively managed to levitate not only the feathers but also my textbook. It was a bit of a stretch to say the textbook was floating smoothly, but it was in mid-air, shakily hovering a full foot above the long rectangular desk.

It may not have been much to another Witch, but it was to me. One, the fact that I was able to do it at all. Two, I did it without the need for an emotional crisis to activate my magik causing an overdrive of power.

It was now three in the morning. Just me and the late night. I gathered my things, preparing to return to the Manor when I heard it.

Laughter.

I found this particularly concerning, considering the fact that this property was exclusively occupied by me at this time of night. More laughter, now from behind me. I quickly turned around and found its source.

Two males now stare angrily at me, but not before I saw them kissing with their hands all over one another. Witches I am sure and almost just as certain, dead Witches.

Gruene and Bexar, their energy glows a light purple. It is pulsating, their presence must cause a reaction to the building because it now illuminates with the same matching aura. It was, after all, their life's work. They were not the sort of ghosts

I had imagined or seen on television. They were not transparent but rather full looking, but very dead looking. Like zombies, except without seeming rabid.

Until they vanished. They must have been 30 feet from me but suddenly I was face to face with them. The smaller of the two speaks first.

What are you doing here little Witch?

His voice crackles throughout the room. Without thinking, I turn around and run away, leaving my things behind, but his voice echoes in the hallway like an intercom. Frantically, I search for an exit but the sight of them at the end of the hallway immediately causes me to stall, and I stand there motionless.

In one swift motion, the larger one, Bexar I think, is inches from my face. Gruene grabs me by the arm, his skin feels like a shell, cold and empty, and tightens his grip. "I'm sorry. I sometimes come here to think," my voice trembling.

You are a filthy little trespasser, aren't you?

Gruene says accusingly, and then Bexar adds.

We'll teach you a lesson, naughty boy.

He grabs my other arm, reminding me of Charles Daley, and I lose control.

"DON'T TOUCH ME!" I scream, except it does not sound like a boy or me. My voice is more ferocious, like an animal. My magik churns within me, my ocean and its waves crash against me and pours out its fury. Cracks form on the marble floors as well as the walls around me. Meanwhile, the ghosts seem to shudder, as if wincing. They appear more static and scattered like an old television losing reception.

As they backed away, I could see it in their faces. Fear. Did I scare ghosts?

They disappear once more and, in a flash, they are back again, only much farther away, creating space between us, more for them than me. Their appearance changed as well.

They look more typical of what I thought ghosts would look like, translucent and airy.

Geez son, you are on our property, no need to get all huffy. You're the Peeping Tom.

My breathing is rapid, but I don't feel scared anymore, only angry. Judging from their reaction, my anger seemed unnecessary. Remembering to both breathe and mind my manners, I slow down and try to regain control. I cautiously respond, "I wasn't spying on you two. I was just walking," my voice flat and steady.

Walking, at this hour.

In a rapid twist of events, Bexar now sounds concerned.

"Yes, I come here to clear my head."

Well we are sorry too. We were just going to remove you from the premises, but you didn't have to attack us or destroy the place. Says Gruene.

I promised them I would tell Dr. Huebner about the incident first thing tomorrow morning and hopefully would have the damage repaired as soon as possible.

Both start rising higher in the air, *Children should be in bed at this hour, nothing good can be found after midnight,* says Bexar, and they both wistfully vanish once more.

"Thanks," I reply, still in shock, to no one but myself. Putting one foot in front of the other, I return to the East Lab, grab my forgotten bag, and run back to the manor. I arrive just before dawn and Morning Meds.

Later that day Maria and I are having lunch and I share my progress on levitation. Maria congratulated me with a little too much enthusiasm. After all, I only floated a textbook, it was only a miniscule accomplishment, but I appreciated the gesture.

Unintentionally, I neglected to disclose my encounter with ghosts to her. Dr. Huebner was out of the office this morning. I left him a note about the damage done to the hallway. Since then, it just slipped my mind. Before Philomena, I would have never forgotten to mention meeting ghosts. We had already moved on to another subject, and before I knew it, the thought floated away once more.

Having announced my accomplishments, Maria shares that she is declaring her commitment to abstaining from boys, and anything dating-related, at least until she graduates.

"I give it two weeks, maybe three," I joke with her.

"I'm serious Noah. I am so done with them." She was wearing a standard black pinafore with cute boots. It was a plain outfit, but on Maria, with her pretty green eyes and blonde hair brightening the world around her, it looked like something out of Vogue. It is no wonder she never stays single for long.

I see David in the distance, in a way he reminds me of Maria. He wears standard uniform, grey slacks and a plain white oxford shirt with a tie. His messy dark hair makes me think he just rolled out of bed, and he is still infallibly movie star handsome.

My heart beats faster as he walks toward us. "May I," he asks, referring to the seat next to me, wanting to have lunch with us. He is joined by Todd Ointeros, Maria's ex-boyfriend, who is also in their Coven.

I managed to stutter out something that sounded like "Yes" and they both take a seat.

David greets Maria while Todd remains silent. There is an awkward pause until Maria speaks first, "Hey Todd." Their post break-up relationship was not going well.

In an attempt to fill the quiet space, I share my success at levitating a feather and the textbook with David who seems genuinely impressed and even applauded at the good news. "That's pure barry," a phrase David often uses with me during our tutoring.

Maria and Todd look at David oddly, "What does that mean," she asks.

"It means fantastic, excellent really," he says.

"Got it," Maria says.

"Can we work on that tonight? Except bigger," I ask, returning our conversation to the levitation spell. "I think I could do better. It just seems like something is in the way. I am not sure what exactly, but I kind of think it could be me," I admitted, surprising myself with the realization, "like a confidence issue."

"Yeah, it definitely could be you," Todd says sharply and then looks at Maria, "He doesn't have it in him."

Without skipping a beat, Maria says, "Yeah, he does, what's wrong with you? Why are you being such a dick? It's the same for me, I have a hard time with Divination. I could do better, but my nerves just get the best of me."

Todd rebuttals but is more focused on Maria than myself, "I am just saying, maybe he's just limited, he is a Non-Legacy, right? Hell, even you Maria, I know your mom is a Witch, but your dad was a Mortal, right? Maybe that's why you blew your Evaluations and only managed a few worthwhile scores."

Maria's nostrils flare, but before she has a chance to respond, David says "Shut your mouth Todd. What do you have to say about it, the only reason you're in the Coven is because your mum's an alum. You have no talent to speak of and are more wanker than Witch."

David looks at Maria briefly before staring at something, maybe nothing, in the distance, his jaw tight. Maria adds in a few more shots. I, however, remain silent.

Attempting to diffuse the situation, Todd rescinds his statement. "Hey, I was just joking around, sorry Noah if I offended you."

"It's okay. It's fine. Thanks though," I say, mostly to save myself from this awkward feeling growing inside me.

David and Maria stare at him coldly. In agreement, they both tell me that I am fine, and I get the impression that is a first for them. Todd excuses himself and they continue to talk about how much of an asshole he is and remind me not to think twice about what he said. The feeling starts weighing heavily on my chest and I just want to run away from this spotlight. I don't deserve it and I am embarrassed to need it.

By the grace of some higher power, the conversation shifts and we began to talk about Maria and David's Evaluations.

David, of course, received high marks in every category. "They're no big deal," he boasts.

Maria said that she received mixed results, but David clarifies, "She got high scores, we were in the same testing group. She may not have had high marks in Divination but that doesn't mean she failed, either. Plus, she got high scores on everything else. Receiving any high score is an accomplishment," he says to her encouragingly.

I am so glad to hear it. "I knew you would do well!"

"Thanks," she says humbly. That was uncharacteristic of Maria. She was never one to boast, despite her confidence, but she was always honest. If she could do something well, she would not pretend otherwise, but I guess today was different.

I do not press her for more information. If she wanted to share more she would, instead I ask them, "What were they like?"

Maria, grateful for the change of topic, responds immediately, "There are three proctors. They run through the core magikal skill sets and you give them what you got. If you can't do it, no worries, you move on to the next magik type, like I had to for Divination."

"Just Divination, that's great. I stumble on Divination all the time, including everything else," we both laugh the way we do, even David is grinning, but he does not enjoy it the way we do.

"Yeah, it's just an assessment to track progress, the three C's, I think? What are they again, David," Maria asks?

"The first C stands for Capacity which rates your level of power. The second is Capability, which is not really a test, you don't get a score. The goal is to just figure out what natural gifts a Witch has, so you either got it or you don't. The last C stands for Competence, basically how skilled you are, that's where a student gets tested on expertise in their Craft."

"And you received high marks in every category," I ask him?

"Sorta, I mean yeah, I suppose so." He smiles but it is overcome by self-consciousness and turns into a slight frown.

"That's impressive, so you basically have expertise in every subject," I said positively.

"How is that? You hardly even go to class," Maria asks with notable notes of irritation in her tone.

"I go to class, sometimes, when I need too, but the thing is I don't really need to." Maria's mouth hangs open in disbelief, but before she speaks, David adds, "What you have to understand is my parents have made me study magik for as long as I can remember, even as a wee one. There are lots of times when I am in lecture reviewing something that I already know, it gets a bit boring to be honest."

I am about to ask him more about that, the boredom thing, only because he seemed a little sad when he said it, when the bell rings and lightning erupts from the fountain of Hai-Tai Wussein, reminding us to return to class. I say goodbye to Maria and David confirms the time and location for tutoring tonight, and I am now eager for classes to be over.

Several hours later David and I were at the Castle. We had made the top floor of the gigantic library our unofficial training area. We are trying to cast a more advanced version of the levitation spell, one meant to aid my defiance toward gravity. This Transference spell was a precursor to Transvection. It was like learning to stand if I wanted to run.

The spell requires a meditative state and for some reason I struggle to reach my practice, so David begins to guide me,

"Open up. Now raise your awareness. Let yourself experience it, and then hold it lightly."

He encourages me to be more easy-going about the spell. "Let go of what you think it needs to be and feel the energy around you, let it help you. One more time."

Kindly he tells me, "Everything is exactly where it should be, including you. Otherwise, we wouldn't be us, and, Noah, that just won't do."

He smiles and I laugh, falling a little more in love with him.

"Now hold it again, this time with a little more power. Keep yourself upright, as tall as you can make yourself. Then light it up, Noah. Hold the palm pose. That's it. Okay, now let it go."

I could feel the power pushing and pulling inside me, but the waves are gentle and under my control.

My mind races and wanders and my attention meanders from thought to thought. I See the room, vivid in my mind. The furniture around me, the tall bookshelves, and the transparent ceiling that operated as the Castle's skylight. It is as if my eyes were wide open, only I See the area with Vision beyond my limited sight.

There I was sitting cross-legged in skinny jeans and a loose grey sweater. My locket with the attached cat pendant dangles where my ribs meet my belly, reflecting the light around us. I sit barefoot, David's recommendation, he is across from me in the same position, his long-sleeve V-neck revealing the lines of his chest. Although his shirt was loose, his muscles remained defined.

Feeling self-conscious, I quickly distract myself. Extending my consciousness well beyond my physical body to the world around me, I connect to the bookshelves, the floor, and the air, traveling through the psychic streets that existed beyond perception.

David reminds me to raise my power, tightly holding onto my magik, and gently letting it go. The air sizzled slightly, as if electrified, and the energy pulsed around me.

"When I say it's time, say the spell quickly," I hear his voice, my anchor, distant but strong, tethering me down. "Now." I obey.

Augentin Circe

The words reverberated around us, flying through all those new connections that existed between David, me, and what was around us. I feel as if I am on a roller coaster, and my belly tingles. I am flying.

My many opal pebbles, a significant source of the spell, formed the symbols of Air, Earth, and Sun. They are the first to float slightly, just a few inches above the ground, and then everything else, including us.

We were floating, the sofas, furniture, books, and bookshelves lifted into the air weightlessly. It reminded me of the time at the Mastersons when I caused all the objects in the house to have the same weightless property. Only back then, I did it without knowing how or why I could do such a thing.

I opened my eyes and the first thing I see is David beaming. His smile shines brightly. No one person should be that beautiful.

My heart could have burst from excitement. David wraps his arms around me and holds me in a tight hug. He was so happy, and it was all because of me. I thought for a minute I could die from happiness and it wasn't because I performed the spell. It was because of him.

As we say goodnight heading our separate directions, he yells, "Hey Noah, tonight was pure barry!"

After that, the days started flowing with more ease. I prepared a travel bag for the long days with books, snacks, and anything else I might need. The work was getting easier. I completed whatever work or study was needed in between breaks or at night.

The best part of my day was the end, with David. Our time helped me in more ways than just my magik. He was easy to be with, no pressure. He had a way of making every mistake, flaw, or wherever I was with magik, perfectly okay. Spending time with David made me feel like I was home. Maria's friendship felt similar, and although we were best friends, it was different. Besides, Maria was a wild child. Busy with her own adventures and magikal development, not to mention new boyfriends.

It wasn't like we did not work. David was easy-going but he took his job with me very seriously, making jokes and then always refocusing. I was improving, and I would never say this out loud, but I think the reason I was doing well was that I didn't want to let him down. I wished I could be better, stronger, more impressive, but I was none of those things. The least I could do was try to avoid, at all costs, complete failure.

Chapter Sixteen

The ritual of the golden letters, or the writings-on-the-wall spell, is a prophetic type of magik.
Restricted to seasoned Seers and advanced practitioners of Divination as likelihood of misinterpretation is all but guaranteed.

David is staring at me as I initiate my umpteenth attempt at the Transference spell, one specifically created to move an object, or oneself, by means of levitation.

Standalone levitation spells manifest the effect of floating only. Developing my magikal "fine-motor" skills is the next component needed to achieve successful Transvection.

Initially, I had some success with the spell, and David looked at me with excited focus as he assessed my movements during the levitation. As we continued, the intensity on his face transformed into a furrowed brow with a frown that now seemed affixed to his mouth.

I tried to move with fluidity during those first few attempts and failed miserably, but at least I was able to float upward and touch the ceiling.

Unfortunately, after several hours of repeat attempts, I am unable to reproduce the effect. My results were now more like that of a chicken awkwardly leaping toward the sky in a useless attempt to fly.

The most frustrating part was that I had done the necessary research and preparation. I understood this spell extensively and should have been able to cast it with ease, yet each new attempt became exponentially more futile compared to the one before.

The poses of the spell required steady and pinpoint poise and fatigue was beginning to wear me down. Still looking at the ceiling, trying to muster the will to touch the panel, I say a little too loudly, "I can do this," more to me than David. I stare back at him accusingly, as if he was the cause of my problems.

Magik was complex, but I was learning more and more each day and, as such, it became gradually easier to use. I ask David in earnest, "Why can't I do this, what is wrong with me now?"

"Nothing's wrong with you. Not a single thing," I can sense a "but" approaching, "The thing is Noah, you've used up your tank, why don't you give it a rest," he says matter-of-factly, as if that put an end to it.

I would have been annoyed if not for the look on his face, filled with concern, reminding me of Joan. Not to mention that he was right. Every part of my body weighed heavily, I even moved slowly. Magik is draining.

He looks directly into my eyes for a few brief seconds and seems a little lost.

"What is it?"

He stutters a bit, but only for the briefest moment, "S-Sorry, nothing mate, it's just your eyes, they're pure bonnie." He laughs uncomfortably with a slight smile that made me feel as if I was falling.

"Thanks," and suddenly I don't know what to do with my hands, desperate to find a place for them, and having no luck. I decided to try the spell once more.

His face changes, his mouth closed and jawline tight, attempting to suppress words that are waiting restlessly on his lips, but they will not be contained.

"Don't strain yourself. Over-exertion of magik can cause serious damage."

"I'll be careful," I promise.

I initiate the spell once more but before I can recite the incantation, he shouts, "Stop it, Noah!"

The volume of his voice startled me. Automatically, I hold my breath and obediently shut my magik down.

My focus was entirely now on him. I wonder if he is mad, and if so, was it because of me, and why did my heart continue to beat rapidly, urging me to run?

"Why don't you give it a break?" Even though he asked me, it felt more like a demand than a question.

"But I haven't figured it out yet."

"I know mate, but you look like you are about to fall over." It was strange for him to worry. I was tired and sure I felt like I could sleep for a full day, but I was excited and wasn't ready to stop.

Besides, St. Philomena Academy had several rules regarding the use of magik. There were measures taken to prevent harm both in and out of the classroom. Bindings, suppression charms, and various enchantments were placed throughout Philomena.

This Witchcraft maintains responsible and safe use of magik. Like how I could more easily move objects through Transference in my room than in the halls of Spirit Manor, or how the potency of destructive spells were greatly diminished across the board.

It made it easy for novice Witches to obey the rules. It was the more experienced sorcerers that must practice restraint. For them, the charms operated more like red tape than locked doors. My Witchcraft may have been improving but I still lacked the ability needed to counteract that magik, making David's worry, although endearing, needless.

"Sorry mate, I don't want to hold you back. Say, why don't we get something to eat and try again tomorrow?"

I asked him about the protective charms, "I thought they also prevented magikal exhaustion?"

"They can, but no one spell is perfect, nothing can account for every possibility."

David shuffled his feet, looking away, until returning his pretty brown eyes back to me. It was plain on his face that wheels were churning inside his mind. He weighs options of some sort until settling on a course of action.

"Plus, taking a break gives you time to recharge and you'd probably get better results."

I thought about this, slightly reassured that at least we would try again tomorrow.

"Please, Noah." He gives me this look, these sad eyes, begging me to stop, making my heart hopelessly capsize.

"Sure, I guess a small break would be okay."

He exhales, and relief wipes away the tension from David's eyes. He adds, a little too quickly, "Great, let's go downstairs and get a snack or something. Sorry, Noah, I don't want to be, what do you call it, a micromanager? Yeah, someone who doesn't know when to stop being a pain in the ass, I guess," his smile slowly returns.

He wanted me to stop my practice and I suspect he was close to making it mandatory, something well within his authority as my tutor, but it was as if he was nervous to draw that line, like he wanted me to be okay with his decision.

"Sure, I am kind of hungry," I answer with a soft smile.

At ease again, his parental panic subsided immediately once the danger of my magikal exhaustion was no longer a threat. Even though I wanted to continue the training, I was happy for that so I reassure him once more, "I think a full day recovery is in order."

It was strange to see all the waves of complex emotions roll through him in just one conversation. I wondered what lived inside that head of his, but ever respectful of his privacy, I dare not enter his mind. After we eat our late dinner from the small sandwich shop downstairs, he walks me toward the entrance of the tunnel that would lead me back to the western section of Philomena, returning to Spirit Manor. The Castle and David's own residence is situated on her far eastern face.

As we say goodbye, he says, "Hey Noah, I promise to, as they say, chill."

"You promise?"

"Sure," and winks at me, smiling mischievously, an indication that he will do no such thing.

I roll my eyes, "Bye," as I walk through the tunnel. A few minutes later, I arrive at the East Lab located within Bexar and Gruene Hall and quickly exit the building, grateful to leave without any ghostly encounters. I step onto the cobblestone path that leads to Spirit Manor when suddenly a small cyclone of nearby leaves appears before me, only to dissipate just as quickly, leaving behind the small Owl-like being that happened to be my favorite Faelin. Technically, the only Faelin I knew.

"Hello Aeduou."

We have gotten in the habit of sharing meals; she was a fan of my taste in cuisine and was welcomed to break bread with me anytime. Today was a lox bagel sandwich with cream cheese and avocado, leftovers from dinner with David.

She whistled happily. The tips of her white feathers start to glow with just a touch of pink and blue. It was her way of saying thank you. I cast the translation spell that Maria was kind enough to teach me. I practiced it many times over with all the other ingredients required for the full ritual and, over time, have nearly mastered the spell. I now only need to speak the incantation to cast it.

We have a brief conversation and she tells me she is well, and she asked me the same. I tell her I am fine, and in so many words, she says that I am lying to her or myself, or to both.

Denial is pointless with the Faelin, they read through such false things.

I reassured her that I would be okay, "I just need some sleep." She scolds me, reminding me of her debt to me over the bargain that I have yet to agree to, and Aeduou does not wait for me to decline her help once more. Instead, she soars above me and, in a twist of air, is gone, I assume back to her realm.

"Goodbye, Aeduou."

Once home, I continue practicing the levitation spell well into the night, despite my promise to David. I felt guilty over it but my drive to improve supersedes my conscience. After all, staying up was better than dreaming.

The next morning, I woke up and felt a sense of familiar angst that reminds me of all the times I was placed into a new foster home, the feeling that thrived throughout my time here. The feeling was diminishing as I was actively adapting to my life as a Witch.

It was all starting to become more manageable but this feeling inside contradicts my efforts. It feels like the walls were closing in on me.

The mural in my room reflects the budding flowers of the tree and the subtle hints of dawn approaching. Its beauty does nothing to console me and I realize that I have not been outside the walls of my room, a classroom, or the Castle since visiting Tarias with Maria. I wondered how long it had been, at least a month. I have been so busy adjusting to life at the Academy, busy trying to survive. I had paid little to no attention to anything that was unrelated to improving my powers.

Later that night I stare out from the bay windows of my room with their spectacular view, losing myself in the beauty of Tarias below, a city built of fairy lights. I find myself holding my hands without conscious thought, compulsively wringing them against one another to the point that I was slightly tearing at my skin.

I try to distract myself with my studies, but I am unable to concentrate on any spellwork. Surprisingly, even levitation failed to derail my anxieties, considering I was so close to actual flight.

I decide to forgo further training and make my way to bed, fully aware my bad dreams will return with a vengeance, but at this point I'd rather maintain some sanity in the terror of sleep than feel out of control in the chaos that is me.

Morgan curls himself around me, "What do you think about me taking a day off from all this work," I ask him. He responds by stretching his paws out and rolls over onto his back, exposing his furry belly.

"I take that as a yes," I privately plan a visit to Tarias and commit to ask Maria to join me first thing tomorrow morning. Either way, I would go on my own if necessary. I needed to get out of this house and away from these walls.

The following morning David and I sit together as he eats a breakfast loaded with meats while I drink coffee and stare at my scone. Maria was practicing Conjurations with another student who specialized in that type of magik and, conveniently, is absolutely gorgeous. Ordinarily I would be cheering her on, but today, her budding relationship is delaying me from planning a visit to the city, also known as my attempt to save myself from going crazy.

David asked if something was wrong, which was not unusual for him. These days he is always asking me something out of concern, raising my internal alarm to the growing mountain of evidence further confirming my unwell-ness.

"Nothing," I say, and he effortlessly catches the lie. It is as if he knew my truth even before me.

David had gotten in the habit of asking me a series of inquiries on my knowledge of various activities found in the city, knowing full well I had not been to any of these places.

I decide it is time to confess and reveal to him that I am going stir-crazy and need to spend some time away from magik. He instantly offers to take me to Tarias the following day, Saturday, allowing for a full day of activity.

"Yes! Let's go," I say so fast that I startle myself.

Several hours later, I find myself walking back to the Manor, worrying about the money I would need to visit the city.

Until I remember the stipend afforded to me by the Council for being a Ward. I have only pulled from the account once, back when I visited Tarias with Maria. I wondered how much money would be in the account by now.

Ms. Penelope had assisted me with pulling funds the last time, but everything had been such a blur those first few weeks, I barely recalled asking for the withdrawal.

"Ms. Penelope, I was hoping to go to Tarias tomorrow, with a school mate, could you..." unable to finish my question.

"Oh wonderful love, you'll be needing some money of course, I am sure you'll be doing some shopping while you're in town. I'll ring Dr. Huebner later to sign off on the withdrawal note. He'll take care of it when he can get around to it. That man is terribly busy, but we cannot wait all day for him now. You do need a day to yourself, love."

No wonder I forgot about the stipend, Miss Penelope accommodated and anticipated my needs perfectly, to the point that I did not have to think about these sorts of practical matters.

Grateful for all her help, I made a mental note to buy her something special tomorrow.

She walked to a gold-plated canister that, up until now, I thought contained sugar. She held her hand above it and cast her spell.

Accommodats Gosii Codochaq

Repeating herself, exactly four times and then in plain English says, "100 fold," adding, "With change please?" She then opened the canister and pulled out a neatly tied wad of cash. It looked like standard paper money of America, only with different designs. In the center of the bills were historical figureheads of famous Witches that contributed to the Witchcraft Union or ONCE.

"Thank you very much, Miss Penelope."

"Anytime, love."

No longer worried about finances, I allowed myself to be excited and automatically my thoughts find and linger on David. Overcome with a buzzing anticipation of spending the entire day with him, I suddenly felt simultaneously exhilarated and impatient, tomorrow could not come fast enough. I went to bed early and, despite the plethora of bad dreams, I woke up with the same excited feeling, and practically jumped out of bed ready to prepare for the day.

As I am changing, Miss Penelope sends me a message by means of an acoustic spell that communicates through the air but only becomes audible when the words reach the intended recipient.

It was inspired by psychic messages but is significantly more polite than invading someone's mind and forcing the communication into a person's thoughts.

"A suitor is at the door for you." A suitor, really?

"He's just a friend Ms. Penelope," sending the message back with the same spell.

"Oh relax, Mr. Ellis, it's just a phrase. Your friend has arrived, a very handsome Mr. O'Faolain, a fine young man."

Sometime ago I learned how to open a channel between me and the other Seers, a kind of inner dialogue that could be turned on and off like a light switch, initially with the aid of a spell, but since then I mastered the ability and can now do it independent of ritual.

It was a harmless thing. Technically, I wasn't in the other Seer's minds, but I was Seeing through their physical vision only, never touching their psychic interpretation and perception of the event. Leroy happened to be in the room with David and Ms. Penelope at the time.

I used the connection through him to see the very handsome David O'Faolain. He was shuffling his feet nervously, which I think is a direct result of overhearing the not so quiet Miss Penelope discuss his "handsome" appearance, and here I thought nothing could phase him.

After filling Morgan's food bowl, I rush downstairs in a flurry but stop myself before I reach the first floor. I do not want to appear overly eager.

The thought of David knowing that it felt like my entire mental stability depended on me being able to spend the day with him is horrifying. Minding my pace, I gradually walk down the remaining staircase until I enter the room filled with the morning light.

He wears grey gym shorts and a green athletic shirt, his ruffled hair contained in a baseball cap. He looked like he was running a marathon instead of touring a town, but inevitably manages to look like he is playing the lead of some romance movie, the dreamy guy who everyone falls in love with at the end.

Meanwhile, I was in ordinary jeans and a white hoodie. We were in the thick of spring, yet the mountain remained cold to me. I put on my new coat from Kevin, who was very familiar with my aversion to lower temperatures, during the summers he would stare at the thermostat and check-in with me daily, if it was "too warm".

Anyway, it was lighter than my bulky winter coats but well insulated. I had other lighter coats from Dr. Huebner, they were an optional addition to the standard uniform, and they were just as effective. I think they may have been enchanted, but there was no way I would ever be caught dead wearing those ridiculous robes.

David beams at me when I walk into the room and says, "Morning Noah, don't you look cozy, in all those layers."

"I am, thank you," I respond flatly, but he laughs and I cannot help but smile. We then say goodbye to Ms. Penelope and Leroy. David and I walk the cobblestone path that descended from the Manor to the main academic buildings, but instead of taking the path to the Academy, we turn right and the trail provides a route to the nearest tower of the Carriages of the Aerials, Tarias' primary mode of transportation.

It is easily accessible from Spirit Manor, which makes me wonder why I had not taken advantage of this and visited Tarias earlier.

The spring mountain wind bites at my face as we approach the location. I look at David and his shorts remind me of our first session together.

Lost in my thoughts, I realize that I had not spoken much since we left the Manor. Without training as the focus of our time together, I didn't really know what to say to him. Painfully aware of my own awkwardness, I blurt out the first thing that comes to mind.

"Aren't you cold?"

"Umm, no, not really," he answers honestly. "You really don't like the cold, aye?"

"No, not at all," I answer.

"Even with the enchantments?" David was talking about the spells that help create more oxygen on the mountain in the upper atmosphere and, to some degree, manage weather. The spells had environmentally friendly limitations meant to reduce a negative impact on nature. For example, severe freezing temperatures of the mountains were "less severe", but only by a few degrees, at least in my opinion.

"They don't make enough of a difference."

"But today is perfect, the sun is out and the breeze is mild."

"Well, I take anything below 70 degrees personally."

He laughs to himself, "What do you mean?"

"Well, it's a little rude if you think about it. We need warmth to live, only helium can remain in motion in the absolute absence of heat, the rest of us just die."

"Oh, is that right, Noah Ellis," David pauses for a minute, I am sure hesitant to say something after my dramatic campaign. "Fair enough, cold and Noah, a clear no-go."

A group of students pass us by, they wave at David, of course, "It's not all that bad, look at them. They're wearing shorts and seem to be faring just fine."

"How is everyone here good with the temperature, is it some Witch thing," I ask David.

"No it's not, but aren't you a Witch? If it were a thing, would you not know it," David points out.

"I don't think so," genuinely unsure if I could tell the difference, there were so many things about being a Witch that remained foreign to me.

"Is it hard for you to think of yourself as one of us?"

"No, not at all," but then I consider his question seriously and add, "Yeah, I guess so, the thing is I'm still getting used to it, being one."

"Do you not like being one," and exhales before also asking, "And being here?"

"It's not that, I am still adjusting to the idea. Most of my life I thought I was human, it is not easy realizing that I am something else. I think it takes time to change all these ideas of what I thought I was to what I actually am," answering honestly. I intentionally leave out the main reason I felt so disconnected, the fact that I had to leave the one home that actually felt like mine, a burden David does not need to carry.

He looks at me with kind eyes, "Makes right sense."

He returns to the original topic, "Anyway, I doubt everyone is comfortable with the temperature. Most are probably, if I am being honest," he says with a sly grin, and continues, "I guess if there are some with your similar aversion, they'd likely just use a heat charm and call it a day."

I place my palm on my forehead, "I am so dumb, this entire time I haven't even thought to use magik."

I could have been feeling cozy all winter-long, instead of freezing my ass off when I walked to class, "I really am the worst Witch," I admit.

He frowns, "You are not the worst Witch," and rests his hand on my shoulder, "Besides, you look nice in that coat." He really is the most perfect boy.

"Thank you," I say while a feeling of inadequacy rises within me.

"The entrance is just past these steps," said David, saving me yet again by changing the subject.

We reach the entryway and climb up the huge singular stone structure, one of many scattered across Tarias. It protrudes from the earth as if it were made from the mountain itself. We climb the spiraling steps and enter the pinnacle.

An older male Witch wearing a plain uniform made magnificent by the shine of his long flowing red robe greets us. "Hello David. It is wonderful to see you my boy. Oh, and you have brought a new friend. I don't believe I've seen you before. Hello, young man, who might you be?" He asked with wrinkles happily creasing across his face.

"Hello sir, my name is Noah, I arrived a few months ago," I say suddenly nervous.

"Well it's nice to meet you. I am Mr. Yurzie, the Conductor of this tower. Where are you boys off too?"

"To the squarc, Mr. Yurzic," David announces.

"Fine job, young man," he says while closing his eyes. A powerful breeze sweeps in and out of the windowless and open platform of the gallery. The wind continues to swirl about, and it carries debris of leaves in its wake. The tower croaks like cast iron pipes in an ancient house.

I feel a pull from behind me, like gravity, except the force moves horizontally. I see the floating Carriage a short distance away, like the ones I saw during my arrival not that long ago. I had not felt this then, or at least I don't think I did.

The Conductor's magik continues to sing within the stone walls and there is something else. The tower itself hums in response, like they are talking.

The Carriage quickly approaches and in one swift motion glides into the gallery. It is easily the size of a room. It levitates mere inches above the floor and waits until we step inside before making its leave, jetting off to our destination.

As we float along, we pass over Victorian styled buildings, federal colonials, and other mismatched architectures. Nearly halfway to the market square I ask David what he thought of the energy pattern I had just experienced.

At first he seems confused but politely reasons, "I can't be sure, maybe it's because you're a Seer." I try to explain it once more, although it seemed impossible that anyone could have missed the experience of the magik between the Conductor and the tower.

"Do you mean the wind?"

"No, not the wind. It was the push and pull of their energy and the sounds of their magik, the way they seemed to talk to one another."

We are interrupted as the city center of Tarias fast approaches, the buildings appear to rapidly grow. Philomena is now far away at a higher elevation, the large academic buildings made small by the distance.

We arrive at our destination, the nearest point to the market. Our Carriage rushes in faster than I expected and, upon arrival, I instantly feel the pull of another Conductor somewhere off the eastern face of the mountain, but it waits until we step off before jetting off to the next location.

We step down the stone spiral staircase, continuing our conversation. David tries his best to understand, "Well, I suppose it's the same with me and my own enchanted items. There is a back and forth, between them and me, a sorta chit-chat," chuckling over the word.

He further explains, "Surely it's the same except tenfold with those buggers. There is old magik in them, the strong and stubborn kind, difficult to work with unless you have a relationship between you and the enchantment."

We step out and into the bustling streets of the market, "Anyway, it sounds like the kinda thing only a Seer could know, but Noah that's a good sign, you probably felt it because your powers are growing, congrats." He raises his palm up to give me a high five, and I returned the gesture awkwardly.

"Sorry," apologizing for my social ineptitude.

"Don't worry about it," he says happily. His good mood was contagious and I couldn't help but smile at him. Meanwhile, I discreetly dry my palm with my coat, hopeful that he would fail to notice how my entire body seems to be on fire at the impact of his touch.

We walk toward the market, the bright sunlight and busy streets of Tarias overwhelm me with excitement. I see adult Witches walking or flying various directions and heights. Some rise into the higher elevations of the few skyscrapers here. A street performer magikally juggles fire. At a nearby park, children accompanied by their parents ride Pegasi, gaining a birds-eye view of Tarias' skyline.

Why have I not come here before? I've only just arrived, and I am already feeling a hundred times better. It must show on my face, "Having fun?" David asks with that heartbreaking, crooked grin of his.

I just laugh, "I can't believe I've only been here once."

"Me too. That's why I have been trying to get you out of Philomena for the past month. All work and no play. I suppose that is how it goes? No matter, the point is it's no good No-El."

"Is that my nickname?"

"Depends, do you like it?"

I pause, pretending to think about it. "It's okay, a little religious, especially since my actual name is already biblical, but I don't mind. It reminds me of home." I tell him exactly how I came about my name, which leads to more stories about Joan.

After the explanation of its origin, he says, "Thank you very much for sharing that with me, I'm honored."

"You are welcome," I say lightly and we both smile back at one another.

"Right, so where to now?" David listed out options and surprises me when he mentions going to the movies. "There's theaters here?"

"Aye, sure are, there are several in Tarias and even the Academy has one inside the Pyramid." I had no idea and, frankly, it would have been a nice distraction during the early days of my arrival. Thanks Leroy, most informed House Lead with the least helpful information ever.

We boiled the list down to either walking offbeat trails, visiting Lake Osage, hitting up a restaurant, or watching a movie.

We settled on a movie and the lake, "I want to see it up close. I stare at it each time my Coven passes it by during the Esbat, I think about what it must be like to be close to the lakeshore, not just the harbor."

"The lake and a movie it is." We watched an action movie about superheroes. It felt like it had been forever since I've seen a film. I thought it might have lost its nostalgia, being a Witch with my own sort of superpowers, but a happy ending never gets old. After the movie, hunger pains remind me that I haven't had food since the night before, "Maybe we should eat something before the lake?"

"Not to worry Noah, I have a solution for that," and begins opening his backpack, "Think of me as the most prepared man in the world," revealing sandwiches and a strange drink.

I smile but remember why I wanted to visit the lake, "Never mind, I don't want to miss the sunset, definitely the lake first."

"Alright, this for later," slyly smiling as he returns the orange lava-like elixir into his bag and offers me bottled water instead, "It'll be a surprise."

Once done, we make our way to the skybridge that runs over the large body of water. The lake is in the valley in far western Tarias. A waterfall spills from the mountain's edge and into the lake, and supplies most of the lake's water that descends from Cat's Peak.

The Bridge offers only a few exit points that lead to either its lakeshore or the forested area of Tarias, home to both various animals and supernatural creatures.

The path to the lake's small beach, the most popular destination, takes a little over an hour to hike, but is the perfect spot to watch the sunset. I am grateful I was able to wear comfortable shoes rather than the pointy dress shoes of my uniform.

We make our way down the long stairwell to Lake Osage's shore. It is lined with cherry blossoms. Each one has been enchanted to remain in bloom throughout the seasons. Lake Osage's frigid waters feed a few scattered frozen pools on the beach. They are used as natural ice rinks for young Witch children, who skate along in ordinary ice skates. I guess some things can be timeless and magikal without Witchcraft.

"Glaciated," that is how David described the icy lake with his Scottish accent, hearing him felt like a dream. It was like that most of the time during tutoring, but usually I just refocused on the work in front of me. Without those distractions, all I could do was fall more in love with him.

He grins as he reaches for his backpack, "Almost forgot about the surprise." He holds up the strange concoction I had seen earlier, a glass bottle that reminded me of a lava lamp.

"It's Besnit. It's a type of soda. It's charmed to create euphoria. The best I can compare it to is something like the effect of alcohol and weed, but only for a few seconds, it's really for kids."

"So, Witches give their children booze and pot?"

He burst out in laughter, "No, not at all, it doesn't work that way. It's also known as giggle juice, here, try it."

I stare at the bottle and hesitantly bring it to my lips, deciding to take a sip. My taste buds are overwhelmed by its unnaturally delicious flavor. All at once, the bubbles fly into my mouth, traveling straight to my head. Suddenly, I am loopy and unapologetically giddy.

It was like being tickled without any of the unpleasantness. It tasted like candy and cake, but with the texture of heavy fog, wisping away as I drank it.

We almost fell to the floor from laughing over nothing. We grab our knees to keep us upright as I tear up from the laughter. And then I am back, as if it were nothing at all. We drank it up until it was gone and continued laughing, despite the absence of the tonic's effect.

I return my attention to the view. The lake shines a golden brilliance as the sun sets.

"Isn't it amazing, David."

"Sure is, Noah," but when I turn to face him, I find that he is not looking at the setting sun or the dazzling lake. Instead, his eyes are fixed on me.

Privately, I remind myself that it cannot be real and wonder if Besnit had any other side effects, like delusion. I change the subject by asking to return to the market so I could buy something for Miss Penelope.

It is well into the evening when we return to the main square. I bought her a bouquet of magikal flowers known as Loranae. The flowers change both color and scent based on the seasons and remain in bloom as long as the stems are placed within water. I hope she likes them.

We decide to have dessert and he recommends a local shop specializing in frozen treats. An attendant greets us when we arrive, he also recommends we try something called Elysion, a magikally infused ice cream that causes prolonged weightlessness.

David clarifies that the treat was usually preferred by younger children and points to a rather impressive playground inside the shop. The attendant informs us that there is an obstacle course on the roof. It was reserved for older Witches engaging in more advanced tricks.

"It's a bit of an event and takes a while to wear off. It would make for a late night, and I gotta be heading back soon."

My heart sinks at the thought. I do not want this day to end, as I pay special attention to the sky and the absent sun. I want to stay here forever where everything is fun and there are no bad dreams or reminders of loss, but more importantly, I do not want to leave the place where I get to be with him.

"Oh, yeah, some other time then," desperately trying to hide my disappointment. "Do you want to head back now?"

"No," he says, only to retract, "Well actually, yeah, that might be best. Next time, maybe in a couple of weeks. We can always come after tutoring."

"I'd like to take you to Geovannies. They have the world's best hot dogs."

"What's the magik?"

"No magik, just really good food."

Smiling at him now, "Okay, I'd like that."

Upon our return to Philomena, David walks me home and we end our night at the front door. He steps off the porch while I remain there, still holding Ms. Penelope's bouquet firmly in my arms. I say goodnight as he leaves, making his way back to his Coven's residence.

I call out to him, raising my voice so he can hear me, "David!"

"Yeah," he replies.

"Thanks for today."

He waves his hand in the air, "No worries, No-El," he shouts without looking back.

"You saved me," I say quietly to myself, wishing with a level of desperation I did not know existed, that he would have looked back.

Chapter Seventeen

Note: Barriers are conjured forces of Transference and used to create shields separating objects, people, and or places in various orders. However, they are dissimilar to protection charms, although they are often a component of that type of defensive magik.

Maria and I created our own personal study group. It was originally dedicated to Alchemy, but we were both doing surprisingly well in understanding the many complex sciences involved in successfully brewing potions, that we decided to expand this time to study other subjects.

I take the time to train on Transference while Maria talks to the handsome boy who helped her with Conjuration, Aaron Fuerios, occasionally excusing herself to check on my training since this type of magik was her expertise.

I was supposed to be at an evening session with Madam Reyna. She wanted all the Seers to do an Evening Meditation, like Morning Meds wasn't enough, but not one of my housemates was on board with the addition to the schedule. We made a unanimous psychic pact to boycott the extra Meds.

As much of a firecracker Reyna was, she could not stand against the majority. I am sure the response was reason enough for her not to push the issue.

Returning to my training, I raise my hand toward the outdoor chair in front of me. With a flick of my wrist, I swat at the air and send my energy out. The chair shoots across the courtyard like an arrow, crashing into the exterior wall and breaking into large pieces upon impact. I quietly gasped, as I didn't mean to use that much force.

Magik had a weight to it and each day I grew more accustomed to it, gradually losing my awareness of the sensation. If I paid close attention, I could still notice the distinction. The more laborious a spell the heavier the magik was, like being submerged underwater.

Once a spell had been mastered, it became light like a glove. Since I mastered this Transference spell, the magik came easily but I do not know my own strength. I accidentally used excessive force on the chair.

It is hard to believe the progress I was making. It was not that long ago that I could barely move a pencil by will alone.

Maria startles me, "What did the chair ever do to you?"

"I can't believe I did that!" Nervously, I petition her for assistance, "Can you fix it?"

"For sure big blue," Maria's term of endearment for me. She could use it sparingly, as she knew I found anything referencing my eyes incredibly annoying.

Stretching her hand outwards, she whispers on the wind, it carries her words to the broken pieces of the chair. The pieces lift into the air and twirl around in the shape of a small sphere, gradually attaching to one another until returning to its unbroken form. Maria's magik holds the chair steady in mid-air as the cracks within the object reseal. Once done, it gently floats back to the ground.

"Wow," I say with my mouth half-open, "Incredible, you really are talented."

"And this is news to you, Noah?"

We laugh, "Sorry, yes, I just haven't seen you in action lately."

"I may not be any good in Divination but I'm in the top of my class in everything else. Speaking of, don't we have some studying to do?"

With that, Maria and I settled down to finish reviewing our individual assignments. I work on completing my readings and she busies herself with calculating astronomical phases for specialized lunar magik, her final effort at improving her own psychic abilities.

I was tired, too tired. I stayed up last night to try to complete readings on spell theory. Returning to the magikal concept I left off at 5AM earlier that day, Infusion, the central mechanism involved in enchantments. This type of magik involves possessing an animate or inanimate object with magikal energy.

> Standard enchantments require maintenance magik but advanced Infusion techniques can sustain an enchantment without conscious effort by creating an automatic process. The classic example being the Faemalyr, the bond between a Witch and another living being. An incredibly complex spell and notoriously difficult to cast.
>
> Most Witches that possess a Faemalyr do not have a complete bind with the animal, often settling for a lesser version of the connection. They are willing to receive reduced benefits ordinarily gained with the true enchantment. Often, in lieu of the bind, Witch citizens prefer to create a psychic connection with magikal animals of higher intelligence.

How amazing would it be to make Morgan my Faemalyr? So stereotypical, a Witch with a black cat, but a boy Witch, scratch that, but a gay boy Witch with a black cat, now that is something. It is a shame the enchantment is so difficult to complete. I finish the final portion of my studies and gather my things.

Maria and I say goodbye and send air kisses to each other. There was no booster session with the Doc, he had been away for two weeks, calling to check in regularly, apparently something to do with disturbances, vortexes, and lost Mortals. The U.S. and ONCE were working closely together to resolve the matter.

"Not to worry," he would say, "All is well."

With the extra free time I decide to go back to the Manor and dress in something more comfortable before meeting David later tonight. On my way there, I heard something foreign. It's like static and reminds me of what it was like when I first discovered my powers, like when I was hearing thoughts that were not my own, only it is not just one. The sound was persistent and aggressively increasing in volume.

There are so many voices. It is hard to identify one thought from the other, including my own. A sudden and intense migraine attack comes over me and I fall over from the pain. I kneel to steady my balance, grateful there is no one to see me acting erratically, even by Witch standards. Automatically, I pace my breathing, desperate to regain control. I command with all my being for the voices to stop. It takes an excruciatingly long minute for them to quiet down, but after five more, they finally do.

The migraine stopped once the voices went away. I return to my feet, worried but feeling fine. I decide to discuss this with Madam Reyna tomorrow morning.

Now back at the manor, I get ready to meet David. After a shower, I catch myself in the mirror, skin and bones, but I don't think I look bad and then I get embarrassed for looking at myself. I dress quickly into jeans and a white linen shirt.

Joan said it was all the rage, blouses for men with its buttons on the collarless neck. It was pretty but I wore it mostly because it came from her. As I open the bedroom door to leave Morgan quickly prances into our room. He had been exploring the Manor, probably learning more about this old house than I ever will.

"See you in a bit, handsome boy." He purred as I scratched the back of his ears.

Running late, yet again, I finally meet David at the tower. He was staring up at the starry sky and for just a moment seemed a little sad. It was in his shoulders, the way they sunk down, carrying something heavy filled with loss. I call out to him. However, when he turns around his flat smile turns wide and bright. Maybe I was imagining it.

"About time, No-El," pointing to his watch as he says so.

David had asked if we could have our session near the cliff top, he said he wasn't much in the mood for being cooped up indoors.

We head off using the Carriages, waving goodbye to a different Conductor, an older woman with white hair and a beaming smile. The relationship between Mr. Yurzie and this tower was so strong, I had the impression he couldn't rotate locations easily, but everyone needs a day off. I wondered how the Conductors switched towers, but the Conductor called the nearest Carriage just as easily. It became obvious she too possessed the same relationship as Mr. Yurzie; all the Conductors must have one with every single tower in Tarias. The task must require a staggering amount of work to achieve given the primal power that lived within the structures.

She sends us off toward the mountain's higher elevations on its eastern side. There are more trails and trees in this less populated part of the mountain. David walks ahead of me, all gorgeous in his ball cap and polo shirt. He looks at me with his heavenly smile and I stumble as a result. He should know better not to do that to me. We take the ascending trail up the mountain and arrive at a plateau near its edge.

It was far past Spirit Manor and the primary academic buildings but closer to the Mansion, home of the Lords. I am sure that was not the official name, like Spirit Manor was only a nickname referring to the home filled with nothing but psychics. I had yet to see it myself, but if it is anything like the Manor, I am sure the title fits perfectly.

We stand on Lola's retreat, a mountain cliff. David and I were working on Transvection and, as my powers have developed, I induce some elements of this magik through my own innate ability. However, I have not mastered all the skills for flight, so I still require some spellwork to compensate. It's a bit like riding a bike with training wheels. I had been putting in extra hours for just this occasion, but I had not known all that would be involved with today's tutoring.

He was holding my hands, my sweaty slippery hands, and was reciting the spell. It felt as if the ground beneath was vibrating with the enveloping tenor of his voice, deep and sweet. My mind was transfixed, stumbling on my words and having difficulty focusing on my intention, an absolute must for the spell. All I could manage was to keep my hands that refuse to remain dry, from shaking within his own. I command myself to breathe, short inhales, long exhales.

Finally regaining some component of control, I say the words with certainty, reciting the spell five times.

Adversi Gravos Aeros Luneayr Awnji Phenaciarial

He lets me go.

The spell makes up for the missing components of my magik. There is a subtle change in the atmosphere and my appearance, a result of this push against gravity. My hair and clothes sway as if I was underwater, flowing in the direction of some invisible current. The magik travels within me in a constant wave, it phases in and out of every inch of my body.

The rocks and vegetation around me stir as if being disturbed by the wind. At a snail's pace, I begin to rise into the air, my feet no longer touch the rocky terrain and I hover shakily a few inches above the ground.

I try to use the vibrations of my power to lift me further up. Struggling with my movements, I lower back down for a minute. David instructs me to think and move in an inverted fashion, like piloting an airplane. I concentrate, trying to press down and hover up once more, now three feet above the floor.

It's an odd feeling, levitating felt like falling, but Transvection was like swimming in the sea. It does not require any physical movement, but there is still an element of engagement and is just as effortful as running.

I find myself struggling to control my direction and end up floating in circles. David returns to me, pulling me in close to his chest to keep me steady, as if we were preparing to dance. I could feel the warmth of his breath.

"Is everything alright?" He asks, while maintaining his position and prompting me to adjust mine.

He reaches for my hands, I quickly dry these mutinous palms against my jeans and nod, and he holds them firmly in his own. His face angles and hovers against mine. He arranges his body to enclose my own, something about the way he looks at me spark a memory of home. I quickly push the thought away. My magik failed me just then and was momentarily supported by his alone. I re-chant the incantation and separate myself from him, reorienting to the task.

I refocused, deep down I knew David was not interested in me, not in that way, and it was wrong of me to think differently.

"Sorry," not wanting to be rude, "Thank you for the help, really."

"Not a problem."

"Come on," he says, urging me to fly toward his direction.

"We are going somewhere else," I ask.

Exasperated, "Remember No-El, don't ask a question with a statement."

I roll my eyes and hold my position. Perfect boy or not, I was not in the mood to hurry. I wanted to take my time learning this magik.

"Oh, come on, No-El, please. It's a surprise, a good one."

Intrigued, I gradually float toward him.

"Awesome! It's time for the real thing," he exclaims as he grabs my hand and leads me toward his surprise.

The hell it is!

Ten minutes later, as the setting sun sends its final kiss to Mt. Tarias and her inhabitants, we arrive at our destination. He brought me to the edge of Lola, the mountain's most bizarre cliff edge. He intended on using this spot to serve as a pseudo obstacle course rather than a random training spot, but it was more like a plateau of death.

The drop off was home to a clearing of natural, jagged rock towers that were skinny as trees and tall like skyscrapers. They were spaced apart at various distances with empty crevices in between them. Falls from these heights promised certain death. He wanted me to jump from one rock to another until I crossed the clearing to the safety of solid ground on the other side.

"Let's do this," he says as he lifts himself up, effortlessly gliding toward the next mark. If it were not for my envy, and my utter terror, I would have praised him right then and there for his skill.

Instead, I cry out, "This is too hard. My energy is weak right now." It was not, but my inexperience in flight made me less inclined to continue the exercises.

"No, it's not. Quit your whining and give it a shot."

I grunt and fuss fruitlessly. David would give me no sympathy, and then I thought, wow, normally I would be kind of ticked if someone told me I was whining, a huge blow to my ego. Counterintuitively, I felt a sense of pride. I was growing up.

David was standing, hand outreached, motioning for me to follow suit while I stood there, statue-still. He breaks down in laughter and I struggle to find the humor.

"Okay, you ready," his eyes now set on the first target.

I say nothing.

He looks at me, "Come on No-el," and he returns his gaze to the target, "And stop rolling your eyes at me."

How did he know? "I wasn't."

"Right, sounds like a load of bull," and he laughs as I return to my strike. "Now on your feet soldier." I breathe out deeply and repetitively, or what David likes to call "shamelessly sighing".

"No," I say flatly.

Admittedly, I disliked being told what to do, and worse complying with forced directives, but he turns on the charm now that he knows I am serious. "Please," he implores with his pretty brown eyes. More eye roll, but then I see his desperate face. I roll my eyes once more for good measure, but ultimately give in. "Fine, but if I die it's on you."

We still focused on Transvection, but this training would be different from the spell we used earlier. David had broken down today's exercise to exactly four steps.

Jumping, no magik required, was the first step. Second, push myself up into the air with the same force I used on the chair earlier today. Third, use levitation to float. Finally, gradually release the levitation, allowing my body to float slowly down to the ground. It was like learning different sequences of a dance; separately the moves do not make sense, but create a show when combined.

It was hard. I needed intense concentration and energy, a constant flux of force, and a steady supply of magik. It was difficult to maintain.

I take his hand and we leap toward the first target, and after several leaps, I complain once more, "This is exhausting, I didn't know I was going to be working-out tonight."

Apparently not for David, I had to give it to him. The guy knew what he was doing. He was steady in his movement, unphased by the use of his power. For him, it seemed as effortless as riding an escalator.

"Gross, you're the worst, why are you showing off?" And there he goes, laughing away while I am dying.

Most Witches do not master Transvection, let alone demonstrate such ease and grace during individual flights. Yeah, grace, David flew with grace. I thought if superheroes existed, they would fly like him.

Meanwhile, here I am jumping from rock to rock, spread-eagled with arms flailing about, desperate to catch whatever surface I descend to which were more like crash landings.

We had been practicing for a little over an hour and I was legitimately starting to struggle; David hadn't even broken a sweat. If David knew my eyeballs had fallen out from rolling their way out of their sockets, he gave no hint or clue of the sort. How much of a magik reservoir did he have?

David literally had to play superhero and rescue me, more than once. I fall into his arms for him to catch me, briefly spinning him out of his own orbit, ending with a loud thud once we hit the ground.

It was mortifying.

In any case, David being David did not take long to assess safety concerns. He closes our training session the second he saw my strength truly waver. Oddly, he asked me to stay a bit longer and said he wasn't ready to go home just yet.

"No more practice," he reiterates, ensuring that I did not misunderstand his intentions and think it would be okay for me to push myself any further. "Just to hang out."

His mood suddenly shifted from excited to, I don't know, something different. I thought maybe he was out of sorts, but I couldn't think of a single reason why.

I say yes automatically, not needing a reason to spend more time with him.

We sat at the edge of Lola, drinking water and eating a shared bag of trail mix. We talk well into the night.

He tells me about growing up in the rolling hills and lochs of Scotland, his mother country as he calls it, the one he visits during winter and summer breaks.

David is the eldest of three sons. His family lives in a literal castle. Their estate, as he defines it, is part of another Witch center known as Athru. It is kept hidden from Mortals with similar charms to the ones in Tarias. He mentions a vague reference to his family's extraordinarily private lifestyle, but does not elaborate further, even when I gently pressed for more.

Leroy had once explained to me David's background. I knew that his father's side of the family is one of the most powerful Legacies in the realm. The O'Faolain magikal lineage dates back over three millennia, making them one of the oldest Witch bloodlines. As a result, they are deeply entrenched in political and economic markets and other affluent circles, both Witch and Mortal.

Tonight, I discovered that one of the reasons he attended Tarias was because of a "fit" between his family and the political climate of the time, versus attending Oxford University of Witchcraft, the magik school of Athru.

One of the things I liked most about David was his carefree attitude. He had a way about him, even in the most stressful of times. His calmness was catching, a reminder that everything would be alright.

It was unusual to see him this way, how he looked away when we talked, and how his smile was flat and thin. He stares off, his eyes fixed at some point in the horizon, but I know he is not looking at the night sky or the land beyond. He was staring at something only he could see.

At that moment, it seemed to me that he was the saddest boy in the world.

"Are you alright," I ask quietly.

It is a long time before he says anything at all. The silence screams and for the life of me. It seems to be begging me to say something, anything, to make everything okay, but in all my life, words don't really make anything right again, even magikal ones. Like the chair Maria fixed, it looked essentially the same, but it wasn't. If you compared the original to the repaired one you could tell the slight, subtle, and singular difference between the two.

I decided to wait rather than saying anything. After a few minutes, he shifts in his seat, clears his throat, and looks at me.

"Sorry, everything is fine, just a rough day."

"Did something happen?"

His eyes dart back and forth as he mulls over some thought, scaling out costs and gains of some unknowable kind.

"Yeah, sorta," he pauses. "My parents, they've been arguing lots lately, and they're talking about getting a divorce."

Another devastatingly long pause, "Me da, sorry, I mean my father. He doesn't care about her, only himself, and maybe whatever girl he's picked up for the night."

David tells me about his parents' marriage, which was originally a love story, making it all the more tragic. His father, an aristocrat, and his mother, a Witch raised primarily in the mortal world, the second to Manifest out of her known family line. David's grandmother was the first, a Recessive Witch. She somehow managed to avoid being recruited by any magikal school and was entirely self-taught in her Craft. She provided what little magikal instruction she could to her daughter,

David's mother. They were the equivalent of commoners in the Witch world, very similar to Maria and her mother.

He tells me stories over the kind nature of his mother and grandmother, "They raised me to be humble, to think about others, and to be grateful. To be good, ya know?"

He believed that it was something he would lack, if his father's side of the family had raised him.

"Probably end up just as selfish as him and the other entitled pricks I grew up with."

I cannot think of a single thing to say. Other than what he has told me so far, I don't know anything about his parents. Come to think of it, I don't really know much about him at all, and I suddenly feel very small and out of place.

With all the sincerity inside me, I manage to say, "I'm sorry." The words come out quickly and without hesitation, but I know enough to say that, at least. Something about how David looks at that very moment, lost, I think. Well, it breaks my heart.

For the first time, it seems David O'Faolain is the one who needs help. I was about to start asking all these questions, trying to talk, trying to fix, trying to help, and just trying to know the boy who saw me drowning. The boy who jumped in without any apprehension, to not only save me but also teach me how to save myself.

I did not think I was teaching David how to swim; I don't think I could, but at minimum, I was letting him know he was not alone.

And maybe that was enough, a little bit of peace returned. So, I sat there and listened. After an hour or so, we say our goodbyes and I hug him as tight as I could.

"I'll see you tomorrow."

I take the Carriage back to Spirit Manor and as I lay in bed, my restless thoughts over tonight's events unfold like a tapestry in my mind. I realized that David had never flown like that around me, not before today. I've seen him levitate in our past sessions, but never like today.

I knew he was talented, but I did not know the extent of his abilities. I wondered why he had not shown me his impressive skills before, true I was initially annoyed, but mainly because I thought I was going to die out there at Lola. It is also true that I was envious, but that would never stop me from celebrating him. It might have been helpful back then, offering me some kind of inspiration.

Then again, I wasn't exactly feeling or doing very well, magik wise, for a while when we first started. It may have been more discouraging than motivating. I think he was trying to be nice and I realize that might have been the kindest thing he could have done.

He really was perfect.

I commit to hold this memory tightly in my mind. Maybe one day, years from now, I could look back on this moment with fondness. This moment, filled with so much uncertainty, but without any of the life altering complications so often accompanied by the chaos of my life. One of the precious few afforded to me, to just be an ordinary boy.

Unable to sleep, despite my fatigue, I decide to spend the rest of the night practicing Transvection and eventually exhaust myself enough to let sleep take me away. It would have been a perfect night if not for those insufferable and incessant dreams.

Chapter Eighteen

Tip: Do not invoke the Celestial entity of Chronos when casting Temporal magik, this deity tends to be rather possessive of time.

My bad dreams have gotten worse and I felt dirtier each night that passed by, but even worse were the screams from Sam and Nina. I obsessively send silent prayers throughout the day in the hope that some Heaven existed for them, while sending another prayer for Charles Daley to rot a little more in hell. I hated that I could not think of them without thinking of him.

For the past two weeks I have been staying up late every night, training until the sun nearly rose. It was my hopeless attempt to escape those wretched dreams. My body weighed heavily from sleep deprivation. I feared my insomnia was finally catching up to me, even walking required concentration.

After Conjuration finally ends, I head straight to the Manor. It was my off day from booster sessions and training when I heard David's voice calling my name. I turned around to see him, handsome as ever. It had been two weeks since David and I talked about his parents. Even though he was going through the difficulties and uncertainty of his parent's possible divorce, he managed to maintain his smile and almost palpable indifference that came along with being sure of himself, nothing like me with all my neuroticisms and insecurities. I found myself wishing I could be a little more like him.

Although every now and again I would catch him looking down, his pretty brown eyes listless, as he withdrew himself to the inner workings of his mind. David being David would just as easily return to his old self, causing me to second guess what I saw in the first place.

Every time I asked him how he was doing, David would deepen his voice and say he was "pure barry". When I asked about his parents, he would just sort of grunt, "dunno" and quickly change the subject. After a few tries, and out of respect for his need for privacy, I stopped asking.

Today was easier as David was focused exclusively on one objective, me. He seemed to have an alarm inside him, notifying him anytime I wasn't doing well. He was always calling me out on my moods and, worst of all, would never let it go without asking me at least 20 questions. For the most casual guy in the world, he certainly was not easy-going about my feelings. He was always trying to fix me.

"I'm fine," I say a little too quickly. I tell him I am just tired and want to go home. For anybody else, that would be that, but not with David, it was never that easy.

"Come on No-El."

He insisted on walking me home even though he had his own specialized training to attend, a class focused on some type of advanced magik. He would miss it if he didn't leave now, not that he cared. After I refused to let him walk me home, he followed me like a stray dog. I repeat myself for the fifth time, "I am fine."

He starts making several jokes, awful one-liners that fail to be funny, in an attempt to engage me in conversation. I do a fairly good job at ignoring him, but then he tells me the most terrible joke yet, "You shouldn't be alone. Hey Noah, did you know loneliness can cause mental health issues?"

I remain silent.

"It's true. That's why there's an 'I' in den-I-al."

"What, that barely even makes sense," this guy. It was so bad I couldn't help but burst out laughing. He could always get me.

And that was it. Clearly, I had a love struck crush on David. He is after all the most perfect boy in the world, but I was in love with him in the way all crushes love, with heart-stopping passion, but from a very far off distance. In that moment, I realized I had more than just a crush. I was devastatingly in love with David O'Faolain in the non-refundable kind of way.

"Can I come up," David asked as I turned the knob of the Manor's oversized door.

I should say no, I was tired and needed to rest. Also, I had a funny feeling in the pit of my stomach, like a warning. I think it was trying to tell me to say no and just go to bed. It didn't make sense, it was only David and he would never hurt me, what was there to warn me about?

The thing is, I don't want him to go. "Fine," I say instead, but this time with a smile. I justify to myself that I will have difficulty falling and staying asleep regardless. We head inside the Manor and walk up to my room.

I change into jeans and a sweatshirt while David waits outside the ensuite bathroom. Now that I have admitted to myself that I am indeed infallibly in love with him, changing in front of David felt awkward and wrong. I was in the middle of practicing the pronunciation of an incantation while brushing my teeth when David asked why I was "obsessed" with all this training.

"I wouldn't say I'm obsessed."

"Well you spend every day doing some new spell, it's a lot, No-El," adding "I know I am your tutor, but I like hanging out with you. I wouldn't mind doing, you know, other stuff, like playing a video game or watching one of your feelings films if it would mean I didn't have to do homework to hang out with you."

He likes hanging out with me, I think that is the strangest thing. He was right of course. I had been doing a lot of training and, truthfully, was overly focused on it. I had neglected almost every other component of my life; I do not remember the last time Maria and I hung out. As far as David goes, excluding the night he opened up to me, I could not think of the last time we talked about something other than magik.

"Sorry, I didn't realize how preoccupied I was with my studies. I'll make it up to you."

David considered that for a moment, "Well you have been very inconsiderate, I think you may owe me a movie tonight? In fact, I think I deserve to oversee the selection, something violent."

I roll my eyes so he can see, "Okay," as David obnoxiously grins my not-so-favorite smile of his.

"Is it alright if you come over, we have the movie theatre set up at the Mansion, it makes for great viewing? Plus, I'm getting stir crazy hanging out at my house with those loons running about, you would be a good change of company."

He looked small then. It reminded me of the night he shared with me the things happening with his mother and father. "Sure thing, it'll be a nice change of pace."

Thirty minutes later we arrive at the Mansion, and it is a mansion. A federal colonial style home with wings off to each side and decorative embellishments, announcing wealth and prestige with its ornamentation. Tall columns and grand curved steps lead up to the entrance, with broad windows in perfect symmetry on both sides of the structure. It had a flat-roof wraparound porch on every level, intricately connected and designed into the home.

We walk into the foyer and climb the extravagant winding staircases that zigzag up and into the various floors, with wide hallways and tall ceilings. David leads me forward toward the Lords dormitories, and then to his room.

To say it was untidy would fringe on delusional, his room is distinctly dissimilar to the crisp and clean elegance of the Mansion. I felt unsettled just sitting there, and I am not typically disheveled over clutter, but David's room was a disaster.

Scattered clothes, underwear, I tried not to blush. "Oh my god, how do you live like this?" He laughs, "It's just stuff Noah, it won't hurt you, all this is clean anyway."

It was true. Surprisingly, his room did not smell despite the full trash can and half-eaten pizza box on his desk. David may have been living in an OCD nightmare, but it was relatively clean in terms of hygiene, that or his collection of various colognes masked any offensive odor.

His room smelled of something sweet and robust, a scent that resided in between the world of flowers and forests. I guess that is the intent of colognes, blending beauty and strength.

David is making his way through the room, hurriedly tidying up odds and ends, and apologizes for the clutter. I have not seen him move that fast in all the time we've spent together. Almost nervously I add, "No worries, it's your organized chaos, right," attempting to brush off his frazzled energy.

I sit there on his plush bed and notice something else, a different kind of smell, musky. Then, as if I didn't know it before, I became acutely aware of the fact that I am sitting on the place David sleeps, where he lies in bed and his body touches the sheets.

I wonder if he sleeps without a shirt or with anything, and I feel something in my belly, something new, a combination of exhilaration and terror. I distract myself, forcing my mind to not think about him that way.

In love with him or not, he was my friend, and he did not deserve to be disrespected. He takes a seat beside me. His face is flushed, and he wears this sheepish smile while shoving his hands in his pockets.

"Ready for that movie," he asked, while I tried to avoid eye contact.

"Yup."

"Right, well let's get to it, No-El."

David sits next to me while we watch the aggressive film. He steals glances at me when he laughs at the violent scenes, expecting me to laugh along with him. I purposefully stare away every time he looks in my direction. I found the gory scenes more annoying than comical which was worsened by my sleep-deprived irritability.

In the middle of the movie, he asks, "You seem a wee restless, would you like to take a walk with me instead?"

Absolutely, anything but this, however his sudden indifference did leave me slightly concerned, "This is the movie you've been dying to see, why would you want to stop?"

"Yeah, I know. It's just that, well, it's nice out and I could use the fresh air."

Reason enough, the movie was awful. I needed to return to the Manor and should be heading back, but then I see it in him again, how his eyes grow dull. Only it's different, this time he is smiling calmly but his eyes remain tragically sad. It reminded me of a grieving man accepting his loss. Fatigue aside, David wins me over effortlessly, "Sure," I say easily.

We are by a large willow tree, near Lola. I stare up at the clear sky. It was dark out despite the bright moon and low stars, but the air was cool and pleasant, spring is alive and well.

Feeling scared of getting into trouble was easier to deal with than feeling bad about leaving him alone. I was a little mad about that, not at David, but at me for thinking of him first; so typical of me. However, the reality was, I would hate myself if I left just now.

Although exhausted, it wasn't so bad being out of the house, hanging out with my best friend, breaking the rules and using, albeit clumsily, my newfound power.

Beneath me is clear air and the ground several feet below my dangling feet. I had only recently mastered the bare minimum levels required for Transvection, nowhere near the expertise level of David.

None of that mattered; I loved what I could do.

I stretched my arms out, opening my chest to the sky as I bent backwards. Settling into position while floating higher, my feet naturally point towards the ground when I lay on my back, resting on nothing but magik and air. I allowed the cool breeze to push and pull me a bit, which made me feel like I was the wind, if only for a moment. But something about the air touching me triggers my Sight, making me gasp.

Another invasion of my mind. This time images flash through my Vision. I can make out shapes and colors, but they all seemed blurred into one another. I cannot say what I See because of the sheer overwhelming number of them. I fall to the ground.

David flies down swiftly, catching me.

"You alright," his worry plain on the creases of his brow.

They stop.

"Sorry, I'm okay. I promise, I don't know what happened."

His eyes widened with concern, and I automatically lied, "It was the wind, I got distracted by the wind." He seems unconvinced but does not press. I right my position, backup, and hover once more on my own magik.

The Visions were gone. I had not asked Madam Reyna about these weird disturbances; I had meant to, but my forgetfulness got the best of me. These psychic disturbances were getting worse and increasing in frequency. I promised myself to ask tomorrow and returned my attention to David.

David settles himself on a branch only a short distance away from me. My most handsome distraction. He then announces, "This is my favorite time of the year."

He looks sad again, I have a war with myself to not investigate his mind but decided better of it, I will not do that to him. I was hovering next to him in the literal sense.

"How are you," I ask.

"Fine, I guess." His voice is flat with the faintest tone of struggle. He was not mean, nor did he sound annoyed, but he seemed empty, as if reaching for something. Yeah, that is what it was, he had no feeling at all, and all at once I am worried about him.

I try to remain casual, "So what's going on?"

He looks away and reconsidering something inside for a moment, but then looks directly into my own eyes. His eyes slightly glazed over, ready for tears to escape, and my heart stings at the sight of it. I sink slowly to the ground and catch myself focusing on us, and I rise back up, steady and sure. David is my friend and, no matter what, I am going to be there for him.

The wind tugs our clothes, but I remain unmoving, and ready to listen.

"What's wrong," I ask in unapologetic desperation. He sits there and his tearful, beautiful brown eyes are the only tether holding me to the earth, the only gravity that keeps my position in this spot of the universe. Everything in me was willingly tied to him, for him, my never-ending attempt at saving David.

After a few minutes, he finally talks. There was an unfamiliar hoarseness to his voice, as if strained. He breaks down and tells me about the fighting between his mom and dad. It is the worst it has ever been. His mother is moving out. How his younger brothers call him each night crying and scared, they tell David how they don't want their mum to go. Finally, he reveals, "They're going through with it, to finalize the divorce."

I just hug him and tell him that I am sorry and that I wish it were better, holding him in my arms. I've never felt this feeling, this need in me to protect someone from all the evil in this world.

A few minutes later, David is eager to end the night. I think he might be embarrassed by the sudden display of emotion and insists on taking me home. I tell him I am fine but then he gets upset and even raises his voice when he says my name. He followed his little tantrum with an awkward apology and one last endearing attempt. "Please Noah, let me do this," he says to me with serious eyes.

So, I agree, he rarely calls me by my actual name these days. I have a feeling that is not a good sign, so I concede.

"Okay."

He takes me home and when we get to the Manor, he hugs me closely, so close that his lips are only a few inches away from my neck.

"Thank you for being my very best friend," he says in a whisper.

A half hour later, against my better judgment, I check on him using my Sight. It is a violation of his privacy but I need to be sure he is okay. I See him as he lays in bed, sleeping soundly, and I am glad for that. Now reassured of his safety, I quickly end the Vision, restoring his right to seclusion.

It was late but I decided to shower. I figured it was my best chance at a decent night's rest. It happened while the water softly rained down from the shower. At first, I hear my name being called followed by a repetitive message, *evil is at the wake*. It is neither psychic nor a physical kind of hearing, rather something else and I know with absolute certainty I am hearing voices.

I am losing my mind.

I force myself to lie in bed, but I toss and turn for an hour. Those wretched dreams violate me with scenes of Charles Daley and the screams of Sam and Nina every time I drift off. Too tired to fight it away, I eventually succumb to sleep and remain in the pandemonium.

The next few hours are riddled with nightmares of him, but I no longer have the strength to fight. As in life and now in death, he unravels me once more. Only now there are other dreams, so many of them, dreams that I know do not belong to me, and I am lost all over again.

Chapter Nineteen

To create a talisman of acquiescence, at midnight, enchant your diamond by performing the Nine Celestial Giant sequence while reciting the following incantation:

Duemocion

Repeat this ritual every night for thirteen years.

He sees himself and does not understand.

What is happening? I am in my room floating several feet above my bed, my eyes are shut, and my arms lie limp to my sides. The students of the Manor, including Madam Reyna and Miss Penelope, surround me.

He sees It. He thinks of the sea and lights from the North.

What is that magik emanating from me, or from the body that is supposed to be mine? The energy pushes and pulls at the people and objects near my physical form. It reminds me of the aurora borealis.

He hears It and still does not know.

Who is that talking? Who are you? What do you want?

He sees them. He sees her as she calls to him.

Miss Penelope and my housemates run back and forth bringing supplies to Madam Reyna, all the while dodging objects that fly in a small cyclone around me.

He sees another power and does not approve of the restraint.

There is a force tying me down, tugging at not just me, but everyone and everything.

The energy produced by his planet.

Gravity, is that what this is, can I see gravity?

He is scared.

I try to call out to the others, but I exist in the space of the room and this moment, but I think for a moment that I might be dead.

He wants to run away.

Instead, I inch closer to my own body in search of a connection, a way back inside.

He looks at his physical body. He thinks it glows like moonlight. He goes away now.

My body remains, but I cannot as I stare out at the wonder and enormity of the Moon. I am in the space that holds the luminary giant, then suddenly on her surface, tucked deeply within one of her craters.

Turning my Vision, I See the glory of the Earth in all her majesty. The sound of it is haunting and invigorating all at once, but there are other sounds that I can hear in what seems to be the incredibly far off distance.

He is opening his eyes.

I am transported once more into something beyond anything I have ever experienced. In awe of all the pretty things, I now stare out at the panoramic image of the true galaxy, in its utter glory and impossible size.

It is like seeing the sierra of the Grand Canyon from the eyes of an orbiting shuttle. I notice it all, yet with each time I look upon it, there is something new; something I had not seen before.

What else could I See out there in the vast Universe? The Vision distorts and I go somewhere far away. Upon my arrival, I immediately sense the splitting of boundaries between physical reality and some vast darkness that I cannot give name to, something beyond my comprehension.

It pulls at my psychic self, threatening to tear it apart. I can feel my physical body breathe faster in the vast distance. It is dragging me into something unknown and impossible. I scream for it to stop.

Suddenly I am returned to the Earth's upper atmosphere. I can feel the breath of my body, down far below, slowly return to its normal pace. And I know, without really understanding how, that I was in a black hole.

He is learning.

Looking down at the Earth, I focus on small parts and then, shifting to the broader perspective, try to understand the experience, but I am consumed by the dynamic chaos that exists in life. It is unfathomable.

He remembers the word Occhiolism.

Yes, the awareness of the smallness of your perspective. Everything from the smallest particle to the largest cosmic giant, all maintain their ambiguous wonder.

He sees them, the colors. He is understanding.

It all has an energy, a vibration that impacts and goes beyond all that we think we know about the world. All the colors I could not see.

I smell the rancid odor oozing from today's waste but what I thought was disgusting now contains a certain awe. The invasiveness of it, how it thrusts itself upon the air, the active effort of the odor that is produced by the waste.

It forces the living away in an effort for us to live another day. I can see its purpose, protecting the life growing within to protect the life growing without. I wish David could see all the wonders of the planet.

He is lonely. He thinks of Sonder.

The realization that each passerby has a life as vivid and complex as yours. Life is the most unstable force of all. Those alive are animation in action. They push and pull against the physical world, affecting worlds far beyond.

What is this, a thing that is far away, and yet all around me? It looks like light bending in a mirror's reflection, incomprehensible. An endless world of possibility living in its image.

He sees time.

Lost in the trails of it, I am with David. He is getting off the phone with his father, and then I am with the person on the other side of the call, David's father. He sits in a large circular office, his face reveals a man lost in regret, but it fades quickly and he returns his attention to the papers surrounding him.

In the next moment I am led through Maria's timeline. She pulls her hair up into a ponytail as she walks into class.

She calls him back.

Madam Reyna.

She tries to stop him, but he does not want to go now.

I See Maria and her future. There was a set path in her steps leading toward it. She was in Abjuration. She would struggle to cast the defensive shield to buffer the concussive offensive spell cast by a student named Trae. She would be too late. Her arm would be broken from the blast.

He changes time.

I could sense and See her distracted thoughts during the event. I change her thoughts and redirect them to the assignment, while offering her the words needed to successfully cast the spell. Suddenly, the timeline shifts, and the image vanishes.

The lost future is replaced with something new, and in this version, Maria summoned the defensive spell with ease. She counteracts Trae's spell and avoids ending the day with the Healers. There will be no injury to mend.

She pulls at him.

Madam Reyna is casting some sort of spell. I am back in my own room, but I was not out of this psychic reverie. I have 360-degree awareness, but it was too much. Although I could sense the experience, my mind could not keep up with it. My attention shifted from the ultraviolet rays to the soil of the Earth and the people living and dying on these lands.

I am at a funeral now.

A mother cries as she grabs at the air within the grave, desperate for her baby to return to her, or at the very least, to go along with him.

Unintentionally and unwillingly, I thought of the cursed house on Grayson Road and suddenly I am at the place of my nightmares.

The house where I lived, and Sam and Nina died. Strangely, it remained intact. I thought it had been demolished. I wondered if I was in the past now. It is exactly as I remembered it, sticking out like a crooked tooth and already rotten at the root from the salted earth.

He remembers.

It was as if I was walking. My psychic sense was made small and tight, like how it was during the days I lived here, desperate to avoid being seen or heard. The leaves and grass felt brittle, although they were undisturbed by my psychic presence, it seemed as if they still broke under the intangible pressure. The air reeked of decay.

The smell of the dead.

He feels something that he calls pity.

I felt sorry for it, this house with broken bones. It was like me, it never asked to be here or to receive what it was given. It was made, then used, and ultimately desecrated.

Uselessly, I tried my best to not think of this time and place, but for some unfair reason this reference point would forever be etched in my memory. If this had been any other circumstance, I would have quickly shut the thought out as easily as I would a door, but I could not manage this unfamiliar magik.

I remain frozen, lost in time, in the home that destroyed me.

His monster returns.

And then I hear him.

I think for a moment that he has returned from somewhere deep in hell, even though I understand now that this Vision is of the past.

Charles kicks the younger me in the lower back; forcing me out of the backdoor. I must have been nine years old. He pushes me to the ground and starts tearing into my skin with a thick rope that he used as a whip. This one was reserved specifically for me. He tells me I am a "fucking waste" and that I am "no better than a hole in the ground," and a "nasty faggot, begging to be filled." He unbuckled his belt and brought his jeans down, but not before slamming my face into the ground. I can even now taste the blood.

The horror I thought long forgotten overwhelms me. I feel myself beginning to shatter, cracks into my psyche, their lines form shards ready to break away. All the pieces of me so desperately desire to escape the pain that lives inside.

There is so much anger and sadness and a thousand other things that I do not understand. The war in me implodes and, without meaning to, I send a psychic shockwave that transports me out of this moment in time into something beyond and unknown.

He hears them. All of them. She has called him home.

There is a purple and pulsating energy surrounding and enveloping my Vision, but I am frozen in the grip of fear and unable to do anything to help myself.

I woke up a few hours later, my psychic explosion must have damaged me because, all at once, thousands of voices and images blare at me, both deafening and blinding me.

In pure irony, Madam Reyna turns out to be my savior. She cast many spells to help me contain my power, we sat down in meditation for hours until day turned to night and the moon shone bright and high in the sky.

For two nights I could not keep them out, the voices and Visions, all nonsensical ramblings of a hodgepodge of thoughts and feelings. The noise was everywhere, and I was losing track of what was mine and what was theirs. The experience made me appreciate my own thoughts. As sad and pathetic as they could be, at least they were mine.

It took a herculean effort to organize a thought, and sleep was a nearly hopeless endeavor as I could slip into unconsciousness for only minutes at a time. I should not have been able to hear everyone else's thoughts, not in the Manor, but the spells used to ward that kind of intrusion could not suppress me.

Madam Reyna taught me how to do something known as taking witness, basically experiencing the phenomena without being controlled by it. Finally, late into the night, I started to regain a miniscule amount of control.

Maria was by my side. It was her that I focused on, grounding me.

"The moon, our guardian, she is the Witch's mother and we of the Seer kind are her most favored children," says Madam Reyna, in a sing-song manner.

Closer to dawn, and with my sanity returning, Maria and I look at each other and laugh softly at Reyna's inevitable, bizarre behavior. Our fears of Madam Reyna must be diluted, most likely because of our delirium.

Madam Reyna, in very unlike Madam Reyna fashion, ignores the slight. We resumed our work toward regaining my full self-control. We were calming the storm of my power and closing gates. There were so many, I closed one and felt a little bit more like me.

Once I am stabilized, Madam Reyna gathers her things and prepares to leave. I hug her before she walks out the door. I don't know what came over me. She hugged me back. I don't know what came over her either.

Maria kisses me on the forehead, wishing me a goodnight, despite it being noon. Madam Reyna, in another surprising act of kindness, escorts her home.

I felt disgusting, but I dare not bathe. I was more likely to fall asleep and drown at this point. Instead, I made my way to bed and enjoyed the comfortable silence around me.

I would forever be grateful to Madam Reyna and Maria. They saved me. I had no more thoughts to think, only dreams, but sneaky dreams that I do not recognize, with wild tales find me. I wake up wondering what damn gate I left open. It was an hour after dinner and I felt like a new me, but several days without bathing leaves me smelling like some corpse-version of myself. I head off to take a shower.

I popped up from brushing my teeth, spitting out toothpaste to face my reflection. Many things have changed for me since the episode. Madam Reyna refers to it as my "psychic evolution". Firstly, my eyes now occasionally, and randomly, illuminate a fluorescent blue. They are literally glowing as I stare into the mirror.

I shrug it off, finish changing, and step out of the bathroom. My room was inundated with flowers, balloons, and boxes filled with various food and objects of comfort. Gifts from the Mastersons, Maria, David, my housemates, the Doc and Miss Penelope.

I called the Mastersons to reassure them I was okay. I had spoken with them the night before I returned to sanity. I think that terrified them because they then insisted on speaking to me on the hour and have been doing so non-stop until earlier that day, just like David.

He may have called constantly, but unlike the Mastersons, who were unable to visit, David did not come by to see me, not even once. I want to believe that he was worried about what I might hear, but somehow that makes it worse. Regardless, I could not identify one stream of consciousness from another.

I wondered how to turn it back on for a moment, if only to avoid it, and just like that I am in my mind's eye. I See them, the gates, there were so many of them. There were still some left open, I would have to attend to those later. No harm I guess; I am not hearing voices at present. I took comfort in the fact that I had some control. Shutting and opening these gateways required a conscious choice.

Strangely, each gate had a specific function, like one for hearing thoughts in proximity, a sort of level one in psychic skill, while another was for looking far into the distance, an advanced skill. It was going to take some time to make sense of it all. I decided to ask Naomi about this, or Madam Reyna, rather. She and I were on a first name basis, at least for now.

Maria arrived shortly after my shower. She refused to leave my side despite Madam Reyna's resistance. We didn't talk much as we were both starving and, thankfully, Ms. Penelope laid out one her famous trays filled to the brim with various items. Maria and I gorged on whatever we could fit into our hands. I was charged with seeing the Doctor and I wished I could be summoned for something other than a magikal disaster.

Maria and I must say goodbye preemptively but we promise to see each other soon. Admittedly, we were both being a bit melodramatic. After all, she was going to wait at the Manor until I got back.

Dr. Huebner does not offer me tea or biscuits when I arrive at his office. Instead, he immediately reminds me of an older lesson he covered some time ago, about something known as the Vilix Despirir, a rare gift that is considered to be the source of magik.

"Awareness of all directions Mr. Ellis and beyond that, this is your gift, the potential for omniscience."

He paused for a moment, "Heaven's Eye." The floor was swept underneath me, a phrase that had not made sense to me, until today.

"What? Dr. Huebner, you said very few are gifted, how do you know it's the true gift? I mean, I just saw some things, I didn't see everything or whatever."

"How was it, Mr. Ellis?"

Not wanting to answer, not wanting to admit to anything, I simply say, "It was terrifying." Yet, for some unknown reason, I cannot lie, "And it was beautiful."

"You saw true reality, no longer filtered by the limits of the flawed biological body or your formerly limited psychic powers, that is the first indication. The second was the show," but he abruptly stops, and has a vacant expression for a few brief seconds. What memory is he recalling? He clears his throat, "Excuse me, Mr. Ellis, I appear to have lost my train of thought. Oh yes, there it is, right where I left it."

He chuckles softly, and my panic subsides a bit, like none of this had to be taken seriously.

"During the use of the Vilix Despirir, there is always a tangible and visual appearance, a very peculiar phenomenon. Unlike most magikal abilities, the Vilix has an exceptionally specific type of illumination. Put simply, with the Vilix, you know it when you see it. Only advanced Seers with the gift can suppress this side effect. I, myself, have only seen it once before."

"What are you talking about?"

"The Corona Borealis, or what is also referred to as the Aurora Borealis. Do you not remember? Certainly, you saw yourself while using the Vilix Despirir, it would have been a spectacular light show?"

I remember now, "The Northern Lights."

"All the incredible things you must have witnessed. This is a gift young Ward," I suppose he can see the dissatisfaction on my face. "You have been blessed. There are few Vilix Despirir users to date in history, and even fewer Witches with the gift at present."

"I don't want this. I don't want that kind of power."

Given Dr. Huebner's enthusiasm, this should not have felt like a death sentence, but I cannot help but feel like I have been given one, call it a gut feeling.

"Do not worry, you won't be omniscient, the gift is limitless, and yet remains bound by the limitations of the user. You are a Witch, not a god. You cannot know everything, but you have the option to learn and know whatever you choose, and that is astounding."

We end our conversation anticlimactically. He wants to talk further about the Vilix, but I refuse, claiming fatigue from the event, and I abruptly and rudely excuse myself from the discussion.

As I walk up Spirit Manor's front steps, I find David and Maria waiting at the door, sitting in rocking chairs as they drank Miss Penelope's famous sweet tea. David held flowers and a bear. Maria, bless her, carried food.

They didn't have to do that.

I hug them both deeply. I had to explain the Vilix to Maria, David was already aware of its significance. I review what Dr.

Huebner told me about the Vilix, meanwhile David remains oddly silent.

"I don't understand what the big deal is, honestly, it just seems like a really good satellite," I joke. Maria laughs but then quite seriously asks, "What was it like?"

I hesitate, not wanting to admit the truth, but I have never been any good at pretending. "It's hard to explain. It was scary, overwhelming," I breathe in deeply, "But it was also incredible. I saw the planets. I saw the sun. I still can't make sense of it all."

Maria was briefly speechless until her words finally burst out, "Holy shit, Noah," covering her mouth as she gasps.

Maria had a date planned tonight with Aaron Fuerios, her now official boyfriend, they had been dating for about a month. A big deal for Maria, she refuses to leave but I stubbornly refuse to let her stay. I remind her that she has already stayed with me for well over 48 hours and needs to take a break, "Otherwise you might get sick of me."

We laugh as she hugs me one last time and makes me promise to not have another episode ever again. As she gets ready to leave, I say, "I hope Aaron appreciates his chance to date an amazing girl like you."

"I hope he does too, for his sake," she says as she swings her hair back, "Goodnight David, goodnight Big Blue." She quickly shuts the door before I can speak another word, knowing I hate that name.

Leaving David and I alone in my room. Despite feeling hurt over his absence during my psychic breakdown, I was still glad to see him.

"Thank you for all the flowers, it was very sweet. I missed you."

"Yeah, sorry mate, I had to take care of some things, but I called, did they tell you? I checked up on you a ton. I thought about you all the time," and then his eyes became watery, a very non-David-like behavior. "I was properly worried about you," he manages to mumble out in his endearing Scottish accent. I hug him, desperate to reassurc him that it rcally is all okay.

"Noah, thank the Spirits that you are okay. I am sorry I wasn't there."

"No worries, just thanks for being here now."

Finally, settling down after ten or so minutes, still sounding a bit down as he apologizes a few more times. I smile, and so does he, but his seems to hold a lingering sadness. It leaves me wishing I could cast a spell to banish that sadness so it could never hurt him again.

Chapter Twenty

Frequent and periodic maintenance spells will gradually extend the life of an enchanted or charmed artifact, and eventually require less frequent recharging. An accurate timetable for specific calculations on duration of this magik can be found in Owen Narva's textbook titled, Commitments: The Accumulation of Exhaustive Research on Maintenance Magik Collected over the Course of a Century.

It had been a week since the episode. The whole event seemed to have changed things. I was given attention that I could not stand or avoid. Madam Reyna, no longer on a first name basis with me, had taken it upon herself to privately tutor me on the use of my new power.

The long hours spent with her had quickly developed my access to the Vilix. I could easily summon the skill and was improving my control and use of magik as a result. Despite this, the Vilix was still overwhelming and left me dependent on Madam Reyna for both guidance and grounding.

I sit cross-legged on the hardwood floor facing her. She is wearing a long flowy white dress with her hair tied in a low ponytail. Now that she was being nicer to me, I could once again appreciate the beauty in her high cheekbones and delicate face. "Noah, I would like you to summon the Vilix once more," she instructs. I am not in the mood, but I close my eyes and focus, paying attention to my body.

My breath catches and then there is a sinking sensation in my belly, like falling. There is an abrupt feeling of weightlessness, but I am grounded somewhere in between my body and the area around me. I have a 360-degree view of the Observatory where Madam Reyna prefers to train me. I feel the varying temperatures and shifts of air pressure from one section to the next.

I sense these strange waves that I had not noticed before, they ripple back and forth as they impact the surfaces within the area. As I try to make sense of them, I am reminded of that odd voice I heard during the episode. The one that described what was happening as it was happening to me.

The voice has not returned since the episode. I have come to the belief that it was never there in the first place. Looking back on that night, I did not really hear words. Instead, it was more like ideas from some other perspective.

The Vilix is fundamentally pure and unfiltered awareness. If I were scared, it would recognize my fear. If I was in awe of the galaxy, it noticed my reaction to the cosmic bodies. The Vilix sees things as they exist, no more, no less. I think it was my own judgment of the intuitive knowledge that is the Vilix that caused the false perception of another entity's presence.

I can still feel that sensation, but it no longer seems two-sided. It's like wearing glasses. The Vilix offers clarity, but behind those glasses are my infinite number of thoughts that distort the truth. I understand what the strange waves are now.

Sound.

Madam Reyna's voice, the clock tower ticking away, and the sound of my own breath echo throughout the room. They are only a few of the many sources of the waves. It's incredible the way it lives, a true wrecking ball demolishing the air. Oh, and air, what a funny thing! It can be entirely disturbed and reconstructed in the same instant from the displacement.

Madam Reyna prompts me to "steer" the Vilix, but deliberate shifting was difficult. As it was, I was still learning how to stay in one vantage point, and I rarely changed focus by choice. One moment I was staring out at the Grand Canyon in all its wonder and in the next, a single pebble in the flowing riverbeds within its depths consumes me.

Lost in the texture and color of that pebble, and then to its subtle erosion caused by the running water, something that I would fail to notice with my limited physical vision. I follow its trails in time and take on each event, from being one with the warmth of the sun and another with the cold desert night. I can see its creation and destruction, scattered into nothing but particles and dust. Although its existence is transformed, that pebble maintains an enduring connection to all things. Witnessed by me, all from a spot many miles away, at the hidden realm of Witches inside the Rocky Mountains, specifically Madam Reyna's classroom.

There was a growing sense of gratitude building within me toward the Divination teacher. Her instruction has allowed me to experience the Vilix in this truly phenomenal way. If it were not for the extra training, I probably would have convinced myself that the Vilix was nothing more than a glorified spy cam, and it is so much more.

I want to dig deeper, but using it, especially in this way, is draining me. Fully aware that exhaustion leaves me vulnerable to an episode, I tread carefully in my prolonged use of the power. I decided to focus on the steering, and I am automatically taken to him, the most beautiful boy. This could be my favorite way of using the Vilix. He was walking down the spiral staircase of the Castle. I connected with the physical world around him, adjusting my vantage point within the air as he moved.

I dare not enter his thoughts, I have always disliked reading people's minds and invading their privacy, but ever since the episode I find the act particularly disdainful. Besides, I would never do that to David.

Guilt and anxiety suddenly overcome me. I didn't mean to spy on him, at least not with ill-intentions. What if he found out I was using the Vilix to watch him? I try to convince myself that it is impossible for him or any psychic to detect the gift. He would be furious if he knew, I think. All these fears, yet I continue to watch him, justifying that one more moment longer won't hurt. I did want to feel his lips, but I will not and at least I restrain myself from violating him in such a way, not my David.

My ethics finally win over my desire and I turn my attention elsewhere. I decided to focus on the Earth attempting to push the limits of this power. The sensations of life on Earth floods my senses and I gasp for air during the experience. It was too vast, I couldn't imagine what it would require connecting to everything, to experience the entire planet all at once; it is inconceivable. That is what they say the Vilix can do. It is only limited by the user, so I guess its limit is me. Realistically, though, how much can one person take?

Stubbornly, I pushed farther to challenge myself, the image shifts into something outside of perception. It is the world of thought. I marvel at the effect it has on our Universe. I see it in the future of a woman that is self-possessed, she believes in herself and her business. She is trying to create a legacy and one day she will. She does not know it yet, but her small business will be a Fortune 500 company, a self-fulfilling prophecy.

It is in the power of a dying man's prayer for the loved ones he will leave behind. It somehow maintains his presence after his death, providing them the solace he desperately prayed they would be given. It is in a novel thought, inventions that can and do change the world by convention, some cause war and others end them. The power to create and destroy.

Then I See something else, the only words I can find to describe it are Order and Chaos, these energies are reciprocally influential and binding.

I struggle to hold it and then I hear with my physical ears the sound of chanting. The melodic noise seeped into my mind until I finally open my eyes. I am back in the office and my body felt strange to me. My breathing is heavy and rapid, and I am crying.

The room has been destroyed, the walls are scorched, and the furniture burnt. There appears to be no evidence of the source responsible for the damage, until I look around me. Within the protective circle Madam Reyna and I routinely cast for my training is the only space in the room left mostly unaffected, as there are a few charred marks that infringe at its edge.

Surveying the damage, I am horrified by it and me, "What happened?"

"It's okay Noah, everything is alright, this is still very new for you," she says with sympathy, the kind of look people would give me when they found out I was a foster kid. My reaction is automatic, bringing me back to those days and the hell that lived there. It is in the way I always felt responsible for all the bad things that happened, as if I deserved it. I feel like that now, only a thousand times more intense because I was the reason for all the destruction.

"I'm so sorry," the tears fall without consent. Madam Reyna responds with uncharacteristic kindness, "Emotions are both a strength and an impediment for your abilities, strengthening and dampening your effectiveness. A quote from your beloved Guardian Crown, Dr. Huebner," something I read before in his lesson book, A Magikal Theory.

"Managing your emotions is top priority to gain mastery of your own mind and the Vilix Despirir," she says.

"Yes, ma'am." Madam Reyna requested my tutoring with David begin focusing on my use of the Vilix from an active magik perspective.

She reasons that because the Vilix is essentially the ultimate form of connection, the passive portion of magik, it was critical I rapidly develop mastery over as many active types of magik as possible.

Otherwise, I would be left vulnerable to influence either from my own emotions, as in the case of me nearly burning down the Observatory, or coerced through external sources, but she does not provide any specific information on who or what exactly would want to influence me. I asked her to elaborate on this several times, which only agitates her, and she shortly ends the session. She urges me out the door, insisting that she needed to place an emergency maintenance order to repair the damages to the classroom. I offered further apologies, but no longer sympathetic, she began yelling at me and demanded I leave immediately. She shuts the door as I walk out, and I can hear her complaint from the hallway, "Ever the same, insufferable child."

David and I sit on the top floor of the Castle the following day. It is entirely empty like it was reserved for our own personal use. We sit in meditation style; the oversized skylight reveals the bright stars and moonless sky.

Tall wooden bookshelves are scattered randomly throughout the room, along with low tables and variously colored low plush chairs. Splendid hunter green carpet mimics grass, simulating quite effectively the outdoors.

We have been meditating for an hour and my mind is restless. My legs have started twitching, I feel the edges of my skin and I cannot help but think of it as a cage. Every nerve in my body wants to burst out of itself and run for freedom from the jail sentence that is further meditation.

Unfortunately, each time I opened my eyes David, shortly after, opened his own. It's like he can sense me disengaging and is actively prompting me to return my focus.

"Ease back in. Just return your attention when it gets away from you," he says.

"It's so hard," and for some reason today it truly is more difficult than it has ever been to sustain my focus. I would rather spend time with David doing something fun or go downtown with Maria, anything but be stuck inside the Castle for another hour. A lightbulb turns on for me just then, I am obviously bored to tears but only because I'd rather be doing something else.

For the first time, I was not struggling to perform the magik. I just wasn't in the mood and that felt incredible. I would rather be lazy than incompetent. This was a first for me and the milestone offers a boost to my self-esteem, providing a renewed sense of energy and anticipation to the practice.

I activated the Vilix with ease and allowed myself to enjoy the rush of it. It was like skydiving, not that I have ever skydived, but I imagined that is what it would feel like.

I See us, David sits across from me and we are barely a foot apart. The world seems to slow down. The sounds of cars and birds and people began to fade, sounding further and further away.

There is a subtle pulling sensation that grabs every object and being, from the building to the birds. It is deliberate, steady, and continuous. I already know this one, it's gravity, holding us here. I see both the sky and the room as if I am looking at it from above, piercing through the walls, like x-ray vision, except I see the wall as well.

I began casting my power into the objects around me, levitating them with control, slowly and purposefully. I breathe in and out, and as my tension increased, so did the movements of my magik, each time feeling the object as it floated along, while I led the way. The Vilix expanded my range of magikal influence and enhanced its effect until every object, including the bookshelves and books placed within them, floated above us in circular patterns across the entire top floor.

After long hours with few breaks, Professor Libiski, the Librarian, tells us it is time to leave and I easily return every item to its original location. He ushers us out so that he can close the library from Preparatory students; the evening after-hours were reserved for older students completing their Dedication or Witches working on their Transcendence, the equivalent of a PhD.

It was a great day. I was able to use my gift and control it and was eager to generalize it with my other skills. All these months here I had struggled to keep pace and find my place as a Witch, but now it was all finally coming together.

David invites me to a camping trip this Saturday as we leave the Castle. He and his friends would be celebrating his birthday, "Would you be up for it?"

"Of course." Obviously I would do anything for David, especially for his birthday. I had to make time to visit the market to get him a gift, something special.

David yawns deeply, no doubt sleepy from all the meditation, his brown eyes look much darker in the absence of the Sun, but always retain their beauty. My appreciation for him skyrockets. The time he spent with me has made all the difference. In a rush, I hug him deeply, "Thank you David, for everything."

"It's been my pleasure, No-El," as he wraps his arms around me, at least until his body begins to stiffen, the event rapidly becomes terribly awkward. To my surprise, I had been hugging him for nearly twenty seconds, which does not seem significant, but friendly hugs don't usually last that long.

"Sorry," embarrassed, I stared down. "I'm just really grateful for everything, I couldn't have gone this far without you, thank you," I wanted to add, "for being you", but thought otherwise of it and said no more.

"You're alright, mate, hey and Noah, I may have helped, but you did this all on your own. You are more talented and courageous than you give yourself credit for."

"Thanks," in more ways than one. We smile at each other and we end the night walking our separate ways. I was barely able to keep my eyes open as I made my way to bed. Although I am excited over my own development as a Witch, and for the upcoming trip, I am exhausted from the intense and long hours.

I held Morgan close to my side and saw through the Vilix all his perfection. I drift into dreams and they are of benign things. One more generosity afforded to me and, tonight, my gratitude knows no bounds.

Chapter Twenty-One

Charisma
At the rising sun, and for seven days, in skyclad, conduct the Celestial Dance.
Invoke Eros at both the Start and the End.

"Sorry, I'm not going to be able to make it." My stomach dropped. It was the morning of his celebratory camping trip. I was still asleep when he called. He was supposed to pick me up. We were going to spend a whole night under the stars. Him and his friends of course, which thankfully included Maria, but it was a night with David. Now it wasn't going to happen.

"Sorry mate, something's come up."

I had secretly thought this trip was his way of making up for his absence during my most recent episode, but his last-minute cancellation leaves me doubting. I had to remind myself that it is his birthday and scold my mind for having such selfish thoughts. Still, why did it feel like the world was ending?

It was just disappointment. I knew what catastrophic days felt like and this was not one of them. While on the phone with him, I refrained from any kind of emotional expression, despite my desperation. I quietly say, "That's okay, I understand," even though I didn't, and kindly release him from his commitment,

"Take care of whatever you need to take care of, maybe next time?"

Silence.

And then David says, "Okay" and he struggles with what to say next and blurts out an "umm," and "mate," ending with a "dunno." I can hear him breathe, evaluating something I think, and I am tempted to use the Vilix, but I do not.

"No-El, uhm, we'll talk real soon, okay?" It wasn't what he said, but how he said it, slow and unsteady. I wondered if he was regretting the change of plans or maybe just regretting inviting me? My insecurities were threatening to tear me down, so I decided to shut them out by returning to bed. I thankfully fall asleep within minutes of laying my head on the pillow.

About a half hour later, loud knocking at my bedroom door rudely awakens me. My immediate thought was of the worst, my greatest fear brought to fruition, that behind that door was a school official charged with notifying me of some tragedy involving the Mastersons. I rush out of bed to answer but trip over my own two feet, landing on the floor. I hurriedly stand back up and open the door.

To my surprise and relief, I found David standing across the way. His eyes seem wet, his pupils dark and large, but there are no tears.

"Noah, I am sorry! I didn't mean it."

Still in my stupor, "What?"

"I wasn't canceling the trip. I thought it would be funny to pretend, like an April Fools' Day joke. I know it's not April. It was dumb. I really am sorry mate," he catches his breath. He must have ran all the way here.

He was playing a joke. "So, you are still going," I ask, trying to make sense of the situation.

"Yes, and I hope you will too," he replies.

He still wanted to go with me, but I wondered why he would play such a mean joke? However, looking at the boy in front of me, all sulk and sweat, I couldn't believe anything malicious could come from David O'Faolain.

"Well, I don't know, since then I've kind of madc plans," I said with an exaggerated shrug.

He looks at me with a half-raised eyebrow, suspicious of the validity of my statement, certainly over my current appearance. I was still in pajamas, a result of his last-minute cancellation, and my hair most likely resembled a small bird's nest.

"Later on, tonight," I add expertly, stunned at my own quick thinking.

"Well, what are you going to do?"

Shit.

"Study," great, there goes the quick thinking.

"Noah, please, I didn't mean to be mean or anything."

"I guess, but still that was really rude of you," as I theatrically stare off, obviously avoiding eye contact, with a heavy sigh, unwilling to let him off the hook easily. He grins obnoxiously. He knows I will cave, he walks up to me, leaving barely six inches between us.

"Please, Noah, I don't want to spend my birthday without you." Placing his hands on my shoulders, he smiles my favorite smile.

He brings his face close to my own, inches from my mouth. My chest is tight and filled with air, and for a second I could not recall how to exhale. Then I remember that I have not brushed my teeth. I could've died, but I am not fortunate that way. Instead, I move aside so he can step into the room and carefully exhale my stinky breath away from him.

David takes off his shoes and climbs onto my bed. He seemed awfully comfortable lying there snuggling with Morgan. His reasoning for the false cancellation was to build suspense, and after a half-dozen more apologies, he ends his explanation by shamelessly using a guilt-trip, "You did promise you'd come Noah, remember? It is my birthday after all."

In truth, he didn't need to give me much reason to forgive him. David could have called me, and I would have still said yes, "I guess I could forgive you, but just this once."

"Never again," he promises while making a mock salute, simultaneously causing me to involuntarily laugh. I start gathering my things to prepare for the day when Ms. Penelope knocks on the frame of my open door. She holds a tray filled with several types of snacks and drinks, "Boys, you all must have some of these cookies before you leave, made them from scratch myself. They'll give you immunity to poisonous bites and toxic plants," she says as she enters the room.

"Sure," David eagerly agrees, eating two right away, then manages to mumble out a thank you. "At the Mansion we never get treated this well, everything has to be requested through the kitchen. The food's great, but it doesn't taste like this, like a home-cooked meal, ya know," he says to Miss Penelope.

"Oh, you are too sweet love," crooning over David's compliment. I don't blame her.

"Thank you, I'll have one in a bit," I say, but Ms. Penelope insists I try one right away. So I stuff one in my mouth, "So good Ms. Penelope, but I have to get ready now." Pleased, she wished us both safe travels before leaving the room, blowing me a kiss as she walked out the door.

David puts another mouthful of cookies in his mouth and washes it down with a glass of milk. He gets ready to leave and we confirm that I will be meeting him at the Mansion, a deviation from the original plan because of David's practical joke. There were still some preparations left for him to complete. He had only come over to offer his apology in person. The worried, beautiful boy at the door was now looking full of relief.

Either way I needed to change and clean up before I could leave with him. Once done, I pack my overnight bag and make my way to the Mansion.

I climbed the grandiose exterior staircase of his Coven's home. As I am about to lift the latch of the iron gothic knocker, the door swings open and David comes barreling forward, trudging along a large yellow backpack. He and I are on a collision course, but he avoids the crash and nearly trips over himself in the process. He regains his balance easily enough, standing tall, he turns to face me and slicks back his hair as if the maneuver were on purpose.

He is dressed in navy blue crew shorts, an oversized shirt, and a camo hat. He wears a wide grin, unable to look like anything less than a teenage dream. My heart aches at the sight of him but quickly sinks when I see the various outdoor equipment. I started reassessing my initial agreement to attend since I have never been on an actual camping trip.

Technically, I have been on one trip, but it doesn't really count. Joan had taken us on a pseudo-outdoors vacation, but it was a blend between glamor and true camping. She rented air-conditioned tents in barricaded outdoor facilities to prevent any interaction with the animals. "Glamping" is what I think it was called. I try to force a smile, but it comes out awkwardly.

"What's wrong?"

"Nothing, just a little tired," and unconvincingly pretend to stifle a yawn. "I've never been camping before. This should be fun."

We stumble over each other as I try to help with the gear, but I end up being more of a hindrance than aid. David remains stupidly happy, despite my clumsiness. He pats the small but formidable-looking truck. David, now 15 according to Witch law, is fully eligible for driving privileges as well as flight, something he was intent on exploiting.

"All done, get in cowboy," sounding terribly off even with his well-done impression of an American accent. Regardless, he still manages to make me laugh. I think he might even sound a bit romantic. I might be the only one in the world who would think that, so I may not be the best judge on the matter.

I step inside the passenger seat as he revs the engine excitedly and we drive off. "So where are we going?" David shrugs his shoulders, "Guess you are just going to have to wait and see." He pauses, wrinkling his forehead as he ponders something, "And no cheating," pointing to his head, indicating the Vilix.

"I am not a cheat," I protest. "Not like you, remember Duchovny's exam," I say in defense.

"I didn't say I wasn't a cheat, at least I'm an honest cheat," boasts David, shrugging his shoulders, smiling roguishly.

"I think that's an oxymoron, no such thing as an honest cheat," and roll my eyes.

Yet he further condemns himself, "Besides, that class was impossible, and if memory serves, you helped me, you are not a complete Angel, No-El," he says with a laugh, "but close." He ends his defense with a grin.

"Well then, I am mostly not a cheat," smiling for him in return.

We drove for about an hour and the roads have remained empty. I struggle to remember the last time I saw a Carriage fly by in the high sky. I breathe in and out steadily. We have driven higher in elevation. The air seems thinner here, further away from the magik that kept the air pressure regulated on Tarias.

He asks me then that seemingly innocuous question, "What are your plans for summer?" The school year was coming to an end and plans were needed to be made.

"I get to spend four weeks with the Mastersons and then I'll take a short summer course, I guess. After that, I don't know, Doctor Huebner had talked about me visiting the Isles of Phoenician; supposedly it would be a good learning opportunity. A powerful Seer with the Vilix lives there."

David makes a face. Evidently, he finds educational opportunities during summer particularly disdainful. "You are going to spend your summer studying? Come on No El, you gotta give yourself a break, do something fun."

As if reading my mind, or reminding himself of the limits of being a Ward of the Council, he follows with, "How about you come with me on my family vacation? My parents are splitting their time in their summer home in Hawaii." It is on a small island still owned by both. One month for him and one month for her. "Most likely I'll only spend the last week with my father and the rest with me mum. It'd be great to have a friend there, and since you'll be with your kind, it shouldn't be a problem if you talk to the Doc."

Immediately I am overcome with rightful suspicion, "You don't have friends there, really?" He laughs indignantly. "Not good friends, acquaintances really, not friends like you. Come on, please, I don't know what I am going to do for a whole summer without you," shamelessly pouting, grossly dominating my summer that I had resigned to exclusive and obsessive studying.

"I mean it, ask the Doc, he is going to say yes. He gives you everything you want. Please?"

He looks at me with those big eyelashes, pretty eyes, and that damn half grin of his, and I just melt. Losing before I even started, "Okay, sure, I'll ask, but I don't know."

"Fantastic, this is really going to be a terrific summer, I'll call my father."

"You haven't asked your dad, what the hell David?"

"Mate you're fine, Doc's gonna say yes and so will my parents. The only person that I wasn't sure would agree, was you. Now that you have, go ahead and send the Doc a note, or better yet some psychic message, however your lot communicates."

Despite David's own expertise in psychic spellwork, he had limited knowledge over the dynamics of being a Seer.

"I think you are talking about Altars," the equivalent of astral projection, happy to be the one offering corrections for once. Telepathic messages were incredibly invasive. Using Altars is more appropriate, but even then a bit of a faux pas unless sent from a person of authority.

"And I just send him notes, like the written kind, it's rude to send out messages like that. He's busy, plus he's too far, distance matters, ya know?" Although with the Vilix, distance was no longer a barrier for me.

It was surprising that none of the scenery was familiar. Lately I found myself exploring these mountains to escape difficult memories. I felt as if I had become somewhat of an expert on these lands.

"How many times have you been out here?" I ask.

"Eh, a couple, it's kind of special to me." There was a pause, the look on David's face stirred concern within me. I asked him if something was wrong, but he said he was completely fine.

Other students have described David as apathetic but as I have gotten to know him, I found that was not really the case. Sure, he put little effort into his own classes, and when asked about his goals for the future, he typically would say, "It'll all be pure barry," or some other Scottish slang equivalent, but without actually providing a single detail on his plans. There was not really a need to worry because, for all technical purposes, he was always doing extraordinarily well.

A quick learner with natural gifts, he had no need to worry about assignments. He never was stuck on some major loss or disappointment, mainly because he never failed at anything. I think people mistook his confidence for indifference, but when he smiled just now, something about the way it didn't meet his eyes made me doubt what I thought I knew. When I asked him if he was okay a second time, he said, "pure barry," adding to my concern that he is not fine at all.

We drove for another hour while the road transformed from the paved cobblestone of Tarias to the rough terrain of the Rocky Mountains. I closed my eyes for just a moment and, somewhere along the setting sun, fell asleep.

My eyes slowly open to initial darkness, awoken by the discomfort of the awkward position I had taken while asleep. I turn to my left and find David's face directly in front of my own. The low blue light from the interior of the truck illuminates his wide wild smile, "Wake up sleeping beauty!" He grabs my shoulder, shaking me and, frankly, belaboring the point.

"Tonight, will be class," his voice shines in the darkness.

"I'm up." Pausing to gather myself, "Where is everyone?"

"Sit tight," David jumps out of the car and disappears into the pitch black. I had this reflexive urge to use the Vilix, but decided against it, after all, I promised him I would not cheat. Besides, David's enthusiasm was rapidly shifting my apprehension into excitement, as was usually the case when I was with him.

My chest tightens when I hear two loud bangs at my window.

"Noah!" Maria screams through the glass barrier. Excitedly I rushed out of the truck, stumbling awkwardly from the needlessly raised suspension and oversized tires.

Maria helps hold me steady, "Why didn't you just float down?" I notice her eyes are slightly glossy, a sure sign of drinking, and it takes me back to a time and place that I refuse to go, so I don't, "Because my dumb ass can't seem to remember to use magik."

We laugh and she gives me a quick hug. I tell her how much I've missed her, most of my time was divided between school and training with David. It felt like I hardly saw her.

"Same, it's been like a whole day."

"Too long," I play along.

"Exactly," as she laughs loudly. "Anyway, it's going to be so much fun, it's not here, obviously," gesturing to the empty area that currently served as a natural parking lot. "It's just up there," and she points toward the floating lights several yards above, casting shadows of David's friends. Their dark silhouettes walk back and forth, "We have to hike a little way up to get back to the camp, come on."

Initially, I was worried David had not invited her, but to my relief she had already promised to join in on the festivities, albeit contingent on my attendance. Apparently, Maria and David had become nearly friends since we started my tutoring. She and I went to Tarias just yesterday to shop for his birthday gift. Maria had been sore that David and I had gone to Tarias without her some time ago, a fact she did not fail to reiterate while we were out in the town. Regardless, she was still kind enough to purchase a gift for him, a six-pack of Besnit.

There is an unexpected boom of hoots and howls, its source only a few feet away. David's friend, Gerald Harish-Mal, magikally amplifies the volume of his inner animal voice. It initiates a sense of inhibition, setting a precedence for the night.

"I have to help David with all the stuff," I announced. At the same time, a few of his friends arrive to assist with unpacking.

"Oh, I'll help too then," she offers, and we levitate the rest of the items from the truck and make our way up to the main campgrounds.

The camp was in the center of clearing located on the mountain's saddle with looming woods rising on its shoulder.

The area was illuminated by floating Edison bulbs that lined up to appear as if they were hung from various invisible strings. Large enchanted white sheets formed into tents, held up by their own accord, stood on the flat grassy grounds surrounding the center where the unlit fire-pit lived.

It's cold and I realize that I forgot the supplies for my warmth spell, "How about we get a fire going, isn't that how these trips are supposed to work?"

David, incessantly bragging over his camping expertise, reassures me he will handle the matter. He grabs his supplies while providing a tutorial on the gear necessary for a "Successful night in the great outdoors." He stops when he finds it.

"What's this," he asks as he holds the large box that I managed to sneak aboard the truck using a concealment spell.

"Happy Birthday, David O'Faolain," I yell with all the smiles that exist within me.

He unpacks the box and dozens of enchanted balloons are released into the night air. They float to the edge of the campgrounds, falling in line one in front of the other, until they form a ring that surrounds the party and then steadily hold their place. He empties the box of the many bottles stored within it, "Booze," he excitedly announces. A wide grin is shared between the group.

"Can you put the box on that table," I ask him. He looks at me with a quizzical brow, "Trust me," I reassure him. He rests the box atop a nearby table and its sides fall loose revealing a gigantic German chocolate cake, his favorite.

I steal him away for just a moment, "And one small thing," as I hand him the small box wrapped in blue. "Do me a favor and open it later, okay?" He nods in agreement and gives me a quick hug. "Thanks, Noah," his smile is small and shy.

Someone hands me a beer and I take a large gulp, nearly gagging as I do so. I take a few more small sips, providing me time to adjust to the bitter flavor. David starts the campfire the Mortal way.

Oddly enough, David is often frustrated by his own magik, at least in terms of the immediate results it manifests. Although some could argue Witchcraft was not so instantaneous since mastering spellwork still required practice and labor to achieve successful outcomes.

However, for David, the physical part of the work made him feel more talented than any magik he could produce. It was that way for him for most of his hobbies. He loved things like skiing, surfing, and all things that require movement. He seemed the proudest of his achievements in Mortal skills. I think that is why he favored Transvection, it requires more physical presence than any other magik.

I finished the beer and now feel lightheaded as Maria and I sing along with the jukebox set up by her boyfriend, Aaron Fuerios. He is a member of the Coven of Magia Correllium, where the Witches specialize in Conjuration to include enchantments, charms, and sympathetic magik.

They had been dating for nearly two months now. She continues to claim he is temporary, but I think Maria may like the "Tall-Dark-and-Handsome," and sweet, Mr. Fuerios more than she lets on.

I see David encircled by a small crowd of his friends. Most of them are from the Mansion and only a few from the other Covens. I recognized Luke Stein immediately. I forgot that he and David played on the same Sorcellirae team. It was a Witch sport, like soccer with one distinct difference; players use Transvection magik, no brooms allowed, within the boundary of the field.

Luke plays with the campfire using his elemental magik, creating a magnificent show, while boasting about his skills, which admittedly were impressive. He created a concert out of the flames, mimicking the music as it played.

Then I remember the time he asked me out and feel immediately awkward. I looked away, focusing on the conversation Maria was having with Aaron. She was upset with him for spending an "extra" amount of time with Katherine, AKA Kady. "She's just a friend," he responds in a panicked defense.

"Fine," she says, but in a way that indicates she is not. I wonder if she would still be making a fuss about this if she were sober.

I look around and realize there are no other members from Spirit Manor. I thought our Covens were supposed to be like family, yet I am the only Seer here.

I remind myself it was not my party. Even if it were, I would not invite them. It is not that I dislike my housemates, but I do not particularly enjoy their company either. Besides, my birthday party would be a small affair. After all I only have two friends.

Wow, that's sad. I wondered what spells, if any, were cast on this beer.

Maria and Aaron continue to argue, and I ask a random question to change the subject, "So when do we stop ageing?"

They both laugh at my off-topic question, that's a relief. Hearing people fight makes me uncomfortable. "I mean, we don't age like Mortals, so how does that work?"

Aaron answers, "Shortly after you reach physical maturity, like the peak, the ageing slows down, almost stops for a century, give or take a few years."

Maria chimes in, "It's usually around the age of 25."

We go on to discuss all the things to do with our extended life. Aaron, a Legacy Witch with two Witch parents does not participate much, extended life and ageing is old news for him.

Luke walks up to me just then and asked how I was doing. Alcohol, a potion in and of itself, surely provides liquid courage. "Hey Noah, how are you?" He is very handsome, like a star quarterback kind of handsome, but he was not David.

"I'm good and you?"

"Same, hey quick question," he says with a sheepish smile.

"Sure."

"You and David, are you all a thing," Luke asked nervously.

"No, he's my tutor and well, we're friends, but that's all."

"Okay cool, I thought it was strange, I know that he and Owen Liu were going hot and heavy for a while, then you came along and then they weren't."

"What? I didn't know that," and I look over at David as he hugs Owen tightly to his body. David is interested in guys like him. He is handsome, athletic, and nothing like me.

"Well hey, how about hanging out sometime, like a date," as he looks into my eyes. I had not noticed the pretty shade of pale blue of his own.

I say yes without thinking, likely out of a need to fall a little less in love with David O'Faolain.

Damn beer.

We play a card game that I win. Everyone claims I cheated since I am a Seer. I am beginning to understand why no other Seers were invited. Other Witches never know what secrets are being uncovered with us around. David comes to my defense, "He's not a cheater!"

"Actually, I kind of did," I say apologetically. "Your minds were so loud. I tried to shut them out but it was too late, I already knew your cards."

"Then why didn't you say something and ask for a re-deal," asked Maria.

"I wanted to win, obviously," and the others laughed in response. David raises up his drink for a toast, "But an honest cheat, cheers."

"Exactly," I say, laughing as well, but the thought of David and Owen Liu intrudes my mind, prematurely ending it. The night goes on with further laughs and euphoric smiles. We make plans to visit Denver on brooms. Finally, we sing happy birthday and David hugs his friends endearingly. I am glad for one thing; that tonight seemed to be perfect for him. People are lost in conversations or games, and others lost in each other behind the privacy of their tents. I look up at the sky.

There is only a glimmer of moon tonight but there are stars. Oh, so many stars.

For a second, I lose myself in their magnificence. I return my attention to the party only to catch David's eyes on mine. He then stares up at the same bright stars.

"It's beautiful, isn't it," I ask, but it wasn't really a question. We stared at each other for a moment. It is the most vulnerable I have ever felt, and it terrifies me.

"Sure is, Noah Ellis."

A few hours later, as dawn approaches, we make our way into the tent that he and I share. He drank too much and fell asleep quickly. He is wearing my gift. I guess he didn't want to wait. It's a ring, a wax seal of his family's crest, the sort of tool used by nobility to sign letters and contracts. The symbol has the sun in the center with many stars in the background. It has magik as well. It can link up with other charms, sort of like walkie-talkies. I was going to link it to the charm he gave me for my own birthday all those months ago, but decided against it. I figured it was his charm to use how he saw fit.

He looks so handsome, the glow of the rising sun revealing the subtle stubble growing on his cheeks and chin, surrounding his lips. He is becoming a man. I am tempted to touch his face at that moment. I refrain and let myself sleep, praying that I do not dream.

Chapter Twenty-Two

Family Ribbon Binding Spell
Incantation: Juno, Freya, St. Anthony
One item of significance is needed from each family member.
At the Moon's height, recite seven times while binding items with velvet.

It was the last day of classes for St. Philomena. David and I are at our spot, Lola, near the cliffs edge. We already completed our required finals and could skip the remaining courses left of the school day. We had spent the majority of our time training. I should have been ecstatic to spend the extra time with him, but for some unfortunate reason I could not shake this uncomfortable feeling lingering in the air like an unpleasant odor.

Things were changing. I have been practicing magik with the Vilix more often. I was taking more risks and it was paying off. I was getting stronger, but there was something else changing about me. It felt like I was becoming someone else and I was not entirely sure what I thought about that.

He and I were reviewing Transvection skills, even though I have already mastered them. This was to be our last session for the year. Our tutoring would be delayed the following semester and was tentatively set to resume in late October.

Dr. Huebner was all but certain that tutoring was no longer necessary. He said I still required some fine tuning but argued that my classes would address those details.

David was limited in his tutoring capacities when it came to that type of magik. He had helped me tremendously, but his helpfulness had peaked as my own training and experience is now, in some ways, beyond him. I was realizing that my time spent with him was becoming superfluous, a secret I would take to my grave. Spending time with David was worth its weight in gold. Nonetheless, there he was, staring up at me with those big brown eyes, beaming, as I lifted higher and higher into the air, now hovering 10 feet above him.

"I think you're ready."

My stomach drops, "Yeah, you think I am a full-fledged flying Witch," I asked as I adjusted my body to face the sky. And then David took ascent, with no effort at all, he positioned himself next to me as if we were laying on top of an invisible hammock and we float side-by-side. I am steady in my position, my magik now deliberate and controlled.

He rolls his eyes at me, annoyed with my sarcasm.

"Right, just need to get you a broom," he says without joking and, with a softness to his face, he declares, "I am a proud teacher." I noticed the ring I had given him glisten in the sunlight, he seemed to never take it off.

"You really have come a long way, guess you don't need me anymore."

We stared up at the twilight sky. He looked a little sad, but then made this mock cry, and that look vanished, replaced by his sly grin.

It is silly, but I cannot help but feel unreasonably despondent just then, I wanted him to miss me. "I'll always need you," I say impulsively, followed by immediate regret.

"Guess we'll just have to hang out like regular friends, what do you say, No-El?" Although he had been joking, I realized that he was indeed asking me.

"I thought that's what we were doing."

He exhales a polite laugh, "I suppose you're right, husband." He had gotten into the habit of referring to me as husband or "Noah O'Faolain," after I told him about Luke questioning our relationship. He thought it was funny that other Witches had thought of us as secret boyfriends.

"So, when do you and Luke go on that date," he asked coolly.

"Next semester, probably, it was a little too late in the year, what with exams," I responded shyly.

"Makes right sense," he sinks back to the ground and I follow him down. "It's getting late and I still haven't packed," he announces.

Most of the students were returning home for the summer. Tomorrow, David will return to his family's' estate in Athru. As for me, I would travel to the Mastersons and spend two weeks with them. Despite their partial custodianship over me, the Witch Council still possessed the authority to impose limitations on my time in the Mortal world. Thankfully, I was able to spend four weeks with them during summer break, two at the beginning and two at the end.

After a small delay, I finally respond, "Yeah, I haven't packed either, guess we should get going."

"I suppose so," he says nonchalantly and pauses briefly, "see you in a few months No-El."

We say goodbye, but as we walk away, he shouts out, "I promise to wait for you," and I find myself, for the first time, not wanting to leave the city of Witches.

The visit with the Mastersons was too short. Time is a greedy thing. Regardless, it was exactly what I needed. My mind must have kept the pain of their absence from my awareness, an action needed in order to survive the drastic changes of my life over the past several months.

Joan cooked every meal and we ate together as a family for each one and played games every night after dinner. I may have broken a record for most consecutive games lost in the family, but I didn't care because it felt like I had already won.

Joan took me to a spa, and I really like spas. I talked to her in more detail about the magik I was learning and shared stories about David and Maria. She was probably Maria's number two fan behind Maria's own mother, and she fell in love with the beautiful boy who she said, "saved my son."

We all cried when it was time to say goodbye, again. I remind them, and me, it is only eight more weeks until I return. Darcy Hutchins, Dr. Huebner's assistant, stands at their front door ready to take me back to Tarias just as she did so many months ago. This time she arrives alone and is met with less hostility. This was a first for me, coming back to a place I had been removed from, returning to a family and a home, my home.

I start my summer course at St. Philomena the following day, which I had elected to take during the time in between my visits at home. It was also to fine-tune my skills in the Craft of Versation, or transformative magik, but mostly it was to occupy my time.

David decided to participate in a paid internship for a collaborative project between the St. Philomena Academy and Oxford University of Witchcraft. We spent our days studying and our nights staring up at the moon. A small part of me thought he agreed to the position because of me. If so, I hope it was not out of pity. He understood I was only authorized to reside with the Mastersons for four weeks during the summer. He obviously had no need for the money and was not the type to be worried about gaining prestige or accolades. He once said, "I want to be self-sufficient." I think it was because he did not want to rely on his father's money for the rest of his life. His parent's divorce was conflictual and left both parties injured to some degree or another. David and his brothers were the primary casualties of their war.

The days went by quickly that summer and, suddenly, there is only one month left of it. I had promised David to join him on his family's vacation in Hawaii and we were leaving that very night. After the trip, I would fly directly to the Mastersons for the remainder of the break.

David and I sit outside a popular café nestled in downtown Tarias. He seemed genuinely excited about his internship. The research conducted was focused on Translocation or Transdimensional-something, "It's groundbreaking Noah, their accomplishments are right quality. They're doing more with magik than I thought possible." This was the first time I saw this side of David, at least when it came to school. It was sweet.

He went on to explain, in excruciatingly technical jargon, something about the planes and dimensions.

"I didn't take you much for a scientist," voicing my observation.

"Huh," now distracted from his emphatic review over the magikal project.

"Sorry, I didn't mean to interrupt, I was just surprised. You're really into this?"

"Statement Noah, not a question." I groan and he laughs in response. "Yeah, suppose I am, sorta," and we enjoy the humor in the irony that David O'Faolain was scholarly after all.

We finish our tracofes, essentially enchanted coffee that increases focus and energy. The magik is in the absence of aversive side effects like restlessness or euphoria commonly experienced in illicit stimulants. The effect evaporates within an hour after the last ingestion.

"Besides, I couldn't leave my best friend." He starts singing, rather terribly with his accent, some random song about loneliness.

"Some best friend," I say in exasperation as he puts his arms around me. With all his bravado and charm, he stretches his broad chest around me and boastfully deepens his voice as he whispers in my ear, "It's going to be okay, mate. Your husband is here now. You'll be right as rain, bonnie."

"I didn't know my best friend could be so full of crap," still, I laugh at his ridiculousness. He releases me from his arms, chuckling maniacally at his irreverent public display of affection.

Unable to help myself, "Thank you, though, honestly."

"For what?"

"For being my best friend, along with Maria"

"What a load of nonsense, don't thank me, but you're welcome all the same," and gives me his obnoxious grin now coupled with a new arrogant wink.

"Okay, only a few more hours and we are off to Hawaii, set your alarm clock, No-El"

"I will," as we make our way toward the nearest tower.

I couldn't sleep. I was going to Hawaii! It's hard to believe he invited me or that the trip was really happening. I felt as if I was taking advantage of his family. I did not want to be a charity case, but in all honesty, I don't believe David thinks of me that way. Not after all we have been through the past few months. We were, after all, best friends. At the same time, I did not want to seem ungrateful. It was incredibly sweet of him to think of me.

We would spend one week of the trip with his father at one of the O'Faolain's hidden islands. Since Ms. O'Faolain had equal ownership of the O'Faolain assets, she would arrive the following week to close out the family trip. This would be my first time visiting the state known as paradise.

We were leaving on their private jet. A private jet, how is that even possible? I would think that becoming a Witch would have been more astonishing than a private jet, but there is something about the familiarity of an aircraft, call it the Mortal element, that makes the experience more exciting. It was a safe kind of exhilaration, which was unlike being a Witch. That came with a host of new and foreign threats that were more terrifying than invigorating.

The loud chiming of the antique clock notifies me that it is one in the morning and time to get out of bed. I walked out of the Manor in the dead of night and found David standing at the Manor's front door with a slight shiver to his body. Despite it being summer, the high Rocky Mountains sent a chill through the air.

"Wasn't I supposed to meet you by the tower?"

"Yeah, but I thought it would be easier if I just came to you."

"How long have you been waiting?"

"Not long."

We arrive to the pick-up point. A limousine waits outside Tarias' magikal border. The driver takes our luggage and carefully packs them into the trunk. I climb into the luxurious vehicle and we drive off to the airport. The night was pitch black, the moon hung back, shrouded by the cover of lingering post-midnight clouds. The Colorado sky occasionally allows the stars to shine.

It was a surprisingly long drive. "I thought the airport was near Tarias?"

"It is, we had to change plans. We'll leave from the Denver airport now."

"Why, what happened?"

"I guess I got the time wrong, my father wanted us to be on a midnight flight."

"We missed the flight?"

"It's all squared away Noah. My father rented another jet for us."

I felt terrible, "When did all this happen?"

"I don't know, earlier, couldn't be helped."

He was keeping something from me. He normally didn't respond with simple short answers, that was not his way. "David, when did you find out?" I said his name because that usually got him to open up.

"Around 11 last night, I suppose. You were already in bed and I wasn't going to wake you up. It's his own damn fault for changing the plans last minute. Seriously Noah, it's all good."

"Is your dad mad?"

"No, not anymore. We exchanged some words, but it's fine now."

I felt like the worst guest in the world. "How much does a private jet cost?"

And on a side note, how much money does David's parents have? Nevertheless, David said everything was "fine," a sure sign everything was not fine. There was no point in asking any more questions. It was his way of saying no more.

We arrived at the airport and were given special access to board the plane. I had never felt so, well important. The airport staff treated us like we were celebrities, waited on us hand and foot. They talked to me instead of at me like most adults did growing up. And the plane!

It was something you would see on a show. David was unaffected by the splendor of the aircraft, preoccupied with thoughts most likely involving his father, but I was in awe over it all. I guess my excitement was catching because David seemed to have a bit of respite from whatever situation he was rumbling back and forth in that head of his.

He was laughing, I guess at me, or with me. His smile was loud, and his laugh was large. A drastic improvement in his mood compared to the grouch he was earlier.

"Have you ever been on a plane before," David asked.

"Once, but that was to take me from Washington to Massachusetts to live with the Mastersons, Family Services arranged the transportation and I was escorted by a caseworker. I don't really remember much of it to be honest."

"Oh," he said. He looks so unbelievably sad. I sometimes forget how crappy my life has been and how it sounds to other people.

"Don't feel sorry for me, it's not a big deal. I am on one now, and it's fantastic being here, with my best friend, doing something fun and, oh my god, there's a television!"

He laughed, I mean he really laughed, and then I laughed because he thought what I said was so damn funny. It was a glorious thing to hear. We had so much fun on the flight over. I secretly hoped that these fleeting moments would never come to an end.

We arrived at Honolulu International Airport a few hours later. From there, we took a smaller plane and were forced to go "Island Hopping".

A terrifying ordeal given that the Mortal pilot had to be enchanted since the O'Faolain's island was magikally hidden. I was convinced David cast the wrong spell and just made the man drunk. It took several self-reminders that I could fly to de-escalate my anxiety.

Finally, I allow myself to take in the view. Hawaii was beautiful, the wind and air, the spontaneous and brief showers, the smell of the ocean and palms, they carried all my worries away; it truly was paradise. We finally landed on the O'Faolain's private island. It was breathtaking.

The inviting cool blue waters come in waves onto the white sand of their personal beach. The island mansion has clear glass for walls and a wrap-around infinity pool, and behind the mansion was a lush botanical garden.

We walk toward the home on a suspended bamboo bridge and on the other side stands David's family. Well, his father, and his girlfriend Denise, as well as his two younger brothers who looked nothing like David with their blonde hair and blue eyes. Bryan was the older of the two and the youngest was Scott. David's father, Douglas, was blonde haired and blue eyed as well. It made me wonder if David inherited his dark hair and brown eyes from his mother.

Although he did not have the exact features of his father, they remained similar in appearance, both the same kind of handsome. As it is, I felt like a freeloader and extremely uncomfortable, and it didn't help that they were all so extraordinarily beautiful like they could be models.

His father would be on some cover of a men's health magazine, and David on Teen Cosmo, where all the girls could crush on his layout. The girlfriend was an actual model, my guess mid-20s, and wasn't a Witch. On the flight over, David explained that none of us were allowed to practice magik around her.

I felt out of place, but they didn't treat me that way, they were all polite. David was the grumpy one. He was even more irritable when his dad and Denise were around and, god forbid they tried to talk to him, he would respond with one of three one-worded responses: "No," "Yes," and "Fine."

Privately, I begged him to be more polite. I told him how uncomfortable I was and how that made it even more awkward. That settled him a bit, he wasn't exactly giving hugs or engaging in deep conversations, but he was more civil. I appreciated that.

We took trips inland to dine at gourmet restaurants. Since his father's girlfriend was Mortal, we did human stuff, which David seemed to enjoy, including parasailing, jet-skiing, surfing, and at one point, water waking, surfing that required being dragged by a boat.

Dragged.

I almost died.

David came to my rescue, although, thanks to a life-vest, I wasn't actually drowning and probably didn't need rescuing despite my cries for help. So other than my ego being bruised, no real harm.

It was when the activities ended that things would get uncomfortable. The silence between them during their dinners was deafening.

Finally, the week came to an end. Douglas and Denise left before the arrival of David's mother, approximately 25 hours prior to her landing. I guess David's father wanted to avoid any interaction at all, or he was eager to enjoy the freedom of bachelor life. Denise, after all, was headed to her hometown in Switzerland while he was off to Brazil, for his "second-vacation".

The entire attitude of the home shifted when his mother arrived. No longer did it feel like we were walking on eggshells. Instead, there was a lightness in the air, like the feeling of flying.

Fiona O'Faolain, David's mother, was beautiful. She maintained her married name because, after all, it is hers to claim. She confirmed where David got his eyes and dark hair. She moved like a ballerina, elegant, and laughed like how grandma Masterson laughed, full and robust. She hugged deeply and fell in love quickly.

His maternal grandmother, Emilia Walsh, accompanied David's mother. A true force of a woman and in her strength was just as much kindness.

"Well, aren't you the most beautiful sight I have ever seen, look at those eyes David. I am sure you get that a lot but indulge me dear, they are so pretty. They look like stars." I usually hated hearing that kind of crap but not with Ms. Walsh, in fact, it was probably the first time I actually felt good about the compliment.

Now free of our inhibitions with the Mortal girlfriend no longer near, we could do magikal things and visit magikal places. We met Myre-people. Their origin legitimately traced back to Atlantis. Conspiracy theorists around the world, I applaud your perseverance.

By the aid of a powerful Versation spell, we were able to meet them without the cumbersome and suffocating scuba gear. The spell required eating fish, which felt very sacrificial to me, but I love seafood, which made the experience tolerable.

I was beside myself, it was as if I was meeting rock stars instead of supernatural beings. David, who knew about them since he was a child, was less impressed.

"They're kind of gross, not pretty like the little mermaids told in fairy tales," he said in utter blasphemy. It is true, they were more fish than people-like but it did not matter.

They were magnificent.

There were different types, like hand-on-heart there was even an actual octopus-like Myre-person. Bonus, they were actually really, really, nice.

After our meet and greet, David and I were able to go off and explore the deep waters. The sea truly is the origin of life. It would be unjust of me to attempt to properly describe the vast and majestic world underneath the water, so I will not, but it was something of the divine.

The rest of the trip itself was a blur. We walked sandy trails and laid in worship of the sun. We allowed the days to drift lazily on by and it would seem paradise could last forever, that is until the final days, when one of my insipid waves would tear through this dream, stealing summer in its wake.

It was a nightmare.

I woke up screaming. David and his mother were at my side, my breathing rapid. Grandma Walsh checked my temperature and cast a few wordless spells. It was innate and rural magik, but it felt like warmth and honey, better than any magik used by Healers in the Infirmary.

"You gave us a fright, No-El, seeing you scared like that, are you okay?"

"Yeah, I get them randomly, sometimes. Thanks though, I promise. I am okay."

David was kind enough not to press.

The previous day, David and I decided to spend the day at the beach. The rest of the family flew off to visit the Draegons of Kohala. It surprised me that these beings would maintain their home on the Big Island.

After a day in the sun, we decided to make a night of it and camp on the island's shore underneath the big blue sky. We were walking along the edge of the water when, uncharacteristically, I told him more about my nightmares. There must be something in the water.

"They're mostly about a man who hurts children."

He asks more questions, I selectively answer some and others I avoid, falsely denying that I remember details. Unexpectedly, he shares his own similar experience.

"I was 9 years old; I woke up screaming, drenched in sweat. My grandmother came to check on me, not even my own father, and my mum was on a business trip," chuckling nervously, a bit embarrassed, I think.

"She did her best to console me, but it was no good, I was in a bit of a state," as he recalls that night with exquisite detail.

"A man, a murderous man, a dead man, that's what I remember." I couldn't sleep without having the same nightmare, only it changed, became less detailed, and less about the man, and more about just the fear." He said his parents sought both magikal and medical aid.

"To help with my sleep and crap mood they put me on Prozac and made me attend weekly sessions with a shrink and a Healer for about a year. It went away after a while. Still though, I never could quite shake the memory of it. It's like a scar. Sometimes it comes back to life, reminding me of the original wound, but I'm not scared anymore, just angry. I know it's strange, being mad at dreams."

"I get that. I get mad at monsters too," and I say nothing more. Avoiding the topic, I asked to play a game, specifically one that involved Transvection. We went flying off, two boys making a game of water and magik.

The stars seemed as if they lived in the sea and danced around him as he came toward me, larger than life, every stroke disturbing the summer night sky's reflection, our home for tonight. We dived into the water, as deep as we could go until we could go no further.

And then we fly, racing to the surface, escaping the waters, the wake evidence of our wreckage. We violently inhaled the sweet air as we floated above the waters, allowing the warm breeze to kiss our bare skin while our soaked shorts weighed heavy on our weightless bodies.

The smell of the sea and sand sent messages of infinite possibilities. The air was filled with bliss and inevitability. It was the ending days of summer passing us by, dragging our youth in its undertow, allowing a few hours of innocence and joy before, like all things, comes to an end.

"Tag, you're it," I quickly zoom away, levitating backwards toward the sea. He floated toward me with impossible speed and precision, hugging me, interfering with my focus, causing me to flail and him to flinch, and we both fell into the water.

We return to the surface and regain our bearings as we tread the water. My heartbeat races when he looks at me.

I remember this one insignificant time I was training with David. He touched the small of my back; slightly nudging me into the correct stance required for the spell. He was so soft and careful. The touch of his hand lingered there for maybe a few seconds, but I could still feel the outline of his palm as if it never left.

We laugh hysterically as we return to our game of flying tag, zip lining through the air and diving into the water only to spout out once more as we continue the chase. Having tired ourselves out, we make our way back to the shore for a break. David stands before me, built like a young Greek God in wet shorts and shaggy, perfectly messy hair, with that dangerously beautiful smile of his.

David kicks the ground beneath him. He stares down and grabs the back of his neck as if he is debating whether to dive off the cliff or remain on solid ground.

"What's wrong," I ask.

"I'm alright, just been thinking about some things lately."

"Well that's very specific," I say with a smile, "Is it anything I can help you with?"

"Maybe, I have been racking my brain over it, trying to figure things out."

He breathes, and softly says, "'I've been thinking about me," he pauses, "And you."

"What," I ask, legitimately confused.

He walks toward me, rapidly closing in the space that lies between us, his face moving toward my own. He stands nearly a foot taller than me and stares into my eyes, "Stars," he says.

My heartbeat is pounding, and I wonder if he can hear it. He angles his face against mine.

I stumble over my words and by some miracle manage to make out a coherent sentence, "What about me and you?"

He breathes deeply. "That maybe, you, might let me kiss you?"

The sound of David's voice is deep and gentle. His words seem to dance like a song in my ears. His beautiful brown eyes bore into mine, pleading for permission.

He slides his hands across my waist, wrapping his arms around me. Slowly he pulls me in closer, holding me tight. His bare chest against my own, his body curving with mine.

I wrap my arms across his broad shoulders and rest my hands on the back of his neck.

David leans in and kisses me.

It was warm. Our lips perfectly fit each other as we pressed them against one another, at last finding their home.

I lose myself in him, completely and utterly consumed by the boy I was always and irrevocably in love with.

I was dizzy. I felt weightless, but gravity pulled me toward him, overcoming me. I realized I was hovering a couple of inches off the ground and not by my own magik, but his.

"Sorry," he shrugs. "I had to give it a shot," he says with my favorite smile.

Still in each other's arms, we descend, lying on the beach shore, as he carefully lays my head against the soft sand, his body on top of my own, "I like holding you," and just like that, we were back where we started. I see and touch his sun-kissed skin. Even in the dark I can see the beet red tinge of his sunburn.

Touch was supposed to be meaningless. That was the belief I held onto, a belief that made the things that came before acceptable. Yet here I am, compulsively reaching out for his body, no longer resisting or denying the magnetic pull that pushes me deeper into him. I was lost in his warmth, forbidding me to leave.

I think back to the time my powers overwhelmed me and I accidentally cast the psychic domination over the entire class.

Even then, my very essence knew not to hurt him, not the perfect boy. I loved him the moment he said my name, all those months ago. I know that now. Fearful of rejection, I refused to consider the possibility.

Now in this moment, I allowed myself to see the inherent reality that could no longer be shadowed by my own defenses. David O'Faolain loved me back. It is the reason he has always been there for me. It is the reason he stays with me. I am only now willing to accept this truth along with the immeasurable bliss alongside it.

He digs deeper now, taking possession of me. First my heart and now my body. If only I could stay here, I wish for a time loop so I may replay this moment of heaven, endlessly.

But, I don't have that kind of magik.

His bare chest lays on top of mine as he tries to dig deeper into me. His hands move lower and press into my bottom. Too fast, I thought. Not with him, I don't want to ruin this.

Softly I say, "Not yet."

He presses himself in-between my legs. I feel himself on me, hard and strong.

And why, oh why, did I think of him?

"Sorry," he says and I can almost hear his eyes staring at the floor, I am sure bashful over his eagerness, but it is too late for me.

My eyes already burn bright blue in the dark night, and the Vision surfaces.

Damn, damn Charles Daley.

I had just turned 8 years old. His rancid breath permeates the sheets. He was taking his time, pacing himself, carefully cherishing every moment of sick pleasure.

He grabs my throat and squeezes it shut. I gasped for air and he slaps me across the face and then proceeds to continue strangling me.

Sweaty and reeking of beer, he lays on top of me, suffocating me now with his overweight body. He shoved himself inside me and squealed like an excited pig at the sound of my screams. A trickle of blood runs down my leg, cooling my skin.

I thought for a moment that I had died.

"You want more bitch," and punches me in the face. "Look how you are begging to be fucked you little faggot," but I remain quiet. My body lays limp and unconscious from the blow.

No, don't let it be true.

David jumps off me, scared and disgusted, he vomits at the side of me.

I gasp. Pleading to some unknown force to change reality.

No.

I feel the ties of my sanity began to unravel. He knows. With the Vilix, I somehow shared this memory of me with him. Only it was more than a memory, I relived the event as if I had time-traveled, seeing the event from my own perspective with the Vilix and all its cursed clarity.

Don't let it be true.

"What was that," gagging the words out, disgusted with me I am sure, as I felt the same.

My rising panic obliterates my coherency. Some of his vomit splattered on me. The strong and putrid smell of it barely registered to my awareness. A storm was coming, rapidly forming around us, pulling at the sea for fuel. I didn't see it coming, if I had, maybe I could have stopped it.

The air is charged with electricity, it quickly changes direction, forming a vortex above me. I stand in the eye of a hurricane.

"Noah. What are you doing?" For the first time, David looks scared. The skies far above separate as if Moses is parting the sea. My eyes feel like fire and I know they are shining like dying stars.

"Noah, please stop. Please." He is yelling and crying.

The ground shakes, a mini earthquake, until the vibrations reach their peak. And there it is, way up in the cosmic space between us and the stars. A hole opens in the atmosphere, allowing bright Celestial light to burn down on me.

It should have killed me, but it does not, and I do not know why. I wish it did. Instead, it enveloped me, sizzling the ground around me. And just like that, the area surrounding me is transformed, black, like the launching pad of fireworks on Independence Day. Scorched but empty now. I am gone.

Chapter Twenty-Three

For providence on journeys, scatter solar Faelin dust precisely on the spot of the first step outside the door, and recite the spell.
Thrice said, Abraxis Malik Ophei

It had been two weeks since that night. Two weeks since I saw David. I am with the Mastersons now, the Council agreed to extend my stay per Dr. Huebner's request, delaying my start to school by a few weeks.

That night my magik somehow unconsciously transported me to Spirit Manor. I figured it didn't bring me to the Mastersons in the first place because it would be a violation of the rules and risk their safety.

The events of that night replayed itself repetitively and automatically throughout my waking hours. I was with David and then unfathomably back at Spirit Manor, still barefoot, shirtless, and soaking wet from the island water.

Nauseous and beyond myself, my gagging and physical cries turned telepathic, announcing my arrival to the Manor's psychic residents that remained during the summer break. I am still unsure how long I was out there, alone in the dark, the only thing I remember were the dark woods.

Madam Reyna was the first to arrive. She rocked me back and forth like a child, but I felt like a child, so I let her.

The exceeding irony is not lost on me that the unwelcoming woman who made my life miserable in those first few weeks at the Academy has become one of my greatest allies. She has been in attendance to every single one of my catastrophes, thus far.

In search of me, David and his family had contacted the Mastersons and Spirit Manor just prior to my arrival. They thought I went missing, or worse, since even Madam Reyna was not able to identify my location.

The Mastersons had called non-stop for hours during my still unaccounted for time in the woods. I had no idea how Translocation worked, and I was beginning to doubt that I was lost in some forest of Tarias. It was a forest. I just don't think it was the literal kind.

The phone rang the second I entered the Manor. Madam Reyna answered the call and informed Joan that I had returned safe and unharmed. She thanked Jesus the second she heard my voice, and after the emotions settled, she told me that David claimed I teleported, "Is that right, Noah?"

"I think so," and she gasped, "How is that possible?" I answer honestly, "I don't know."

They demanded to see me at once. With perfect timing, Dr. Huebner arrived at the door, standing tall in a plaid nightshirt, essentially a nightgown, that I thought was somewhat cute and was considering getting one.

Dr. Huebner reassures the Mastersons that I would be there tomorrow. He secured the authorization for my extended trip that very morning. I vividly remember forcing myself to end the call, saying goodbye and goodnight to them and even Rocky, damn dog barked up a storm at the sound of my voice.

Regrettably, David's worry and excessive attempts to locate me prompted the need to have a conversation with him and his family that same night, at the very least to reassure them that their houseguest was indeed alive.

David answered immediately and sounded exquisitely relieved to hear me speak, but that moment was fleeting. In a low voice, almost a whisper, he asked if I was *alright*. His tone referencing the disappearance and the thing that lived underneath it, the secret held between us, that was now a wall. Something that was not there before, "Yeah, I'm fine."

He deferred the conversation to his mother and then he was gone.

Fiona O'Faolain, slightly sobbing, thanked the Spirits I was safe, while David's grandmother loudly thanked many goddesses for my confirmed arrival in the background. Thanking higher powers seems to be a common trait for Mortal and Witch mothers alike.

Fiona cried and laughed a bit, overjoyed that I was not hurt and excited over the feat I had accomplished in the Translocation.

She asked what prompted me to use that sort of magik. I skirted around several topics until landing on the most reasonable excuse I could surmise in the moment. I told her I had seen something in the water and panicked, "And then I was here." My mouth feels unclean, as lies seem to stain.

We ended the call with her promising she would see me soon, contracting me to spend time with the family at my earliest convenience. I said goodbye without speaking to David and, finally, that night of crossed stars ends. I was unsure of whether I was grateful or devastated to speak to him no further.

I take the Walk-Easy to return home, unable to replicate the magikal act. I have cried myself to sleep every night so far. It was still difficult to get out of bed.

My sadness was a heavy thing. I was remiss, and regretful over being remiss, wishing I could appreciate the time here more generously. On the plus side, I had no bad dreams, as my current reality is enough of a nightmare.

Thank god, goddess, or whatever is out there for my family. Unable to keep it entirely secret, I revealed most details of the whole David fiasco to Joan, censoring the sections that she did not need to know. Joan, who feared that she would be unable to tend to my first broken heart so long ago, feared needlessly.

I cried into her shoulder begging for the pain to stop. She responds very Joan-like, kind and easy, and lets me talk openly before aggressively insulting him.

She claimed she never liked him, which I know for a fact is an outright lie. Joan loved him, a direct result of my late-night phone conversations about his kind nature toward me as a tutor, I don't blame her.

I occupied my spare time by working on a special gift to the family. I was able to conduct an enchantment for them, self-cleaning floors. The activating word for the spell was Abracadabra, Jake's choice. Debris, small trash, and dust and dander would pile itself into the garbage.

Morgan, being too small, was dragged by the magik more than once. He had to be carried or rest atop the furniture while the Witchcraft was in use. It also required an annual maintenance spell to recharge its battery, so to speak. I don't mind, it was nice to have an obligation to them, a chance to contribute to the household. After all, chores are good for the soul.

Randomly, I was also baptized. Leave it to Joan to find some hippie Christian sect that was willing to baptize a Witch. The Mastersons had converted prior to my arrival. Frankly, I was just grateful for the distraction.

It was odd to see Joan singing enthusiastically during the service. Her gospel soprano was a clear polarity to the simplistic and soft Indie music of the hippie church, self-proclaimed as the Church of Movement and Sound. I read the Pastor's mind when she dunked me into a tub of water. I had to be certain she was not some radical cult leader.

No, just a regular kindergarten teacher who also happened to be transgendered as well as a practicing Buddhist. Joan, the ultimate advocate of human rights, was already her best friend. They were already planning campaigns and protests for various institutional inequities.

I wasn't sure any kind of specific god existed, but I do believe there was something more out there and even further beyond. Life may have its challenges, but I have to believe it always maintains its beauty. Look at all the magik.

My time there ended too quickly, but it, nor school, could be refused. I end up crying aggressively during my goodbyes, surprising everyone and even myself.

Joan, without skipping a beat, performs an in-depth interrogation that is only missing a dark room and a bright spotlight on my face. She cross-examines all aspects of my life at Philomena with every potential harmful scenario from sexual abuse to bullying.

"No, I promise, nothing's wrong, I am just going to miss you all so much," not a lie, but not the exact truth, either.

The following morning Dr. Huebner meets me at the front door and we return to Philomena using the same Walk-Easy that now feels familiar. During the trip he digressed into several topics that held little interest to me, until he brought up the O'Faolains, specifically David's recent encounter with a Vampyre. My heart beat faster and uncontrollably at the news.

It only slowed after several requests for repeated confirmations that he was indeed safe and untouched. David successfully suppressed the Vampyre through his telepathic abilities and even managed to coerce the being's agreement for detainment. Once stabilized, the afflicted individual consented to treatment at a local rehabilitation center specializing in curing infectious magik and other curses like Vampyrism.

I was relatively quiet for the rest of the trip. He asked me how I was doing, and I told him I was fine. The look on his face said he did not believe me, but he kindly did not press for more.

Once back at Philomena, I take a rather immediate exit to Spirit Manor and ride the Carriages alone instead of riding with Dr. Huebner via the Coachman and Tiny, my beloved Corrorabador. There are only a few individuals awake when I arrive at the Manor, but I manage to sneak up into my room without saying hello to any of them, even Ms. Penelope. Morgan and I lay in bed as I cried myself to sleep.

It had been nearly a full week of coursework. I have been busy catching up from my initial absence. Everything here felt the same and entirely different all at once. I now sit in Dr. Huebner's office drinking tea. He asked me to visit with him so we could discuss my schedule.

He wanted to modify my courses to better fit my current skill level based on my most recent display of power, "Translocation is a remarkable achievement, as is the power it must have required." Evidently, the Council ordered a team of Seers to investigate the scene. I panicked at the idea of the psychics reviewing the events of that night.

They said I produced some type of higher order magik, well beyond the scope of my age. They could not make heads or tails of how I achieved such a task. Apparently there were some missing events of that night that were hidden from their Vision, and they believe it was a side effect of the Vilix. Dr. Huebner was smiling from ear to ear during his review of the report.

"Was anything exciting or scary happening at the time of the incident?"

"I was scared something was in the water, I did it without thinking and that's pretty much all I remember," repeating the lie I used for Ms. O'Faolain. The partially false words defiled my mouth all over again.

"Perhaps it was merely adrenaline," he says dismissively. We finished reviewing my courses. I will be resuming my training with Madam Reyna for the Vilix, as well as covering additional spellwork on dimensional magik. I have no idea what that means, and I don't care enough to ask. He then tells me that my tutoring sessions with David will resume immediately, "You two shall focus on specific spells that I will review with both of you at our next meeting."

"But sir, I thought the tutoring was supposed to be re-evaluated in late October, to see if I still needed the training?" David and I have not spoken to each other since that night. He says he has been busy.

I know he is not.

I hate that I still look for him. It feels awful to invade his privacy, but I hate what I See even more, he is avoiding me. I do not look at his thoughts for several reasons. Reading someone's mind is invasive and requires a lack of regard for the person. Ultimately, that is the main reason why I keep out of the inner workings of his psyche, but I also think I am avoiding too.

I don't want to know what he thinks about me, it would be too devastating, and my fragile heart may not withstand the impact. I allow fear, shame, and guilt to do their work and hope it can keep me from watching him at all, eventually.

Seeing from a distance is not like knowing his thoughts, it is the difference between watching him or being him. I know he takes the long way to class. I know that when he sees me having lunch at the Pillar, he turns around and makes his way to the Castle.

From a bird's eye-view, I See him read during his free time instead of practicing Sorcellirae with his teammates. I forbid myself from zooming in out of respect.

"Dear Mr. Ellis, no rest for the wicked, life favors the prepared and tutoring will give you exactly the preparation needed for your advancement. Now run along, class is in session," commands Dr. Huebner.

I am almost out the door when he reminds me about my Evaluations scheduled for mid-November. I asked if I should be worried and he laughed indignantly, "Of course not dear boy, you will be fabulous."

Still feeling dejected, I walk rather slowly to Advanced Conjuration. I was not sure which was more devastating, David having to be forced to spend time with me, or the reason for his disdain. I wrap my grey trench coat even more tightly around me, and hope it will warm this cold and numbing feeling growing inside.

My eyes glow a soft blue, the random byproduct of the Vilix seems to be increasing in frequency. The color is oppositional against the dark sky. The other students' eyes on my own confirm my observation. I look away but end up finding two, particularly pretty, brown eyes that I have not seen since summer. He takes my breath away, in typical David O'Faolain fashion.

It had only been a few weeks since the trip, but he is even more handsome than before. All debonair without any pretentiousness, the rest of the summer had been good to him. Maybe it was because I missed him, but he seemed taller, broader, his body responding perfectly to time and sunlight.

I felt like some naked degenerate in that moment, as if I had come upon him intentionally. I feared desperation was stamped on my face for the entire world to see. Like the truth had finally been revealed, I do not belong here, near him, or anywhere.

Suddenly he stood before me, taller, that was confirmed, and more handsome, a shattering defiance against probability. How can someone be more perfect?

"Hey Noah," his voice slightly deeper, his muscles distinct in the outline of his sweater and slacks. I barely managed to speak, let alone make sense. I rambled on about classes and non-significant things like today's lunch choices, until I blurt out, "I've missed you." Catching myself, I quickly looked away and forced my mouth to remain silent.

"I missed you too," he says back. I stared up at him, but he was looking far past me.

"Listen Noah, about this summer."

We talk, rather, he talks for less than five minutes. That is all the time he needs to effectively devastate my world. Once he is done, I carefully step aside to reveal nothing and simply say, "Okay," and as I say so I hear him whisper, "Noah."

"It's fine, I have to get class, see ya," and I walk away. I felt his eyes on me. My own were distraught to not meet his, they dared me to turn around, but fearful my deviant tears would rage against me and invariably win their war. I keep walking with my eyes dry.

I ended the school day early, citing a stomach bug to Professor Duchovny, who discharged me to the Infirmary. The Healers cannot find or treat the ailment. I was not lying, my stomach did hurt, but for other reasons. They sent me home with tonics and restorative healing stones to be placed underneath my bed. They glow a soft amber.

It was unpleasant, I felt like a hole was growing in my belly. I finally crawl my way into the soft sheets of my bed when Maria calls to check up on me, "I'm okay."

"Are they going to make you go to the Esbat?"

"Shit, I forgot that was tonight." All I wanted to do was be consumed by this bed and sleep the day away.

"Do you think I can weasel my way out of it?"

"Are you bleeding?"

"No."

"Hmm," scheming for a plausible solution, "Did you go to the Infirmary?"

"Yes."

"Did they give you a tonic or some kind of charm?"

"These yellow charms."

"Damn. Unless you pass out there is no way Madam Reyna is letting you off the hook." I groan and use more profanities than I am used to, but finally accept reality.

"Sorry Noah, meet you in a few hours my Crown," she says sympathetically. "Thanks, my Lord," I say in sardonic contrast.

"I'll see you soon Maria," this time, a little more pleasantly.

Chapter Twenty-Four

Mimicry magik, better known as mirroring, a type of Witchcraft meant for copying the physical and intellectual skills of others. Please note advanced mastery of telepathy is critical for successful mirroring.

The other Seers and I take the Bridge to the Palladium, Philomena's central stadium, and we are crossing over Lake Osage nearly reaching our destination. We participate in our part for the Drawing of the Moon as David's coven sings their song to call us forward. I use the Vilix to hear his voice, it is clear and distinguished from the choir, haunting me in unimaginable ways.

I start complaining to Leroy, "This is pointless, we do this for some make-believe union between our Covens. Honestly, who thought up this bullshit?" He almost dropped his lantern at my outburst. I didn't mean to shout but I was tired and desperate to make this hole in my heart go away.

He does not realize I genuinely want an answer, but quickly gains this insight when I stubbornly refuse to walk any further, at least until I am provided an explanation. Derailed by my tantrum, he needs me to repeat the question, "I guess, What's the point? And don't give me some nonsense about Divine right or whatever the hell you call it."

He cautiously responds, "I guess the best explanation would probably be our Grimoires."

Each Coven has their own magikal book, a sacred text that contains specialized spells and history of the Coven. Leroy explained that unlike other Covens, the Crowns and Lords have one additional Grimoire that is shared between the two. Neither of us have even seen the separate or shared magikal texts, but Leroy's mother, a Seer, worked closely with them during her Dedication.

"She once told me a story she read in our shared Grimoire, about the origin of our Covens, a myth to be sure." He grinned awkwardly before he spoke, "Supposedly, we are descended from the First Witch, the oldest of the Ancient Ones, interestingly enough she was the First of the Recessive origin." He looks away, giving me the impression he was embarrassed to discuss the fable, "What's the story?" My interest must have shown because when he returns his attention, so too did my reliable tour guide, and he enthusiastically elaborates.

"They say when she became pregnant with her first-born; she used her Sight and discovered the child was a boy. It is unclear why, but she needed her first child to be a daughter. According to legend, the First cast a spell invoking the dark powers of the Divine to change the child's sex. The spell backfired and split the son into two, a boy and a girl. The First was initially overjoyed by the unexpected results of the spell, at least until their birth. To her delight, the daughter developed vast amounts of power that far surpassed her mother's, but the son inherited all of the First's psychic abilities, leaving her with none. The son, the Seer, and the daughter, the Soldier. Feminist Witches often cite this lore as literary evidence to support the claim that female Witches are far stronger than their male counterparts."

"What do you mean?"

"Well, if you compare the power between a male and female Legacy Witch of similar lineage and skill, almost always the female is more powerful. But no scientific researcher in their right mind would use this myth to explain that unusual phenomenon."

It is interesting, according to genetics Mortals and Witches alike all start female, only by mutation do we become males. The story reminds me of a mathematical theory on probability based on the idea of necessity and possibility. Of what is, and what could be, given the opportunity. In some ways, females were the first primal force needed for life, while males, existing out of need and circumstance, were secondary.

Leroy goes on to say that the twins were stolen from the First, but with the absence of her Sight, she was unable to find them. Defeated but unable to cease living, she continued to live a half-life, giving birth to other children, "Supposedly, Legacy Witches found in lesser Covens."

"Lesser, that's an awful thing to say."

He laughs, "You have to keep in mind these ancient books are sometimes filled with stories no more magikal than the stories told to Mortal children." Leroy lacks appreciation for the power that lives inside words.

"What happened to the twins?"

"Well, according to the translations of the meticulous prophecies from the famous Seer Aritoles, they are believed to have been abducted by Mortals. He claimed he was victimized by Visions of the twins being forced to reproduce. Supposedly, their descendants are said to be the Crowns and Lords of our Covens. Seers are born from the son and Lords from the Daughter. Based on the lore, their blood eagerly searches for the other so they can once again be whole, hence the shared Grimoire and the supposed union between us. Then again, Aritoles also had a reputation for being a bit of a loon."

"Still sounds like a tragedy," I say quietly, but I don't have a chance to ask anything further. We have arrived at the Palladium and now face the entire student body of Philomena. My anxiety creeps into my throat like a chokehold, but I put one foot in front of the other and it eventually subsides. I place my lantern on the large stone table and the light inside floats out and travels further up the Palladium, offering its shine for the night's work. David stands only a few feet in front of me, I try my best to avoid his gaze.

Their song comes to an end and Dean Tetson steps up to the podium. Tonight was a special ceremony honoring the Autumn Equinox. After we are served cakes and ale, the Dean instructs the student body to sit in self-reflection in celebration of the coming fall. She allows for individual pairs or collectives, as she calls it, to gather.

Maria and I claimed dibs on one another. We sit in a circle of white tall candles underneath a bizarrely oversized oak tree. The scent of the charred wick lingers in the air. The students of Philomena and the citizens of Tarias scatter about and light their own circle of candles. Dancing starlight litters the mountainside, revealing its slope while making the night come alive.

"Have you talked to David, he has been a little off, like, I don't know, just not very David-like?"

"No."

"Why, what happened to you two?"

"Nothing, sorry, I forgot we talked earlier today," I felt feverish just mentioning his name. "He and I have both been really busy," I uselessly lie to the girl that knows me too well.

"So," looking directly into my eyes, "How was your summer?" Not so discreetly asking me to spill, she has already heard my benign answer on my first day back.

"Good, yours?"

"You know how my summer went, boring as all get out." She pauses, "But I don't really know all that much about yours," hitting the bullseye with her arrow of accusation, "You haven't even told me about Hawaii."

"Everything is fine, I promise," I tried my best to sound upbeat, but my voice sounded flat and empty, even to me.

"Noah, what's wrong?" She pauses for only a moment. "You've been quiet all week long, upset or something, you don't seem right. I say that as one of your best friends. Speaking of, where is David, anyway?"

She looks around as if he would appear out of the candle's vapors, "So, currently I am your only friend." I chuckle more bitterly than I intended, "Thanks."

She adds, "I say that with all the love in the world. Neither of us are swimming with besties, I mean hell, I can't even keep a man." She and Aaron had recently broken up. He claimed it was because of Maria's "emotional reactions", though some would say overreactions. If I am honest, she could be a bit high-strung, a fact that I would deny and contend all the way to the end. Maria was strong and I loved her for it.

We can't help but break down in laughter, the kind that bubbles out at first and then turns into a roar, regardless of my own obstinance to feel anything but self-pity. We laugh at our own ridiculousness and reclusiveness. We are loners that do not want to be alone. Thank goodness we have each other, besides we don't need more best friends, well maybe one more, at least for me.

After a minute or so, the surge of giggles recedes as things of that nature usually do.

She sighs, collecting herself, no longer joking, refusing to be distracted from our original topic. I think she saw what lived on my face. Concerned, she tried to remove the worried mark and will not be refused.

"Seriously, Noah, what happened?"

"Nothing." Silence fills the void as we play secrets and chicken. "Nothing really," breathe, I remind myself, "something though, I don't know, I think, I'm not sure."

"What the hell did you just say?"

I laugh, "Sorry for rambling."

"I didn't know how I really felt before, I guess I always knew but wouldn't let myself believe it," pausing and breathing for good measure, wanting to be stronger than I was, "I am," breathe, "in love with him." I expected Maria to tell me something along the lines of *duh* while rolling her eyes in her harmless joking way.

It leaves me speechless to see my sweet best friend, and yes only friend, with tears shamelessly streaming down her beautiful face. All my defenses begin to fall unwillingly as a result, but I am rapidly losing the power to sustain them.

"I am so sorry Noah. What did he do, did he do something to you? Tell me."

"No, nothing like that, he didn't hurt me."

"Okay good, cause I would've killed him," she sighs in relief with persistent tears in her eyes. "Then what?"

I hesitate, so many walls of mine are crashing down. All the secret corners of my hidden world transform eerily into focus, "We kissed, and a little more, but not much more, and then something else happened." I choke on the last part, "There's something you should know about me, about the things I've been through."

Pausing and breathing some more, I share the details of that night with her, but only the parts that directly relate to it and without excess, I guess some walls remain. The flames of our candles begin to dim despite the still air and plentiful supply of wick and wax. Maria is crying in such a way that makes me think that the world may have come to an end, "He hasn't talked to me much since then, except just to say that it was a mistake."

My hands hold each other like it's the last time they'll meet, "I didn't think it was a mistake, not for me," I say in a whisper, "I don't know how to stop myself from loving him."

Maria leans in to hug me and the pieces of me fall apart. I think maybe her hug broke me, the capacity of my well too full to tolerate any more emotions. Although maybe I was already falling apart and her knowing hands came to catch what she could. She holds me tightly, trying to contain all that remained.

Finally accepting her help, I allow myself to fall into her shoulder as I cry rivers into the world. At the same time, a gust of wind surged from our circle extinguishing our candles. It spreads across Tarias in a perfect ring, disturbing the meadows and trees as it travels throughout the mountain, taking the light from every burning candle along with it, banishing the stars on the ground. Their owners hopelessly attempt to relight them with fire and magik, but those candles died that night, and would never burn again.

The ceremony abruptly ends shortly after, Maria offers, more like begs, to come to the Manor with me at least a dozen times. She is afraid to leave me alone. I reassured her that I would be okay, "Honestly, I actually feel a little bit better, just tired and ready for bed." We said goodbye and once I managed to release myself from her cage of a hug, I returned to the Manor with the rest of the Seers.

Restless and unable to find sleep, I lay in bed with Morgan wrestling with thoughts that demanded to be heard; all were about David. He told me we were better off as friends. I have to come to terms with the undeniable truth that he doesn't want me. There is an awful feeling growing in the pit of my stomach, it threatens to swallow me whole.

Morgan purrs softly and sweetly in my arms while I breathe through this sudden wave of pain, nudging his head into my arm until I calm myself. I love him so much, but then an uninvited and most terrible thought manifests within me, Morgan's life will not last as long as my own.

My mind is flooded with fear. He is the only thing that has stayed with me all this time. The one part of my life that has remained constant. I couldn't lose him. I was so tired of losing people.

He purrs louder now as I cry persistently. He suddenly stops to stare up into my eyes, his way of reminding me to pet him. I do so obligingly, but only for a conservatively short duration of time. Morgan, my special one, runs his own show. He leaps out of bed to stalk the corridors of the Manor. My bedroom door automatically reacts to his request, slightly opening so he can nudge his way through before gently re-shutting itself. I know when he returns the door will respond agreeably and reopen automatically, it seemed like Morgan had his own bit of magik.

Magikal pets, that reminds me of something extraordinary, Faemalyrs, the Witch's pet offers a potential solution to my crisis. The life of a Faemalyr can be extended by casting a magikal bind between it and the life force of its Witch. It is a rare magik, only a few have been successful in achieving that level of a bond. My insecurities rapidly rise within me forcing me to doubt my abilities, but another part of me contests its logic. Maybe I can do it. Everyone keeps telling me that my powers are miraculous, and if that is the case, then why couldn't I attempt one more incredible feat. I have a longer life span regardless and I refuse to live it alone.

No longer crying, I get out of bed and grab the book to reread the concept of Faemalyrs and bindings. My plan brews as I furiously take notes into the late night and only begrudgingly return to bed once I've read all there is to read on the section. There is nowhere near enough information on the topic. The first step in completing Project Morgan is to conduct an exhaustive study on all things related to Faemalyrs. Tomorrow evening I will make a special trip to the Castle to research the topic. Back in bed, I fall asleep surprisingly fast. My mind and body must have relaxed with the plan in place.

Unfortunately, Dr. Huebner, in his typical fashion, impulsively ordered the meeting for David and myself that following morning. I arrived half an hour early to avoid running into David while in the building, but he was already seated when I entered the Doctor's office. Dr. Huebner does not waste time providing his directives. Starting today, I am obligated to attend training with Madam Reyna followed by tutoring with David every evening, Monday through Thursday. It would seem my plans to visit the Castle tonight would have to wait until Friday.

Dr. Huebner informs us of the specific training regimen. He would tutor me on eight particular spells. He took notes with impeccable scrutiny and is unwilling to take his pretty brown eyes off the page, consequently making my chest feel tight. Thankfully, the Doctor discharged David to his classes before dismissing me, an unintentional kindness. I was dreading walking out the door alone with him.

Dr. Huebner asked me to stay so that he could give me the textbooks needed for training. He puts several healthy, heavy volumes of books into my magikal, and seemingly bottomless, bookbag before sending me on my way.

I met Maria in Alchemy. She wears this sad familiar expression on her face, one that I cannot allow. "Don't you dare feel sorry for me," I condemn.

"I don't," says the liar. I stared at her indignantly.

"Okay, okay, I won't. Do you want to talk about it?"

"Nope."

"Okay, that's fine," raising her hands to surrender, "Changing topics then, how about we have dinner this Friday at the Stables?"

"That's perfect," I say excitedly. The Stables are a training ground for supernatural creatures that happens to have a detached bistro with an entirely vegetarian menu. It is conveniently close to the Castle, I could go there right after dinner.

Surprised at my instantaneous reaction, "Awesome, the cheese enchiladas there are so good. I can't wait."

After school, Madam Reyna and I meet at the renovated Observatory. She is predictably meditating. Legacy or not, she is a true devout Witch.

"Have a seat, Noah."

She provides an overview of Dr. Huebner's requested training. It is all related to Nekromancy, magik involving the dead. The Doctor requested I focus on a specific ritual that challenged even the more advanced Nekromancers, one that required several types of magik. Madam Reyna discusses it further, "In order to open the gates between our realm and the realm of the dead, a Witch must possess Transdimensional abilities, the Divine skills of a Seer, and an exceptional power source required in any Celestial spell."

"Geez, all that to basically create a door?"

Madam Reyna looks at me with ice in her eyes, "Additionally, advanced skills are needed in Evocation to summon the dead and Abjuration to send them back. We will not be practicing the spell, obviously."

Apparently these acts of magik come at a great strain to the Witch performing the spell. Many Witches have died to accomplish this type of Craft. Madam Reyna tells me she will teach me components of the spell, perfecting my skills in those areas.

"You must first learn to summon gates and then to close them. We begin practice tomorrow evening, 5PM sharp."

"Yes, ma'am."

Our session ends, and for the first time ever, I do not want to leave her classroom, but I am supposed to meet David. I walk slowly and deliberately to the meeting place, dreading each step that brought me closer to the perfect boy.

Chapter Twenty-Five

Be warned; Magik carries a signature, like thumb prints.

Training with David turned out to be more pleasant than I was expecting.

He had invited a few of his friends to help. I think to reduce the tension between us. Thankfully, we had the spell to focus on, and his friends, Wryder Rodriguez and Gerald Harish-Mal, were jovial and blessedly distracting.

We started right away, I was practicing the Hand of Fatima, a barrier that is impenetrable from psychic, cosmic, and elemental attacks.

I have mastered some spells in forming barriers, so I am not starting from scratch like back in the early days of my tutoring.

We practiced late into the evening, casting the spell several times. To my surprise, I mastered the magik that same night, creating the specific barrier with ease and, not to boast, expertise.

The barrier was meant to be malleable and I successfully changed its form and size, as well as its layers of protection effortlessly.

I held the transparent energy around me, allowing for the breeze to enter but kept back the torrents of rain and devastating winds sent from David. I was even able to block Wryder Rodriguez. He was from the Coven of Astrylum, whose members all specialize in Celestial magik.

He threw a Heavenly Earthquake, an offensive spell channeled from the cosmic giant Jupiter, known only for its capacity to destroy.

It didn't even shake me.

Unfortunately, the outdoor space we practiced in did not fare so well. It was like a bomb went off and resembled a battlefield more than a courtyard.

David casts a spell to repair the damage inflicted by Wryder's magik, signaling the end of our session. His friends leave as the spell takes effect.

It was different from the spell Maria used to reassemble the chair I accidentally destroyed last spring. His magik seemed to move time backwards. The shattered concrete and stone structures reenact the destruction, only in reverse, before returning to their original form.

It took five minutes for the spell to finish the job. Those five minutes should have been devastatingly awkward but wasn't because I was too busy marveling at the sophistication of his magik.

After those five minutes, he turns to me and says, "You did well Noah, it's impressive how much you've improved." He literally pats my shoulder as if I have shingles, "Are you going to be alright to walk home alone?"

"Yeah, I'll be fine, thanks for the help. I'll see you tomorrow."

"Yup, same time, same place. Have a good night Noah, sleep well."

"Thanks, you too," I say without a smile and turn to walk away, looking back out of habit, but he is far away now. He must have used a Versation type of power to travel the distance in such a short amount of time. I can barely make out his silhouette in the distance.

"I miss you," I whisper to myself and walk back to the Manor to end the night.

Maria and I meet at the Stables that following evening. Over dinner, I confess my plans to make Morgan a Faemalyr, "I want one too," she said excitedly.

"Of course! As soon as I figure it out, I think you have to bond with a pet first," I advise.

"I want a bird, a big one, like a condor."

"I don't think you can have a condor as a pet, isn't that like animal cruelty?"

"Is it?" We brainstorm on condor alternatives, still uncertain she announces, "Whatever, I'll figure it out." We finish our vegetarian meals and a glass of red wine; we are only allowed one.

She gossips about a new love interest from the Coven of the Pentacle, the elemental Coven, a rugged and well-built Witch named Allen Casta.

After a bit more conversation, we end the evening and say goodnight. She returns to the Mansion as I head southward toward the Castle. She asked to come but I told her it was going to be boring and not to worry about it.

In truth, the reason I didn't invite her was that it felt like a private matter, something just between Morgan and me.

Each step toward the Castle fills me with a newfound sense of reverence for the building. Its stone gargoyles with their intimidating size and sharply pointed spires most assuredly qualify it as the most supernatural-looking thing in all of Tarias.

Once inside, I beeline it to the card catalogs and make quick work to pull every text I could find on the history and principles on everything containing the word

"Faemalyr".

My first query leads me to a reference used in the Mortal world.

> Familiar - noun, a demon attending to the demands of a Witch. Origin - Latin - servant.

I still sometimes misinterpret words or phrases in the Witch world, their meaning and spelling could vary tremendously from the world I used to know so well. Daemon, for example, refers to destructive magik and not some devil or king of hell. I scan the texts and find the proper reference to my search.

> A Faemalyr is an infused living organism that has developed a psychic bond with a Witch. This connection can be developed into a Bind, in which case the Faemalyr is linked to the Witch's life force and magikal properties.

Morgan and I have achieved a bond, but I wondered if "Bind" represented something else, I continued my search using various names with slight discrepancies and alternative words altogether.

> Bind. Bond. Bound. Binding.

The last query leads to a plethora of articles related to bindings of the more adult and non-magik variety.

I feel defeated. Maybe there wasn't a spell, or if there was, maybe it was so old that it was forgotten. I could use the Vilix to search the past, but to search all of history was an impossible task. Or maybe I can figure it on my own. I knew I needed to infuse my magik with him, binding him to me I guess, and then I remembered something Dr. Huebner once explained to me.

The second Origin of a Witch, the Blessed origin. A Mortal and a supernatural force bind their energies, blessing the person with magik, creating a Witch. I scroll through the catalogs cross-referencing

Faemalyrs

and

blessings

and finally, with a bit of luck:

> The Challenges of the Blessed Bind of the Faemalyr. Also known as Servant of thy Wise One.
>
> Few Witches have successfully cast this spell. Many problematic components to the ritual contribute to the severely limited successful executions of this Witchcraft. It requires mastery over several Transdimensional and Celestial magikal abilities, notoriously difficult skills to master.
>
> A Witch must have a large reserve of magik and incredible endurance to create the Blessing. The spell does put the Witch at risk of death. A final barrier includes the attachment between the animal and the Witch. It is said that the entity chosen to receive the blessing must accept it, willingly. Otherwise, all her effort will be for nothing, and will quite possibly result in the death of both the Witch and the animal.

Never have I felt so certain about something, Morgan would choose me. Unfortunately, I found nothing further on the subject. I thought that maybe I could make sense of the magik required using the Vilix, but the spell involves magik with other realms.

The dynamic of spiritual energies is complex, and my mind could not possibly comprehend the vastness of those energies.

I needed a spell. I continue searching for the better part of two hours, but I am finally forced to surrender. I pack up my things and return to the Manor.

The next morning, I wake up late and rush to Morning Meds. Madam Reyna, despite her sympathies toward me, was not opposed to having a full fit over my tardiness.

Sure enough, "So nice of you to join us," she said with spite.

"You will not improve Mr. Ellis if you are unable to practice your meditative state, and you cannot improve if you do not attend to your gift. Clearly, something you are in desperate need of, given your inability to simply arrive on time, disgraceful."

My face flushes with heat as the entire classroom turns to see my embarrassment. I breathe in deep. I want to cry and yell at her.

"I'm sorry, Madam Reyna." I stare at the jewel centered on her forehead just to avoid meeting her condemning eyes. It was only 10 minutes. I bring my eyes to meet hers, "I will be on time going forward."

"Have a seat."

Already dreading tonight, I don't need to be a Seer to know my tardiness will negatively affect my training with her. I had no idea how accurate my prediction would be, as several hours later I took cover underneath a table made of stone.

Madam Reyna borrowed Professor's Sutton's Detention Room for Misbehaved and Delinquent Witches for our exercises.

It is a Spirit Trap, a vortex meant to contain Witches. The vortex was designed in the style of a dungeon with a dragon, the beast kind, breathing fire from far above me. While I could feel pain, I couldn't actually get hurt in this pocket dimension. Earlier, she had reviewed a section of the Nekromancy spell,

Despirir Nekroncia.

My job was to summon a dimensional doorway. The vortex offered me the ideal opportunity to open a gateway, and as she put it, "It is good motivation to get out quickly."

In terms of procedure, opening and closing gates was the relatively easy part, all that was required was an iron lantern that burned primordial oil, myrth, and grinded coal. Its flame is not easily extinguished, and its scent assaults the senses.

Alongside my locket and cat charm was a small vial filled with condensed and crushed dark purple petals, an attempt to aid my magikal ability.

Per Madam Reyna's instruction, I cast the sigil by carving into the ground with Transference magik, destroying the floor, and stretch my hands out high while casting the incantation.

Nexia, Septus, Despirorian.

Then, in my native tongue, ***Open Thy Gates***.

The Sigil of Nekros, the gateway of the dead, appears beneath the ground below me, marking the Transdimensional door.

Only nothing happened, and I dive to the next cover as the dragon prepares his next bout of fiery burps to be hurled in my direction.

Madam Reyna is forced to release me. She wore a face filled with pure bewilderment, as if I somehow managed to stoop even further below her expectations. She assigns me an excessive amount of homework, magikal exercises designed to increase my stamina.

I wasn't even angry, there was a satisfaction in the notion that I could very well be Madam Reyna's greatest disappointment. She provided a small pharmacy of herbs and potions to enhance my strength and resilience.

The charms originally placed after my first incident here at St. Philomena are to be removed. The initial purpose of these spells was to subdue my powers while I gained control of them, but they were now a hindrance to my success.

David waits outside the Observatory's main entrance, leaning against the exterior wall looking like some 80s heartthrob, all classic and gorgeous.

"You okay?"

He seemed worried about me. I thought I would never see that on his face again, "Yup, right as rain," as I wipe the dirt that covered my face, a direct result from rolling on the dungeon floor, "Just a rough day."

"Oh shit, did Reyna ream into you?"

"Something like that, what are you doing here? I thought I was meeting you at Lola?"

"I have a Healing class this semester, figured I would wait for you."

The intrusive memory of that night with him flashes vividly in my mind. A reminder that David would never want to be with me.

I want to hate him, but I think that is impossible, because I cannot help but still be in love with him.

"Oh," I say finally.

I felt so alone, and it seems like the air grows thin. I thought of Morgan. I don't know what came over me but before my mind could catch up with my mouth, "Hey, do you know anything about Faemalyrs?"

David was superior over me in both skill and knowledge; maybe he would have more practical information than what I could find in textbooks.

"That's random," he says, raising a quizzical brow, but quickly concedes after a second of my silence, "A bit, never been my sort of thing."

"How is it done? Is there a spell?"

"In theory, it probably just requires a combination of Binding, Conjuration, and Evocation. I suppose it also depends on the kind of bond you are creating. A generic one should be relatively easy."

I nod "But how is it done, the non-generic kind?"

"That type of magik is advanced, it's not even taught in the normal curriculum. It requires summoning loads of energies and probably dangerous. Why do you ask, trying to upgrade the black cat?"

Asshole, "Yes, by the way, that black cat has a name." I say with no inflection or smile, "Don't call Morgan a cat, as if he doesn't matter."

He puts his hands up in the air, surrendering, "Alright, white flag No-" he was almost going to call me No-El. Things were too different now, we were too different, "I'm sorry Noah, Morgan it is."

"Thanks, apology accepted."

He sports a grin that would have been perfect if not for the sadness in them. He lifts his backpack with an empty smile, and I return it with my own absent one.

We walk together toward Lola. I think that as some sort of reparation, he explains his understanding of the magik behind Faemalyrs.

"Have you ever heard of a weaving loom?"

"Like a spindle?"

"Something like that, the weaver looms with perfect accuracy each string of yarn or twill. The magik is something like that, except the strings you'd be weaving represent all the forces of life and death, up to and including time, and probably even gravity, because you are dealing with souls."

"That reminds me of the Vilix."

"Suppose you are right, if anyone can do it, it would be you," and if it is possible, I think he blushed.

"Maybe, I am not so sure. Although I can connect to those energies, I don't know if I could do the weaving."

Unfortunately, I had limitations. Although my abilities have improved generally, my use of them in the Vilix state could use some development, and in all honesty, I had been on a bit of a hiatus in terms of training it.

"Noah, you can't use that kind of magik, that's why those sorts of magikal books are in the Controlled Section, reserved for dark magik, texts that deal with dangerous and sometimes deadly Witchcraft." I guess he sees the hurt on my face, he quickly adds, "But don't worry about it, you will probably be able to do it in the future, in a few decades or so, maybe then you can try?"

I stay quiet. A few decades, Morgan would die by then, I don't have that kind of time.

"Where is the Controlled Section?"

"Beneath the Castle. Noah, you can't go down there without authorization. There are loads of protective charms and curses shielding the place from intruders."

"Right, what if I talked to Dr. Huebner about it, maybe they'll give me permission?"

He sighs and seems relieved, "Sure, I don't know if he'll give in, even if it is *you* asking, but you never know. There's no harm in giving it a shot," he says, eyes looking away now.

Eventually we arrived at Lola for training. Today we are working on the second task Doctor Huebner assigned to me, something called a Cardinal Bind, which refers to control over at least one of the four primary elements. I had none.

The Elements are challenging. The Cardinal Bind was a lot like the Blessed Bind. It was a sacred thing, like being chosen.

David has all four of the Cardinal powers, is there nothing that he cannot do?

He lays out an assortment of books and supplies prepared to test which element I would have the most innate talent to develop. I had some talent in influencing the weather, but that magik is not a Cardinal Bind.

He recommended I start with Fyre since I had some skills in conjuring flames to candle, but in the end, it was Aer that I had the most propensity to develop.

I finally managed to summon a breeze at the end of our session, it did not qualify as a Cardinal Bind, but it was a start.

I hurried back to the Manor as soon as our training was complete, eager to ask Dr. Huebner for permission to enter the Controlled Section. I write the letter quickly and send it off with the magikal box that Translocates its contents to the intended recipients.

Closing the lid once and just as quickly reopening it, the box was now empty, proof that my letter had been delivered.

Chapter Twenty-Six

Shed fur from Golden Tibetan Monkeys to add an excellent addition to any fate and luck potion.

Lavender dances in the air but does nothing to soothe me. Dr. Huebner has refused my request. He provided his response earlier that morning through the post.

> I am sorry Mr. Ellis, but that type of material simply is not appropriate for a young Witch. Those texts contain dangerous magik, and as your Crown Guardian, I must think of your safety first.

I had even gone so far as to ask Madam Reyna for permission, figuring she would agree to anything that would enhance my psychic skills, but she just laughed at me and said, "Absurd, get control of your punctuality first."

Attempting to negotiate, I came to his office after training with David, but ended up uselessly pleading with him. Frustrated, I start packing my things, "It's okay, Doctor," fighting back these damn tears. I felt so powerless. I wish the Doctor goodnight and leave his office.

As I walk downstairs, I reflexively feel for my locket, but touch empty air. In a panic, I search for it using my Sight. It hangs on the hook of my towel rack back at the Manor. I forgot to put it back on after I showered this morning.

It dawns on me to use the Vilix to enter the Controlled Section, if one of those books do contain the spell of the Blessed Bind, maybe I can learn it without physically having the book. Instead of going back to the Manor, I decided to return to the Castle, determined to search the Controlled Section.

On my way to the East Lab located in Bexar and Gruene Hall, I spot the two gay ghosts canoodling in the upper level.

"Get a room," I said playfully, now in a much better mood.

We are not doing anything, says Bexar, the larger of the two.

It is not a crime to hug the man you love, adds Gruene, as the two refasten their canvas breeches and dull colored frock coats.

"I didn't know you were supposed to hump when you hug?"

You Peeping Tom! Good day, Noah Ellis, says Gruene while he resets his powdered wig.

Bexar laughing, quips, *Go find a boyfriend.* They turn translucent and vanish, "Tried that, but not one of my gifts." I say to only myself.

I arrive at the Castle twenty minutes later. I could have used the Vilix back at the Manor, but it was best to be as close as possible to the Castle's Dungeon below since this would be a first for me.

I thought it best to start with my Altar, a manifestation of myself that can extend beyond me. Most Seers tend to be exceptionally skilled in this Witchcraft. For us it is like riding a bike, mostly everyone can do it. This kind of Seeing was nowhere near as clear as the Vilix, but my Altar was far less distracting. I had more control going this route.

Everything has a unique energy pattern. Some things are relatively similar, but there are still subtle differences. Usually, when I am searching for someone or something, I have a familiarity with what that thing or person.

The more familiar I am with them, the easier it is to find their unique pattern. If I do not, I can find them through a small trace, like a place or person that has interacted with them. That is how I intended to find the Controlled Section. I would use the Castle's proximity to the Dungeon as my starting point.

It takes less than a minute for my energy to separate from my body, and then I See myself. I am sitting upright on a plain wooden chair, in a white shirt and red cardigan, my eyes are closed and my palms rest on my lap.

My Altar phases through the floors below in search of the room. I experience the textures of the objects through this psychic extension of me. Then I find myself in a tunnel with long winding stone stairs that further descend. The hall is dimly lit by enchanted blue fire held high above by some invisible force. I make my way down the steps into the heart of the mountain. It takes nearly an hour, but I finally reach my destination.

Unfortunately, it is located on the opposite side of large iron gates. There are words and symbols carved into them, written in old Witch language, one of the hidden dead languages, something I was still learning to translate. I already know what they are, I can feel it, curses meant to keep out invaders. My Altar is unable to pass through the barricade of enchantments.

I call the Vilix now, its mystical power rises within me, expectantly. My Altar returns as my mind opens. I feel the room around me. It shifts into the Castle and the caves of the mountain and then the earth below, followed by the air above. I See my body tucked away in an isolated section of the library, on the seventh floor.

This level primarily housed large volumes of reference material seldom used by the student body. The faculty typically have whatever material they need delivered by magikal means. Tall shelves huddle close together throughout the entire floor.

I chose this secluded back corner for its privacy, knowing that I would need to use the Vilix.

The Northern Lights produced by the Vilix calls too much attention to itself. I couldn't risk anyone figuring out what I was doing and prohibit me from going further.

The sensation is still strange. I can See the cryptic Castle, but at the same time, I exist within it and everything beyond. It was still a bit overwhelming. Even though my psychic eye was set here in Tarias, the power of the Vilix could easily locate energy forces outside of this space. The familiar ones were almost automatically made known to me. One swept me away like a hurricane.

One minute I am viewing myself in the room and the next I am back home in the quiet suburbs of Westchester. The Mastersons lie in their beds, peacefully asleep. The neighborhood, a living, breathing system, couples fighting, a child with a fever, a woman exercising, and the earth below shifting and the air racing.

I think of David, and I am exceptionally and extraordinarily familiar with David O'Faolain. Instantly I am with him. He sits in one of the Mansions' common rooms, but there are too many sensations and I am derailed once more.

The Visions are of things David had recently interacted with like the gym, his bedroom at the Mansion, then his family home in Athru, and finally back to him. I ground myself to the area around David, focusing on the sound reverberating off the air to slow my mind.

Once my Sight is steady, I return my attention to the mission and think of Morgan. All at once I am taken back to the Manor. He is sleeping lazily on the bed, his head jerks up almost as if he knows I am here. He stretches his feline body and yawns widely. A desperate feeling grows within me. I want to have him for the rest of my life.

Something shifts and it all goes blurry. Everything zooms past me. It seems as if I was moving forward and not moving at all and, suddenly, I am back at the Dungeon facing the iron gates that guard the Controlled Section.

Only with the full plethora of my psychic powers, the curses are now unable to restrict my access as I exist within them and this place.

Thinking of what I want, I search using words from the spell's name.

Blessed.

Bind.

Servant of Thy Wise One.

Faemalyr.

There it is, the pattern, it leads me to a brown leather-bound book held within a glass case. It is much larger than I expected, about the size of a small portrait. Words of the dead Witch language are written on its cover, the same type of language carved into the iron gates.

Through the Vilix their meaning is revealed to me, both a warning to intruders and instructions for welcomed guests. To use the magik found within its pages, a Witch must provide a prerequisite of blood. The book reveals itself to me, Grimoire Despiraes, owned by Covens Divina Diademate and Ius Divinum, the shared Grimoire of the Crowns and Lords.

Inside its contents were spells written in many languages, most were somewhat familiar, yet there were texts and symbols that seemed entirely alien. Eventually, I locate the ritual of the Blessed Bind. I try to memorize it, but the words shift into another language, a ward for those who would attempt to invade its pages.

I attempt to reach further into the Grimoire's contents, but the extensive barriers give me cause to hesitate. This magik was thoroughly on another level than any magik I have experienced thus far.

Something about forcing my way into this book evoked an intense feeling of trepidation, as if it would be offended; such an act would be met with serious consequences. It was intimidating.

This book is more than just a container of ancient spells, it held a power within, it held the magik necessary to complete all its spells, including the Blessed Bind. Not only did I not have the spell, but I need to physically possess the book in order to cast it.

My Vision returns to my physical body. I make my way to the staircase that would lead to the Controlled Section. I was hopeful that I could retrieve the book on my own but Professor Libiski, the Librarian, cuts me off, "Library closes in an hour for Preparatory Witches. I do believe it is past your curfew, Mr. Ellis."

How was I going to get that damn book? I couldn't influence him, could I? Well, I can at least try, but I hesitate, weighing my options. Professor Libiski grows impatient and I just blurt out, "Why is there a locked room in the Dungeon?"

"Because it is restricted, restricted to those who have special authorizations to retrieve the items within the room. You will need to reach out to either your Crown Guardian or House Chair to grant you access. Now, be on your way or I shall give you detention for the next two weeks."

"Okay, sorry, yes sir," hurriedly picking up my bag and walking toward the door. "Have a good umm, night, thank you," I say nervously.

Now back at the Manor, ruminating over the night's events, calculating plan after plan, I decide it is time to call for reinforcements. David could help but I was not sure I wanted him to, not after everything. Besides, he was not exactly eager for me to have access to the material.

I didn't want to impose on Maria, she was busy completing the advanced coursework that she signed up for last year, but

I couldn't do this on my own. Somewhat apprehensively, I decided to enlist the aid of my best friend. I call her and share the details of the night, "The spell I need is in the Despiraes, our Covens shared Grimoire."

She expressed her concern that it might be dangerous for me to cast such a spell, siding with David. She softly asked, "Maybe once you get better at the Vilix?"

"I got this, trust me," I say confidently and she instantaneously caves. Unable to resist the opportunity for adventure, "I'm down, besides if anyone can do it, it's you. And me of course."

I smile and I am sure she can hear it, "Thank you."

"Of course, ride or die Big Blue," and I allow her to use the offensive name.

Now more than ever, I was determined to make this happen. I caress Morgan as he presses his head against my hand.

My mandatory training forces me to take a slight detour from my mission. There is little I can do throughout the week to prepare for Project Morgan.

Time with Reyna proves to be unnecessary. I do not have an authentic opportunity to practice the Nekromanic Ritual. Summoning the dead is not like taking a leisurely stroll across the park. The use of this type of magik must be justified and approved by the Witch Council.

Other than memorizing the details of the ritual, and attempting to open a dimensional doorway out of Professor Sutton's detention, admittedly failing to do so, there was not much I could do in terms of practice.

Although, I do think I am getting close to summoning the door out of the Spirit Trap. After my time in the ring of fire with Madam Reyna, I swiftly leave for the additional training with David. We continued our work on developing a Cardinal Bind with some progress gradually being made. I asked him if we could end early and he rather swiftly agreed.

Maria had promised to meet me at the Manor to work on our plan to get the book. I justify that if I had clearance this would be a non-issue; it was after all a library book. I rushed to the Manor to meet her.

"The Despiraes and the other sacred texts are powerful magik, not to be played with. These spells can do some serious damage, which is why that kind of material is restricted and protected by charms," says Maria.

"How do you know all this stuff?"

"It's a part of my training, my specialized classes are a little different than the spacey ones you Seers take." Fortunately, Maria had several volumes on defensive and dark magik.

For the next week we conduct research on the Controlled Section and its restrictions. With Maria's technical knowledge and the Vilix we were able to identify and gain a better understanding of the curses that guard the Controlled Section.

The area was protected with blood charms and other types of old dark magik, crude, but effective. It was significantly stronger than some of the more modern spells, and capable of withstanding the test of time.

However, no spellwork was perfect, everything had its limits. It took weeks to prepare the spells needed to counteract all the Castle's defenses, but finally we are now ready to infiltrate the Dungeon.

Our first barrier was the Castle's magikal alarm system. Turning it off was going to require powerful Witchcraft. This type of magik went beyond the scope of the spells I have cast so far. It was its own entity, more of a living thing, and whatever magik we cast would only last for so long.

We settled on an antiquated somnolence spell, better known as a sleep enchantment, used in the times of Ancient Greece.

The spell's foundation was based on a type of suppression magik that drew its powers from the Celestial entities Hypnos and Morpheus, the Greek primordial gods of sleep and dreams.

The spell was excellent to quiet both animate beings and inanimate objects, one of the few incantations that could dull the senses of the natural world and Spirits.

We used the Vilix to enhance our power during the spell.

It was relatively simple, but effective. We were able to cast the spell from the comfort of my room.

The chant sounded like a nursery rhyme. The success of the spell came down to who could outlast the other, a battle between us and the living security system.

We stand facing each other with our arms spread wide. The Sigil of the Luna Crest, representing Nyx, begins to glow as we sing the ancient words.

Prosefchómaste ston Theó tis Nýchtas
Nyx
Prosefchómaste ston Theó ton Oneíron
Morféas
Prosefchómaste ston Theó ton Oneíron
Hypnos
Evlogiménos Na eínai skotádi
Boreí Na sas tragoudísei stin Eirini
Kai sas stélnoun sto kenó
Timitheíte
Nýchta

I was vaguely aware of my body, like the way one is aware of feet on the ground while looking up at the sky. Maria had once asked me about that, how I See things through the Vilix.

There were no words to accurately convey the experience. It was like trying to explain how to ride a bike. You need to do it to get it. The best comparison I could come up with was the nervous system. People cannot feel those synapses charge and respond to one another, linking one part of our body to another, just the effect, like riding a bike. With the Vilix, I had full awareness of all those gateways and explosions that run the body and engage with the world outside.

Interestingly, our nervous system closely resembles the universe. All cause and effect, bridges between the two, things rippling against one another, and the gateways that connected one world to the next.

We continue chanting. Our words are carried through the air, lulling St. Philomena into a very mild and fleeting drowsiness as they journey to their destination. Reaching for the Castle, they invade its walls, dig below to its Dungeon and meet its guard. With the Vilix, I see the spell crash with the magik of its guard, and it responds like a raging tyrant.

It all seemed to be going well until the power of the guard almost brought us to our knees. It was strong magik, but I was determined, so it pushed us, and we pushed back. It claws and charges but grasps nothing.

Gradually, our chains of submission began to subdue him and I could feel the thing try to drag itself out of those chains, but it was too late. It ebbs and flows, but eventually succumbs to our spell and then, like falling asleep, is entirely submerged; turning that angry man into a sleeping infant, whose fatigue outweighs its fussy nature.

Chapter Twenty-Seven

Unless a Witch is exceptionally skilled in Illusionary magik, glamours must be persistently maintained on the hour lest they be washed away by mere rain, talismans tend to do the trick.

We did not know the precise duration of the sleeping spell, the alarm could turn back on in a few days or a few hours, so we had to act quickly.

Still in uniforms, we take the East Lab tunnel to the Castle, arriving there close to midnight. Maria cast a camouflage spell just before we sneak out of the Manor. I projected a psychic barrier that distorted the perception of others. It kept our presence out of onlooker's conscious awareness. With our spells still intact, we enter the building.

There are only a few students studying this late at night. Professor Libiski sits in the center of the main hall, books float beautifully above him, spiraling up into the cathedral-esque ceiling. He reviews each one, as it hovers at eye-level for a moment, evaluating its condition.

Once approved, it joins a line of floating books that rise toward the higher levels in a synchronized spiral.

Books veer off into various directions as they ascend the atrium, making their way to their respective homes until the final few reach the top floor and return to their shelves.

It is where David and I used to train, that used to be one of our spots. I force myself to ignore the memory.

Maria and I internally gasp when the Professor suddenly looks up and stares directly at us. He continues to look in our direction for what feels like an eternity, before shaking his head as if trying to remember something, and then returns his gaze back to the book hovering in front of him. We dare not linger. I don't even try to read his mind as we rush past him.

We reach the office section of the library. The entire space serves as the foyer to the Dungeon's stairway. The wide steps begin to narrow as we descend further below. It takes on a tomb-like design, with darkness suffocating the space. The eerie blue fire barely produces enough light to see the stone floor underneath us.

There is an expected, but still startling, blood-curdling scream out of the darkness up ahead.

"Here we go," says Maria, but I am unable to respond. We hear the shriek again, but this time much closer than before. Finally, a third time, now continuous and deafening and directly into our ears. It rattles me down to the core.

Murderer. Tear him apart. Rip him from his dirty parts. The ones he covers.

I felt as if I would come undone and concave into my stomach and all the rest of me. Unsure of what Maria's assailant had screeched into her own ear, whatever it may have been, it was enough to shake her out of its grip.

"Noah cast the circle!" Maria commanded. It took a moment for me to realize she was speaking. I look down and see the vial in my left hand. Inside it, the purple potion we created for just this occasion glows against the First Seal, Maldición de Miedo. The curse of fear.

It invoked visions from our own personal hells. I think I hear Charles Daley groaning in the background, and that brings me back to reality.

With surprising speed, I smash the vile against the floor and spread my palms above the spilled contents, with Maria following suit.

A simple mix of Florida water, Solomon's seal root, preferred herbs for smell, and enough magik to thoroughly bring a house down. The potion pools in a controlled motion forming into a perfect hexagram, reflective and luminescent.

Maria and I start the chant.

Abraxas, Mysterious One
Look upon our enemy
Ereshkigal, Queen of the Dead
Open thy gates
Hecate, Goddess of Witches
Drag them below

Exactly six times, shouting on the last round. Each word synchronized with the growing light of the sigil, lighting up the dark hallway in impossible brightness.

The Curse was furious, manifested into a snake-like smoke, and wrapped itself around us. Nonetheless, it is useless against the spell. The sigil shines like a small sun and begins consuming the writhing vapor until its swallowed whole, taking the immobilizing fear along with it. A lost battle.

"Holy shit, it worked," Maria says, breathing heavily.

"One down."

The spell would only bind the Curse if we were in its keep. It would be released, from whatever dark place held such creatures, once we leave the Dungeon. This was important, we needed to return things exactly as we left it or else we risk someone discovering us. I prayed these halls would remain empty during our time here.

Maria and I follow the winding steps, descending deep below the Castle, until entering the inner caves of Mt. Tarias, which served as natural walls. The steps transform into a narrow bridge held within the open and wide space.

I hear the river that runs through the mountain to the lake faintly echoing as it travels its long journey to the sea, a sign of the cave's intimidating depth, and I genuinely had to remind myself that I could fly, thanks to David. Again, I do not let my thoughts linger on him.

I gasp loudly when we finally reach the iron gates. "We're here," I announce. Maria looks at me with knowing eyes. It was time to face the Second Seal.

"Ow." I groan at the sharp pain.

"What's wrong," she whispers in a fury.

"My face, it scratched me," I touched my cheek and felt something wet.

Elumiscent

A glow spell. It took a second for it to register that the bright red liquid on my hand was blood, my blood.

Out of nowhere, a gust of air sweeps past us and in an instant, Maria is lifted into the air by the invisible force. The light from the spell barely illuminates her figure against the pitch-black surroundings. She screams out, ***Taesdae Onya***, a powerful offensive spell.

She ignites into a magik white fire that gives light to the deep crevices of this vast underground dwelling. The invisible entity holding Maria releases her, its harsh scream is the only indication of its existence.

She drops low into the cave's depth for the briefest of moments before catching herself, now hovering in the air, supported by her own power.

The Second Seal was demons, not to be confused with the supernatural entity of Daemons. These beasts' magik was exclusively purposed for longevity and durability. Dark beings, with the power of invisibility that have existed in these caves for eons, bound to the Dungeon by our ancestors. They transformed them into soldiers for the sole purpose of keeping those without clearance out.

I activate the Vilix and See the demon that attacked Maria who now lays dead on the ground far below. They were humanoid-like, but larger than the average adult, with scales for skin and leather wings. Their arms moved independently from their wings and they use their thick hind legs to launch themselves into the air.

At first, it was just the one that attacked her but a new demon dives down like a kamikaze from far above. Its large canines protrude out of its mouth like fangs and a thick ooze drips out of them. It aims its talons toward Maria's heart.

"Now," I shout to her.

Maria casts a shockwave of Transference energy, bombarding it backward to the far wall. Then I See them, the rest of them.

Dozens of these beasts crawl up the cave walls, lifting off once high enough to generate enough lift to carry their large bodies, abiding by their obligations to protect this part of the Dungeon from trespassers.

I had used retrocognition to prepare for this moment, it wasn't too difficult, I found one event, Professor Libiski returning a dark book to the Controlled Section.

He returned it by hand, because apparently these items tend to be resistant to magik. The demons swarmed around him when he approached the iron gates, but the Professor was now glowing a soft green light. The demons shied away from the librarian.

The green aura was his clearance. An enchantment that could only be cast upon approval of St. Philomena's Board. The process of gaining this clearance was at least seven months.

That was seven months too long, so Maria and I were able to devise a substitution for the spell.

Maria holds them back while I steady my mind to cast this intricate magik. This is the part I had been dreading most but my options were limited. Using the Vilix, I connect to them, all of them, and become them. My physical body nearly gags as a result.

Monsters.

"Hurry, Noah, I don't know how much longer I can hold on," she says, close to a panic as more demons dive toward her, eager to feast on my best friend. A most unacceptable thing.

"ENOUGH," I say. My voice booms and echoes much louder than possible, a direct result of my psychic attack.

All at once the demons fall from the sky, barreling down to the deep ground below. Unfortunately, the demons are durable. A few hit the ground and either lay broken or dead, while some catch the cave walls or the solid limestone towers just before impact. Most spread out their wings and catch the air. They effortlessly fly back to the bridge, eager to finish the job.

Maria floats beside me, her long blonde hair flowing with her power, but her fire is dimming out. She descends onto the bridge floor.

I see myself through their crystal-clear vision, my eyes shining a blinding blue while the Northern Lights of the Vilix cascade and envelop the cave in brilliant colors.

Only now the demons perceive Maria and I with a slight difference. Their minds now distorted, they look upon us and see a glowing green aura, the same as Professor Libiski.

They somehow manage to appear confused despite their monstrous features, or maybe that was just the Vilix allowing me to be privy to the inner workings of their minds. Regardless, they thankfully do not question their vision.

One by one, the demons fly off in random directions, making their way toward the crevices within the caves, returning to whatever meal was left behind at our arrival. The path was now clear.

We both suffered damage from the attack, the gash across my face begins to sting now that I have the capacity to pay it mind. Maria received the worst of it. She has several cuts and slashes across her body. Her clothes magikally repair themselves, as do my own.

I give her all my healing yellow amber stones. She holds them tightly and their light seeps into her skin and travels through her bloodstream. The gashes begin to heal, and her skin reseals itself as if the wounds were never there.

She grabs my hands and places the stones within them, forcing me to retain my grip. "I'm all healed-up Noah. They still have enough juice to take care of that nasty cut."

The stones have a faint light to them but that fades away as my body absorbs their magik. The pain fades away as my skin eerily closes in on itself, leaving only the stain of blood as proof of its existence. My clothes are unmarked, another magikal convenience.

Maria looks up at the iron gates and asks if I am ready.

"Ready as I'll ever be," this night had been more of an ordeal than either of us anticipated. I was reevaluating my life choices, but what could I do, we had gone too far to turn back.

We walk toward them in silence. They opened easily. We look at each other for approval and enter the dark room, ready to meet the Third and final Seal.

The iron gates instantaneously transform into large double-sided red doors. We are in an empty windowless room with high ceilings. On the opposite side of the room stood identical doors.

Confused, we cautiously walked toward it. This was not what I originally saw with the Vilix, it was supposed to be a battle with a Daemonic spirit, but there was no supernatural force in sight.

Our footsteps echoed as they hit the marbled floor. The whole place was in stark contrast to the underground bridge and cavernous walls outside it. We gently pull the red doors open and walk into the next room only to enter the same room once more.

We turn around and run backwards several times, hoping to return to the cave. When that does not work, we run forwards for good measure, but arrive at the same place, only to face those devil doors.

I used my power to See the room and realize my mistake.

It was an impression of another spell, a sort of illusion that used to deceive Seers. It was done perfectly. It never occurred to me to search for that type of magik.

"I am so sorry, Maria, I had no idea this was the Last Seal, it was covered up with a glamour."

"Oh my god, we're going to get caught and my mom is going to kill me." I hope that given her expertise on this type of magik, she might know a way out of here. I shifted nervously, "Do you know what this is?"

"Yeah, it's a Spirit Trap, but I have no idea how to get out of one," she says in a panic.

"Wait, like detention with Professor Sutton?"

"Yeah, it's the same thing, those dimensions come in all sorts of shapes and sizes," says Maria. Although the room is empty, it somehow is worse than Professor Sutton's detention, at least in his room there is some action with its false dragon. This pocket felt like something brought from hell.

"I think I can get us out. Madam Reyna has been training me on this kind of magik since the beginning of the semester. We need a door, a Spirit Door; all I have to do is summon one. I haven't been able to just yet, but I have come close."

"Are you sure Noah, isn't that dangerous?"

"No, I got this," I was not going to lose, not when I was this close to the book. I could practically feel it in my hands. Thankfully, I still carried the glass vial of precious flowers on my locket used for training with Madam Reyna.

"Besides, summoning the door is like Translocation, and I've already done that," even though it was only the one time. I was hopeful that I sounded convincing, but it seems to reassure her. It never was an expectation to repeat the event, as that Witchcraft is incredibly difficult to manifest. It takes either a natural disposition or extraordinary practice to cast successfully. Very few found the time or energy needed for that kind of development, which was the same for me, at least until today.

Focusing my power, I raise my open palms above me and begin searching for the way out of the Spirit Trap. Traveling into the galaxy and in-between realms, I lose track of time, too busy being consumed by the stars.

My body began levitating, and without realizing it, my legs took a cross-legged position. It finally makes sense why that loon Reyna was always meditating. This was addictive. The Vilix reveals a void, the Betwixt, a rift in space and time, and on the other side is a world not unlike my own. I remembered the lesson Dr. Huebner gave on multi-dimensions, the force that laid between these Universes.

I thought maybe it is my world at another time, but deep down I already know the truth. It is a world far away from my own, similar, but from an entirely different universe.

Something even more peculiar happens then. Even though I am in my psychic presence, it feels like my very own particles are pulling itself toward something. And then I understand what my atoms seem to be reaching for, our Universe. They want to go home.

In seconds I am brought back to the Spirit Trap. I See us trapped within the pocket dimension, tucked away within our reality. The Betwixt divides the two like a line in the sand, and just past this cage is the Controlled Section.

I am ready to summon the door. I cast the spell, and, like a gunshot, a small explosion ensued.

Nexia

Septus

Despirorian

The Sigil of Nekros forms.

Open thy gates

It feels like I am being pulled in and out of myself by something unstoppable. I hold myself to this trap, linking me across the darkness to the Despiraes sitting in its glass container, surrounded by all the other Controlled Materials.

It feels like I explode, like a burning star for the briefest of moments. I see only darkness and I felt so very far away, as if I had forgotten myself.

What was I doing?

The last thing I remember was invoking those words. What if I didn't? My silent words echoed in the void that might be me. Am I stuck in this empty space, or did I die?

Is there a difference?

"Noah, you did it," Maria's voice breaks me from the trance. I opened my eyes and there before us is the door, more like waves of distortion, but still a door. Maria encourages me to walk but it takes me a moment to regain myself, so she uses Transference and basically tosses me out like a bag of trash.

Once through, I crash onto the cold hard marble floor of the Controlled Section, Maria now joins my side. She and I looked at each other excitedly, we made it.

Floating tall white candles scattered throughout the space dimly light the room, they gently bob up and down and travel throughout the area in the most subtle movements as they make their way toward us. Only a few tables laid in between the shelves that held the ancient books, with various items encased in glass with one that contained the Despiraes.

"Let's go, Noah. I heard something," Maria says quietly. She re-casts the camouflage spell as I uncase the Grimoire, removing the book from its home. As I do so, I sense the magikal alarm stir, slightly detecting the intrusion but it remains quiet. The somnolence spell maintains its sedation.

Quickly, I join Maria, we race out of the Dungeon, and I produce the psychic barrier as a second safeguard to prevent discovery. We pass the demons, who can only perceive the green aura zoom by on the skinny bridge.

We hurry past the First Seal. It is released once we cross its borders, but it pays us no mind. Its role was to prevent entrance not departure. We hear Professor Libisiki's footsteps when we near the Dungeon's exit.

We huddle close to the stone walls of the winding stairs and dare not breathe. He totes a handful of Controlled Materials, on his way to return the items. He turns around for a moment and looks back at us, taking notice of the slight distortion caused by Maria's camouflage spell.

He walks toward us. My own spell takes effect and derails his attention. It buries his concern deep below his conscious awareness. He nods the thought away.

I exhale my bated breath, not only thankful that he did not catch us, but because he arrived just prior to the First Seal being released. He would have noticed its absence and investigated the matter, and easily discovered the spell that had trapped the Curse, as well as identify the culprits. After all, magik carries a signature.

We resumed our flight up the stairs and exited the Castle in leaps and bounds. We don't even leave time to discuss the adventure. Instead, we both rush back to our homes. Now realizing the depths of our culpability, we are desperate to avoid being caught.

It surprised me to find Leroy still awake in the common room when I returned to the Manor. I managed to hide the book into my bookbag just before entering the home. Leroy was busy practicing a spell. I quickly walked past him, afraid that he would sense the Grimoire and discover my delinquent act.

In an attempt to calm my nerves, I force myself to remember that the other Seers never attempt to invade my space or mind.

Needless worries, he neither asked nor demonstrated any kind of reaction, other than disinterest at my arrival. Leroy greets me with a nod and silence, his attention never straying from the spell at hand.

“Have a goodnight,” I say and rush up to my room. I collapse on my bed once I am there and allow dreams to steal my shock and awe over tonight's events.

Chapter Twenty-Eight

The Staff of Dagda, an ancient Witch relic, is held in Oxford University of Witchcraft. Known for its enduring enchantment that does not require routine maintenance spells, it has the power to distort both time and weather.

The scenic route of Mt. Tarias' slope flashes by as the Carriage glides in descension toward the bustling city. It was the morning after my larceny of the Despiraes, Maria and I have plans to meet later this afternoon. I had woken up early to visit the local shops in hopes of getting something special for her.

It does not take long to find the perfect gift along with something for the Mastersons. I bought her a butterfly charm and individual cat charms for Joan, Kevin, and Jake.

I return to the Manor shortly after and enchant all four, linking them to my own so we could send messages in the form of text. Words would literally form out of objects or loose debris near the receiver to spell out the message.

Maria's charm receives a second, more substantial, enchantment that takes two hours to create. It can manifest nine psychic projections in the form of butterflies. Each one could latch onto and bewitch a living entity, allowing the Charm Wielder both access and control over the mind and body.

I send the Mastersons their charms using the Manor's magikal mailbox, opening and closing its lid to verify its empty contents, a sure sign it was on its way to them, then head off to meet Maria at the Mansion. She smiled broadly when she unwrapped the gift but burst into tears when I explained its use, immediately attaching it to her silver bracelet.

Nine luminescent butterflies materialize around us, fluttering in rotations to Maria, like planets to the sun.

"Oh my Spirits," and I can see the marvel in her eyes as she experiences the Divination. "Thank you, Noah," she says in a gasp.

She had to do routine magik on it for recharging. She simply had to meditate under the full moon every three months while channeling her energy into the charm. Just doing this practice almost guaranteed that she would eventually master the magik.

We do not chat for very long. She is eager to test their powers and I have my own plans for the day. She found a willing test subject in Allen Casta, who serendipitously arrives at the Mansion. He planned on formally inviting her to lunch. He looks at her with innocent eyes and a handsome smile and, rather eagerly, agrees to her request.

I leave them to it as one of Maria's butterflies turn transparent and intangible, perceptible now to only her and Seers, it lands on Allen's face and she inhales sharply as she enters the surface of his consciousness. A bold move on his part to allow the girl he seems so enamored with into his mind.

"Have fun," I wave goodbye and set off.

It is a short walk to the willow tree. The very same place David opened up about the challenges of his parent's divorce. I hoped he was doing well now. During my training with him, it seemed like he was holding something back. I am not sure how to explain it. He just wasn't the same anymore. I was uncertain whether it was because of what happened to us or something else. For his sake, I hoped to be wrong on both accounts.

I set two tall pink candles on top of the picnic table underneath the tree. Randomly unclear why I chose to come here to study the Despiraes, it seems I am a glutton for obvious punishment. My incense burner sits at the center permeating the air with the scent of verbena. Last night's escapades and activating the charms earlier this morning has left me significantly drained, leaving me unable to innately cast the translation spell or use the Vilix, at least efficiently. Fortunately, I can use the full ritual to compensate for my lack of energy.

I recite the chant seven times and my looking-glass charm begins to levitate, stopping at eye-level. The book stands on its spine upright in front of me. The spell translates the foreign words, but in the next instant, the words shift into an entirely different language. I had to recast the spell every time the language changed. At one point, the words transform into words so foreign that it rendered my spell's interpretation useless.

"It's Enochian," flinching at the sound of him. Behind my shoulder stands David, strong and dapper, he leans and looks over the Despiraes. Why did he have to get so close?

"Sorry, mate, didn't mean to scare you," he looks back at the book once more, and his eyes grow wide with recognition of the textbook.

"Crivens Noah! Did you steal the Despiraes?"

I say nothing at first but eventually cave to his accusing eyes, "Sort of," I say with my eyes cast down, "I am going to return it as soon I am done borrowing it."

"How did you manage to pull this off?"

I recount the story of the burglary, all the while his unblinking eyes strain from astonishment. He stares at me for a bit longer until finally he regains his words, "I knew you were cannie," slang for brilliant, "Noah, but this takes it to a whole other level."

"Thanks," hesitantly responding. Something about his smile told me he was more concerned than impressed.

"Was all that for the Faemalyr business you were asking about?"

I nod and his mood abruptly shifts. He shoots me an uncharacteristically agitated look while I remain quiet, confused by his sudden irritation. He seems to catch himself and tries to relax his face with a loud exhale. He sits down across from me, his long legs spread out so they rest outside of my own, as if he is trying to hug me.

"It's risky, Noah," his deep, normally steady voice now shaky. He leans in, his broad chest open as he rests his elbows on the table. His right hand stretches out toward me, only to rest lazily on the picnic table at the center of the space between us. The way he managed to bring his body close to mine reminds me of the prior semester, like nothing has changed, but we both knew nothing was the same. I inched away out of respect for him, and me. He frowns then, making me doubt my actions.

In frustration, I look straight into his eyes, "What's the problem?"

He stares at me with furrowed brows and his pupils run back and forth, a man deep in contemplation, running scenarios in his head.

"What if you get in trouble with the Council or hurt, or something worse?"

I am sure he thinks this is another desperate attempt to improve my magik, I can't blame him for that, my past justifies that as a likely motive.

"You don't understand how important this is to me, I have to try something."

"Why Noah? What's so important about this that you would risk your life?"

"I don't want to lose him. I am so sick and tired of losing the people I love," and my stubborn breath catches and I have to bite back my tears.

He stumbles, his resolve wavering. He looks away from me but eventually meets my gaze. "Okay, right, I'm sorry, it's just, well this magik is dangerous and I worry about you."

"Don't you dare," my voice cracking from the surface of a cry.

I breathe, "Don't worry about me, I'll be fine," I say without inflection.

David hesitantly smiles, but it is filled with consternation. Even so, he manages to lean closer to me and softly says, "I hate to see you upset, even more when it's my fault."

"It's fine. Besides, I can't read it for now anyway." I explain to him why I am unable use the Vilix and the challenges with the shifting words of the book.

Avoiding my gaze, he extends an offer, "I can help, if you like?"

Still slightly irritated yet eager for the assistance, I accepted his offer, "That would be really helpful," regretting the degree of excitement in my voice.

"When? I have some time right now if you like," he asks.

"It's still the weekend, don't you have plans?"

With his stupidly beautiful grin he says, "Sure enough, I am helping my best friend make his black cat, umm, I mean Morgan, the best damn Faemalyr in the world."

I cannot help but smile back, my mood was, and may always be, vulnerable to his unsolicited influence. "Thank you, you don't have to, but thank you." I want to tell him to go have fun with the people he does want to be around, for both our sakes, but in my selfish aspiration I accept the offer.

We returned to the Manor to study the book. David sits on my large bed. My new sheets surround him in shades of blue and green, the colors of the sea. We talked for nearly an hour, catching up on inane things, until finally returning our attention to the book.

"How long ago did you submit the offering," asked David.

"What offering?"

He responds, his face perplexed by my confusion to the obvious, "The blood offering?"

"Oh my god, I can't believe I forgot about the blood sacrifice," I say in honest embarrassment.

It was information revealed to me when I originally located the text that somehow escaped my memory in between the preparations and actual infiltration of the Dungeon.

"No wonder the book has been such a complete ass."

David rolls over in laughter at my expense.

"Are you done?" My smile is flat, finding the moment a little less hilarious.

He raises his palms to me in acquiescence, "No offense meant by it, promise," chuckling to himself, "It was just so obvious."

I respond with silence.

After settling himself, he lays back placing his hands behind his head, stretching his shoulders, opening his muscular chest.

"Relaxed," I ask as I raise my eyebrows to him. In truth, it was nice to see him like this, to be like this with him again. All the tension and uneasiness between us seems to float away.

"God this bed is comfortable. Do they give you some special deal for having the Vilix?"

"No, everyone at Spirit Manor has the same standard bed, I'm afraid."

"Right, suspicious I think," he says with a wink.

I rolled my eyes hard at him in turn and refocused on the matter at hand. Pulling out my lower Athame, the more utilitarian Witch blade that, until now, was only used for cutting various herbs. I place my hand above the book, raising the blade toward my palm, and breathe in deep.

"Wait," David shouts, "let me try first."

"Why?"

"It could be dangerous," he replies.

"Exactly, I'll go first," I respond in opposition.

David rolls his eyes at me and, before I knew it, grabs his own pocketknife and slashes into his palm. A trickle of scarlet liquid drips down onto the book cover. For a few seconds, nothing happens. Concerned, my eyes remain fixed on David. The dark book begins to pulsate and sends a small vibration into the floor and suddenly burns bright red, the color of David's blood, ready to serve its master.

"Are you okay," my attention now on his wound, worried over the potential costs there could be for his sacrifice.

"Pure barry, mate, honestly, I feel a bit buzzed, it's like I am connected to it."

"Okay," I say cautiously.

"But I don't think the sacrifice lasts for very long, it feels like sand falling through my fingers, I suppose."

I grab him a towel and some healing ointment from the bathroom cupboard, "You're alright, Noah, why don't you open the book?"

I look at him in bewilderment, but he refuses to let me dress the wound and motions for me to get the book.

"Right," I walk over and grab it, but the light fades the second I touch it.

Immediately understanding, "It needs to be my blood."

"Looks like," and he nods in agreement.

"I wonder if that would work since you just offered your own, if we could double up like that?"

"Only one way to find out," slyly smiling.

I pick up my blade once more and, in a rush, like jumping into a pool, I bring the blade down to the skin of my palm, and swiftly pull back. Sighing in exaggerated relief once done, I caused enough damage to produce a single drop of my red substance, the equivalent of a paper cut.

"Really went for the gold on that one, didn't you Noah."

"Shut up," I huff, returning my attention to the Despiraes.

"Well, it was enough or was it not David O'Faolain?" I say sarcastically, as the book shines in response to my own gift. Meanwhile David is chuckling in the corner. He is right though, it does feel like a fading thing, fire with only so much fuel to maintain its flame. Gently, I turned back the ridiculously large cover. I flipped the durable pages back; it was like they were made of steel rather than wood pulp.

The book, now cooperative, changes to an alternative old Witch language, but at least the language remains the same, a language that David could easily translate. At last, I turn to the page of the Blessed Bind.

My blood sacrifice leaves the book wanting as I feel the contracted time end. Its light fades once more at my touch.

David's time lasts longer and is maintained by the droplets of blood that occasionally fall onto the book as he translates the spell. I sit beside him and try my best to help by taking notes, but I have difficulty concentrating. Being close to David was like using the Vilix, easily captured and spirited away without a chance to be scared.

Thankfully I have the spell to refocus my attention. We discuss the components of the ritual. There was an entire section devoted to the significance of having a loving relationship with the Faemalyr. It had to be a mutual choice. Anything but could result in the death and devastation for both the Witch and Faemalyr.

The first half of the ritual consisted of preparatory ceremonial procedures like daily magikal baths and other sundries. I nearly spit out my tea when David told me about a prerequisite potion that took a year to create. Thankfully, the potion's purpose was to aid the common Witch in contacting the Divine. In other words, it compensated for limited psychic abilities of both Seer and Non-Seer Witches.

The spell would be like traveling to some foreign land. A Witch needed a ship to go there and to come back, a map to show the way, and a compass to stay on track. Thanks to the Vilix, my ship was a plane, and instead of a map and compass, I had a fully functioning navigation system born within me.

"Seems like you've got the hard part done, Noah."

"That's a relief," I say genuinely.

David finishes writing the instructions and procedures for the spell and hands his journal to me. Although the ritual is complicated, the magik required is relatively simple. It boils down to a direction of energies. If I can connect to those energies then it is only a matter of moving a piece of me, my magik, and placing them inside Morgan's own energy, assuming the two get along. My primary concern was that the spell required sustained attention, and with the Vilix, a mere thought can kidnap me to an entirely different reality.

"I guess that's it."

"You do need the book, it acts like a key to the spell, and I think it's also meant to help protect you. After all, you haven't spent a lot of time in the Spirit world or dealt much with ghosts."

"What? Yes, I have, I talk to Bexar and Gruene all the time."

"Who is Burr and Green," he asks, and I privately smile, oh how I loved the sound of his voice.

"Bexar and Gruene, the ghosts, or Spirits, from Bexar and Gruene Hall."

"You've seen ghosts, No-El?"

"Don't ask a question with a statement."

He looks annoyed just then and I laugh in response.

"I'm being serious, have you seen ghosts?" He breathes restlessly.

"Yeah," timidly answering him. I was taken aback by his raised voice.

"Were you using the Vilix?"

"No, why does it matter," I was thoroughly confused on where he was going with his questioning.

"Seeing the dead is no common skill for Seers or non-Seers."

"I don't understand, Dr. Huebner once talked about ghosts with me like he was discussing the weather. Why are you so worried?"

"Most of the time 'ghosts' are a reference to Poltergeists, apparitions that are reflections of the past. True Spirits reveal themselves by their own choice, not ours. Advanced spellwork or active use of an innate skill are needed to force their revealment, and even then, only advanced Nekromancers can see the dead easily. If you were using the Vilix that would make sense, but you weren't."

He is talking so fast and there is a fury in him, it makes me uncomfortable. I remain silent. Recognizing my reaction, he says, "I am sorry Noah, I don't mean to scare you," and I believe him.

"Have you told anyone else? Maria?"

"No," and he looks at me with suspicion. "I haven't, I promise," to reassure him.

"Okay," he sighs softly.

Although I cannot share in his relief, "I still don't understand."

"Noah, it's complicated, just do me a favor and please keep the ghost thing to yourself, promise?"

Concerned and uncertain, I hesitantly agree, "Okay."

He apologizes to me once more, adding, "Noah, I just worry about you." He comes in close and grabs my shoulders.

Feeling his touch and hearing the worry that lives in his voice right now unravels me. For a moment, I allow myself to believe we might be soul mates, until the memory of that night floats to my surface, reminding me of what cannot be, followed by an immediate need to be rid of him.

I want to tell him not to worry about me. I want to remind him of the disgust that laid bare on his face that night, and that he is the one that rejected me. I want to tell him to go home and stop hurting me all over again. However, that would require strength I do not have.

Instead, “It’s fine, David, no big deal. To be honest, I am kind of tired, but thank you so much for all your help today. Here, take some scones with you, my first gift of gratitude, with more to come.” I try my hardest to wink but just end up blinking.

He laughs a laugh that does not touch his eyes.

I try to convince myself that soul mates don’t have to be in love, we could be perfect for each other as friends.

“I guess I’ll be going then. One last thing, if you do use the spell, if it’s alright, I would like to be here with you when you do it?”

“Yeah, that sounds good.” I do not know why I lied to him; maybe I was afraid of him trying to stop me. Maybe I was just afraid to be near him. Maybe it was because I was lying to myself, we are not soul mates after all, and the thought crushes me. It is too much hurt for one night.

“Okay, Noah, I’ll see you soon.”

“Perfect. See you then,” trying to smile. We ended the night in an awkward hug, my failed attempt to say goodbye.

“It was nice hanging out again, we should do it more often. I missed you,” he says with a tiny grin.

“Same,” in thousands of ways you will never know, David O’Faolain.

Chapter Twenty-Nine

With or without innate skill any Witch can summon the misplaced and missing.
Supplies: Globe.
Sigil of Eros: Traced above or below.
Prerequisite: Powerful dependency to the lost artifact you seek.

All week long I perform the preparatory acts for the spell.

For six days at dawn and dusk, I cleansed the sacred space where the ritual would be performed, also known as my room, along with a nightly purification bath.

The steamy waters had to be mixed with a combination of pungent herbs and a specialized oil that had an unfortunately thick sludge-like texture.

Lastly, the book required daily blood offerings to use the spell. It was recommended I give as many offerings as I could, but I was not about to feed that blood-sucking textbook any more than the minimum.

Besides, the Healers at the Infirmary started to give me suspicious looks when I arrived with the same wound from the day before. Dr. Statton, the Lead Healer, told me on day number three he would be making a psychological referral on my behalf. In a panic, I partially revealed the reason behind the concerning wounds. The need for my blood.

"It's an ancient magik project for my theory class," I explained.

"Why didn't you say so, dear," and offered to draw my blood, "This is far less barbaric than the crude methods you were using before, I am sure." Surprised, I graciously accepted his offer.

One at a time, he placed a vial on the crease of my elbow that filled with my blood without ever breaching my skin. He had me stay at the Infirmary for an hour for monitoring and forced me to consume at least one cookie and juice box before I could leave. Once done, he handed me several vials of my blood, just enough for the remaining days needed for the spell, "Good luck, Mr. Ellis."

"Thank you, Doctor," I said as I walked out the door, shocked by the convenience of the visit.

On the sixth day I went to bed particularly early in preparation for tomorrow's spellwork. It is near midnight when I hear the soft persistent taps at my window, disturbing the still quiet of my room. Once fully out of my sleep-induced stupor, I rise out of bed to locate the source of the noise and find it behind the large bay windows.

Uneasy about the mysterious noise, but too tired to think about using my Sight, I shakily pull the heavy curtains aside. I exhale in sweet relief at the sight of him. David hovers outside my bedroom window, four stories above the ground, and smiling in that crooked pretty way of his.

What was he thinking? I unhook the sash, allowing him to smoothly glide inside onto my bedroom floor. He stands there in blue jeans and a polo, all charm without any assumption.

"What are you doing here," I ask quietly. He walks closer to me and whispers, "Get ready, we're going on a trip."

Thrown off by the impromptu late-night visit, I remain speechless for an extended amount of time, preoccupied with my own inner ramblings.

David looks at me with an odd expression, waiting for me to say something, “Is something wrong Noah?”

Pulling me out of my awkward reverie, “No, nothing, sorry. What trip?”

“Me and a few lads are headed off to Denver, to see the city. I'd like it very much if you could come along?” He says it excitedly, all smiles, but with an intense gaze. He closes in the distance between us.

His pupils seem large even in the darkness of my room. The light of the silver moon outlines his features, emphasizing the strapping nature of his body.

I haven't even asked for permission?” I was lost again, now by my thoughts of him.

“Since when has that ever stopped you,” he gently jabs. David reviews the specifics of the events of tonight, things like “brooms”, “hopscotch”, and worst of all “skyscrapers”.

“You want me to fly to Denver, on a broom, are you crazy?”

Yes, I technically could fly, but I had never crossed that kind of distance and I've never been on a broom.

He smiles broadly, “It's going to be alright, no better than that, it's going to be spectacular. I promise you, trust me?”

“Don't ask a question with a statement.”

He chuckles, “Sorry, do you trust me?”

“Always,” I say on an impulse.

Realizing now that I was still in pajamas with my hair probably resembling some fashion of a tumbleweed, while he was standing there looking like a movie star.

He lies in my bed while he waits for me to get ready, looking more relaxed than I have seen him since summer.

It was cold again in Tarias, I cast the warmth enchantment on my charm given to me so many months ago. I changed into blue jeans, a long sleeve shirt and green sweater, with a mid-length gray trench coat. The spell was effective but wearing winter clothes gave me a warmth that the spell could not provide.

I pause in front of the mirror to evaluate my appearance, noticing all the changes in me since my arrival here.

For the first time, I like what I see in front of me. My eyes shine blue, the Vilix waits to be called, and I shut down the reaction. Not tonight, I say privately, and return to David.

He helps me out the Manor's window and does not let go until I am on the ground. We walk toward the meet-up point. Winter was at our heels and the wind was strong. It carries pricks of ice that aim for our bare faces when we arrive to the relief of Cat's Peak. Down below is the city and across is the valley. I can make out the Palladium in the distance beyond Lake Osage, which serves as a natural divider. The Bridge maintains an enduring connection.

David invited his other friends, which thankfully includes Maria. Also, Gerald Harish-Mal, Amelia Sycamore, Kady Zilberman and Maria's newest beau, Allen.

It surprises me to see Kady there, the Lords do not normally invite other Seers to their events, but Gerald resolves my confusion when he intimately wraps his arms around her waist. They all have brooms and are giddy with anticipation.

Two more of David's friends arrive, his Sorcellirae teammates Wryder Rodriguez and Owen Liu. The sight of Owen makes my heart stop. I try my best to avoid making eye contact with him, the boy who David could love.

"This is going to be so much fun," Maria squeals, "I was going to call you, but David said he was going to the Manor to sneak you out." She looks at me with knowing eyes. I was about to ask her if David and Owen were seeing each other again, but David shouts over the noise of the wind and group chatter, prompting us to move toward the drop off point.

I am no more than a foot away from the Peak's edge and down below is a seemingly bottomless black pit. It stares back at me, convincing me that this was an impossible task. I thought I might fall over at any moment. Tightening my grip on David's coat, my fear of heights fuels my anxiety and grips me tightly to the ground.

The easiest ways out of Tarias were either the Translocative mists of Lake Osage or the Walk-Easy. None of us possessed a boat and no one was willing to take the long walk into random parts of the world that would eventually lead to Denver, except me.

"You're riding with me Noah," says David enthusiastically.

For some unfathomable reason, Gerald steps back to have a running start toward the peak's verge and somersaults himself over the drop off point.

He holds his broom steadily as he falls headfirst into the deep, but centers the broom underneath him, right before he is consumed by the darkness. For a few seconds he is nowhere in sight and I appear to be the only one concerned, until he shoots straight out of the pit and into the star-filled sky.

Incredible.

It dawns on me this trip was more about the journey than the destination.

One by one the other Witches either fall or float into flight toward the sky. I guess there are always people that either play it safe, or don't.

"You ready," David asks, nudging his shoulder against mine. The proximity of his face to mine leaves me dizzy and bright red. He looks toward my clenched hands on his jacket. Under normal circumstances I would have let go, but fear is a powerful thing.

"No," I shout over the booming wind.

David holds his lips close to my ear, and must be using magik, because I can clearly hear his whisper over the furious gusts.

"It's gonna be okay, trust me Noah."

Every sense in me wants to run away, back to the safety and comfort of the grounded Manor. I must be a fool because I don't. Instead, my head, without approval, nods agreeably.

David sits atop the broom as if he were on a bicycle. He hangs mid-air, almost perfectly still, with only the tiniest indication of a restless sway and not because of the wind. The broom seemed almost eager to be taken out for a spin.

He lowers the broom back to the ground, then extends his hand toward me, and simultaneously kills my last reserve.

"I won't let anything happen to you, on my word."

My legs move of their own accord. First the right, bastard, and then the left. The broom rises but does not lift me off the ground and is unexpectedly comfortable. It has an enchantment that creates a cushion like a bicycle seat.

David then mounts the broom and, surprisingly, sits behind me. He said it makes it easier to keep his eyes and magik on me.

David wraps his arms around my waist and reaches out to grip the end of the broom's handle for steering, making my heart race in the process.

We are now at the edge; a slight lean could easily result in a fall into the abyss. I think for a minute that David is going to dive like Gerald, who is circling high above, waiting for us along with the others.

"Alright No-El, here we go."

Without apology, I fiercely cling to his arms that are tightly holding onto me and close my eyes as we slowly lift off. My toes stretch for the briefest moment, desperately extending to maintain contact with the ground, until I feel nothing but empty air.

The violent winds push and pull at us as we lift higher. For a second, I thought I was going to fall off this damn stick, but David's magik steadies us through the cyclonic winds.

Finally, I open my eyes and the vision leaves me breathless. The clouds formed castles in the sky, as far as the eye could see. I dazzle at the world before us as we fly forward until David derails my attention by resting his chin on my shoulder.

His mouth is so close to my neck that I can hear his breath. It makes it difficult to focus on the path in the sky and makes me wish I could live here forever with him, but that is not how the world works.

We approach the bright downtown of Denver and begin our descension. David mimicked the sound of a Pilot on the overhead. "Attention passengers, we are now beginning our descent, it's a cool 30 degrees in Denver, please sit tight and welcome to the Mile-High City."

"Your accent makes you the worst announcer," playfully mocking him, ignoring the fact that the sound of his voice still makes me swoon.

"Oh, breaking my heart No-El, who knew you could be so cruel," he says with a false cry.

"At least you would land the plane safely. I'd rather have a qualified unintelligible pilot than a crystal-clear incompetent one."

"How did you know I can pilot a plane? No-El, have you been using the Vilix to spy on me?"

Of course he can fly a plane. "No," not for this at least, "call it an educated guess, after all, aren't you the great David O'Faolain, known as the boy who can do anything?"

"You might be confused, No-El, isn't that boy supposed to be you?"

"No, I'm the boy that screws everything up and then figures it out."

He halts the broom to a complete stop and looks directly into my eyes.

"That's not you, can't you see it, all the incredible things you've done?"

David looks at me with desperate eyes. I think he wants me to see myself the way he sees me.

"Calm down, I was only kidding. Besides, you can't honestly tell me you want me to fly a plane?"

"Absolutely not, you'd get nervous, probably crash it before liftoff."

We both fell into laughter and I worried for a moment that all that laughter would force me off this glorified cleaning tool. I do not think I have ever felt happiness like that before, it was an exhilarating thing, being up here with him.

We catch sight of Maria and the rest of the group further below. They stream forward like rockets, breaking velocity just before they land.

We all arrive at an isolated park, Wryder and Amelia cast a cloaking spell to avoid being seen by Mortals. We could not risk someone posting photos of us on some social media distributor, exposing our unauthorized late-night departure.

A small jungle gym stands in the center of the grounds. It reminds me of my old life and of something else that I cannot remember, it triggers a feeling of unbelievable sadness. I hate that about me. David says something and I refocus on him, not so much to hear what he has to say, but to recover from the pain that lived inside this sudden hole in my heart. Although the sadness feels overwhelming, I do not let myself stay there. I love that about me.

We all sat down to eat Elysion, the magikal ice cream that induces an anti-gravity effect, a helpful component for tonight's aerial game, followed by Besnit, the magikal drink that makes us laugh over nothing. It was a fun, although unnecessary, addition.

We shoot off like arrows toward the rooftop of the Republic Plaza. I tested out my aided flight skills with the extra broom that Maria was kind enough to tote along for me. I felt more confident closer to the ground, even if it was on top of a skyscraper.

Even my best effort could not persuade David into letting me stay there while the others played the game. He stood atop his broom, like a skateboard, flying in circles around me, "It's a little absurd, your fear of heights. Here you are, 40 stories up, and now you're pure barry."

"The rooftop is a very safe distance from me. A fall from here would cause a slight bruise, if that," I remark.

"Well up there you have the height and time to catch yourself if you fall."

It was true, some Witches had been known to have accidents on their brooms, which is why Transvection magik is always practiced prior to aided flight with enchanted objects. It was a preventative measure, if you fall, just fly down. Although some Witches fall off because of intoxication or fatigue and die from the serious lapse in judgment.

"I don't know, something about seeing the ground, it grounds me, I guess" and we both laugh a little.

"Oh No-El."

After a cautious test run, I began to play along and zip from one roof to another, gaining points for leaping over a Witch and losing them based on landings and flight pattern adjustments. Owen, David, and Maria had the highest scores. Meanwhile, I had the worst, but it didn't matter. I was alive with electricity from the night.

The hour eventually grew too late and we had to call the night to an end to start the return flight to Philomena. David and I rode together again. I tried to fly on my own, but David adamantly refused.

"Noah, you've only just now started to use a broom, and it's a bit of distance from here to Philomena. The upper atmosphere is difficult to fly in without experience. It's not the same as the heights of these tall buildings."

Even Maria agreed with him, "I mean he can do it, but it would probably be safer, just in case," as she intentionally walks away from my cold glare.

"Fine," finally conceding. We left the glorious city known for its elevation above the point where sea and land meet.

We land back on Cat's Peak. David and the others return to their respective homes while Kady and I walk back to the Manor together. We sneak in through my window.

She apparently started the evening much earlier with Gerald and forgot to unlock her own. We say goodnight and she tiptoes back to her room.

I sink into my bed while Morgan curls down beside me but it is impossible to sleep. My mind is restless with thoughts of David, flying, magik, friends, and David again. They race back and forth like racquetball.

After 20 minutes of staring out my window at the fading night sky, I decide to test the Binding spell. Originally, I had planned to perform the ritual later that evening, but the preparatory rituals were all complete, so it made no difference if it was then or now.

There was not much time left, dawn was approaching, and I needed to cast the spell during the absence of the sun. My sense of urgency moves me quickly. I sneak into the Manor's storage room to gather the remaining supplies, return to my room, and immediately start the spell.

Per the book's instructions, without ever touching them, I send out the thirteen black candles, no less, no more. They float to their respective spots, creating the 13th dimensional constellation representative of all that is within and without, between the worlds, and beyond even them.

I ground the spell using four ingredients that represent the cardinal elements.

> Watyr: Ice chipped from a northern glacier.
> Eyrth: Primordial oil.
> Ayre: Breath of the Witch.
> Fyre: Flame from the oil of earth.

The blood sacrifice contract now expired; the hungry book requires an additional offering. I pour out the contents of my final vial of blood onto its leather-bound cover.

There are three incantations. The first to open the gates of the Spirit realm. The second to find and access the lifeforce of both Morgan and me. The last to break and bind the pieces of us together.

Activating the Vilix, I recite the first incantation.

Venzoro
Heastr
Ianis
Reland
Metyx
Rusum
Martyree

Igniting the fireplace that is filled with primordial oil, the unlit chimney blazes to life in brilliant flames. The enchanted fire takes the form of tunnels. It tubes itself throughout the room.

The book sits in front of me and I place raw gold on top of it, which instantly turns black and slowly into violet. Using Transference, I levitate the frozen seawater over my head and the fire envelopes the glass until it shatters. The melted ice spreads over me and the book, creating a liquid dome. I breathe in deep and exhale all the air out of my lungs. The water dome expands into an oversized orb and creates a circle of power.

Now time for the second incantation.

Pe

Nek

Ra

Hapo

Ka

Qellis

I see myself, but not the me I know. Something much more, I gasp out loud at the sight.

Then, I hear a meow. Morgan, he reaches for me, barred by the circle of black magik, seeing him clearly for what he truly is, and it is miraculous, every being has magik.

Come here my love, if you wish. I whisper these silent thoughts that travel somewhere in between this world and the next. Just like that, he strides in, tail up high and takes his seat on my lap.

Finally, I chant the last spell completing the Blessed Blind.

Erish

Cathe

Kinan

Horucifa

Lusiris

Galanatos

Heth

Sades

I grab a small piece of my infinite life force and place it within him, he offers me the same, and I accept.

The spell is exceptionally draining and I find it difficult to keep my eyes open. The last thing I see is the hot yellow ball creeping up the mountainside, ending the night in fire. Finally, I fall into nothingness.

Morgan woke me. He rubs his forehead against my cheek, urging me to rise. I felt his invisible touch on the deeper inner workings of my mind. It was the strangest sensation.

Now awake, I lift myself off the floor. Unable to remember what happened after the spell, figuring I was suffering a post-spell blackout, and then I feel it.

A familiar but separate psychic entity has breached my mind. I was well accustomed to sensing the psychic energies from the rest of the Seers in the home. Divinations and psychic events were almost second nature for us, but they could never extend their presence into my own. It understandably comes as a shock to find one clearly inside my own psyche, especially given the source.

Morgan was sending me telepathic messages that I was powerless to block.

He was excited over the Binding and wanted to play with his newfound powers, and then he wondered what other powers he possessed.

For a moment I second guessed my decision to cast the spell.

Morgan suddenly walks away from me, as far as he could manage while still being within eye view, and then gracefully lays down into a regal curl with his back to me. I swear he even flicks his tail contemptuously.

He sends a clear message with both his body and mind, alerting me to my lack of gratitude for him, and my need to remediate my actions, specifically for thinking subversive thoughts of regret over the Bind.

His ideas and opinions, although unspoken, were perfectly clear to me. I could know a lot of things, but always by choice, but now Morgan has unlimited access to my mind.

I apologized and expressed my appreciation of him. He could feel my happiness, now knowing that, for as long as I lived, he would always be there. Knowing my history like no other has ever known, he forgives me easily, as only he can comprehend its significance.

Later that evening Joan calls to catch up. I tell her about Morgan being a Faemalyr, the flying on a broom to Denver, and how I am still inescapably in love with David, despite the continued rejection and subsequent re-wrecking of my heart.

I was about to go into detail over Morgan when she interrupts me, "Noah Ellis, on a broom, oh Jesus, give me strength."

Chapter Thirty

Cledonomancy, a type of Divination used to read the future through scrying random local and global events of the world.

A nightmare woke me up, the first one in a long time, but this one was different. Nina, Sam, and I were on a small boat. They fell into the water and were drowning. I dove in and pulled them back onto the boat. They were fine, scared, but alive. I looked away for a second and they were back in the water, gasping for air, again and again. I kept diving in, but eventually fatigue set in. Nina died first, and then Sam.

I woke up drenched in sweat. It seems impossible to shake this growing tightness in my chest and I try my best to distract myself with homework.

Morgan is rolling around and swatting at a card while I am knee-deep in research on a Versation spell that Dr. Huebner requested I study. As if speaking of the devil, his Altar appears in front of me by the fireplace, a first for him. It was unusual for him to break social etiquette. This method of communication in someone's bedroom is considered inappropriate.

"Noah, meet me in my office. It is a matter of urgency."

"Okay," taken aback by the intrusion, but I respectfully comply and gather my things into my bookbag. Dr. Huebner sends one more psychic message that twists my stomach into knots.

"And one last thing, bring the Despiraes."

He knows. A thousand thoughts run through my head all at once. What am I going to do? What about Maria? How much trouble have I gotten us into? I try desperately to think of a lie, some circumstance to get out of this situation. Maybe I could go back in time and change the past?

Ridiculous.

My breathing is rapid and panic constricts my airflow. Now dizzy, I sit on the floor to avoid falling over and try to fill my mind with rational thoughts, like the fact that there is no need to be afraid of Dr. Huebner. It was certain I would have some consequences, but he will not hurt me, or Maria.

It is going to be okay. I say this repetitively to control my breathing.

Exhaling and inhaling to calm myself, I stand back up and make my way into the closet to grab the Despiraes. I rescind the concealment spell over the book and it immediately reveals itself. I grab the book and shut the door behind me, accidentally trapping Morgan inside, but he phases right through the solid piece of wood like a ghost.

Morgan.

Calling him telepathically, I pick him up and hold him close to me, "What else can you do, handsome guy?"

He nudges in my mind for me to put him down and to focus my attention on the card he carried in his mouth.

> Congratulations Mr. Noah Ellis,
> The Coventry of the High Crown has selected you to test for High Crown Candidacy. Your Evaluations are to be performed in witness of two members of the Coventry and one of the Crowned Nine.
> Date: Twenty-First of November

Time: Twilight
Location: Hamptons
Room: 404-A
Sincerely,
Ensemble of the Nine

A few minutes later Dr. Huebner, looking rather sophisticated in his tailored suit, sits across from me behind his broad oak desk with a crystal orb at his far right.

I handed him the book the moment I arrived and to my relief he did not seem upset by my actions in the slightest. If anything, he seemed impressed. It affords me the opportunity to discuss my more pressing concern.

"Dr. Huebner, what does this mean," shakily handing him the invitation, the glow of the letters slowly fading away. I knew that my first annual Evaluation would be due soon, but this invitation looked nothing like Kady Zilberman's.

He clears his throat, preparing himself, "It is an invitation. It is, well, err the same Evaluation, per se," nervously stumbling over his words, another first for him.

"You have been identified as a candidate for the High Crown by the Ensemble of the Nine."

"What does that even mean?"

He smiles patiently, "I apologize, Mr. Ellis, it refers to the attendance of all Nine Seats of the High Crown."

I remembered our discussion so long ago, the High Crown was a legendary Witch, some would say mythical, who rises to power in times of need. Supposedly, there had not been a true High Crown for many centuries, so instead, the Council elected Witches identified for their superior magikal abilities. None of the individual Witches on their own is more powerful than any other gifted Witch in their craft, but together, they are capable of manifesting extraordinary power that mimics the legend, making them the most powerful force in Witch nation.

"Why me?"

"Review your history, Noah Ellis, Translocation at the O'Faolain's summer home, the Transdimensional door you summed as in the case of the Despiraes, let alone the magik you used to raise your Mortal family's pet from the dead. Your psychic prowess, including the Vilix Despirir, is in and of itself miraculous and now most recently, the powerful magik you used in the Blessed Bind. Do you not understand, few Witches are strong enough to cast such a spell, to link the meta-bodies of your life force to that or another is beyond the skills of even the most advanced Witch." His eyes glean with awe.

"I'm confused, I know that Faemalyrs of the Blessed Bind are rare, but not impossible to create, at least for the Witch who has access to the Despiraes."

"Yes, Noah, there are Witches that have cast this spell successfully. Even then, nothing to the effect of your own spell."

"Your housemates and faculty, including myself, can sense the Divine power of your magikal pet. Even your House Lead has made me aware of accounts where it has demonstrated innate magik. I had to alert the Coventry of the High Crown of your skills. Frankly, I am surprised they have not already identified your talent."

A huge lump grows in my throat and chest, "So what do they have planned for me?"

"After the Evaluation, Candidacy will advance and your training will be resumed with select Coventry members. They will also prepare you for the Final Trials, your chance to be selected for one of the Seats at the High Crown."

I struggle to maintain attention; the walls feel like they are closing in on me, and the floors seem to be shaking. It occurs to me that the Doctor said my training would be "resumed", meaning there would be a disturbance to my current education. A question grows within me, so obvious, I wonder why it did not come before.

"Dr. Huebner, where will I receive this training?"

He clears his throat, and then finally speaks, "At their city center, located near Seattle, Washington, known as Avalon."

"Near Seattle? That's where they found me, as a baby. It's where I was abandoned. Did you know that Dr. Huebner?"

"I am sorry, Mr. Ellis."

I felt a familiar surge of blood rush through my veins and it feels like I am about to burst. The sensation begs me to run away.

Quietly, I ask him, "What if I fail, on purpose?"

"The Evaluations are not based on a pass or fail score, regardless, Candidates of the High Crown are pre-approved by the Ensemble of the Nine. However, it is traditional for one of the Nine to be present to offer the formal invitation. I believe the Crown of the East has volunteered."

In other words, I was already damned to be spirited away, again.

A single tear falls, but nothing more. Its existence only proved by the cold air against my skin left vulnerable by its trail. I was so tired of crying and I am not sure there was enough left in me to spare.

"What if I refuse?"

He has this pained look on his face, remorse, "You cannot son, it is a mandatory invitation, the Council will either have you complete the Trials voluntarily or through coercion."

If only I could wish it away. "Don't call me that, I am not your son. What was the point of bringing me here if all you were going to do was force me to lose one more thing all over again?"

I am not safe and probably never was, the Doctor tears up a bit but I hold no sympathy for him.

"Noah, this is an opportunity."

Struggling to contain my frustration I walked out of his office without goodbyes or apologies. He deserved none of them.

There is a trail further below the main buildings of Philomena that leads toward a steep area and a hanging cliff halfway toward the Manor. I chose it as a detour to clear my head. My thoughts are made small by the vastness and majestic sight of Mt. Tarias and her people.

The smell of mountain laurel is in the air. My favorite scent does nothing to help soothe the ache in my heart. And just when I thought I had none left, a reservoir opened within me, unleashing a fury of cries that fell freely to the ground below.

The next day David sits beside me. He had arrived before me and has not spoken a word since I entered the room. Dr. Huebner had asked for our presence in lieu of what would have been our tutoring session.

The Doctor has already updated him on the good news. He has dismissed our training, "Alright," David says with clenched jaws.

"I suppose, is there anything else I can help with Dr. Huebner," his words are pointed and almost manic, "Oh, forgive me Noah." David pauses and then says, "Congratulations."

Surely, he must know what this means, that I am leaving Philomena. I wonder why he would congratulate me. To be fair, David is more likely to be aware of the dynamic of this competition, and all that it symbolizes to the Witch nation. It is possible that he might be genuinely happy for me.

He waits for me outside of Bexar and Gruene Hall.

"Would you walk with me?"

"Sure," and we walked to Lola, the place I learned to fly. We sit at the edge facing the jagged terrain of skinny towers formed out of rock and natural stone, their height rivals that of the great redwoods.

It was our personal spot on the mountain. To my surprise he is reviewing a training plan, hurriedly listing bullet points to focus on, almost desperate to cover all the necessary material for the Evaluation.

"Your magik needs to be," and he struggles with wording.

"Better," I offer.

"A bit more fine-tuned," correcting me. He sighs. "You can do this Noah, we are gonna make sure you can," a slight tremble is in his hands, unable to suppress his worry.

"David, why are you so worked up by this?"

He buries his face in his hands and breathes in and out, "I just want to make sure you are okay. Like it or not, Noah, they are going to send you to Avalon, the problem is," only his voice cracks from the beginnings of a sob.

My heart breaks just then, as he exhales a heavy thing. No wonder he seems so different, what with him carrying all that extra weight. He composes his words carefully, "People die from using the magik they make you do, all the time."

I should be scared but I am not. Dying does not seem like the worst thing in the world, but as I look at David's worried face, I cannot help but say, "Okay, well let's get to work then," as softly and genuinely as I could muster.

David and Maria volunteer to enhance my magikal training. Even Leroy and other members of the Spirit Manor offered to practice with me until the wintery date that marks my end at St. Philomena.

My Evaluation were now two days away. David looks at me carefully, silently assessing my transitional movements for the spell. We were working on my Cardinal Bind.

"I think you just aren't raising enough power, like there is a block or something. You are doing the movements perfectly, it's just not enough," he says as I try to sway the wind.

"Guess you're right," after all, my mind was more on me leaving.

"Maybe I don't have it in me, maybe this is my ceiling," I suggest.

Silence stands between us. It was after all a possibility, as everyone has a magikal limit.

He stands up and places his large hands on my shoulders and stares down at me with his sincere brown eyes and says, "You, Noah Ellis, are going to get this. I will make sure of that."

Looking into the eyes of the perfect boy standing in front of me, in his pull over sweater with shaggy hair, and that beautiful smile, I cannot help but be devastatingly in love with him.

Although I do not want to, I ask to call it a night. I felt so alone these past few nights but being with David somehow made it harder.

"Sure, Noah, you do need your rest. Please sleep well."

"You too, and David?"

"Yeah No-El," looking at me with eager eyes.

"Thank you for everything, really."

"It's no problem, I promise," he pauses and then hugs me like he used to, not awkward or uncomfortable, and then takes my hands in his and offers one last reassurance, "You are more capable than what you think."

He lets go of my hands and walks away.

After he leaves, my impulses get the best of me as I extend my Sight to him and notice how he clenches and unclenches his fist, taking deep inhales and exhales, and I hear the sound of his beating heart and feel the pounding of my own.

The rest of the night is used for practicing the skill. The Vilix connects me to the concept of Ayre and affords me a new appreciation for the element. Its movements were mesmerizing, all hot and cold.

It brings life to the trees from the sky and travels to and from the lungs of the animals, including Mortals and Witch alike. I feel it in my own body and even Morgan's and then in David. In typical fashion, my thoughts always come back to him.

Oh Ayre, messenger of the gods and carrier of life. This being connects all things in its medium like the ocean for its creatures. I did not know how much you love us.

Oh Ayre, that which carries rain, earth, reason, and thought. You are fire and lightning, you are ice and water, you are rock and the Earth, herself.

It is late into the night at this point, happy for the experience, but I am ready to call it.

Oh Ayre, in its fickle ways, shifts around me, introducing itself. It scatters paper all over the room, kissing me on the face and brushing my hair. It fills my lungs with cool inhales and returns itself in warm exhales.

Blessed Ayre, thank you for claiming me in your Bind.

That next evening, Madam Reyna requested that I meet with her. She wanted to educate me on the processions.

"The Coventry of the High Crown identifies candidates by testing for specific areas; the first is Capacity, which refers to the amount of power a Witch possesses. The second is Competency or the Witch's expertise in a particular type of magik. Lastly, Capability which identifies all of the Witch's innate magikal skills."

We sit across each other in her classroom as she repeats information that I already knew. I stare at her with my bright blue eyes, hoping she can read the 'fuck you' inside them.

She explains the Evaluations are essentially a test in every core subject taught at Philomena.

My eyes maintain the same message as I stare back in a fixed gaze. I knew she was not responsible for what was happening to me, but I cannot help but be angry, and my rage was proving impossible to contain.

To my surprise, she responds with a gentle frown, "At the final portion of your Evaluation you will receive an offering, a potion meant to both test and mimic the powers of the Vilix Despirir, a sacred skill of the true High Crown, although an unnecessary requirement to be one of the Nine. For those without the Vilix, the potion will allow access to worlds out of reach for typical psychic gifts, without the Corona Borealis, or as you refer to it, the Northern Lights. However, for those with the Vilix, the potion serves as a stimulant to the sacred power, activating its luminescent side effect in the process."

"But I have the Vilix, why do I have to be tested," reminded of the torment I experienced when first tested for my Witch genetics by Abigail Tetson and, technically, Dr. Huebner.

"It is tradition. The gift has to be verified and every Witch Candidate of the Nine is required to experience the skill at least once in their career toward a Seat at the High Crown."

Annoyed, "It still doesn't make sense."

She sighs, "The tonic has a tertiary function, an enchantment that both bewitches the candidate and manifests a psychic representation of the Witch, one that can be easily manipulated by the proctors and other witnesses."

"Are you kidding me, they want to watch what goes on inside me?"

I think I am delirious at this point because I start laughing hysterically at the absurdity of the whole ordeal, "That's disgusting, so what, they just want to use me to read their fortune, or tell them some dirty secret?"

"It is a foul practice, Mr. Ellis, an unfortunate reality of our kind. Many oracles, Mortal or Witch, have been forced to use their gifts for the desire of others. Seers in ancient Greece were often drugged for compliance by lesser Witches. I am sorry you are burdened with this task."

"Are you going to be there? Are you going to enjoy the show?"

"We're done."

"No," and my eyes glow blue.

"Why does David think I am in danger?"

"Your tutor, the one that rejected you," she says in retort.

Morgan arrives just then, I guess my magik got ahead of me, because all the doors shut, and the room grows heavy with heat.

"It's time for you to leave, now."

She looks at me with condescension, but I do not budge, "If you don't want to tell me, I can just take it from you."

"Calm yourself first."

The room begins to cool, and the doors reopen.

Madam Reyna sits back down, "I suppose Mr. O'Faolain is concerned with the Trials for a High Crown Seat. Some of them have a higher risk of injury or death for the Witch casting the spell. In addition, you do have a severely late start in the specialized education for a Candidate. It is a shame only Nekromancers are automatically transferred to the Colleges of Avalon's School of Oracles. There are many talented Seers that would greatly benefit from their training."

That was the reason David urged me to keep my ability to see ghosts a secret. He was trying to protect me and maybe even keep me here at Philomena.

She goes on, "He worries fruitlessly, you've already demonstrated the Capability for most of the Trials. The Ninth, by far the most dangerous, should not prove problematic for you. After all, you were able to Evoke a dimensional doorway when faced with the Third Seal during your felonious theft of the Despiraes, which is the most difficult component of the Ninth Trial."

Agitated, I ask sharply, "What are the other Trials?"

She reviews them briefly; they are specific acts of magik that must be mastered to be eligible for a Crowned Seat on the Ensemble. Each represent a form of the following magikal subtypes to include Divination, Translocation, Abjuration, Temporal, Evocation, Elemental, Conjuration, Healing, and Nekromancy.

"The first is the Third Eye, an innate skill in Divination, which for obvious reasons is not an issue for you."

She continues to list the skills needed. First is the Gates of Chronos, a celestial Translocation spell that requires using space and gravity to perform the magik. Lorg mór is a magik focused on the manipulation of time. Jericho's Rose, the ability to both resurrect and heal those on the precipice of death. Therianthrope, Versation magik, a specific skill in shape-shifting into animals. The Coire Ansic, a conjuration referenced as the cauldron that never runs dry, its enchantments would supposedly last for an eternity.

They all sound vaguely familiar. It is not until she tells me what the Seventh Trial is that it finally dawns on me, "For Abjuration, you are required to produce a barrier that is impenetrable from varied attacks including psychic, cosmic, and elemental assaults, it is known as the Hand of Fatima."

"Give me a second," I searched my bag for the list of spells Dr. Huebner assigned to me at the start of the year. I feel out of breath as I privately read over the list. David and I only managed to cover two of the seven assigned.

Gates of Chronos
Lorg mór
Jericho's Rose
Therianthrope
Coire Ansic
Hand of Fatima
Cardinal Bind

The

Third Eye,

like Madam Reyna said, was absent for obvious reasons. I then say, "And the Ninth is the Despirir Nekroncia, the one you were teaching me, right?"

"Correct," she answers.

"What's the last one," I ask to confirm what I already knew.

"The Cardinal Bind, of course, a very tricky magik to master."

Dr. Huebner already knew I was leaving Philomena. He always knew.

Chapter Thirty-One

Old antiquated spells abandoned by their ancestral inheritance are difficult to conjure, but can be re-awakened, and make a most formidable magik.

David asked me to step out with him for a few minutes before my Evaluation. It is snowing and I can smell the soft ice falling onto the ground. It's clean, almost like an absence of scent, a result of molecules dancing to the slow closing song of a neglectful heat.

He is staring at his shoes, standing only a foot away, "I really, really don't want you to go."

"Ditto."

There is an energy between us, like gravity, but unlike the orbital relationship of a planet to its sun. This was like a black hole, desperate to remain close to light and matter due to its own emptiness, and I was the void. David is good, and I honestly believe he will miss me, but I am not sure for the right reasons.

"If anyone can do this, it's you No-El."

"Absolutely, it's going to be okay," hoping I sound genuine, and with nothing more to say, we returned to room 404-A.

Maria sits with Leroy, Kady, and Ms. Penelope on the witness side, behind the two-way mirror. She runs out of the room toward me and engulfs me in a deep hug, "Knock 'em out," she says confidently.

Dr. Huebner and Madam Reyna arrive shortly after and do not attempt to greet me, fully aware of my disdain for them. Although I am not sure how much Madam Reyna knew about my inevitable transfer, it seemed as much a surprise to her as it was to me.

The clock chimes, announcing the arrival of twilight. I turn my Sight outside of these four stark walls and See Jake throwing a frisbee back and forth with his friends. Nearby there is a group of girls watching, just like Jake and his friends are watching them. I can See their young excitement over one another, at the same time, I can tell this next stage closes the door on the former, ending their days of innocence. I See the subtle and gigantic rotation of Earth, and then me. I could have looked into my future but decided against it. What was the point? My life was already on the precipice of irrevocable change, again.

The sound of her heels arrogantly announces her arrival from the hallway, and I know it is her before she walks through the door. She wears a black dress that hangs loose against her thin body. The click of her red-bottomed heels increases in volume as she approaches, "Hello, Mr. Ellis."

"Hey," I say flatly.

Three others arrive with Ms. Tetson, all dressed in black, and I correctly assume they are the exam proctors. An older, bald man, with a permanent frown scarred onto his miserable face is the first to introduce himself.

"Nicholas Crouexe," but he does not look at me, not even once. The sight of him sends a tremble throughout my body.

"My name is Tara Norr, 'tis a pleasure to meet you," said the middle-aged woman with red hair and an Irish accent.

"Same to you," I respond sincerely, her accent too endearing to hate. Although the sound of her is unlike David, the similarity to him is enough for me.

Finally, a bizarrely tall and thin man, who could look young if it were not for the lines etched on his face. He wears a traditional Witch's hat with flowing robes and an enchanted train suspended in the air.

"Walzem Valas," says the Crown of the East, one of the Nine.

They have me stand in the center of the empty room. The two-way mirror divides me and the proctors from the others. The proctors sit behind a table across from me with pen and paper at the ready.

Each Witch is offered four hours to complete their Evaluation. Each subject covered at St. Philomena is tested and the student can use a traditional spell to replicate the ability if it has not been mastered. If there are no Capabilities in a subject, then the Witch moves on to the next.

It has been nearly two hours but we are near the end and are now on Abjuration. I chose to demonstrate the Hand of Fatima.

Nicholas Crouexe casts fire against me, followed by a Celestial lightning bolt that was unexpectedly channeled from the Sun's solar force, an unnecessarily dangerous power source given our proximity to the cosmic giant. It forces against my barrier, and I struggle, but the barrier holds.

Tara Norr tests the barriers malleability and attempts to telepathically attack me, but she might as well have been using feathers for knives.

"Very good, Mr. Ellis."

"Thank you, Ms. Norr."

"You may move on to Elemental magik. Please announce your spell or skill, whenever you are ready, dear."

"Cardinal Bind," I stare through the two-way mirror, making direct eye-contact with Dr. Huebner.

Oh Ayre, what would we do without you?

I created a bubble around Nicholas Crouexe, the proctor that attacked me with the force of the Sun, siphoning precious air out of his lungs. I hated him, probably because he reminded me of that dog of a man. I stopped immediately once I sensed he approached suffocation. He takes quite a bit of time to recover, overreacting of course. He was never entirely out of breath.

"Impressive, Mr. Ellis, although you do not need to direct your magik toward the assessors, please avoid doing so, going forward," said Walzem Valas, wearing a slight smile on his face.

"Yes, Crown of the East."

Once the Evaluation is complete, Abigail announces the additional test of High Crown Candidacy, the test of the Vilix.

"When you are ready, Mr. Ellis."

She floats the potion to me that takes a year to create, it is the same one used for compensating psychic gifts in the Blessed Bind and is good for one use.

The concoction has a gaseous form. It has trails swirling inside creating a more solid appearance, but then evaporates and reforms once more in a continuous sequence. If I looked closely, the liquid partially revealed something, maybe the stars? The golden laced vial that holds the element is cold to the touch, absorbing the heat from my fingers causing more frequent and intense colored ripples.

I raise the glass to my lips and swallow all its contents. At first it was like breathing in the winter air, but it instantly became heavy, like swallowing gallons of water all at once. The sensation works its way through my throat, into my chest, and finally settles in the pit of my stomach.

They stand watching, waiting, yet nothing happens.

"Am I supposed to activate the Vilix first?"

The Crown of the East says, "What do you mean activate the Vilix?"

"Turn it on, should I do that first?"

"Oh dear, it appears there is some misinformation being exchanged, you are talking about the Vilix Despirir, correct?"

"Yes," obviously.

"Maybe it is purely semantics, but you don't turn *on* the Vilix. It is not a tool but rather a trait. You don't have the Vilix Despirir," he pauses, reading my face to determine my comprehension of the words he speaks.

"You are the Vilix Despirir."

"Oh." I stay quiet for a moment, unsure of what to say, "Forgive me, Crown of the East."

My agitation takes over just then, "So do I turn myself on now or what?"

Ms. Norr laughs.

Walzem Valas answers, "We have to activate the potion's secondary purpose, are you prepared to proceed?"

"No, but I don't have a choice, so go for it."

He frowns and it seems sincere but cast the spell regardless.

Blue fire burns in my eyes.

I float up, succumbing to the incantation, unable to suppress the ribbons of blues and violets that flow around me, making its way into the group of onlookers.

The proctors audibly gasp at the sight of it.

A form appears before them, an ethereal version of me, but this version seems to shine with the glow of the moon, brightening the world around him.

He speaks while I am suspended mid-air, motionless. My eyes face the high ceiling above, fixed on some nonsignificant point.

"The Spirit is a public representation of the boy's private thoughts, experiences and combined magikal abilities, an Avatar," says the Crown of the East.

"Remarkable," comments Ms. Norr, in equal concurrence. Nicholas Crouexe quietly shudders in response to the vibrations produced by the Vilix.

The Northern Lights entwine in ribbons of light dancing around me, holding on to my Spirit, fueling and minding its presence. Dean Tetson calls from behind the glass window and beseeches the Avatar to share the experience of the Vilix. The room pulsates with magikal energy, challenging the charms previously infused within the room for just this occasion.

We are here.

Though no words were spoken the sound was maintained, both in the physical world and in the privacy of their thoughts. The words produced by this other-worldly entity echo inside the walls and space within them.

Abigail prompts again for a shared experience into my psyche and power.

We know what you seek. We always know.

Walzem Valas speaks, "What are you? I can see the boy in you but there seems to be something more?"

We are the divide between life and death. Mortality and infinity. We are the edges of the universe, and the worlds before and after.

Dr. Huebner stands bravely, "Will you show us?"

We do not show you, as this is his wish.

"Why would Noah wish this," he asks incredulously.

Its image shall obliterate your physical minds. And He will not allow it.

The Avatar looks back at my floating body with obedience and the slightest note of petulance.

I barely notice, lost all over again, vaguely aware of my body. Then I find myself in a nauseatingly familiar place.

It seems no matter where I go, I will always be abducted by these insipid memories, brought to life by the damn Vilix. Well, brought to life by me, back to the home that built and destroyed me, only it is no longer there, in its place is rubble and debris.

Time is still for a moment, and then suddenly rewinds itself in a blur. Grayson House, rebuilt, stands before me.

Three Witches stand in a circle. They surround an unconscious floating boy, a sickly and small thing with dark hair. His eyes are closed but if they were open, I know they would be the color of stars.

Dr. Huebner initiates the spell. An Aquarian star is sliced into the ground by an invisible knife destroying the blades of grass. The other Witch, Abigail Tetson, joins the chant followed by a much older woman who I do not know. They recite the spell in unison.

The air shifts and the winds begin racing. Small mammals and birds are lucky enough to flee the area, but the insects beneath the ground are not so fortunate. Loud cracks of invisible electricity strike the ground, creating small explosions. The spell is like a tornado, slow to form but quick to destroy, because in one swift motion Grayson House is ripped apart. The hard and heavy pieces of the home crash onto the ground.

The final act of their spell settles itself on the marked one.

Me, it lives in my memories. In this moment, a special kind of time loop, hiding it from existence and time. What did they want me to forget?

The Vision changes and Charles Daley shouts out obscene things as he rips off the small jeans of the younger me. I try to push him off, a hopeless attempt to get away. He punches me and blood spills freely from my nose.

The last thing I see is Sam hiding in the corner, right before Charles Daley slams his fist into my eye, and I see no more.

He drags me down to the basement, but the Visions blur at my command. I do not want to See the things he will do. Allowing it to reform a few hours later, my wrists and ankles are chained to the wall, and I am covered in blood. There are distinct bruises on my neck in the shape of his hands. The Vision connects me to the sharp and intense pain inside my childhood body.

The undeniable truth shamelessly reveals itself.

I died that day.

He killed me, and my magik must have somehow brought me back.

The younger me convulses, tears fall from his face, but then he hears him above. Charles is moving heavy things, and a spark of white-hot anger consumes us. His body trembles from our power, every link of the chains that bind him twist and bend and wither away. The fury inside him burns without control. He walks to the door, it cracks until it splits into pieces, shooting away from him to clear the path.

The image shifts and I stare again at that pig of a man. The two bodies of my foster siblings lay motionless in front of me. He was playing a game. One that we could never win. The cost always resulted in blood. Hearing his nauseating thoughts, trying to convince himself that he did not mean to kill them as the realization of their deaths manifest. He had a fleeting moment of guilt, but it is quickly dismissed by his sheer incapability for remorse. In its stead is contempt for Nina and Sam, he reasons their deaths could have been avoided if they had only touched him without argument. He was going to bury their bodies in the empty wilderness. No one would ever find them in their unmarked graves.

I could still hear their screams, it echoed in the woodwork, damning the place forever.

Nina was six and Sam had just turned two.

The younger me stands in front of Charles Daley and he stares at him with uncensored hate, his pupils are narrow with purpose.

"What have you done," the younger me screams. His eyes radiate bright blue.

Charles falls back in a jolt, shocked by the sight of the dead boy now brought back to life. However, the fear of someone discovering his crimes transforms his initial surprise into rage.

He sees me as a threat, and thinks that I am at fault, and deserve to be punished for disobedience.

Charles finishes tying up the trash bag that contained Nina's body. With murder on the mind, he stands up and makes his way toward me, "Get over here you piece of shit."

Our power detonates as he reaches for us. Charles is pushed backward against the wall. Disoriented at first, he stands up slowly, but quickly regains his senses. He dismisses his confusion as to how he fell backwards, refocuses, and runs toward me at full speed.

Our magik envelops him, lifting him off the ground, and tears at his skin. He does not cry out right away, his sudden inability to move disorients him. He uselessly rips his own muscles in his attempt to free himself, but only his eyes maintain their mobility.

I wanted him to see it.

He looks at us, at him, and is momentarily lost in pretty blue stars, until he begins to understand what is happening.

I am going to kill him.

He trembles and pathetically soils himself. A bead of sweat slides down his swollen dirty face. He wonders what kind of freak I am. He calls us a nasty faggot and, in his mind, thinks we may be one of those Witch devils.

His nose pours out blood.

Charles tries to scream, to plead, to justify, but there is nothing that he can say now. Nothing will stop this, stop me, stop us.

And the younger me finishes our work.

"Stop breathing" and the blood vessels of Charles Daley explode.

His dread, his breath, and his life fade away into nothingness.

The childhood me rushes over to the bodies of my foster siblings. He desperately tries to resurrect their bodies, like he did to his own, but to our profound grief and regret, he does not know how.

All he can do is hold their bodies close to his own and scream for them to come back. His cries shatter every glass-surface in the house and cracks the earth below.

That is when I realized why the nightmares continued to haunt me. It was not just my hate for Charles Daley, but also the hatred I held for myself for not saving them.

The Vision fades away, and I am back inside room 404-A, with Walzem Valas pleading with my Avatar to demonstrate its power. Something has changed, because now the Avatar grins.

Yes.

It recites the Nekromanic ritual. The sound of its voice strips paint and twists metal.

Ordinarily this spell required preparation, things like ritual baths with water taken from the lower depths of the sea, where the sun does not touch. The room used for the ritual also had to be hidden from natural light, but continuously illuminated by torches that burned the dust from grinded black diamonds and ancient oils for days. The Door of the Dead had to be marked by dark purple violets scattered onto the floor, shaped into the combined symbol of Hades, Saturn, and the Magik Star.

It is no surprise to see the proctors stare open mouthed at my Avatar successfully casting the spell, using only words, nearly mastering the magik.

Nexia

Septus

Despirorian

The dark sigil carves itself into the ground, desecrating the entire floor. It glows black and drinks the surrounding light, while draining my power.

Orshri

Hathe

Rishkagal

Finishing the spell, the Avatar summons the dead forth.

Krev

Anje

Daehs

My body falls to the ground, the pain from my knees hitting the concrete floor awakens me to this world, but there is no injury that could take me away from the vision in front of me.

Two true Angels slowly approach me. They are covered in starlight and wear diadems made of gold.

Halos.

Hello, Noah.

Forever six years old, pretty in her white dress, beautiful Nina.

She stands in front of her baby brother, a small toddler with an angelic face. He hides behind her.

We miss you.

I want to tell them I miss them every day. I want to say a million things, but all I can do is cry out to them, "I'm sorry. I should have protected you. I'm sorry I couldn't save you."

Its okay Noah, we are safe now.

Her ethereal voice tries to offer reassurance. Sam peeks out from behind Nina, mustering all his two-year-old courage, and finally speaks.

Okay now No-Ow. He never could say my name.

Okay now. Be okay now.

I bury my face to the ground and rock myself back and forth. The first sign of my lost mind.

The screams remind him of blood and monsters.

Chapter Thirty-Two

Please remember spells carry a life of their own, and abandoned magik neither forgets nor forgives those who betrayed them, or their descendants. Hell hath no fury like that of the scorned.

The strange guttural screams sounded much further away, almost like a whisper. It sounded like someone had broken a bone or suffered some other severe injury. The blunt ache in my throat was the only indication that its source was me. I have never been burned severely, not in the literal sense, but I imagined death by fire would feel like what I experienced on that day.

The strain in my vocal cords remind me that I am not dead. That is pain's gift, a reminder of life, but it is then that I recognize the screams are not exclusively my own.

My Avatar screeches while the Spirits of the dead rise in the small room. They crowd against each other, translucent but visible, blinking in and out in the dark space. All from various eras, some are horrified, others surprised, and then there are those who are in an utter rage against the world.

Bexar and Gruene appear in front of me. *Noah, what have you done?*

I don't have time to answer. The Avatar's psychic noise shatters the two-way mirror and then disappears. In his stead is another version of me. Only its eyes are no longer blue or bright, instead, they are shrouded in a glowing void of darkness, and I know unequivocally the pieces of me have been shattered.

It hovers a foot off the ground and is filled with hate and a desire for destruction, a Daemon of Fury.

Impossibly fast, it flies directly toward me and without warning, a second version of me apporates between us. He, or it, is much older and its eyes blazed a brighter blue than my own. Attached to its back are eight wings, like that of a Seraphim, a top-ranking angel in Christian theology. Its wings are translucent. The lines of the luminary appendages are only visible under certain angles of light.

Like a guard, the Seraphim grabs the Daemon by the throat and slams him into the ground, cracking the concrete floor against its head upon impact, but it instantly disappears.

Someone touches my shoulder; I turn around and find a boy beside me. He wears severe concern that does not belong on his perfect face. David wraps his arms around me, his face wet with sweat and fear.

Maria is standing above me. She holds a psychic barrier produced by her butterflies, and I realize she holds it against the Spirits that now swarm around me. Her barrier, fueled by her immense strength, goes beyond the scope of my initial enchantment and holds them at bay. Across the room are the proctors and faculty who all are casting their own spells against the Spirits.

The Daemon reappears in front of us and David casts a banishing spell against it. The spell should send it to the nearest body of saltwater, several leagues under the surface, but it does not even flinch. With a vicious grin, the Daemon flicks its hand and hurls David and Maria into the wall. Thankfully, Bexar and Gruene appear and use their energies to buffer their impact.

The Seraphim attempts to hold it back, but the Daemon's eyes glow black and drain his ethereal light, forcing it to retreat. With the guard gone it returns his attention to me with contempt clear on its face and conjures a psychic blade, raising the weapon over me.

That is when the third arrives, a younger version of me, the boy Charles Daley killed. He faces the Daemon, valiantly using his small body as a wall between his fury and me. Without words, the little boy commands it to stop.

His psychic noise is small and light, but sharp like knives. The Daemon hesitates, its eyes dart back and forth, and I understand now it cannot move. The little boy contained it, at least for the moment.

I turn to the younger me but I am quickly derailed by the sight of him. Across the room, standing beside the fighting proctors is me, at least another psychic piece of me. This one is nearly identical, but I know right away that this version of me is not a Witch, just a boy. He is the *me* that I wished I could have been.

My reverie is disrupted by the deafening crack of the Daemon ripping at the young boy's magikal trap until finally releasing itself. It swiftly hovers toward me and grabs my neck, lifting me into the air, stealing my breath, but the Seraphim returns. Its light is slightly dimmed, but it manages to peel the Daemon off me, and with impossible strength pushes it clear through the wall.

To no avail, the Daemon instantly reappears behind the Seraphim, plunging the psychic blade into its winged back. The Seraphim fades and is gone. Once more, the Daemon lunges toward me. In futility, the child attempts to restrain it by apporating onto its own back but is consumed by fire. He didn't even scream.

From a distance, David desperately yells out to me as he and Maria barricade themselves against the Spirits, as more continuously arrive through the hole in our dimension. They dragged Sam and Nina, prompting me to pick myself up, but I struggled to find my balance and fall back on my knees. Something was wrong. My senses were dulled far beyond the normal state of shock. The spell has drained me beyond any of my experiences.

The Mortal approaches, and to my surprise, the Daemon stands still in abeyance at his arrival. The Mortal leans down to face me as David and Maria's barrier begins to break and the dead prepare to overtake them. He grabs my hands and peers into my eyes with his own. His are a mundane blue, dissimilar to mine, yet still beautiful.

The Seraphim and child return, translucent now, but they too remain still, yielding to the Mortal's presence. I realize what this part of me represents. He is the best of me.

The Mortal speaks to me through thought. *You can stop this. So, stop this.*

He restores something within me. I think it might be hope.

David and Maria's barriers deteriorate and the Spirits pin their bodies into the wall, consuming their lifeforce. Their eyes are cast downward and their faces low, as if they were trapped underwater, and can no longer hold their breath. Nina and Sam try their best to hold their own barrier against them, but even their strength wavers, and I see their light fading.

It is too much pain.

No, not Nina, not Sam, not Maria, and not my David. I was not ready to give up, not on them. I wreathe, broken from my comatose state with a single-minded purpose. So, I held on, knowing the cost, but for me the end justifies the means.

The Mortal vanishes and the Daemon flies toward me, but my own eyes are now on fire.

No more.

It seems the world cracks and rips at my sheer grit, electricity streaking in the space around us. I am lifted into the air by the undiluted force of my power. The Daemon is held to the floor by invisible chains, and I begin to cast the spell to end the ritual of the dead, opening my eyes through the Vilix.

No, that is not right. As Walzem Valas said, I am the Vilix.

Through my eyes.

Without words, in full mastery of the spell, I send the raised Spirits back to where they belong, and restore the strength of those they drained. Bexar and Gruene return to their hall, and I gently return Sam and Nina to their place in Heaven. Stars appear in the room as I do so and then time stops. All is quiet and still.

Now focusing my energies on my broken psyche, I banish the pieces of me to the Betwixt, the space between worlds. Soon I will join them, there is no other way, they are me and I am them. My only regret is Morgan's own Spirit follows the rest of them into the empty place. His body now lies lifeless in my room. He did not have to die today. He could have lived a long and wonderful life had I not been so selfish by binding our Spirits.

Do not worry Morgan. I will be there soon.

My eyes face the sky. The blue in them grow dull and listless. Time begins again and I fall to the ground.

There is a word for a feeling of profound emptiness that can only be experienced by being present in a place that is normally filled with life but now void of it, called kenopsia. That is what I feel here in the Betwixt, although I am not sure life has ever existed here in this place of hyper emptiness.

But when I look beyond its border, I can see an infinite amount of other worlds beyond my own.

All the people and life that exists in this multiverse is inconceivable, and they seem familiar at the same time, like I was connected. I think we all are.

A ripple distorts the vision and is discordant with the vast Betwixt. There is no air or substance to create the disturbance, even gravity and time do not exist in this place, yet it travels to my consciousness, and all at once I feel David's rapid breath against the nape of my neck.

Somehow, I was still connected to my physical body. It occurs to me that this ripple is an enduring connection, and I know now that it is the Vilix in its purest form.

David, in a state of alarm, holds my body tightly and convulses into deep sobs. Those are the ones that suffer, the ones the dead leave behind.

I am sorry.

He casts spell after spell over my rapidly cooling body. I can feel the strain it causes on his heart, and I do not know how far he will push himself. Silently, I plead with him to stop, but he keeps holding me and muttering incantation after another. He trembles, wet scarring tears fill the whole of his face, "Please, No-El, you have to keep trying. Come on Noah, only a little bit more, please."

His tears fall and find me.

I do not know if I have enough in me to fix this, but like with most things, the perfect boy effortlessly succeeds at convincing me to at least try.

Voiceless, David recites the incantation for me through our connection.

Venzoro

Heastr

Ianis

Reland

Metyx

Rusum

Martyree

I claw and tear at the edge of the Betwixt, opening a dimensional doorway using the Blessed Bind. It was not supposed to be used this way and I worry over the consequences for my actions.

David cries out just then, sending my concern away. I can feel his resolve just as easily as his arms around me. He refuses to let go and I can at least do the same.

Pe

Nek

Ra

Hapo

Ka

Qellis

I collect all my shattered pieces. David falters on the spell, not because of him, but me. The connection between my body and Spirit were fading, but my wonderful and absurdly stubborn friend will not concede. He burns me with his own power, giving me a fragment of his own life. A torch, it is not mine to have, but I hold it strong, nonetheless.

Erish

Cathe

Kinan

Horucifa

Lusiris

Galanatos

Heth

Sades

I pull my shattered Spirit against and through the Betwixt and into the voided vessel that is my body. Carefully, I returned Morgan's Spirit and the piece of mine already Binded to him, back to his own. I sense him coming back to life in the distance.

With all my will I use the psychic elemental components; fire to mold, ice to bind, air so they do not break under the pressure, and sealed with the steadiness of earth. I test my Spirit's structural integrity by letting go, and it holds. It was like a broken bone. The end-product resembles the original, but will never be the same.

David calls me, but I am too tired to open my eyes. The perfect boy who keeps saving me pulls me in close as I fade into darkness.

Chapter Thirty-Three

Enchanted brooms, or Besoms, are levitated into the upper atmosphere where they are radiated in moonlight for one lunar cycle. This traditional Witchcraft has been practiced for centuries. To date, this method is the most effective spellwork for longevity of its magikal properties.

Time, in all its insensitivity, parades on. It pushes me forward into the next second, minute, hour, and day, leading me to where I do not want to go.

I woke up two days later in the Infirmary with Morgan at my side. Several tonics were used to restore my strength after the Evaluation. They induce an extended sleep for a minimum of 24 hours and do not reach their full restorative effect for at least an hour after I am fully awake.

Dr. Statton is the first to greet me, "Welcome back, Mr. Ellis." He directs an apprentice to notify my family, and returns two minutes later with the Mastersons.

Joan wraps her arms around me, "Thank God you're finally awake." Kevin and Jake join her as I cry deeply into her shoulders and muffle out, "You're here, how is this possible?" Mortals were forbidden to enter Tarias.

"The Council made an exception for you," explains Dr. Huebner, who is the last to enter the room.

The memories of my Vision flood my mind with a vengeance. “Get out.”

“Noah, bc reasonable.”

“Reasonable? You erased my memory, playing with my mind like a toy. How could you do that to me,” I say with the feeling of bile in my mouth. Dr. Huebner’s treachery and blatant disregard for my own will has left a scar in me, and it is now fresh with re-injury.

“Let me explain.”

Joan looks directly at him with daggers in her eyes, but she and Kevin remain silent and wait for him to speak. Apparently, they have already heard whatever he is about to say.

“By all means Doctor,” my tone drenched with bitterness.

“It was a matter of your personal safety.”

“The hell is wrong with you people,” Kevin barks, unable to censor himself.

“Us people, by that you mean Witch-kind?”

“No Vance, Witches like you,” Joan shouts out.

My concern for the Mastersons bombards me, fearful that Dr. Huebner may try to hurt them. He is not the man I thought I knew and cannot be trusted, but I am still weak from the Evaluation. If need be, I could at least fend off Dr. Huebner to give the Mastersons time to get away, but I do not know if I could do much more. Unwilling to jeopardize their lives, I try my best to remain calm and ask them to stop arguing in a strained voice. Thankfully, they respond to my fragility.

Joan breathes and Dr. Huebner smiles softly and his eyes grow uselessly watery. He tries to mediate, “I know this is difficult to understand, but we had to bind your memory to erase the evidence. If the Mortals knew you killed that vile man, they would have sentenced you to death solely because you are a Witch, and the Council would have been powerless to stop it.”

I think back to that girl in the trailer park, the one that practically burned the whole place down. I never saw her again, maybe the rumors were true, and she killed someone too?

I killed a man.

The heaviness of it begins to sink within me. Somehow, I always knew, the memory lived in the corners of my mind, just out of reach, like a dream, but thoughts of Sam and Nina wipe away any feeling of regret. I don't care what that says about me.

Dr. Huebner goes on, "The spell does more than just block your memory. It removes moments of time into a Loop. It starts from the memories of all living witnesses. We hid the moments that held you responsible for the man's death by using your memory."

"You used me."

"We were trying to protect you, Noah."

"Protect me? If that's the case, why didn't you take me to Tarias right then and there?"

"We could not initiate custodial rights without raising suspicion with the authorities. They would have linked your Manifestation to the murder."

"Then why haven't you told me? I've been here for nearly a year, were you ever going to say something?"

"Please understand, because of your power and unfortunate lack of early training, you lack self-control. You are a safety hazard to yourself and others, as evidenced by your Evaluation."

With unbelievably poor timing, Abigail Tetson enters the room. She re-introduces herself as the *former* Dean of St. Philomena and *current* Ambassador of the Coventry of the High Crown. Without invitation, she confirms my Candidacy and subsequent orders to attend the School of Oracles located in Avalon, the center hidden by mists just west of Seattle.

My rage was close to the surface and I was beginning to feel the healing potions reach their maximum potency.

"Go to hell," snapping at her, "the both of you."

"The insolence," she says haughtily.

Dr. Huebner pleads, "I implore you, Mr. Ellis, please remember we are on your side."

"No, you're not. You are only on one side, yours. Why put me in a home, my only home, just to rip me out, and then do it all over again? Do you know what I've been through, do you?" My tears are too close to the surface but the time for crying is over.

My eyes glow so bright it shades the room blue. Before I can cast a single spell, Dr. Huebner floods the space with his Illusionary magik, showing me the spell used the night I killed Charles Daly.

"Look for yourself. We didn't just erase your memories."

"What do you mean?"

Dr. Huebner shows us the additional spell placed upon me, "Suppressing your powers was our only choice. We had to delay your Manifestation so we tried our best to consider your needs. True age is different for our kind, but we understand the significance of it for Mortals. You were not supposed to Manifest until your eighteenth birthday, to allow you to be raised by the Mastersons, providing you some semblance of normalcy. Unfortunately, you, Noah, are beyond even our magik."

His illusions create the image of a tapestry and I verify its authenticity with my Sight. It is an accurate reflection of that day. The additional spell consisted of many threads that weave around me in my memories and powers. They cast it with enough power to easily last eight orbits around the Sun, but my magik refused to be contained. It started tearing at the threads the moment the spell was placed upon me.

"We didn't want to hurt you."

"What about the School of Oracles and Avalon, you knew and didn't tell me."

Dr. Huebner stares away, "I was wrong, I am sorry for that, it was a mistake. I thought it would distract you. I had no idea how attached you were to your friends and the city."

I remain quiet, unsure of what else can be said.

Abigail returns to the subject of Candidacy. I want to beg her to let me stay, and it gives me a fresh dose of Deja vu, recalling similar pleas to her not that long ago. Realizing the fruitlessness of this endeavor, I did the next best thing.

"I'll go, but on my terms."

I list out my demands, the primary one being my continued contact with the Mastersons, without stipulations, "I want to visit them when I choose to, and I want them to be able to visit me at Avalon."

Dr. Huebner promised me that he would secure this accommodation. Abigail Tetson refuses, "What an absurd idea, Mortals in Avalon. Disgusting."

My eyes shine like a lighthouse when I plunge her into the wall and dominate her psyche. I force her to experience a Witch burning. She tries to resist, an impossible task, and she screams in agony for me to stop.

Not so surprisingly, she eventually agrees to my request, with the condition that I leave by the rising sun. I will say this about Ms. Tetson, that woman sure is tough. She just went through hell and still has the gall to negotiate. I agree, not wanting to press my luck. I thought she would have the Council on me for my little stunt, but she doesn't. For all their alleged strength, it has me wondering who has the real power, them or me.

The next few hours fly by in a blur. It is already near midnight when Dr. Statton finally discharges me. Staff pack my luggage quickly and my goodbyes go far too fast. In the early morning, I hug Ms. Penelope and the residents of Spirit Manor goodbye.

Maria meets me and the rest of my family at Tarias' boundary. Bands of sunlight streak past the dark and menacing clouds, like fingers of some god trying to stop the doom those clouds promise to bring upon the world.

Maria and I cry shamelessly when we say goodbye and do not bother to erase the evidence. "I am really going to miss you," she says and hugs me with a ferocity.

"Same," I say, now quietly sobbing. We promise to remain in contact, my second requirement to Abigail, unlimited contact with whom I choose.

Then there was him.

David had visited while I was unconscious and left flowers on my nightstand, but no note. I asked Maria to invite him since I was so busy with my last-minute move. She wasn't sure where he was, "He said he would be here, maybe he'll meet you at the airport?"

Two cars arrive just then. One is magikal, it would Translocate the Mastersons back home, and the other a standard vehicle, meant to drive me to the Denver airport. My Sight was transfixed on the Mastersons until they arrived back home for the entire commute. I even went so far as to perform an extensive safety-check for any magikal sabotage from the Council. The only magik I find are the charms I personally cast for my family's protection and convenience.

A representative from Avalon opens the door when I arrive at the airport. She was my escort for the trip. She urges me to go inside but I refuse, and she is forced to wait outside with me. I searched through the crowds for him, but he was nowhere in sight. I do not use my abilities because I don't want it to be true. I shift my balance from one foot to the other, Morgan loudly purrs from inside his kennel, reminding me to breath, but I just stand there, sad and pathetic, stupidly waiting. He wasn't even going to say goodbye. I guess I cannot blame him. It was not like being with me was easy.

The Colorado sky darkens, the clouds grow so thick they cast night over the parking lot, almost entirely blocking out the sun. The people outside all raised their heads and pointed to the sudden storm as blue-green light streaks in the distance, followed by the bellowing roar of thunder. I could not stop myself and it did not feel like me, like I wasn't there anymore, but it was me. There was a hole in my heart, and I was stuck somewhere inside it, a hole so deep that I could not see the way out.

The storm continued, thunder and lightning thrash and strike at the world. A part of me knew to stop, but for the life of me, I cannot seem to dig myself out.

A toddler softly cries as he stares up at the black sky, clinging to his mother. He could not be any older than two and he reminds me of Sam. The memory of him raises me out of the hole in my heart, and I immediately release the spell, unsure of how I cast it to begin with. The clouds return to gray overcast, and the thunder and lightning cease their tirade. I grab my luggage and look back one last time, but there was no one there for me.

The escort and I board the plane. We sit across from each other in first-class. It may not have been a private jet, but the Coventry of the High Crown appeared to spare no expense for its Candidates. Morgan crawls about, unseen and untouched by the staff or passengers near our isolated area, mid-length walls offer a slight amount of privacy.

They served me champagne and, the preoccupied escort, who is typing intensely into her laptop, does not seem to care. I privately toast to the staff and aircraft that would take me to my new world.

New, always new, felt old somehow.

I drank until my eyes grew heavy and swallowed more just to be certain that it would take me somewhere else. When I wake up the pilot is preparing for landing, and my first thought is of him. I allowed for just the one. A desire to See him just one more time, but nothing more.

Epilogue

It has been nearly a year since I left Philomena. The bad dreams have not returned. I am not sure what that means. Dr. Huebner kept his promise and convinced the Council to limit their custodianship and authority over me to my magikal education only. I have been able to visit the Mastersons every weekend.

All things considered, Avalon is beautiful. It has waterfalls with rolling hills and true beaches with salt in the air from the Pacific Ocean. The land also serves as a haven for supernatural beings and creatures. I have made friends with Draegons, Phoenixes, but not Unicorns, who are, frankly, overrated.

There is staff available at all hours exclusively focused on attending to my needs. My dormitory is the entire top floor of a magnificent palace that is so exquisite it puts St. Philomena's Castle to shame.

Morgan is faring exceptionally well and loves lurching about Avalon's magikal lands. His powers protect him without so much of a thought on my part. He has died a few times, but always self-resurrects, and will continue to do so as long as I breathe. Thank the Spirits for him.

Beautiful scenery and luxury aside things have not been easy here. The young Witches at the School of Oracles were not like the students of St. Philomena. Competitive does not begin to describe the nature of the Witches here. It was like magikal warfare and I had to learn how to survive, not exactly a new phenomenon for me, but this took things to a whole other level.

On my first day, a Seer ensnared me in a lemniscate, a curious and terrible technique of psychically trapping others by distorting their perception of time. While captive, a person feels as if seconds are hours, minutes more like months, and even broader discrepancies of time. She cast and maintained the spell on me for a whole whopping minute, and that was the last time any of them successfully used their magik against me. After that, I tried my best to remain cordial, considering they tried to imprison me in my mind, at least until the other Seers used their tricks against my family.

A group of them trapped Jake for ten minutes. He lived in their prison for ten months. They are lucky to still be alive. The students now treat my family like royalty; unfortunately, there are always a stubborn few that refuse to change. For those few, I hope in time they learn their lessons, considering their psyches have all the time they need in my own lemniscates. Although my time at the Colleges of Avalon has been relatively unpleasant, the faculty, even the students, have taught me valuable lessons on my abilities.

With that said, I cannot say much about my progress in the way of making friends. Thankfully, Maria and I write to each other regularly. I sent her a letter earlier today on the latest updates, mostly on the recent drama between the water Faelyn and Myre-People. The Faelyn are ruthless and almost always go for the jugular, sometimes literally.

And then there is *him*. I miss him every single day. I can still taste his kiss that summer. It is sweet like honey, but the absence of him lingers like some obscene spice. Everyday requires my best effort to hide him in some corner of my mind, at least until today.

The Final Trials for a Crowned Seat are being hosted at a chosen destination, all the High Crown Candidates are required to go, and we will be leaving in a matter of a few days. My dorm was a chaos of clothes, books, shoes, and products of both ordinary and magik variety. In the beginning, I made an unspoken vow with myself to never unpack, sort of like going on strike.

I have basically lived out of my suitcases and whatever was on the furniture or floor. Now with an urgent need to decide what to pack, I call an end to my protest, and empty the suitcases. I find it tucked away safely in a front main pocket, an obvious place. It took almost a year to find his letter. In very David-like fashion, he once again capsizes my world, tormenting me with his enduring perfection.

Noah,

You will probably be up in the air by the time you get this, I am really going to miss you, like something crazy. Please forgive me for not saying goodbye. I wanted to see you off, well not really, that means seeing you go away and just the thought makes me a right mess and randomly burst into tears, the ugly kind with snot. I can't risk losing all semblance of my manhood, at least not in front of you.

Before I get ahead of myself, I need to confess something to you about that night at the beach. My ability to see the past triggered your memory that night. It was an accident, I just wanted to be close to you, but it happened without me thinking, I swear on my life I didn't do it on purpose. Hurting you like that was unacceptable, I couldn't risk it happening again, so I stayed away. It seemed like the only way to protect you, but it just made it worse, and I hate myself for that. Please know I am truly sorry, and hope you can forgive me, because I really need you to forgive me. Truth is I am desperately in love with you, in a ferocious and all-of-my-being kind of way.

Tonight I stare up at the blue moon and it reminds me of your eyes, I know how you hate hearing that and are probably rolling them right now, but still, I hope you are staring at the same blue moon, like something that could still belong to just us. I will not say goodbye. Instead, I will ask you something No-El. Here is hoping for a yes.

Will you be my pen pal?

That's a thing, right? I am sure lots of blokes do that sort of thing, well maybe not, but I don't care, because this bloke right here in St. Philomena will do it for a pretty boy with pretty eyes, and the most perfect heart.

Love,
David O'Faolain.

I have to sit down. It takes me a minute to compose myself from the initial shock and realization that he loves me too. Finally, I managed to write him back.

David,

I just found your letter. Please forgive me for taking this long to write you back. I would love to be your pen pal, but I have news; I will be back in Tarias in a few days. Would you like to still write to each other, just for the hell of it? I hope it's not too late, because the truth is, I am still hopelessly, and probably always will be, in love with you, Mr. O'Faolain.

Yours,
Noah Ellis
AKA No-El

Wrapping my letter tightly in enchanted cloth bindings, I cast a small spell over it ensuring its return if it were to be lost. Then placing it carefully into the envelope with the official stationery of the School of Oracles, authorizing its delivery outside of Avalon.

My formal title is listed on top of the address as Noah Ellis, High Crown Candidate.

"Aeduou," calling my favorite Faelin. In a wisp of wind, she appears, manifesting out of thin air. Her wings, white with magnificent colors at the tips, move quickly with the speed of a hummingbird.

"Hello Aeduou, can I ask for a favor," she cheers in excitement, making various sounds of her people's language and nature. I hand her my letter, "For David," she squeals happily, she too could not help but be in love with David O'Faolain. She flies up to my face, pressing her forehead against my own, careful to not poke me with her antler crown.

"Thank you," I say quietly. She vanishes in a brief and strong gust that makes me take a step back. I walk outside on my balcony, "David, I am coming back to you," looking at the full, bluc moon and the great big sky, a little late. I pray not too late.

Acknowledgments

Writing this story took years to create and has been a labor of love. I started writing Noah the Witch during some challenging times and this book has carried me through several more. I have wanted to write a story about magik since I was child. As an adult, I now understand that ultimately I wanted to write a story about the impossible. To make something so unbelievable, into a type of reality, a reminder to others and myself to never give up hope, and never stop believing in magik.

A special thanks to my amazing and wonderful children that inspire me every day.

I wrapped up the manuscript during the COVID-19 pandemic and, with the exclusion of my family, much of the interaction I had with the people were through various electronic means, but somehow we made it work in our attempt to protect others and ourselves during the crisis.

I want to take the time to offer my appreciation to all the wonderful people in my life that have supported me along this fascinating, albeit time-consuming, experience.

Cheers to my fabulous beta readers. Each of you helped me maintain my excitement and perseverance to complete this dream of mine.

Natasha Pedraza, thank you cousin for your constant encouragement and honest feedback. Kimberly Goodwin for your continued support and open ear. Kady Maltos, your words kept me going. Thank you for re-reading the final-final draft. I am infinitely grateful for you, comadre.

I appreciate all of you, mainly for the many, many virtual wine-down sessions.

Thank you to my loving husband, Logan Sparrow. I do not know what I would have done without you. From the nightly repetitive read-throughs and my shameless demands for constant praise to help me manage my insecurities. You have been with me through it all. You have been my cheerleader, my objective reader, an editor, and my biggest support. I love you.

All of you helped give me confidence and feel like a real author and actually give this writing-business a shot. Thank you for reading the story and thank you for loving it the way that I do.

Senovio C. Sparrow was raised in the Rio Grande Valley and now lives in San Antonio, Texas with his husband and two daughters. From a very young age, he has believed in the power of lighting candles and wishful thinking. This is his first novel and he hopes you enjoy it as much as he enjoyed writing about Noah the Witch.

www.ingramcontent.com/pod-product-compliance
Lightning Source LLC
Chambersburg PA
CBHW030629310726
48979CB00003B/931

* 9 7 8 1 7 3 5 2 9 5 9 3 0 *